POSTCOLONIAL NATURALISM

POSTCOLONIAL NATURALISM

Periodization, World-Literature, and the Anglophone Novel

ERIC D. SMITH

LIVERPOOL UNIVERSITY PRESS

First published 2023 by
Liverpool University Press
4 Cambridge Street
Liverpool
L69 7ZU

Copyright © 2023 Eric D. Smith

Eric D. Smith has asserted the right to be identified as
the author of this book in accordance with the Copyright, Designs and
Patents Act 1988.

All rights reserved. No part of this book may be reproduced, stored
in a retrieval system, or transmitted, in any form or by any means,
electronic, mechanical, photocopying, recording, or otherwise, without
the prior written permission of the publisher.

British Library Cataloguing-in-Publication data
A British Library CIP record is available

ISBN 978-1-83764-050-8

Typeset by Carnegie Book Production, Lancaster
Printed and bound by CPI Group (UK) Ltd, Croydon CR0 4YY

Contents

Acknowledgments	vii
Introduction: Naturalism, Postcolonialism, and World-Literature	1
1 Narrative Desolation and Postcolonial Naturalism in V.S. Naipaul's *Guerrillas*	39
2 Neither Us nor Ours: The Dialectic of Hysteria and the Beautiful Soul in the Novels of Lewis Nkosi	65
3 Heredity and Horizon in the Postcolonial Bildungsroman: Rhys, Cliff, and Adiga	99
4 Future Perfect and the Impossible Present: Two Faces of Postcolonial Anti-Utopianism	151
Conclusion: Naturalism, or, the Cultural Logic of Capital in Crisis	203
Works Cited	211
Index	223

For my parents, William "Crockett" and Sherry Smith
Now, I know, it's a long, hard road.

Acknowledgments

This book was initially composed over a six-year period that proved, for a variety of reasons both personal and public, to be one of the most challenging in my life and in our collective lives. It would not have been possible without the encouragement and support of many dear friends, family members, and fellow travelers. Specifically, I thank my colleagues at the University of Alabama in Huntsville, particularly Angela Balla, without whom this book would likely not exist, along with Alanna Frost, Rolf Goebel, Christine Sears, Bill Wilkerson, Stephen Waring, and especially John Harfouch, who provided valuable feedback and much encouragement on the first draft. Many thanks as well to José Betancourt, who graciously provided the book's cover art and to Graham Gotvald for his expertise. Deepest appreciation goes to my dear friend and mentor, Phil Wegner, as well as to Tom Moylan, Fredric Jameson, and Darko Suvin for their encouragement and enduring inspiration. I am once again grateful to the many students with whom I've had the privilege to share these texts and discuss many of these ideas over the last several years, none more so than my friend Tim Farrell, who also composed the index for this volume. I'd like to acknowledge the UAH College of Arts, Humanities, and Social Sciences as well as the UAH Humanities Center for research support and for the sabbatical that enabled me to complete this manuscript. Sincerest appreciation must also go to the editors at Liverpool University Press and the anonymous readers who provided invaluable suggestions for improving the book. To my daughter Alysse, all my love and thanks for your patience. I began this book when you were six and completed it before your thirteenth birthday. Finally, loving gratitude to my first, best reader, Meg, my partner on this "tenacious adventure" who reminds me day by day and in ways great and small that, as Badiou puts it, "Real love is one that triumphs lastingly, sometimes painfully, over the hurdles erected by time, space and the world." The next one is yours.

A version of chapter one and a portion of chapter two were previously published in the following journals, and I thank the publishers for allowing me to include that material here:

"Narrative Desolation and Postcolonial Naturalism in V. S. Naipaul's *Guerrillas*," in *Genre: Forms of Discourse and Culture* vol. 50, no. 3, pp. 371–395. Copyright 2017, University of Oklahoma. All rights reserved. Republished by permission of the publisher. www.dukeupress.edu

"Seeds of Destruction: Naturalism, Hysteria, and the Beautiful Soul in Lewis Nkosi's *Mating Birds*." *Cambridge Journal of Postcolonial Literary Inquiry* vol. 7, no. 2, pp. 158–175. Copyright 2020, Cambridge University Press. All rights reserved. Republished by permission of the publisher. www.cambridge.org

Introduction
Naturalism, Postcolonialism, and World-Literature

This book argues for aesthetic naturalism as a coherent cultural logic emerging within the world-system of capitalist modernity. As the developmental trajectory of the world-system pursues flexible accumulation and the spatial fix for its internal contradictions, it produces underdevelopment and reinforces an experience of chronological and ontological disjunction across the face of what remains, despite appearances, an integrated global totality. Thinking of naturalism as a structurally determined cultural logic rather than as a discrete chronological epoch or mobile array of literary techniques helps us to understand its local recurrence within world-literature as a periodizing concept. One such site of naturalist recurrence is in the aftermath of anti-colonial resistance—when the independent nation is faced at once with the realization of its political ambitions and their immediate nullification in the recognition of an emergent new world order. Naturalism expresses the anxiety of the national bourgeoisie caught between the inadmissible political demands of the masses, in whose name it has legitimated its rule, and a recalibrating global empire. The concept of postcolonial naturalism thus enables a mapping of both the dynamic ideological valences of postcolonial world-literature and the structural determinations of literary naturalism more generally.

    Amid the flurry of post-millennial re-examinations of Goethean *Weltliteratur* and its conceptual utility for the present, Christopher L. Hill cautions against what he identifies as a model of diffusion that explicitly or implicitly informs some of the more prominent of these theoretical proposals. Acknowledging that the work of Franco Moretti and Pascale Casanova more "boldly addresses the impact of global systems on literary practice" than many previous accounts, Hill avers that each is nevertheless hampered by an underlying presumption of internationalist diffusion that tacitly posits "a world of national (or regional) literatures interacting globally" through an ultimately developmentalist spatiotemporal logic of "departures and arrivals" in which, originating from the privileged locus of the European metropolitan center, expressive cultural forms then radiate out through peripheral and semi-peripheral subsidiaries (2009: 1198). Thus, he observes, "At a time when transnational movements of capital and people have exposed the historicity of national culture, we should ask whether an international logic can grasp the history of literary forms on a planetary scale" (Hill 2009: 1198).

As an alternative, Hill adduces the global development of literary naturalism. Defying explanatory models of "origination and reception" and other such "linear teleologies," this fictional modality "flourished in distant parts of the world at the same time as its triumph in Europe" (Hill 2009: 1198). The unique historical contexts and often surprising trajectories of these simultaneous global expressions thus "reveal multiple, overlapping histories that make up the heterogeneous, planetary history of the form" (Hill 2009: 1198). Against the interior evolution of an originary European naturalism prompting successive waves of global diffusion, as in the paradigm influentially proposed by Yves Chevrel,[1] Hill points to Argentine and Brazilian naturalisms, among others, that are contemporaneous with "the moment of naturalism's European triumph" and therefore not merely derivative of it (Hill 2009: 1201). Importantly, Hill's transnational model does not deny influence as such. Rather, it rejects the assumption of a unilinear influence in which the European form is taken up and given merely idiomatic inflection in (semi-)peripheral national cultures. The history he proposes thus reveals multiple, intersecting chronologies and conjunctural spaces "that together constitute the heterogeneous history of a transnational cultural phenomenon" even as it rejects the totalizing aspirations of the primary models that he contests (2009: 1201).

Ramifying the constellation of scalar and temporal concurrency that Hill's reading proposes, however, is what he describes as "the condition of unevenness and simultaneity in what by the late 19th century was a planet-scale intellectual culture" (2009: 1202). This near echoing of Leon Trotsky's familiar formula of "combined and uneven development"—however subtly appropriated here for a generalized strategy of what Mahmood Mamdani might well call the culturalization of material processes[2]—likewise directs us not only back to Moretti, who is perhaps

---

[1] See Chevrel, Yves 1993 [1982]. *Le Naturalisme: Étude d'un mouvement littéraire international* (Paris: Presses Universitaires de France).

[2] See Mamdani, Mahmood 2004. *Good Muslim, Bad Muslim: America, the Cold War and the Roots of Terror* (New York: Pantheon).

more sensitive to the complex cultural dynamics, simultaneities, and asymmetries of the capitalist world-system than Hill sometimes credits him (and, indeed, who also makes effective use of Trotsky's concept),[3] but also to the more recent efforts of the Warwick Research Collective (WReC) to "grasp world-literature as the literary registration of modernity under the sign of combined and uneven development" (WReC 2015: 17). This model, which Hill's study neither engages nor acknowledges, offers a totalizing framework that also countenances cultural difference and local specificity.

Starkly opposing a plurality of *alternative modernities*[4] as well as the bold, humanist universalisms of recent comparatist approaches,[5] the WReC authors follow Fredric Jameson's insistence on a *singular modernity* as the complexly variegated, necessarily local experience of what is nonetheless a dynamically integrated process of the capitalist world-system. Such a paradigm would seem to satisfy Hill's recommendation that expressive cultural forms like naturalist fiction ought to be approached as "synchronically organized, diachronically evolving transnational fields" (2020: 183) whose complexly overdetermined histories nevertheless "cannot be separated from material, political, and intellectual histories that [are] not simply 'parallel' to literary history but really should be considered part of the history of naturalism per se" (2020: 180).

Emphasizing both the singularity and simultaneity of the capitalist world-system and underscoring its asymmetries of political and economic dispensation, Jameson's model, as deployed by the WReC, thereby annuls diffusionist or developmentalist projections of homogenizing cultural expression and the sequential march of consecutive periods even as it refuses the proliferation of discretely local modernities. The differential idioms and seeming incommensurabilities of the latter are rather discernible, through a process of allegorical mediation, as the "everywhere irreducibly specific" registrations and locally inflected encodings of a "globally dispersed general 'situation'" (WReC 2015: 12). Taking up this theorization of a singular, simultaneous modernity and underscoring its resonance with the cultural implications of Trotsky's recognition of uneven development's "amalgam of archaic with more contemporary forms" (2015: 6), the WReC conclude that

---

[3] See Moretti's much-discussed essay "Conjectures on World Literature," *New Left Review* 1 (Jan/Feb 2000): 1–12.
[4] See, for example, Gaonkar, Dilip Parameshwar 2001. *Alternative Modernities* (Durham: Duke University Press).
[5] They cite, among others, Apter, Emily 2019. *Against World Literature: On the Politics of Untranslatability* (New York: Verso).

[m]odernity is neither a chronological nor a geographical category. It is not something that happens—or even happens *first*—in 'the west' and to which others can subsequently gain access; or that happens in cities rather than in the countryside; or that, on the basis of a deep-set sexual division of labour, men tend to exemplify in their social practice rather than women. Capitalist modernisation entails development, yes—but this 'development' takes the forms also of the development of underdevelopment, of maldevelopment, and dependent development. (2015: 13)

World-literature, as the cultural expression of the system's endemic unevenness, will thus necessarily express its "juxtaposition of asynchronous orders and levels of historical experience, its barometric indications of invisible forces acting from a distance on the local and familiar—as these manifest themselves in literary forms, genres and aesthetic strategies" (WReC 2015: 17).

Roberto Schwarz already makes a comparable observation, specifically regarding the challenge to realism and naturalism posed in the work of Brazilian writer Joaquim Maria Machado de Assis. As he writes,

For literary forms may not mean the same in the core and at the periphery of our world. Time can become so uneven, when it is stretched far across space, that artistic forms which are already dead in the first may still be alive in the second. Such contrasts can be viewed with regret or satisfaction. (Schwarz 2005: n.p.)

Though Schwarz does not identify Machado de Assis as a modernist (as other critics, like K. David Jackson, have more recently done[6]), a glancing evocation of the Brechtian *Verfremdungseffekt* sets up an implicit opposition between the "unspiritual materialism" of what are here called naturalist "servitudes of physiology and climate, temper and heredity" on one hand and the structurally determined necessity of modernism's devices of abstraction and critical estrangement in relation to a crisis of realist representation on the other:

Brecht, who did not want to lag behind his epoch, said it was futile for a realist to stare at workers trudging through the gates of Krupp in the morning. Once reality has migrated into abstract economic functions, it can no longer be read in human faces. Observation of

---

[6] See Jackson, K. David 2015. *Machado de Assis: A Literary Life* (New Haven: Yale University Press).

life in a former colony, where social divisions remain stark, might then seem more rewarding. But such concreteness too is suspect, since the abstractions of the world market are never far away, and belie the fullness of spontaneous perception at every moment. (Schwarz 2005: n.p.)

Hence, the "correlative realities" of core and periphery structuring the impossible situation of post-independence, in which "there was no way either to escape from the terms that European developments imposed on Brazil, or to live up to them," places tremendous pressure on the hegemon of realism itself, which thence becomes emblematic of both successful modernization *and* a critical cognizance thereof— though the latter, Schwarz suggests, is more often than not perfunctory (2005: n.p.). In Machado de Assis, however, much as in the mature Joyce, the vicissitudes of capitalist modernity—its frank brutality coupled with its veneer of conspicuous civility—are exposed through a guerilla misappropriation of the late realist style that throws into relief its ideological mechanisms in ways that transcend the explanation of cultural derivation and implicate instead a global class dynamic.

Such emphasis on formal discontinuity as a registering of what the philosopher of utopia Ernst Bloch calls the "simultaneity of the non-simultaneous" (qtd. in WReC 2015: 12) similarly leads the WReC to the Jamesonian triptych *modernization/modernity/modernism*, in which the first concept-term indicates capitalist subsumption as both an extensive and intensive material process, the second marks the lived condition or broad social precinct of this process, and the third delineates the general cultural *habitus* of the material/social condition. Refuting Adorno's privileging of an exclusively oppositional or critical modernism, the WReC authors call for a radical expansion of the temporal and spatial province of literary modernism "to incorporate the great wave of writing from the mid-nineteenth century onwards that is construable...as an encoding of the capitalisation of the world" (2015: 17–18). Equally discarding conventional and "still-dominant" accounts of modernism deriving from aesthetic criteria "that situate it in terms of writerly technique (self-conscious, anti- or at least post-realist, etc.)"[7] and those that remain reliant on geo-culturalist distinctions (as in much postcolonial theory) that count it as a primarily Western European phenomenon, the authors of the WReC look to the relentless, violently erratic process of capitalist subsumption to explain

---

[7] This formal codification Jameson deems "late modernism" or the "ideology of modernism" (2002: 150).

the shifting temporal parameters of modernism and its multiple loci of expression (2015: 18).

Periodization and the Cultural Logics of Modernity

Such a critical remapping and radical dilation of the aesthetic and geo-spatial contours of modernism[8] necessitate a corollary rethinking of modernism's conventionally defined horizon of non-identity: literary realism. Having dismissed the standard sequence of literary periods evolving organically in relatively homogenous, empty time—impelled either by the happy accidents of intrepid genius or some internally coherent, metamorphic process of natural selection—the WReC instead situates the morphology of form in the Wallersteinian world-system's dialectic of core and periphery, such that all forms "are brought into being (and often into collision with other, pre-existing forms) through the long wave of the capitalisation of the world" (2015: 51).

Within this paradigm, all forms of cultural expression under the regime of capital are effectively *modernized*, and the problem of "realism" is displaced or fundamentally reimagined. Indeed, rightly calling into question the reductive *realism-modernism* binary—in which the latter is cast as the progressive, experimental, and iconoclastic antagonist to the former's stultifying, decorously self-assured conventionality—the collective shows, by way of the paradigmatic Adorno/Lukács debate, that what Adorno privileges in modernism is precisely "the pertinence of its grasp of contemporary reality," while what Lukács recognizes in the "delirious, hallucinatory realism" of a writer like Dostoevsky is, in fact, the critical gauging of modernization's fitfully conjunctive unevenness in the semi-periphery (WReC 2015: 61–62). Again, following Jameson's lead in the dialectical recognition of "modernistic realisms" and "realistic modernisms," the WReC claims that the two forms are never to be understood as stages in a unilinear, literary-historical teleology, but as specific responses to or from corresponding positions within the cyclical fluxions, incessant reorganizations, and contingent respatializations of the modern world-system itself (2015: 67). That is, the WReC offers a periodizing logic that designates *structural* rather than *chronological* or *geographical* indices of cultural response.

---

[8] Lazarus productively expounds upon this radical expansion of the geographical and temporal provinces of modernism in his new book. See Lazarus, Neil 2022. *Into Our Labors: Work and its World-Literary Perspective* (Liverpool: Liverpool University Press).

The WReC's commitment to this model of structural causality and the dialectical method also obliges its members to recognize the union of oppositional tendencies within each of these aesthetic formations. While they follow Joe Cleary's argument that modernism is the cultural form concomitant with the nascent transition from the old order of European empires to what will finally emerge as the new imperialist dispensation presided over by Cold-War polarities, they distinguish between two tendential forms of aesthetic realism: on one hand, realism of the "ideal-type," which, expressive of the relatively stable material and existential substance of the core, depends on what Jameson describes as the "conviction as to the massive weight and persistence of the present as such" (Jameson 2007: 263); and, on the other, the "irrealism" of the (semi-)periphery, from which "the 'shock' of combined unevenness is registered with particular intensity and resonance" (WReC 2015: 72). The latter also takes as its object an unremittingly "realist" representation of the present, including its contradictions and violent deformations. Its historicizing logic is attentive, however, not only to the task of producing a history of the present but also to the recuperation of "alternative histories that might have been but were not, yet that (paradoxically) might still be" (WReC 2015: 72).

As the authors note, complicating such an exercise in standpoint epistemology is the recognition that even monumental works of the ideal-type frequently encode the splits and contradictions of capital's constitutive antagonisms in marbleized veins of irrealist expression (WReC 2015: 72), much as detected through Edward Said's practice of "contrapuntal" reading (Said 1993: 66). Thus, the ideal-type's projection of solidity and permanence must be understood neither as objective fact nor as an ideological blind born of either deception or naïveté. As the WReC notes by way of Jameson, this type rather arises from a situation in which "a history in movement and a future on the point of emergence" can be imaginatively—if not always concretely—realized (qtd. in WReC 2015: 78).

Realism in this sense is what Jameson elsewhere describes as "a demiurgic "...practice" or:

> as a component in a vaster historical process that can be identified as none other than the capitalist (or *bourgeois*) cultural revolution itself...namely, the moment in which an entire last surviving feudal "world" (power, culture, economic production, space, the psychic subject, the structure of groups, the Imaginary) is systematically dismantled in order for a radically different one to be set in place. (1992: 226)

This identification of realism with the process of cultural revolution—in which an ascendant class or class fraction for the first time universalizes its parochial codes and values and undertakes to "invent the life habits of the new social world" (Jameson 1992: 226) in a situation in which social transformation is imaginatively proximate—is evident in the WReC's assertion that the most successful or dominant forms of this realist impulse are those associated with revolutionary or liberationist movements (2015: 77).

Aligning the revolutionary mode of realism of the ideal-type with what Frantz Fanon calls the "fighting phase" of cultural nationalism, the WReC also acknowledges that the historical specifications necessary for its emergence are rare and decidedly short lived. The contradictions of history and what seems the increasingly evanescent *ignis fatuus* of revolutionary transformation tend more frequently to yield a (modernist) irrealism commensurate to peripheral or marginal existence, where structural discontinuity and the co-existence of multiple chronologies (as in magical realism or, as I have argued, its inheritor postcolonial science fiction[9]) yet persist.

Realism of the ideal-type is therefore, as Jameson suggests, "a peculiarly unstable concept" and a rarity due both to the inherent paradox of its incompatible aesthetic and epistemological claims as *a representation of reality* and to the delicate balance of antinomies imposed by the historical situation that conjures the form into brief, urgent existence (1992: 217).[10] Having distinguished between the ideal and estranging forms of realism (dialectically folding the realism-modernism antinomy back into the practice of realism itself) and thus refuting denunciations of realism as irredeemably bound to narratives of either obsolete cultural nationalism or European derivation, the WReC theory of world-literature proceeds under the premise that "an elective affinity exists between the general situation(s) of peripherality and irrealist aesthetics" (2015: 68). By privileging writings that reject the revolutionary narrative of anticolonial nationalism in favor of those that "inscribe the techniques of hybridity, pastiche, irony and defamiliarization," postcolonial literary studies has, in the group's view, both ignored vast numbers of texts that do not suit this paradigm and tendentiously misread the irrealism of many others under the sign of a putatively subversive (*postmodernist?*) anti-representationalism.

---

[9] See Smith, Eric D. 2012. *Globalization, Utopia, and Postcolonial Science Fiction: New Maps of Hope* (Basingstoke: Palgrave).

[10] He elaborates on the delicate antinomy that sustains the rarity of realism in Jameson 2013. *The Antinomies of Realism* (New York: Verso).

In the WReC's "remappings of both the history of modernism and the intertwined trajectories of world-literary wave formations" (2015: 19), however, a significant lacuna opens up between realism in its fighting mode and its imminent cancellation in the practice of irrealism. If, following Jameson's periodizing logic, as the WReC authors do, we understand the morphology of form to be "governed by the historic logic of the three fundamental stages in secular bourgeois or capitalist culture as a whole" (realism-modernism-postmodernism), we must likewise consider the "technical problem of constructing a mediation between a formal or aesthetic concept and a periodizing or historiographic one" (Jameson 1992: 213), however provisional. Yet, the technical defamiliarizations, temporal juxtapositions, anarchic hybridities, and exilic meditations that define the canonic texts and reading protocols favored by much postcolonial theorizing cannot primarily be those of postmodernism, which is, in Jameson's view, the ethos of a "whole new class fraction... a new petit bourgeoisie, a professional-managerial class;" postmodernism thus serves as the "dominant ideological and cultural paradigm" for the moment of late capitalism—"moment" here again designating relative structural positionality in an inherently unstable system rather than any chronologically linear or developmentalist telos (Jameson 1991: 407).

While the WReC paradigm makes effective use of the essay on magical realism, Jameson in fact offers the most expansive discussion of the periodizing dialectic of realism-modernism-postmodernism in the monumental essay "The Existence of Italy," which directly follows the essay on magical realism and makes up approximately one third of his 1992 volume on film *Signatures of the Visible*. Here, Jameson outlines the three moments or stages, which, he insists, are not to be thought as "particularly 'linear' or even evolutionary" but always in dialectical tension and simultaneous interrelation, combined though unevenly distributed. *Realism* corresponds to "the conquest of a kind of cultural, ideological, and narrative literacy by a new class or group" and should therefore be thought as inventive and innovative rather than passively reflective of reality as objectively given (1992: 214). *Modernism*, which he elsewhere associates with the allegorical registration of colonialist horrors and the spatial dilemmas of empire upon metropolitan consciousness (Jameson 1990: 43–68), corresponds with a broader crisis of representation within narrative realism, which, in its late form, now functions as the familiar hegemon, whose staid, superegoic authority and complacent conventionality we will belatedly imagine modernism to have made obsolete.

While we might think of modernism as the literature at the margins of realist hegemony, its estrangements need not always be progressively oppositional. As the WReC authors point out, an Adornian strong identification of modernism with or as resistance too readily neglects the "celebratory wing of fascist modernism (as in Marinetti) and the contradictory juxtapositions of reactionary plots and vanguard formal structures (as in *The Waste Land*, for instance)" (2015: 20), a seeming paradox that Jameson also captures in his own paradigmatic, odd-couple pairing of James Joyce with Wyndham Lewis (1979: 20). More important for Jameson than its oppositional charge, then, is the way in which modernism in its own early, demiurgic moment corresponds to a shift in the mode of production (here, to imperialism or Lenin's "highest stage of capitalism"[11]) and thus to a supersession of the nation-centric paradigms of an antecedent stage "for a world poised on the edge of some thoroughgoing metamorphosis" (2002: 136).

Postmodernism, which attends the spatial and psychical saturation of the "world" by a universal process of commodification, marks the subsumption of modernism's margins (oppositional as well as reactive) and thus full submersion marked by three major systemic transformations: first, the emergence of the multinational corporation and the consolidation of a new, global class of the capitalist elite; second, the concomitant reorganization of the old European empires and national sovereignty itself to accommodate the structural demands of the former; and, facilitating both of these, the emergence of mass mediation and data production under the regime of electronic information processing and telecommunications technologies. Postmodernism is therefore the historically myopic and "inhumanly impoverishing" perspective informing Jameson's imagined 'First-World reader,' whose restricted sympathies and simplifying binaries presume both the impossibility of social solidarity and, as a corollary, the civilizational difference of the Other (1986: 66). That Jameson's critical diagnosis of this ideological effect has been tendentiously misread as evidence of the latter in his own thought is perhaps the surest index of its tenacious ubiquity.

---

[11] See Lenin, Vladimir 2010 [1917]. *Imperialism: The Highest Stage of Capitalism* (New York: Penguin).

Neither "Fighting Phase" Realism nor Postcolonial (Post)Modernism

What Fanon criticized as the national bourgeoisie, fighting for political independence in the name of the masses, emerges as a postcolonial comprador elite, the local liaisons of the protracted capitalist crisis formation that Kwame Nkrumah names "neo-colonialism" or the "last stage of imperialism" (1965: 1). But, despite this forced fealty to the interests of global capital, the national situation in many, if not most of these (semi-) peripheral structural locations in the world-system does not provide the requisite conditions for the ahistorical, planar social existence that Jameson describes "in the negative terms of anxiety and loss of reality, but which one could just as well imagine in the positive terms of euphoria, a high, an intoxicatory or hallucinogenic intensity" as defining the vertiginous cultural formations of postmodernism (1991: 28–29). Indeed, it is fitting that, as Phillip E. Wegner points out, exactly contemporaneous with Jameson's first major articulations of his theory of postmodernism is his much-polemicized essay "Third World Literature in the Era of Multinational Capitalism." Building on the theory tentatively developed in *Fables of Aggression*, Jameson argues that, as Wegner puts it, "the essentially modernist practice" of national allegory "finds a new lease on life in the emergent conditions of the decolonizing Third World" (2014: 74), where, as Jameson writes, the "'mapping' or the grasping of the social totality is structurally available to the dominated rather than to the dominating classes" (1986: 88).

Here again, though, a significant gap appears between the anticolonial nationalist impetus of realism and the modernist practice of irrealism—which undertakes a cognitive mapping of the new historical configuration of multinational capitalism—not to mention the "posthistorical" logic of postmodernism. For between this "fighting phase" realism and its irrealist permutation lies perhaps the vast majority of the melancholic, forlornly retrospective narrative practice that is conventionally privileged (particularly by a First-World readership) as "postcolonial literature," a cultural expression that cannot be adequately captured under the rubric of postmodernism, despite the considerable efforts of some theorists and scholars in the 1990s to affiliate the two under a common "post-." As Ato Quayson puts it, the variances between the postcolonial and the postmodern readily appear "when their different social referents are disentangled from their representational domains," however much a Du Boisian optic of double-consciousness or parallax perception might reveal them to be structurally complementary sides of the same global construct (or singular modernity) (2007: 652). That is, if postmodernism "generaliz[es] about global economics and culture

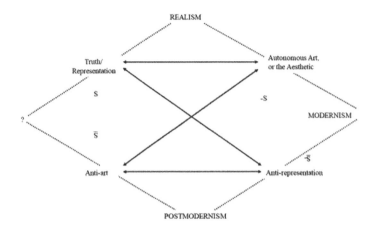

Figure 1, Jameson 1992. Signatures of the Visible, 222.

as they are seen from the vantage point of the Western metropolis"—a point of view characterized by the infamous "waning of affect" as well as "multiple and shifting subjectivities, and the total subordination of the real under the irreality of the images generated by visual culture under capitalism"—postcolonialism dramatizes the historical copula linking "a seeming situation of ontological crisis" with its determinate material conditions (Quayson 2007: 652). Such conditions are nevertheless also mediated through images that "alienate the racialized consciousness from itself and obscure the conditions that sustain the ontological split in the first place" (Quayson 2007: 652).

In the book that follows, I hope to address this lacuna in both the WReC model and the periodizing schema proposed by Jameson, who continues to view naturalism as an empirically-inclined subcategory of realism. I contend that what is defined above as the postcolonial within the domain of world-literature *structurally* coincides with the late, reactionary deviation from realism called naturalism, a move that retains Hill's recognition of the transnational dynamism of the form while nevertheless refusing the category of "World Lit" and subjecting it to the historicist critique of "planetarity" waged by the WReC. I again draw guidance here from Jameson's "The Existence of Italy," where he deploys the semiotic square of A.J. Greimas to map out the array of "formal and ideological combinations available *within* the closure of contemporary culture" (1992: 221):

If what Greimas calls the *complex* term in the square's top position "name[s] the totality" of the Symbolic constellation—as Wegner puts it in a generative superimposition of the Greimas square onto Lacan's three orders, which I adapt below (2014: 98)—then what is mapped in this instance is the semic universe of possible orientations within realism itself. *Realism* is thus the name given to a novel dialectical tension between epistemology and art, sustained in a moment of social transformation under the consolidation of a national bourgeoisie. If the *neutral* bottom position (which Wegner identifies as "homologous to the Lacanian Real" [2014: 99]) exceeds the Symbolic authority of this named universal, rendering it "not-all," then Jameson's location of postmodernism here indicates the point at which realism fails fully to "suture" the historical and ideological reality that it names. "Postmodernism" therefore marks the ultimate deformation of the national capitalist topology and its revolutionary historical transformation into the moment (structural locus) of late or multinational capitalism (Wegner 2014: 99).

What will chiefly concern me here, though, are the diagram's two middle terms, corresponding in Wegner's novel reframing to the order of the Lacanian Imaginary, which is comprised of the binary oppositions and "antimonies whose apparent irresolvability constitutes the lived experience of a particular situation" (Wegner 2014: 98). The two outer positions along the square's horizontal axis "name the two poles of a historical contradiction whose logical matrix is composed by the four internal terms of the square" (Wegner 2014: 98). If the constellation

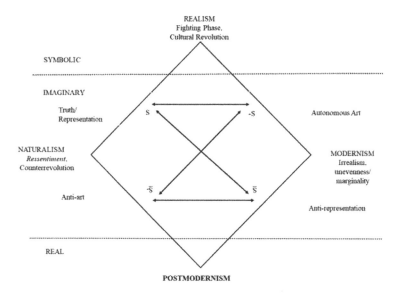

Figure 2 Four Cultural Periods of Modernity.

named by *realism* is marked by the fitful reconciliation of truth claims with aesthetic autonomy, then *modernism* nominates a radical deviation toward symbolic autonomy and a simultaneous cancellation of realism's mimetic claims to truthful representation. As this semiotic plotting reveals, the formal contrary to modernism is not realism (which the latter formally presupposes) but rather a deviation from realism in the direction of representational claims to truth and the repudiation of aesthetic autonomy: a form that purports not to create but to document. While Jameson leaves this position unnamed, suggesting that it might be filled by some new variety of the documentary film, it seems clear that within the totality of literary realism, the formal contrary to modernism is, in fact, the practice of naturalism.

Indeed, the two forms are nearly historically contemporaneous, each emerging—in the European context—out of the late nineteenth-century commodification of everyday life, the paroxysms of imperial expansion, and the tumult of revolution. Moreover, each can be regarded in some sense as a *succès de scandale* predicated on the shared imperative to demystify the ideological compass of what had by that time solidified into hegemonic realist convention. That James Joyce (early devotee of Ibsen) was initially read as a scion of the naturalist movement is well established, as Philip Raiser summarizes:

> Much of the early criticism argued that Joyce absorbed a good deal from naturalism before he willingly allowed it to abandon him to his stammering conscience. Not only were *Dubliners* and *A Portrait of the Artist* termed (by Edmund Wilson) "straight works of Naturalistic fiction," *Ulysses* also was considered by more than one reviewer as the "*ne plus ultra of naturalism.*" Using a synonym, George Bernard Shaw, in praising the work, claimed that "*Ulysses* is a document" whose authenticity he would, as a Dubliner, verify. (Raiser 1974: 460)

Shaw's estimation registers the documentary impulse of naturalism; this despite the fact that, as David Baguley observes, "most naturalist writers, certainly in France, were refined aesthetes" (1990: 3). Thus again, we observe the dialectical compresence of oppositional tendencies in each antipodal aesthetic expression. Therefore, if modernism breaks from realist hegemony in the exaltation of representational autonomy or abstract totalization, it takes the form, as we have already seen, of either a right or left deviation: Lewis or Joyce, Marinetti or Lawrence.

The same holds true for naturalism, which departs from realism in similarly progressive and/or reactionary attitudes. While it is true that many naturalist writers in both a European and American context identify as Leftist to some degree (notably Zola, Alexis, Dreiser, London, Norris, Bellamy, and Gilman), others evince a fundamental conservativism (most emphatically in the minor aristocratic Goncourt brothers, whose *Germinie Lacerteux* [1865] "unequivocally establishes a pattern for naturalist tragedy" [Baguley 1990: 80]). What unites modernists like Joyce, Marinetti, Lewis, and Lawrence, despite their evident political and ideological divergence, is the shared commitment to the practice of remaking the present through the visionary audacity of symbolic mediation. Likewise, what unites the naturalist writers under a common classification is a shared presumption of the primacy and ineluctability of natural forces and processes verified through empirical observation and normative valuation. In addition to Jameson's oppositional pairings of "Truth or Representation" and "Autonomous Art or the Aesthetic," we can therefore add that of "Nature or History."

For even the radical politics of these Leftist writers is grounded in and therefore constrained by naturalistic theories of evolution and social Darwinism. As Eric Carl Link observes in his study of American naturalism, even a work of progressive speculation like Edward Bellamy's millennialist utopian vision *Looking Backward: 2000-1887* (1888), which draws directly upon the more optimistic evolutionary paradigms of John Fiske and Herbert Spencer, figures its future utopian society as the inevitable outcome of an organic telos. Bellamy follows Spencer's confident assurance that social injustice, like all other systemic inefficiencies, is gradually selected out of existence:

> The ultimate development of the ideal man is logically certain—as certain as any conclusion in which we place the most implicit faith; for instance, that all men will die.... Progress, therefore, is not an accident, but a necessity. Instead of civilization being artificial, it is a part of nature: all of a piece with the development of the embryo or the unfolding of a flower. (qtd. in Link 2004: 82)

As a consequence, Bellamy's progressive vision ultimately outflanks and neutralizes the need for deliberate revolutionary action.

Deeply influenced by Bellamy and the Nationalist Clubs party of Christian Socialists that *Looking Backward* directly inspired, the American feminist and socialist Charlotte Perkins Gilman similarly "advocated a revised version of social Darwinism in which human cooperative enterprise allows for social reform and progress within a Darwinian framework," a notion that inspired her own narrative utopia,

Herland (1915) (Link 2004: 85). Even London's great dystopian novel *The Iron Heel* (1908), composed in the dismal aftermath of the failed 1905 Russian revolution and the rise of the great U.S. trusts, places its utopian "Brotherhood of Man" in a remotely distant future inaccessible by any political mediation extant or imagined such that, despite their many differences, London effectively reproduces the progressive-evolutionary temporality of Bellamy and all but forecloses the revolutionary project that he would otherwise appear to advocate.[12]

This adherence to natural theory and its grim social Darwinist twin, communicated through entropic narration, ultimately reveals what Jameson calls naturalism's *"authentic ressentiment,"* not only in the naturalists' ultimate capitulation before an implacable and indifferent Nature but most especially in their consistently reformist message and troubling uneasiness before the radical political desire embodied in the masses (Jameson 1981: 185). While the socialist loyalties of Gilman and London could not be more starkly opposed to the fretful class elitism of the Goncourt brothers or semi-conservative neurosis of George Gissing, for example, they each share a comparable anxiety before (if not outright contempt for) what London memorably names "the people of the abyss," most vividly rendered in a ruthless and stylistically relentless sentence from *The Iron Heel*:

> It surged past my vision in concrete waves of wrath, snarling and growling, carnivorous, drunk with whisky from pillaged warehouses, drunk with hatred, drunk with lust for blood—men, women, and children in rags, and tatters, dim ferocious intelligences with all the godlike blotted from their features and all the fiendlike stamped in, apes and tigers, anaemic consumptives and great hairy beasts of burden, wan faces from which vampire society had sucked the juice of life, bloated forms swollen with physical grossness and corruption, withered hags and death's-heads bearded like patriarchs, festering youth and festering age, faces of fiends, crooked, twisted, misshapen monsters blasted with the ravages of disease and all the horrors of chronic innutrition—the refuse and the scum of life, a raging, screaming, screeching, demoniacal horde. (London 2006: 232)

---

[12] Wegner productively situates London's novel at the contentious standoff between the respectively "radical and reformist elements of the American labor movement," the Industrial Workers of the World and the American Federation of Labor (2002: 137).

The overwhelming preponderance of static description in passages such as these, as I hope to make clear in chapter one, is the formal (syntactical) correlative of the naturalist inscription of ontological (or biological) Being upon radical historical Becoming. The people of the abyss, the text makes clear, are "not our comrades"; indeed, they are a politically incoherent "mob, an awful river that filled the street" in a drunken lust for blood and destruction that must be curtailed by the forceful intercession of the party vanguard, who will oversee the necessary reforms to keep this destabilizing, chthonic vexation at bay (London 2006: 232). As such, their agency is subsumed in a naturalizing ontology in the same instant that description overtakes narration.

The *revolutionary* politics of both London and Gilman are thus directly contradicted and enfeebled by an anxiety before the masses, one underwritten in each case by notoriously nativist and racist sentiments, which they largely share with the Goncourts (not to mention, as Hill himself notes, the racial stereotypes that readily appear in the fiction of Frank Norris or the dramatization of the liberal "whitening solution" in Brazilian naturalist Aluísio Azevedo [Hill 2020: 84, 21]). In each case, this is predicated on a fundamental commitment to an evolutionary social anthropology in which what Gilman refers to as the "inferior" peoples (qtd. in Knight 2000: 161) must follow the superintendence of the vanguard white elite. In its depiction of the suffering individual as an exemplary social type, naturalism hence recognizes its subject as a victim of historical injustice in the very instant that it subordinates the latter to preeminent forces of natural existence that may be sympathetically documented and, at best, fitfully mitigated but never actively resisted through efforts of collective intervention. Such liberal depictions offer up what Marx and Engels describe as the "spectacle of a class without any historical initiative or any independent political movement" (2022: 212). Like the liberal utopianists condemned in the *Manifesto*, the naturalist unease with political revolt from below is accompanied by the ethical imperative of pity:

> In the formation of their plans they are conscious of caring chiefly for the interests of the working class, as being the most suffering class. Only from the point of view of being the most suffering class does the proletariat exist for them. (Marx and Engels 2022: 213)

A contemporary postcolonial iteration of this sentiment, which can also serve as a general description of the aesthetic/political sensibility that I am tracking here, can be found in a 2015 essay by Neel Mukherjee. Appearing in *The Guardian* shortly after the publication of his celebrated second novel *The Lives of Others* (2015) (see chapter four), "Neel Mukherjee's Top 10 Books about Revolutionaries" offers the author's reflection on those literary works that he has

> found useful, over the years, in thinking about revolutions and armed struggles, and people caught up in them, both activists and those on the receiving end. A common theme in most of these books is how revolutionary action is foredoomed to failure and revolutionaries are either deluded, or wrong, or both; at worst, they are psychopaths and criminals. Idealism seems to be vitiated the moment it is translated into (usually misguided) action. (2015b: n.p.)

The destabilizing possibility of political action from below is thereby neutralized by liberal compassion for the "most suffering class," an affective recontainment of material opposition.

This tension between sympathetic empirical observation and assiduous documentation, on the one hand, and stoic resignation before the inflexible laws of primal nature, on the other, marks the ideological and narrative contradiction dwelling at the heart of the naturalist aesthetic. In its "penetration into the essentials of life and [simultaneous] withdrawal from them" and its presentation of "compelling dramas of suffering and degradation, transformed into a decorous description," the naturalist novel invents almost despite itself a cultural formula of liberal sympathetic detachment and genial counterrevolution as reform (Baguley 1990: 82). It is for this reason that, mindful of Eleni Coundouriotis's recent recovery of documentation and visuality in contemporary African literature from Lukács's critique of naturalist description,[13] I wish to retain as useful the latter's much-debated distinction between description and narration.

Hill likewise recognizes the "contradiction in naturalist fiction between reformist intent and deterministic theory" in the identification of the Zolian trope that he calls the "degenerate body" in Tōson Shimazaki's *Spring* (1908). Thus, he writes, in naturalist works "the closed circuit of heredity and social determinism that is a basic part of their social analytic seems to exclude the possibility of change" (Hill 2020: 95). To the extent that historical contingency is in fact reckoned into the naturalist worldview, it is so only by way of the neutralizing force of

---

[13] See Coundouriotis, Eleni 2022. "Narrate or Describe," in *Landscapes of Realism*. Eds. Sven Erik Larsen, Margaret R. Higonnet, and Steen Bille Jørgensen (Amsterdam: John Benjamins).

"deterministic theories of ethnic atavism and nervous degeneration" (Hill 2020: 95). Naturalism thus consolidates, as Jameson puts it, the "narrative paradigms that organize middle-class fantasies about those slums and about 'solutions' that might resolve, manage, or repress the evident class anxieties aroused by the existence of an industrial working class and an urban lumpenproletariat" (1981: 186).

However, social class as such is frequently repressed in the naturalist novel, which offers in its stead the compensatory "notion of 'the people,' as a kind of general grouping of the poor and 'underprivileged' of all kinds, from which one can recoil in revulsion, but to which one can also, as in some political populisms, nostalgically 'return' as to some telluric source of strength" (Jameson 1981: 189). Indeed, London's fiendish denizens of the abyss and Gilman's social inferiors are already prefigured in what the Goncourt brothers call "the rabble" (*"la canaille"*), the term with which they unfailingly refer to 'the people,' whom, as Baguley notes, "they held more in disgust than in sympathy" and who "represented for them some base and alien species on which they had happened to stumble" (1990: 82). As the Goncourts confide in their journals:

> People will never realize our natural timidity, our discomfort in the middle of a working-class crowd, our horror of the rabble, and how much the beastly and ugly document on which we have built our books has cost us. This trade of behaving like a conscientious police agent is quite the most abominable business to which a man with an aristocratic mind can turn. (1900: 228)

Such conscientious policing of the masses requires the cultivation of a dispassionate and meticulous objectivity. Thus, what Baguley calls the "dialectic of (realist) involvement and (artistic) detachment" recommends the putatively apolitical character of naturalist writing, its utter disavowal of history and agency in a posture of neutral observation and diagnostic truth telling (1990: 82).

While the Goncourts' aesthetic approach was conceived in opposition to the romantic view of urban life and especially the 1862 June Rebellion depicted in Hugo's *Les Misérables* (1862), Zola's monumental Rougon-Macquart series bears the indelible impression of the progressive author's deeply ambivalent, ultimately reactionary response to the uprising of the 1871 Paris Commune, as David Charles has convincingly claimed (2017: 111). The Paris revolution was perpetrated by what Zola in his turn called the "scum" (qtd. in Weinberg 1979: 86) of French and European political life. Jameson observes in a reflection on the emergence of naturalism as a crisis response to revolutionary insurgency that these bourgeois realists, whom he characterizes as "'shepherds of Being' of a very special, ideological type," are thereby compelled into a

> repudiation of revolutionary change and an ultimate stake in the status quo such that they then deploy in their experimental fictions a host of containment strategies, which seek to fold everything which is not-being, desire, hope, and transformational praxis, back into the status of nature; these impulses toward the future and toward radical change must systematically be reified, transformed into 'feelings' and psychological attributes [...]. (1981: 193)

Though he does not underscore the fact, a number of works cited as exemplary by Hill express a similarly reactionary, reformist, or defeatist political sentiment following upon the failure or compromised success of fighting realism or revolutionary romanticism. Thus, the failure of Korean resistance to Japanese colonial rule in 1919, for instance, gave rise to an era of literary naturalism that Hill describes as "permeated by a sense of hopelessness" (2020: 24). Such defeatism is almost always accompanied by a retreat into the psychological and somatic (or affective), in which the material terms of history are transformed by way of the naturalist alembic into eloquent diagnoses of organic maladies and constitutional distempers.

This book will pursue the claim that the ambiguous historical and cultural period of the postcolonial, caught between the revolutionary moment of anticolonial nationalism (in realism) and the ongoing cognitive mapping of late capital's spatio-temporal, political, and cultural renovations (in modernist irrealism; or what Neil Lazarus also calls the literature of "disconsolation" [2011: 31]) is most productively read against the aesthetic and ideological lineaments of naturalism. It is the unacknowledged aesthetic contours of naturalism, I claim here, that impose the criteria through which "a certain limited optic on the world, a *'selective tradition,'* has been imagined, and is proposed, as a universal" (Lazarus 2011: 32). The "pomo-postcolonialism" of Homi Bhabha and his followers instantiates a paradigm that opposes what Arif Dirlik is compelled, as Lazarus notes, to describe as the "metanarrative of progress," which was "conceived by modernizationalists and radicals alike in the decades after World War II" (qtd. in Lazarus 2014: 14). Its opposition to totalizing historicity and promotion of irreducible difference, hybridity, and a well-nigh Huntingtonian civilizational discourse redounds, however, to modernism's dialectical opposite in naturalism. Vasant Kaiwar holds that, in replicating the "Orientalist geography of Asia-Europe, East-West," what he derides as the "postcolonialist" approach perpetuates "a hostile takeover of the idea of class contradiction by a class-free civilizational consciousness" (2014: 95). Following a poststructuralist intolerance for totalization-as-totalitarian, postcolonial theory's investment in geo-cultural identity consequently replaces the grand narrative of history with the organic plurality of nature either in "naturalising inequalities under ascriptive titles" or in "the further naturalising effects of the displacement of categories like 'hybridity' from animal breeding to cultural identities" (Kaiwar 2014: 108).

The approach of this book is therefore to view naturalism less as a method, mode, or style, which is either dutifully followed or so radically reinterpreted as to annul the form altogether, than as a coherent cultural logic determined by structural location in the capitalist world-system. Naturalism names neither a chronology nor a technique. Thus, unlike Hill, for whom naturalism is a matter of conscious (subjective) practice,[14] I maintain that a writer might well be practicing naturalism without claiming or even knowing it and that naturalism itself (as an objective cultural logic) might take on a variety of appearances and might or might not feature the tropes of categorical convention.

In a postcolonial historical context, the naturalist position coincides with the era following decolonization and formal independence during the late twentieth-century transition from an imperialist to a multinational or neo-imperialist stage of capitalism. Furthermore, postcolonial naturalism is the field of cultural influence (uneven, certainly, but pervasively present) associated with the Third-World national bourgeoisie in the aftermath of independence and therefore reflects or refracts the embattled interests of this class standpoint (frequently validated through appeals to cultural identity, which is itself naturalized), just as European naturalism reflected bourgeois anxiety in the face of revolutionary upheaval. Therefore, we can also revise to some degree Jameson's own periodization of naturalism. By extending the structural causality that he claims for modernism to its aesthetic counter pole in naturalism (as a cultural logic in its own right), we find that—like modernism—naturalism must, too,

> be seen as a project that re-emerges over and over again with the various national situations as a specific and unique national-literary

---

[14] Hill writes, "When it comes to definition, then, I propose taking writers and critics at their word: if they called it naturalism, then naturalism it was" (2020: 11).

task or imperative, whose cross-cultural kinship with its neighbors is not always evident (either at home or abroad). (Jameson 2002: 180)

Accounts of the rise of Shizenshugi (Japanese naturalism) and its retreat from socially-engaged realism, for instance, might consider the form's emergence in what was effectively the bourgeois revolution of the Meiji Restoration and its subsequent suppression of labor unrest rather than as the merely derivative cultural appropriation of European aesthetic models.[15] Such a materialist reframing helps to counter still-prevalent assessments of, for example, Tsugi Tengai's *Hatsusugata* (1900) as merely a failed attempt to write the Japanese *Nana*. Similarly, Lebanese Civil War novels by internationally celebrated writers like Hassan Daoud, Elias Khoury, and Rashid al-Daif, despite their respective differences, all share a broadly liberal-humanist inclination, a preoccupation with subjective trauma and destruction, and a pronounced disenchantment with Leftist revolutionary ideals (despite bearing Leftist sympathies). In addition, they tend toward a fragmentary narrative sensibility (one often mistaken for modernism or postmodernism[16]) that could, in fact, qualify such works as expressions of literary naturalism.[17] The primacy of affect, image, recursivity, and passive voice in Khoury's hauntingly elegiac *Little Mountain* (1977), for instance, is expressive not only of the repudiation of narrative, but of other intolerable totalizations as well (nation, party, class, history) and a Leftist disconsolation that reactively enshrines the sensual individual consciousness as the inviolable measure of history. Estranged from conventional stylistic categories, *Little Mountain* is perhaps most productively read alongside Orwell's *Homage to Catalonia* or, as we shall see, Mariano Azuela's *The Underdogs*, a novel of frustrated utopian hope that lapses into what I discuss in chapter four as a species of anti-utopianism reliant upon naturalistic metaphor.

To extend Jameson's structuralist claims for modernism to such a global theory of naturalism (and to do so in terms that explicitly square Hill's intellectual project with that of the WReC) is also to posit that

---

[15] For a useful discussion see Henshall, Ken 2010. "The Puzzling Perception of Japanese Naturalism," *Japan Forum* 22.3–4: 331–356.

[16] Indeed, debates over the novel's style describe it variously as modernist or postmodernist. Edward Said himself unequivocally declares Khoury a postmodernist: "At great personal risk...Khoury has forged (in the Joycean sense) a national and novel, unconventional, fundamentally postmodern literary career" (2000: 323).

[17] See Lang, Felix 2016. *The Lebanese Post-Civil War Novel: Memory, Trauma, and Capital* (Basingstoke: Palgrave).

when we reckon in that unevenness of development... a multitemporal and multilinear picture of [naturalism] emerges which cannot be flattened out into any simple model of influence or of cultural and poetic imperialism, of cross-cultural diffusion or of teleological virtuality [...]. (Jameson 2002: 180)

As Hill puts it, naturalism is neither simply local nor "'about' the global in the immediate and mediated ways that Debjani Ganguly and Pheng Cheah, for example, have traced in later twentieth- and twenty-first century fiction about globalization and postcoloniality" (2020: 169). Yet, the conditions for its local apparitions are nevertheless precipitated by global forces of combined and uneven development. As Hill himself crucially recognizes, "the world political economy reverberates in them" (2020: 169).

Hill notes that, "on a large scale, literary tendencies conventionally treated as sequential 'eras' may be coeval" (2020: 183)—a claim that perhaps surprisingly accords with Jameson's own theory of cultural periodization. However, he also claims that the inherent instability of the transnational naturalist field (largely the result of its "monocentric" reliance on the discursive authority of the figure "Zola" and a lack of "multidirectional citations" in its varied peripheral expressions) ultimately precipitated its disintegration in the mid-1970s (2020: 182). While he recognizes, as many critics have done, naturalism's influence on many postcolonial writers like Naguib Mahfouz, Ngũgĩ wa Thiong'o, Cyprian Ekwensi, and Bessie Head, then, Hill's study shows little interest in the specific phenomenon of postcolonial literary naturalism and in fact holds that naturalism as a transnational movement had, by the first decade following decolonization, effectively arrived at its end.

Postcolonial Naturalism and/as Narrative Entropy

The undoubtedly paradigmatic statement on postcolonial naturalism remains Neil Lazarus's seminal 1987 essay "Realism and Naturalism in African Fiction," which compares Njabulo Ndebele's theory of "spectacular" and "ordinary" African fictional modalities with Lukács's influential distinction between naturalist description and realist narration (Lazarus 2007: 340). Considering the radical socialist realism of Ngũgĩ's *Petals of Blood* alongside what ostensibly presents as the abject defeatism of Meja Mwangi's *Going Down River*, Lazarus questions whether the classic Lukácsian critique of naturalism as a "degraded form, one whose effective politicality emerges as contrary to its radical intent" can effectively be applied to postcolonial African literatures (2007: 341). The radicalism inherent in African naturalism, Lazarus contends, in fact lies in its subversion of the "totalizing, rationalistic progressivism" privileged in Lukácsian realism and in an alternative emphasis on the "indeterminacy of the political action to which it points" (2007: 342).

Coundouriotis takes up Lazarus's theorization of postcolonial naturalism as a literature of "sheer resistance" (Lazarus 2007: 342) in her own study of the African war novel, which countenances "ordinary people and places their fate at the center of the nation's concerns" in the form of a "people's history" (Coundouriotis 2014: 11). This concern for the lives of ordinary people Coundouriotis traces back, somewhat surprisingly, to the Goncourts and Zola. These naturalist writers, she avers, opposed a sentimental "politics of pity" (Arendt) with an effort to bestow "dignity" upon the lives of the poor by granting them the right to representation or, rather, the right to be represented in fiction, which she views as the cultural complement to an expanded political franchise (Coundouriotis 2014: 6). Echoing the appraisals of Arendt, Coundouriotis thus presents the French naturalists as fully "progressive" and in "solidarity with the people" on whose behalf their fictions labor (2014: 7). Putting aside the question of slippage here between the political and cultural forms of representation that Spivak famously distinguishes as *Vertretung* and *Darstellung* (Spivak 1988: 277), this book, as suggested above, will take a less sanguine view of naturalist political attitudes than do the accounts of Arendt and Coundouriotis.

What Lazarus's essay does not provide, however, is a theory of postcolonial naturalism that troubles the presumption—familiar from the Goncourts to Zola to London—to represent 'the people.' If Coundouriotis's "people's right to the novel" is reducible to the right to be rendered the scandalous object of the bourgeois gaze, then it does not yet satisfy the radically universal demand informing what Brazilian writer and critic Antônio Cândido famously calls "O direito à literatura" ["The right to literature"] or even what (as Stefan Helgesson observes) Homi Bhabha's long forthcoming book names "the right to narrate" (Helgesson 2022: 99). As Helgesson puts it, Cândido's late essay, published in 1988, represents his "effort to square the circle on social justice and aesthetic discrimination" by arguing for an egalitarian model of broad literary inclusion (indeed, a World-Literature) that retains a sensitivity to aesthetic complexity and the overdetermined interanimation of global forms. His invocation of literature as a universal human right is therefore ultimately utopian and, in the face of postmodernist pluralism, defiantly modernist. Helgesson characterizes

Cândido's rights discourse in precisely such terms as "proleptic" and aspirational rather than empirically descriptive. Thus,

> it speaks to the present by anticipating a possible future. But this is *not* a teleology of the future anterior ('it *will* have been')—instead, it is an open future in which the right to literature enables the continued, dialectical and above all unpredictable labour of making society inhabitable and more just. (Helgesson 2022: 99)

Such fragmentary resistance to totalizing, progressivist grand narratives (like the universal 'right to literature') and concomitant favoring of indeterminate potential action that is not yet codifiable as a politics could, at first sight, also just as easily fall under the heading of *postmodernism*, which likewise "rejects the master narrative of realism" and ostensibly favors a populist pluralism (Lazarus 2007: 343). Therefore, if naturalism is defined simply as the fictional representation of "a localistic welter of abstract facts straining towards but failing to reach their social truth," it stands to reason that the "implicit utopianism," "pragmatism," and "sensitivity to the materiality of everyday life" that Lazarus observes in the fiction of Bessie Head, for instance, are not incompatible with the "naturalist idiom" (2007: 342–343).

The periodizing schematic that I advocate here aims to resist this very conflation. A theory of postcolonial naturalism that thinks its relation to European naturalism in structuralist rather than stylistic or derivatively cultural terms could suggest, much to the contrary, that Head's materialist and utopianist "challenge to the credentials of realism" is, despite its idiomatic resemblance to some cosmetic features of naturalism, resolutely modernist in its orientation to capitalist modernity (Lazarus 2007: 343). This can especially be observed in the way that the realist elements of Head's *When Rain Clouds Gather* (1972), which critically anatomizes the social and natural forces of inertial and active opposition to revolution in rural Botswana, are juxtaposed with bursts of delirious estrangement in *A Question of Power* (1974). Hence, the consonance that Lazarus observes of Head's work with Gabriel Garcia Marquez and Salman Rushdie is less surprising than it might initially appear (2007: 343). Each is a practitioner of modernism. Similarly, emphasis on the realist, observational style of a writer like Amitav Ghosh might belie the historicizing labors of his work, which consist of dragging into historical and agential consciousness social phenomena and even non-human voices that have been relegated to the unconscious domain of nature. Through the conventions of the realist novel, then (and with the exception of his speculative fiction

The Calcutta Chromosome), Ghosh's project can be seen as deviating in an arguably modernist direction despite its cosmetic adherence to the naturalist aesthetic.

In this light, we might also consider Anita Duneer's recent claim of a "direct evolutionary lineage" connecting the postcolonial novel to American literary naturalism (2020: 72). Though she concedes that the two might seem incomparable in their philosophical hues and political implications, Duneer claims, like Coundouriotis, that "at their core, the urgent matter for both American literary naturalism and postcolonial literature is the plight of characters trying to maintain humanity and dignity while subjected to forces beyond their control" (2020: 49). Against such invocations of subjective dignity, however, one might usefully recall Fanon's observation that the resistance of the colonized "has nothing to do with 'human' dignity" because the "colonized subject has never heard of such an ideal" (2004: 9).

Duneer defines literary naturalism as saliently concerned with the universal problem of human nature or "how to maintain our humanity when social, economic, and/or environmental conditions elicit survival instincts of the animal within" (2020: 49). Significantly underscoring both the epistemological and empirical foundations of naturalism and what I will call its anti-utopian inclinations, she observes,

> The tendency for naturalistic characters to make poor choices and sabotage their endeavors to improve their conditions often emerges as a result of limited understanding of themselves and their circumstances. While naturalist characters may not grasp the larger forces at play, a fuller picture is typically conveyed through the ostensibly objective scientific lens of the narrator. (Duneer 2020: 49)

Hampering this deployment of standpoint epistemology, however, is its reliance on the subjectivist implication that the woeful circumstance of the naturalist character is the result of poor choices predicated on the lack of objective point of view, which the naturalist diagnostic confidently provides. In chapter two, I will associate such self-exemption of representation from the dynamics of immanent history with Hegel's notion of the Beautiful Soul.

With its emphasis on the cultivation of exceptional dignity, Duneer's theory of literary naturalism is derived almost exclusively from the influential work of Donald Pizer, for whom the form (in its distinctively North American manifestation, at least) is chiefly concerned with probing the desperate lives of its impoverished, uneducated, or otherwise precarious subjects for signs of what he calls the "extraordinary and excessive in human nature" (1984: 11). Pizer likewise reads American naturalism as closely affiliated to modernism in its elevation of banality and vulgarity (he cites Joyce), its confounding of progressive temporality, and its acclamation of subjective experience. Thus, he avers that the

> distinctiveness of the form of the naturalistic novel lies in the attempt of that form to persuade us, in the context of a fully depicted concrete world, that only the questioning, seeking, timeless self is real, that the temporal world outside the self is often treacherous and always apparent. The naturalistic novel thus reflects our doubts about conventional notions of character and experience while continuing to affirm through its symbolism both the sanctity of the self and the bedrock emotional reality of our basic physical nature and acts. (Pizer 1984: 39–40)

Given Pizer's emphasis on the sanctity of subjective experience/truth and the derangement of linear temporality, it is not wholly unexpected that Duneer should find the postcolonial iteration of American naturalism homologous to, perhaps even continuous with postmodernism. Indeed, she presents a table, explicitly modeled after Ihab Hassan's well-known charting of modernist and postmodernist features, that delineates what she calls the fluid "evolution of naturalistic concerns influenced by the global and postmodern concerns of postcolonialism" (Duneer 2020: 51).

However, with what is by now an obligatory acknowledgement of the contentious "debates about the universalist and essentialist assumptions implied in his distinction between 'Third World' and 'First World,'" Duneer also refers postcolonial naturalism to Jameson's theory of national allegory in the "era of globalization," which would seem to incline her theorization away from Pizer's model of the universally subjective search for human dignity and the postmodern inflections that she otherwise prioritizes (2020: 61).[18] For instance, Duneer's

---

[18] Duneer's essay offers a brief but sweepingly eclectic survey of such works spanning the long twentieth century: Native American writer/activist Zitkála-Šá's "The Soft-Hearted Sioux" (1901), Caribbean writer Eric Walrand's short story collection *Tropic Death* (1926), Saudi Arabian writer Abdelrahman Munif's great petrofiction novel *City of Salt* (1984), Indian novelist Aravind Adiga's *The White Tiger* (2008), Cuban-American writer Achy Obejas's *Ruins* (2009), Sinha's *Animal's People* (2009), and South Korean filmmaker Bong Joon-ho's sensational *Parasite* (2019). Her brief but insightful discussion of Adiga's *The White Tiger* (a novel that I also explore here as an example

assertion that works of postcolonial naturalism present "perspectives of the subaltern condition that reveal larger forces characters do not fully understand" (2020: 72) departs sharply from the perhaps immoderate claim she makes of British Indian novelist Indra Sinha's *Animal's People*—that here we find "the voice of the subaltern who *can* and does speak" and "claims a sense of agency, self-acceptance, and dignity in defiance of the forces that he cannot see or control" (2020: 66)—toward a critical allegorization of the limits that such subjectivism imposes on one's capacity to map (or speak to) the global present.

Here, Duneer's analysis comes closest to grasping the ideological content of postcolonial naturalism, which is predicated not on the subjective quest for human dignity but on the elision of history and class struggle by the rhetoric of ontological difference, cynicism, and entropic degeneration. Thus, what she recognizes as the stylistic "gritty realism" of *Parasite* (2019) cannot alone sustain its categorization as a work of postcolonial naturalism, just as Head's early objective style does not in itself qualify her work as naturalist. Rather, it seems to me, Bong's film, like Head's fiction, presents precisely the inverse operation: the domestic enclave is demystified in a fierce, global class antagonism, and the seemingly neutral spatial coordinates of late capitalist life are thereby summarily *denaturalized* not merely as the *"site* of politics, conflict and struggle, but also the very thing being fought over" (Wegner 2002: 179), much in the sense that Henri Lefebvre observes of the ideological imperatives of domestic spatiality:

> Familial space, linked to naturalness through genitality, is the guarantor of meaning as well as of social (spatial) practice. Shattered by a host of separations and segregations, social unity is able to reconstitute itself at the level of the family unity, for the purpose of, and by means of, generalized production. The reproduction of production relations continues apace amid (and on the basis of) the destruction of social bonds to the extent that the symbolic space of 'familiarity' (family life, everyday life), the only such space to be appropriated, continues to hold sway. (1991: 232)

of the postcolonial Bildungsroman) exposes the valorization of subjective experience as both an instrument and an effect of neoliberal ideology, such that even the novel's celebrated critique of Indian casteism is "inspired by the ethos of American individualism"; therefore, despite the narrator's "compelling story of personal struggle," Duneer notes that "his actions lacks [sic] the solidarity of class consciousness" and therefore merely allow him "mobility within the established system" (2020: 68).

Thus, the critical force of Bong's film lies principally in its *derealization* of the ideological structures and instrumental spatializations of the contemporary world-system (or of what the late Mark Fisher famously calls "capitalist realism"[19]) as these are anchored in the domestic locus. In this sense, the film's punctual moments of surreal excess may recommend it as a work of what the WReC identifies as irrealism—or perhaps even of the critical operation that science fiction theorist Darko Suvin calls *cognitive estrangement*;[20] both, I argue, are forms of modernist praxis and thus the polar opposite of naturalism.

Postcolonial Naturalism and Mariano Azuela's *The Underdogs*

The value of the theory of postcolonial naturalism that I am proposing here, then, is that it enables one to make such granular distinctions within a general periodizing framework. We can even discern finer gradations and torsions within a single work along the axial continuum defined by these two poles. A naturalist reading might, for instance, productively supplement the WReC's discussion of Mariano Azuela's novel of the Mexican Revolution *The Underdogs* (1920) as a work of peripheral realism. The novel's unstable point of view and fragmentary, picaresque narrative structure[21] as well as its "attempt to incorporate indigenous and residual folk values" disrupt, the group contends, what is otherwise a realist narrative of the ideal-type with "surrealist, avant-garde, and vanguardia" flourishes (WReC 2015: 79). The limitation of such a reading, however, is that it again duplicates the split figure of realism-modernism that risks obscuring from view other dynamics in the text that more clearly exemplify what the WReC authors describe as the book's "attempt to give voice to the collective forces of the period, albeit through a liberal bourgeois rather than a properly radical perspective of the revolution, thus reflecting the ambivalent role of the middle classes" (2015: 79).

Outside the text, the clearest anecdotal/biographical suggestion that Azuela's liberal bourgeois reaction to revolution betrays currents of naturalism is surely the author's lifelong, unwavering devotion

---

[19] See Fisher, Mark 2009. *Capitalist Realism: Is There No Alternative?* (New York: Zero).
[20] See Suvin, Darko 2016 [1979]. *Metamorphoses of Science Fiction*. Ed. Gerry Canavan (Oxford: Peter Lang), 24.
[21] The work was originally published as newspaper episodes beginning in 1915, which might equally explain this narrative effect.

to Zola. As Salvador Azuela writes in the prologue to Frances Kellam Hendricks and Beatrice Berler's translation of *The Underdogs*, his father "felt profoundly the influence of Émile Zola in his works," so much so that a framed portrait of the great naturalist "presided over the daily tasks" of Azuela's writing desk as he composed his best-known novel (1963: ix). Among his favorite works, according to Salvador, was Zola's *Germinal* (1885), a novel that expresses both a fulsome sympathy for striking coal miners in 1860s Northern France and the liberal reformist's ambivalent dread at the infamous "black and avenging army of men, germinating slowly in its furrows, growing upwards in readiness for harvests to come, until one day soon their ripening would burst open the earth itself" (Zola 2004: 523). The other is Zola's late novel of the Franco-Prussian War and the Paris Commune, *La Débâcle* (1892), the closing pages of which express the author's vexed mixture of equal parts contempt for the uprising and sympathy for the brutality of what is rendered as its historically necessary suppression:

> He [Maurice] was losing all faith in mankind, and he felt that the Commune was impotent, being torn asunder by too many contradictory elements, getting more frenzied, incoherent and stupid as it was increasingly threatened. It had not been able to carry out a single one of all the social reforms it had promised, and it was already certain that it would leave no lasting achievement behind. (Zola 1972: 474)

Despite Azuela's disavowal of the technical particulars of Zola's experimental method and his misgivings regarding the latter's notion that "the novel should be treated as means for the scientific enlightenment of people," one does not have to probe too deeply in *The Underdogs* for evidence of Zola's prominent artistic and philosophical influence (S. Azuela 1963: ix). A man of science himself, a licensed physician, Azuela confesses, "I found the 'bad' men for my novels in my practice of medicine in the villages and the rural districts. When they solicited my professional help, I had many occasions to observe them in their most intimate moments and *in their own lairs*" (M. Azuela 1963: xvi, emphasis added). This penchant for observation of the bestial masses is intensified following Azuela's personal disappointment in the wake of the Madero Revolution of 1911, which had roused the previously apolitical physician to a fervent support. After his appointment as *jefe politico* (or local prefect) of Lagos de Moreno is obstructed by local authorities and "pseudo-*maderistas*," he writes that the incident "revealed to me that the revolution would be a great failure"; furthermore, he intimates,

"It disillusioned me and from then on I determined to be a calm and impartial observer" after the model of the naturalist documentarian (M. Azuela 1963: xvii).

With the defeat of Pancho Villa in 1915, Azuela, who was treating wounded soldiers in Lagos, was forced to flee into the sierras. Here, he endured intense hardship and hunger and was harried by the forces of Venustiano Carranza, who had supported Madero's overthrow of the *ancien régime* of Porfirio Díaz but who subsequently led the northern Constitutionalist Army against Zapata and Villa in the civil war that followed Madero's assassination by the rightwing coup of 1913. The personal suffering and political disillusionment that came as a result inspired Azuela's art, however, and his abandonment of political life soon proved a boon for his writing:

> That is the reason the novels I wrote in these months of bitterness were conceived, expanded, and completely impregnated with stinging mordacity. My defeat was twofold: I had lost economically as well—all my savings for the past two years went up in smoke and without ideals, full of disenchantment I had to face the facts and perform my immediate duty—the maintenance of my family. (M. Azuela 1963: xviii)

A mordant spirit of failure certainly permeates *The Underdogs*, particularly in the brutal disillusionment of its explicitly 'quixotic' protagonist, Luis Cervantes, a journalist and medical student, who is briefly caught up in the ardor of a revolutionary idealism of which he is then painfully disabused. Cervantes's intellectual and moral superiority to the uneducated and boorish revolutionaries is repeatedly made explicit; he perceives more clearly than they both the broadly emancipatory potential and the locally situated strategic logic of the movement. Despite his idealistic speeches, however, Cervantes's initial encounter with the "scrofulous" and "reckless" soldiers inspires a premonitory vision of the inevitable failure to come: "Luis Cervantes, who shared with the troops a hidden, implacable, mortal hatred of the upper classes and officials, felt that the last veil had fallen from his eyes and that he could see clearly the final outcome of the struggle" (M. Azuela 1963: 77). Cervantes's efforts to maintain his motivating idealism are most sorely tested by his encounter with Captain Alberto Solís, who chastises him for his callow enthusiasm and relates his own anti-utopian disillusionment:

> 'I dreamed of a flowery meadow at the end of the road; I found a swamp.' My friend, there are deeds and there are men which

> are nothing but pure bitterness. And that bitterness falls drop by drop on the soul; it embitters everything; it poisons everything. Enthusiasm, hopes, ideals, happiness—nothing! Soon nothing remains: either you turn into a bandit like the rest, or you withdraw, hiding yourself behind the walls of an impenetrable and ferocious selfishness. (M. Azeula 1963: 204–205)

"The revolution," Solís concludes in one of the more striking of the novel's many naturalistic conceits, "is a hurricane. The man who is swept up in it is no longer a man; he is a wretched dry leaf snatched away by the gale" (205). The tragic irony, he further suggests, is that "we who come to offer our whole enthusiasm, our very lives to crush one miserable assassin turn out to be the builders of an enormous pedestal on which a hundred or two hundred thousand monsters of the same species may be raised up!" (212).

The romantic Valderrama later responds to the news of Villa's defeat in terms that similarly depict revolution as an unbridled natural force, this one chthonic and sublimely indifferent to the destruction that it leaves behind:

> Villa? Obregón? Carranza? X, Y, Z! What difference does it make to me? I love the Revolution the way I love an erupting volcano! The volcano because it is a volcano; the Revolution because it is the Revolution! But the stones left above or below after the cataclysm, what do they matter to me? (252–253)

Azuela thus calls into question not only the legitimacy and purpose of this revolution but of revolution as such. Surveying a scene of destroyed houses and smoking rifles, Cervantes "believed he had discovered a symbol of revolution in those clouds of smoke and those clouds of dust which in brotherly fashion rose arm in arm, intermingled, then faded away" (212). When Demetrio Macías, who has dreamt of returning to his family, at long last embraces his wife and son, she tearfully begs him not to return to the fight. When he answers with grimly suggestive silence, she asks for what purpose they are now fighting. As an answer, Demetrio hurls a stone into the deep canyon before them, saying only, "See how that rock keeps on falling—falling?" (259). The historical content of revolutionary strife is thus displaced into nature, which dumbly refuses any signification other than itself.

Cervantes eventually concedes the wisdom of Solís's words and, like the author, renounces political struggle. He later writes to his former comrade Venancio from El Paso, Texas, inviting the latter to partner with him in opening a "genuine Mexican restaurant," where, he writes, "we will make ourselves rich in a very short time," perhaps prefiguring the latter-day culturalization and commodification of the political (249). The letter also sarcastically denigrates his fellow revolutionaries. Initially offering his condolences for the loss of two former comrades, Cervantes nevertheless admits that he was not surprised to learn "that they stabbed one another on account of a game of cards"; likewise, he expresses regret at being unable to extend to the unscrupulous Margarito his "fervent congratulations upon the most noble and admirable act of his life—that of committing suicide" (249). Cervantes's characterizations here are consistent with those throughout the novel: the revolutionaries are repeatedly portrayed either as cloddish, humorous foils to Cervantes's romantic rhetoric and steady virtue or as an ignorant, haphazardly organized mob of basely opportunistic looters and rapists, who chiefly use the uprising as the mendacious pretext for lawless indulgence.

A naturalistic reading of the novel would also reveal what I will discuss in chapter one as the trammeling encroachment of scenic stasis (or description), upon narrative momentum, which might further suggest an alternative accounting of the book's fragmented, episodic structure following Lukács's suggestion that naturalism presents "a series of static pictures, of still lives connected only through the relations of objects arrayed one beside the other according to their own inner logic, never following one from the other, never one out of the other" (Lukács 2005: 144). While I do not have the space here to treat fully this theme in *The Underdogs*, one might consider Azuela's tendency toward poetic fallacy or the projection onto an encompassing and pitiless landscape of an acute, if unnamable, political despair:

> The mountains stood out like great stretched-out monsters with angular backbones. There were hills which looked like the heads of colossal Aztec idols with gigantic frightening faces and grotesque grimaces which now made one smile, then aroused a vague fear—a sort of mysterious foreboding. (224)

Strolling their encampment at sunset, Demetrio and Camila survey the idyllic farmland nearby: "Stripped clean of vegetation, the golden earth of the plain ploughed ready for sowing spread out in an immense desolation" save for the "veritable miracles" of three large ash trees, whose foliage bends forlornly to the earth: "I can't make out what there is round here that makes me feel so sad," Demetrio confesses (235).

Beyond mourning the specific failures of the Mexican Revolution and the corruption of its political ideals, the naturalist abjuration of Azuela's novel impeaches revolution in principle and would appear to have more in common with George Orwell's bitter testament to revolutionary disillusionment in *Homage to Catalonia* (1938) than, as the WReC authors suggest (2015: 79), with José Eustasio Rivera's *The Vortex* (1924). The latter attempts the very different project, it seems, of articulating a historicizing account of the rubber trade in the Amazon basin *despite* the imposing threats of the rainforest and the caprices of human psychic and moral frailty, an agenda that it bears in common with Head's *When Rain Clouds Gather*. The latter novels' departure from realism of the "ideal-type" thus marks them (like *Parasite*) as modernist in their Imaginary orientation, while Azuela's despairing surrender to a tendentiously anti-symbolic nature indicates a naturalist deviation. All four of these texts, however, operate in relation to the Imaginary poles of naturalism and modernism as described above within the broad historical situation that they define.

Here, I attempt to outline the narratological and ideological contours of this periodizing concept in which the form of postcolonial naturalism emerges as an historical (and hysterical) symptom, an anxious response to the crisis of representation in the postcolony. Postcolonial naturalism designates the complementary opposite of the modernist pole, though the texts placed under its mostly unacknowledged imprimatur or read according to its tacitly inscribed interpretive protocols are often disproportionately favored as representative of the "postcolonial condition." In the first chapter, I offer a narratological analysis of V.S. Naipaul's *Guerillas* as a work of the naturalist aesthetic exemplary in the tension that it manifests between the contrary operations of Lukácsian description and narration. I also argue that the novel demonstrates what Gilles Deleuze, in his writing on cinema, terms *the impulse-image*, a deviation from what he theorizes as the (realist) *movement-image*. Between the kinetic action of realism and the affective ideation of surrealism lies the impulse-image, which Deleuze explicitly associates with Zolian naturalism in its positing of an inescapably *originary milieu* and its simultaneous refusal of realist totalization on the one hand and surrealist fragmentation on the other.

Chapter two focuses on the novels of South African writer and critic Lewis Nkosi, where I examine postcolonial naturalism's management of the dilemma that finds a resistant national consciousness suddenly without a definite oppositional object (the loss of object being a Freudian precondition for melancholia) and risks withdrawal into resignedly ironic and subjective self-reference and self-acquittal. This defining quandary, which registers on one level as that between the personal and the political, I here thematize as hysteria versus the condition that Hegel identifies as the Beautiful Soul. In the intimate politics of Nkosi's *Mating Birds*, we find a formal and ethical solipsism, which provides the subjectivist criteria against which the novel's presentation of middle-class anxiety must be read. Conversely, his late novel of revolution, *Underground People*, gives voice, despite Nkosi's arch disregard for South African solidarity criticism and his skeptical view of revolutionary resistance, to the hysteric's desire—ever deferred—to think simultaneously the immiscible domains of the personal and political, the natural and historical.

Chapter three examines the play between what I call heredity and horizon in three exemplary works of the form that, in some sense, remains the presiding genre of postcolonial literature: the Bildungsroman. Engaging important recent considerations by Jed Esty, Maria Helena Lima, Simon Hay, Pheng Cheah, and others, I argue that the central impasse defining the postcolonial Bildungsroman arises from the structural inability of the national bourgeoise to manifest the destiny exemplified (however imperfectly) in the classical form, caught as it is between the political demands of the masses and the nonplace of the new Empire, from which national independence has provided no safeguard. In the frustrated teleology or unrealized *Bildung* of these texts, we find the naturalist crisis of narrative, which here expresses itself in the overwhelming of realism's horizonal ambition by the foreclosed temporality of heredity. In Jean Rhys's *Wide Sargasso Sea*, I argue that the novel's defining thematic and formal retreat into the bitter consolation of inherited form and arrested temporality can be read in part as a response to the rise of the socialist Dominica Labour Party and the influence of the Black Power movement.

However, the task throughout this book will be to regard such responses (reactionary or otherwise) not merely as subjective—as attitudes or claims to be refuted or dismissed as such—but rather as conditioned by a unique historical situation and structural orientation from which voluntary exemption is not wholly possible. Therefore, turning next to Michelle Cliff's *Abeng*, a novel that might be read as a direct riposte to *Wide Sargasso Sea*, I examine the narrative arc of protagonist Clare Savage's physical, sexual, personal, cultural, and ideological development, one in which her every effort at Becoming is hampered by the inertial force of Being. Even the novel's celebrated reclamation of a suppressed maternal history and communal solidarity must contend with, as Jennifer J. Smith's reading of its sequel *No Telephone to Heaven* suggests, the way in which the return to the body as the site of political praxis also imposes the limits of the cycle, destiny, and non-futurity upon any radical agenda. In Aravind Adiga's *The White Tiger*, we see the persistence of this dilemma (and of Zola's explicit influence) into the twenty-first century and the further mutation of late capital. Here, what is frequently hailed as a thoroughgoing critique of neoliberalism and the entrepreneurialist ethic rather enacts what Slavoj Žižek (after Peter Sloterdijk) calls *cynical reason*, ironically reaffirming the very system it ostensibly critiques by neutralizing in advance the possibility of any alternative.

Following the intimation expressed in Naipaul's *Guerillas* that the political imagination has, along with history and narrative, exhausted itself such that we are unable to imagine a social order that is not simply the prolongation of this one, chapter four posits the presence of the anti-utopian temperament as a defining feature of postcolonial naturalism. This anti-utopianism bears two faces: first, in refusing or negating the imaginative possibility of revolutionary change, one current of anti-utopianism naturalizes the social status quo; alternatively, the second form is born of a desire for social transformation that has been thwarted precisely through its realization and thus evacuated of its utopian content. First, in Neel Mukherjee's widely celebrated novel *The Lives of Others*, which instructively juxtaposes a tale of multi-generational domestic conflict with that of the Naxalite insurgency, we find a variant of the solipsism seen earlier in what Mukherjee calls the "great circularity," a kind of natural law or gravitational force superintending the individual and familial destinies of the characters as well as the distribution of material resources. This concept-term, which provides the novel's philosophical and formal logic, is echoed in the book's curious use of the future perfect tense and narrative prolepsis. Here, too, I suggest, we find the influence of a specifically Orwellian brand of anti-utopianism, not least in Mukherjee's concluding reauthoring of the Ministry of Love.

Finally, I identify the second current of anti-utopianism (frustrated utopianism) in Orlando Patterson's *The Children of Sisyphus*. Situating the novel within the tragic foreclosure of emancipatory horizons and reading it alongside theories of Rastafarian resistance, I argue that it enacts a paradoxical *active nihilism*, the recognition of which helps to elucidate Patterson's balefully masochistic and fatalistic themes. Patterson's anti-utopianism is therefore distinct from Mukherjee's in that it offers not a moralizing affirmation of neoliberalism but a bitter anatomy of the broken promises of prior utopianisms and a scorched-earth purgation of mendacious hope. Nonetheless, in either case, we find the definitive expression of *ressentiment* that Jameson identifies as the political desire impelling naturalist figuration (1981: 201).

This book thus aims to contribute to the WReC's groundbreaking project of a periodizing theory of world-literature by way of both extension and revision. Supplementing the structural causalitity of the WReC's emphasis on peripheral irrealism, this book argues for a structurally intelligible account of "postcolonial literature" as organized under the aesthetic regime of naturalism. Equally, while I continue to be instructed by and principally uphold to one degree or another the thoroughgoing critiques of postcolonial theory offered by thinkers like Benita Parry, Neil Lazarus, Vivek Chibber, and Vasant Kaiwar, among others, the approach of the present study will be to consider "postcolonial literature" less as the invention of a theoretical enterprise whose methods or interests misconstrue its cultural object than as the crystallization of germinative historical forces, the hypogeal vitalizations of which elicit, nourish, discipline, or inhibit the flowering of distinctly expressive forms, which, as Jameson teaches, never fail to communicate their own political unconscious. Postcolonial naturalism is the name that I give to the crisis response within the nationalist culture endorsed by local bourgeois interests in the period following formal independence, when the marginal *desire called modernism* (for history, for narrative, for utopia) is met with a forlornly fatalistic return to instinct or essence and the (ahistorical, anti-narrative, anti-utopian) *desire called nature*.

Chapter 1

Narrative Desolation and Postcolonial Naturalism in V.S. Naipaul's *Guerrillas*

The world is what it is; men who are nothing, who allow themselves to become nothing, have no place in it.
—V.S. Naipaul, *A Bend in the River* (1989a: 3)

'Life is simpler than that' Zola says at the end of one of his criticisms of Stendhal. He thus completes the transition from the old realism to the new, from realism proper to naturalism... The writer no longer participates in the great struggles of his time, but is reduced to a mere spectator and chronicler of public life.
—Georg Lukács, "The Zola Centenary" (2002: 89)

Later nature, being there, makes itself felt, or at least that part of nature of which science has given us the secret, and about which we have no longer any right to romance.
—Émile Zola, "The Experimental Novel" (1964: 53)

As much is made of the Victorian cast of V.S. Naipaul's stately, scrupulous prose as of the writer's emphatic self-construction as a detached gentleman observer in the model of Anthony Trollope, Charles Kingsley, or James Anthony Froude (1988: 7). Detecting a distinctly "Victorian residue" in Naipaul's *The Enigma of Arrival*, Chu-chueh Cheng claims, for example, that the author's mature work might well be regarded as "a geographical and historical extension of Victorian literature" itself, illuminating an abiding if not wholly unexpected "imbrication of the postcolonial era and the Victorian period" (2006: 1, 4). Naipaul, Cheng concludes, is a "belated" Victorian who, much like the melancholic narrator of *The Enigma of Arrival*, arrives "too late to find the England, the heart of Empire" (Naipaul 1987: 130) from which he seeks an ever-deferred affirmation. More characteristic of conventional criticisms is Pascale Casanova's condemnation of what she views as Naipaul's shrewd reproduction of "the narrative models of 19th century writers" (Casanova 2001). Equating Naipaul's 2001 Nobel Prize for Literature with Henry Kissinger's 1973 Nobel Prize for Peace, Casanova offers the analogic reduction that Naipaul's "conventional style is to literature what his conservative public pronouncements are to politics" (Casanova 2001).

Yet, as Sara Suleri and Timothy Bewes also suggest, Naipaulian style is perhaps less attributable to the imaginative or even moral failure of the ambitious colonial subject than to the objective historical circumstances that produce him, and Naipaul's re-authoring of colonial tropes—as in his misappropriation of the imperialist traveler's gaze in *An Area of Darkness*—is neither naïve nor blindly derivative. Countering a chorus of universal indictments, Suleri argues that, "located as they are at the intersection of the colonial and postcolonial worlds, Naipaul's narratives are forced to record the astonishment of the initiate" even as they ultimately reveal his inevitable disappointment and pitiless self-incrimination (Suleri 1992: 152). Similarly, Bewes considers Naipaul's stylistic belatedness as both symptom and condition of the ethico-formal quandary that he names postcolonial shame, which may be defined as the moral imperative to bear witness borne under the formal incapacity to do so. Naipaul's Victorian gestures therefore acknowledge the incapacity of borrowed forms (perhaps of forms more generally) to express the historical and political conundrum of postcolonial reality.

Where such reconsiderations regard the author's "dangerously anachronistic literariness" as the tortured self-examination of the postcolonial subject—and, indeed, as the demonstrated failure of the literary as such—this chapter will attempt to identify more precisely the substance of that shameful literary inheritance, which perhaps has more in common with the entropic fatalisms and anxious sublimations of Zola and of Gissing than with the confident Victorian realisms of Trollope, Froude, or even Naipaul's own once-cherished model, Dickens (Suleri 1992: 173). Reducible neither to a "pessimistic materialistic determinism" (Becker 1963: 35) nor to a resilient liberal humanism (Pizer 1993: 6), the postcolonial naturalism of Naipaul manifests through its spectacles of scenic description and its dim intimations of affect a crisis of narrative that is also a crisis of history as well as futurity. Yet this foreclosing of temporality by what I will term here naturalism's death drive nevertheless portends the presence of something historically new as the exhausted and reified forms of a prior historical situation are cast aside and new forms are sought to address a moment that as yet knows neither historical nor narrative horizons of intelligibility.

Predicating the "characteristic naturalist elements of disintegration, of loss of self, substance and humanity" and "the ultimate fall into anonymity and death" is the literary movement's foundational "dialectic of (realist) involvement and (artistic) detachment," the presumption of a neutral representation of the world as given and of the author's objective laying bare of reality's inexorable and determinate laws (Baguley 1990: 79, 81). The heroic ambitions of the epic and the world-building industry of high realism give way in the naturalist aesthetic to the ignominies of hereditary repetition, while the transgressive impulses of romanticism are met with the pitiless enclosures of insuperable natural law. The naturalist writer transforms the socially or environmentally conditioned subjective response—found in Marx's *The German Ideology*, for instance—into the extrojection of the subjective onto a "natural world," which, like a geologic lithosection, is then interpreted as the externalized sediment of an objective moral inheritance. Through this "transformation of physical into psychological states," naturalism paradoxically reinterprets the determining environment as "the physical manifestations of moral conditions" that are themselves naturally and therefore inescapably recurrent (Baguley 1990: 86). David Baguley observes that Zola, naturalism's most systematic proponent and indefatigable practitioner, "directs the reader to believe that certain moral conditions (passion, remorse, homicide, suicide) are logically, fatally, determined according to the operation of certain general laws," which, therefore, lie beyond the grasp of history and agency (86).

In Lukács's influential critique, the naturalist elision of the socio-political with the moral and the biological neutralizes any progressive political or cultural agenda (such as Zola's sympathy for proletarian struggle or his intervention in the Dreyfus affair) that naturalism might pursue (Lukács 2002: 91). Once the epic and romantic heroes have been reduced to naturalism's notorious "grey statistical mean" (Lukács 2002: 91), then "mechanical average takes the place of the dialectic unity of type and individual; description and analysis [are] substituted for epic situations and epic plots" (Lukács 2002: 89), and the percussive dissonance of socio-political strife dissolves back into the organic constancy of nature itself. Social pathologies are thereby routinized as hereditary psychopathologies.

Naturalism nullifies the epic ambitions of the realist novel—with its purposive action, progressive temporality, and socio-historical vocation—by halting the constitutive dialectic theorized in Lukács's distinction between narration and description. Naturalist description, having achieved a kind of formal autonomy, overtakes narrative motivation, cancelling out the spatio-temporal dynamism and social orientation of the latter with the leveling equivalence of all objects and, as corollary to this absence of principled selection, arriving at the cessation of movement and of history itself. Hill suggests that Lukács's pointed critique (or at least the subsequent application of it) is in many ways responsible for the decline of naturalism in the mid-twentieth century partly because it prompts the wrong question: "The issue may not be whether naturalism narrates or describes, but what it narrates: 'history,' or something else" (Hill 2020: 136). Thus, if the critic sets out to locate in naturalist fiction "a Marxian dialectic of history," they will inevitably be disappointed by its "static view of society" (Hill 2020: 136). Perhaps, Hill offers, naturalist novels "narrate *structure* rather than History, as Lukács wanted," and do so in the figuration of a "narrative sociology" (2020: 136).

The distinction here, however, seems to depend upon the perception of an ethical critical modality in the latter, discriminating between "good" and "bad" ways of writing/reading. Thus, the issue for Lukács is not that naturalism fails to provide any narrative at all or even that it refuses to represent the occluded narrative of an ultimate economic determinism; rather, as Jameson puts it, "It is as if, in the works of Zola, the idea, the preconceived theory, intervened between the work of art and the reality to be presented: Zola already knows what the basic structure of society is," and it is one "determined in advance" (Jameson 1970: 27). This is to be distinguished from the heroic or demiurgic impetus of realism, whose author, Jameson observes in regard to Balzac, "does not really know what he will find beforehand" (Jameson 1970: 27). Rather than functioning as the "privileged instrument of the analysis of reality," then, the realist novel under naturalism is "degraded to a mere illustration of a thesis" (Jameson 1970: 27). The issue is therefore that a tenacious bourgeois subjectivism projects its own presumptive universals onto the unfinished object world, which is then seen to mirror rather than challenge or disrupt those presumptions. The great innovation of Zola, Jameson argues in defense of Lukács's critique is thence the "transformation of description into action" (Jameson 2013: 50).

Nevertheless, such an internal tension between the poles of narration and description, while present in any narrative fiction, holds a conspicuous place in Naipaul's work from its inception—as may be superficially indexed by a 1960 endorsement by reviewer Robert Payne that yet adorns the most recent editions of *Miguel Street*: "Naipaul does not *tell* stories. By some sleight-of-hand he takes you to Port of Spain and *shows* you the rich, bawdy, consequential lives of the Trinidadians, *as though there were no intervening veil of words...*" (Payne 1960, emphasis added). If *Miguel Street* is celebrated for its anecdotal immediacy, its "swift caricatures" of the "loony multitude," *A House for Mr. Biswas* would seem rather to present Naipaul at his most unabashedly and expansively Dickensian, the episodic hesitancy of his early fictions having given way to the fluent indulgences of a mature realism (Payne 1960).

Yet, as Bhabha has observed, even this supreme instance of Naipaul's fidelity to classical realism—with its formal and ideological commitments to "individualism, progressivism, and the autonomy of character" on full serio-comic display—is internally disrupted by "the uncanny ambivalence of fantasy" (Bhabha 1984: 116). The "driving desire of 'Biswas'," Bhabha contends,

> conceals a much graver subject: the subject of madness, illness and loss; the repetition of failure and the deferral of desire; the trauma of being always inscribed between the unwritten—Biswas' narcissistic fables; and the endlessly rewritten—the beginning of the novel re-writes the end, and in that sense it never really begins or ends. It is here that the fantasy of the text lies; a fantasy that is resistant to the tension releases of humor, and so to the structural resolutions of comedy. (1984: 118)

But where Bhabha considers this formal tension in terms of generic or modal discontinuity—with the unruly desires of the postcolonial fantastic harrying and momentarily dirempting the "myth of realist narrative—its grand syntagms and sequentiality, its pleasure, irony, comedy, characters and consolations, its historic utterances and easy identifications between I and you" (1984: 119)—I want instead to identify it with the struggle between narrative and descriptive tendencies *within* the practice of realism itself, a form that, in Naipaul's work as well as Zola's, finds itself increasingly incommensurate to the representational demands of its present. Furthermore, far from repudiating narrative, Naipaul's mature fiction rather expresses it as the impossible object of its own constrained or derelict desire.

Hence, Mr. Biswas's frustration at the *Sentinel's* revised reportorial directive, "REPORT NOT DISTORT," has perhaps less to do with the proscription of romantic fantasy than the displacement of narrative kinesis within statically objective formulae comprising arbitrary and utterly fungible elements of descriptive detail: "'Write?' he said to

Shama. 'I don't call that writing. Is more like filling up a form. X, aged so much, was yesterday fined so much by Mr Y at this court for doing that. The prosecution alleged" (Naipaul 1989b: 355–356). The objectivism of the *Sentinel*'s new standards bears as much in common with Zola's "experimental method" as its erstwhile sensationalism does with literary naturalism's journalistic precursor, the *fait divers*. And the phrase with which Biswas repeatedly opens his innumerable unfinished stories, "*At the age of thirty-three, when he was already the father of four children,*" evokes less the estranging powers of fantasy than the compulsive passion for narrative under conditions inhospitable to it.

The chief threat in *A House for Mr. Biswas* seems most nearly that of narrative exhaustion, of story's final capitulation to pure description, to undifferentiated landscape, sheer subjectivism, and the irrevocable loss of historical temporality, such as we glimpse in Biswas's extended dark night of the soul at the Green Vale:

> People. He could hear them next door and all down the barracks. No road was without them, no house. They were in the newspapers on the wall, in the photographs, in the simple drawings in advertisements. They were in the book he was holding. They were in all books. He tried to think of landscapes without people: sand and sand and sand, without the 'oses' Lal had spoken about; vast white plateaux, with himself safely alone, a speck in the centre. (Naipaul 1989b: 254–255)

Biswas's immediate fear of the vengeful cane workers stimulates deeper anxieties regarding his own social precarity. Thus does class anxiety converge with the interruption of narrative by the spectacle of timeless, spaceless scene, bearing out Jameson's observation that "[w]hat stands at the center of the naturalist narrative paradigm is the perspective of the bourgeoisie and its vision of the other (lower) classes" and, moreover, his claim that "included in this collective 'point of view' is a desperate fear: that of déclassement, of slipping down the painfully climbed slope of class position" from which vantage Biswas consistently repudiates the rural, religious, and folkloric as symptoms of the anonymous peasant masses from whom he, like Naipaul, struggles mightily to distinguish himself (Jameson 1981: 284). The interlude at Green Vale is thus less that of the disruptive postcolonial fantastic than of a pronounced class anxiety, specifically of petite bourgeois déclassement.

The limits of Bhabha's reading of *A House for Mr. Biswas* are more starkly revealed, however, in the function of the Gothic divergence in Naipaul's late-period novel *Guerrillas* (1975), which may be said to herald the full emergence of postcolonial naturalism in the post-independence, post-Vietnam, post-OPEC era, when the transnational and domestic forces soon to be codified under the heading "globalization" have already begun rapidly to coalesce and the imaginative possibilities of revolution to grow less proximate. Indeed, only with the publication of *Guerrillas*, Naipaul's most explicitly anti-utopian novel, was he received by a wide readership in the United States, an occurrence that one might argue was at least as important for shaping both the institutional reception and disciplinary contours of 'postcolonial studies' in the West as was the publication of Edward Said's *Orientalism* only three years later.

Inspired partly by Naipaul's trip to Uruguay and his horrified reaction to the communist National Liberation Movement's guerrilla insurgency against the oppressive regime of Jorge Pacheco, *Guerrillas* was eagerly received by a U.S. readership also weary of Third-World political resistance. Reviewer Hilton Kramer places *Guerrillas* alongside the works of Conrad and Turgenev "in the great tradition of novels that anatomize the effect of ideology on the lives of those it has thoroughly 'possessed' and destroyed" and marvels approvingly at Naipaul's shrewdly judged political-sexual equations, of which he wonders "how a writer of similar gifts and similar beliefs, but one less favorably situated in relation to the Third World would fare in the ideological jungles of the West" (Kramer 1976). Thus, *Guerrillas* clears space for a Third-World literature for the First-World reader, reassuringly melancholic and retrospective, safely divested of any foolhardy radicalism. From this political void, this uncertain life between the death of colonial rule and the death of the Cold War (which lingered on in an uncertain afterlife until its symbolic termination in the 9/11 attacks on the World Trade Center[1]), emerged the discipline of postcolonial studies in the western academy, the ambivalence of the much-debated "post-" marking the scarred site of an excision, of the anxious "culturalization of the political" (Mamdani 2004: 172).

As Lazarus observes, "After 1975, the prevailing political sentiment in the West turned sharply against anticolonial nationalist insurgency and revolutionary imperialism;" thus, he argues, "The decisive defeat of liberationist ideologies...was fundamental to the emergent field, whose subsequent consolidation, during the 1980s and early 1990s, might then be seen, at least in part, as a function of its articulation of a complex intellectual response to this defeat" (Lazarus 2011: 9). That

---

[1] See Wegner, Phillip E. 2009. *Life Between Two Deaths, 1989-2001: U.S. Culture in the Long Nineties* (Durham: Duke University Press).

is, postcolonial studies provided a theoretically sophisticated "rationalization of, and pragmatic adjustment to, the demise of the ideologies that had flourished during the 'Bandung' years" (Lazarus 2011: 9). Rejecting nationalist anti-imperialism, postcolonial studies—insomuch as it remains under the intellectual imprimatur of Bhabha—"refuses an antagonistic or struggle-based model of politics in favor of one that emphasises 'cultural difference', 'ambivalence', and 'the more complex cultural and political boundaries that exist on the cusp' of what 'modern' philosophy had imagined as the determinate categories of social reality" (Lazarus 2011: 12). Naturalism, I contend, is the unnamed aesthetic complement and ideological axis of this mid-70s turn.

Guerrillas and Narrative Logic

In *Guerrillas*, Bhabhaesque fantasy (assuming accents of what has come to be known as the postcolonial Gothic[2]) is presented as more nearly a symptom of neurosis in a moment when, having exhausted its spatio-temporal dynamism, the living impulse of narrative dissipates into utter immobility, directing its productive energies back in an attitude of pure subjectivism, generating spectral narratives that can only be flickering ersatz perversions founded on either symbolic idiocentrism or sterile plagiarism. In this way we might account for the Gothic pretense of the formally eccentric journals and letters of Naipaul's Jimmy Ahmed, a former black power leader and aspiring revolutionary who, with characteristic grandiosity, dubs his ramshackle commune "Thrushcross Grange" to indicate at once its heterotopic social agenda and his own overweening literary aspiration. But just as this spatial secession is doomed to fail in its project either to transform or defend against the desolation of its surroundings, so too must its Gothic narrative counterpart surrender up its own romantic stridencies to the paralytic density of pure scene.

For Jaye Berman, who also detects naturalistic resonances in *Guerrillas*, these inherited literary conventions are given a postmodernist inflection through the periodic interpolation of Jimmy's writing. This technique, he contends, "infuses an otherwise realistic narrative with the irrationality that serves as its theme," formally accentuating the book's elision of politics with madness (Berman 1986: 29). By enumerating the "repeated references to madness which begin in a kind

---

[2] See, for instance, Holden, Philip 2009. "The 'Postcolonial Gothic': Absent Histories, Present Contexts," *Textual Practice* 23.3: 353–372.

of litany at the novel's midpoint," Berman underscores the portrayal of a "general state of confusion on the island and the deterioration of reason among its inhabitants" (1986: 31). While it is Jimmy's insistence on supplementing reality with the literary, an effort to forge "a self made entirely out of language to replace, however feebly and temporarily, the pieces of his disintegrated personality," that indicates for Berman the book's anticipation of postmodernity's schizoid character (which, as Susan Harrow argues, is already evident in Zola as well), perhaps there is another way to read this formal juxtaposition (Berman 1986: 33).

In "Michael X and the Black Power Killings in Trinidad," the essay that preceded publication of the novel and serves as its key intertext, Naipaul reserves as much vituperative judgment for the writerly presumption of would-be revolutionary Michael Abdul Malik (whom *Guerrillas* makes over as Jimmy Ahmed) as for his role in the murders of commune members Gale Benson and Joseph Skerritt. Naipaul seems in fact to regard the latter failure as wholly continuous with, if not directly predicated on, the former, noting that Malik's own unfinished "primitive novel is like a pattern book, a guide to later events" (Naipaul 1980: 63). Proclaiming Benson's "a literary murder if ever there was one," Naipaul suggests that Malik's fundamental error lay in the fact that, for him, "writing had for too long been a public relations exercise, a form of applauded lie, *a fantasy*" (1980: 73). Simply, by recalling the plot of Malik's own writing—in which the narrator, a white, middle-class Englishwoman, conducts a passionate affair with "Mike Malik"—the arrival of the white Englishwoman Benson encourages the personal fantasy that "his novel began to come to life" (Naipaul 1980: 74).

Concerning the belabored rituals that followed Benson's murder—a communal ablution in the sea, then a solemn gathering around the fire in which Benson's belongings had earlier been burned—Naipaul suggests that Malik intentionally manipulated reality as material for his literary work-in-progress:

> That bathing party, with the fire on the riverbank: it was the crowning conception of an intricate day. Like an episode in a dense novel, it served many purposes and had many meanings. And it had been devised by a man who was writing a novel about himself, settling accounts with the world, filling pages of the cheap writing pad and counting the precious words as he wrote, anxious for world fame (including literary fame) [...]. (1980: 87)

Naipaul seems almost to suggest here that Malik's lack of novelistic skill ("not even an elementary gift of language") is in some way complicit with the disastrous consequences that follow "when he transferred his fantasy to real life:" "Such plotting, such symbolism! The blood of the calf at Christmas time, the blood of Gale Benson in the new year" (Naipaul 1980: 88). Malik's recourse both to "fantasy" (a term Naipaul elsewhere derisively applies to the failed "utopia" of Guyana's Jonestown[3]) and self-conscious symbolism are thus singled out as indicators of imaginative weakness and, therefore, Naipaul implies, the threat of violence.

Expressing disdain for the fantastic estrangements of literary modernism and declaring its utter lack of influence on his own style, Naipaul insists that "writing should not call attention to itself" (qtd. in French 2008: 13). In a list of "rules" for aspiring writers published by the Indian website *Tehelka*, Naipaul recommends disciplined economy, the principles of style inherited from his father: short sentences, short words, sparing use of adjectives and adverbs, and the strict avoidance of verbal abstraction ("Always go for the concrete" [qtd. in French 2008: 45]). Naipaul's impatience with abstraction and symbol is no mere demonstration of artistic caprice, nor the anxiety of influence, nor the retrograde reverences exhibited by the belated postcolonial novelist.

For Bewes, Naipaul's assertion that "displays of overt technique" are "an embarrassment"—a sentiment that would seem to bear out Casanova's dismissive claim that "Naipaul has invented nothing in his novels" (Casanova 2001)—are more productively read alongside both Theodor Adorno's theory of "late style" and Gilles Deleuze's meditations on modern cinema, each of which views the registration of formal incommensurability as immanent to artistic expression. Against Casanova, then, Bewes insists that "Naipaul's work is intimately formed by historical circumstance; that his style, far from being anachronistic or 'behind the times,' is generated by *or as* a 'lateness' that is both personal and historical, but that cannot be understood merely chronologically" or even subjectively (Bewes 2011: 80). Read this way, Naipaul's literary critique of the Michael X murders may be seen as self-directed, as already implicating the novel that will follow. In Naipaul's fiction, as Suleri observes, "the writer is never exempted from the text's graphic indictment of the postcolonial world" (1992: 154).

---

[3] Naipaul, V.S. 2003. "A Handful of Dust: Cheddi Jagan and the Revolution in Guyana," in *The Writer and the World* (New York: Vintage), 485.

Naturalism's Impulse-Image and the Return of the Originary World

Bewes recommends that Naipaul's preoccupation with what *The Enigma of Arrival* describes as "the possibility, the certainty of ruin, even at the moment of creation" inaugurates a "trajectory away from literariness" and toward the ambivalent aesthetic of late twentieth-century cinema's self-interrogation or exhaustion of narrative form (2011: 99, 98). Here, he superimposes Bhabha's figure of an internally divided colonial discourse—in which one regime of thought maintains a custodial attitude toward "reality" while another discursively reframes it through the ambivalent practice of mimicry—upon Deleuze's distinction between the organic movement-image of the late-nineteenth and early twentieth century and the fragmentary time-image of postwar cinema. The result of this juxtaposition is the recognition that

> Naipaul's late work shares the characteristics that Deleuze attributes to the "new kind of image" in postwar cinema: the replacement of a unified, "organic" situation with a "dispersive" one; the irruption of incommensurability, or ellipsis, into the substance of the tale, rather than remaining a mode of the telling; the introduction of an open "stroll/voyage" narrative form in place of the closed quest/search form; a strong, irresolvable consciousness of clichés; and the expansion of this consciousness to such a level that all possibilities of a meaningful whole become suspect. (Bewes 2011: 98)

To equate Naipaul's novel with the postmodern time-image, however, collapses into near indistinction its foremost aesthetic achievements and historical insights. Subtly but significantly revising Bewes's account, I argue that more apposite for *Guerrillas*, if not for Naipaul's later period on the whole, is the curiously intermediate *impulse-image* that Deleuze locates within the organic regime of movement itself: a variant or aberrant suspension of the movement-image, caught between the sensory-motor unity of action (realism) within a determined milieu and the unlocalizable idealism of affect (surrealism). Following Zola's positioning of his experimental method between realism and idealism (the latter designating a modernism that Zola could not yet name), Deleuze identifies the cinematic impulse-image with the broad aesthetic of naturalism, which, he claims, "is not opposed to realism, but on the contrary accentuates its features by extending them in an idiosyncratic surrealism" (Deleuze 1986: 124). Zola, Deleuze suggests, frequently plots a rationally extensive "real" milieu or "set" that is distended and finally sundered by the iterative irruptions of an "originary world" and the base impulses it stimulates. The originary world is "made up of outlines and fragments, heads without necks, eyes without faces, arms without shoulders, gestures without form," yet it also forms the foundational matrix that "unites everything, not in an organization, but [in] making all the parts converge in an immense rubbish-dump or swamp, and all the impulses in a great death-impulse" (Deleuze 1986: 1, 124). The impulse-image is thus suspended, like literary naturalism, between realist totalization and surrealist fragmentation, caught in a repetition compulsion from which it cannot summon the means to free itself.

However, the impulse-image and the time-image are easily mistaken, as Deleuze himself notes, for in its depiction of curved or cyclical time, understood as either entropic death wish or eternal return, the naturalist impulse-image begins dimly to think the temporal and historical as such. Deleuze remarks that "it is undoubtedly one of the naturalist cinema's great achievements to have come so close to a time-image" (1986: 1, 127). Yet, because of its final subordination of history to the insurmountable impulses derived from a timeless and archetypal originary world, "naturalism could only grasp the negative effects of time; attrition, degradation, wastage, destruction, loss, or simply oblivion" (Deleuze 1986: 127). Given all this, one might therefore suggest that Naipaul's historically "belated" work (especially *Guerrillas*) does not yet approximate, as Bewes has it, the allochronic crystallization, the dramatically revealed "coexistence of distinct durations, or of levels of duration" that Deleuze finds in postwar cinema's Surreal time-image (Deleuze 1989: xii); rather, Naipaul relentlessly restages the naturalistic irruption of an originary world upon an exhausted and incommensurable milieu (which is at once that of realism and nationalism) in the moment of an emergent globalization that cannot as yet be named and so can only be regarded as the necessary return of a primeval, ancestral impulse or a fragile, all-too-human nature, confirming yet again Marx's insight that it is "the fate of completely new historical creations to be mistaken for the counterpart of older and even defunct forms of social life" (Marx 1993: 59).

Scenic Description and the End of Temporality

Considered in the light of both Naipaul's severe literary critique of Malik and a Deleuzean cinematic naturalism, Jimmy's narrative digressions seem to function not simply as late symptoms of the linguistic turn, nor as Bhabhaesque fantastical alternatives to realism's ironic containments, but rather as hypersubjectivist (even romantic) responses to the pervasive paralysis of the surrounding object world and the intrusion of aboriginal nature. Necessarily, however, these futile strivings after narrative orientation—which, as Jameson notes, are always also the desire for historical thought[4]—are revealed as mere plagiaries and already testament to narrative's inevitable failure to resist the gravitational contraction of an approaching historical singularity.

Of Jimmy's appropriation of *Wuthering Heights*—which "makes you believe in heredity" (Naipaul 1990: 34)—Roche dismissively observes: "I don't think it means anything. I don't think Jimmy sees himself as Heathcliff or anything like that. He took a writing course, and it was one of the books he had to read. I think he just likes the name" (Naipaul 1990: 4). Perusing Jimmy's "Communique No. 1. CLASSIFIED," presented with comical solemnity, Jane finds it "a fairy story, a school composition, ungrammatical and confused" (Naipaul 1990: 11). Jimmy, who "began to feel unsupported by his words" and experiences the Biswasian "vision of darkness, of the world lost forever, and his own life ending on that bit of wasteland," also begins to glimpse the belatedness of his romantic pose (Naipaul 1990: 32). Unable to resume writing,

> he became aware of the night and the bush; and he was undermined again. Melancholy came over him like fatigue, like rage, like a sense of doom; and when he went back to the desk he found that the writing excitement had broken and was impossible to reenter. The words on the pad were again just like words, false. (Naipaul 1990: 35)

In a passing reference to *Guerrillas*, Bewes observes that, in the novel,

> everything strains to escape the merely verbal; passages of pure visual description contrast with the emotional and intellectual dependence of each of the characters on totemic phrases, most obviously the writer-character Jimmy Ahmed, hopelessly aware that the failure of his writing is apparent in its inertness ("words alone"), its refusal to leave the page. (2011: 92)

---

[4] As Jameson writes, "The 'desire for Marx' can therefore also be called a desire for *narrative*, if by this we understand, not some vacuous concept of 'linearity' or even *telos*, but rather the impossible attempt to give representation to the multiple and immensurable temporalities in which each of us exists." In Jameson, Fredric 1988. *The Ideologies of Theory Vol. 1* (Minneapolis: University of Minnesota Press), xxviii.

As in the magnificently ambivalent concluding passage of Zola's novel of failed (or perhaps deferred) revolution, *Germinal*, the scenic recurrence of Naipaul's blighted vegetable world is also the site where the quickening of revolutionary ambition is conflated with both the ascension of the descriptive mode and the return of an aboriginal violence:

> An amber light fell on the brown vegetation of the hills. But in that vegetation, which to Jane when she had first arrived had only seemed part of the view, there was strangeness and danger: the wild disordered men, tramping along old paths, across gardens, between houses, and through what remained of woodland, like aborigines recognizing only the ancestral landscape and insisting on some ancient right of way. Wild men in rags, with long, matted hair; wild men with unseeing red eyes. And bandits. Police cars patrolled these hillside suburbs. Sometimes at night and in the early morning there was the sound of gunfire. The newspapers, the radio, and the television spoke of guerrillas. (Naipaul 1990: 124–125)

Like Zola's, Naipaul's poetic description ambivalently presents revolutionary germination as an extensive manifestation of a necessarily cyclical nature.[5] Naipaul's "guerrillas," co-extensive with the surrounding landscape, are merely the lingering fever dream of a previously determined milieu in which the fierce agents of yesterday's anti-colonial narrative are banished to the bracken of the Fanonian romance with which the feckless liberal Jane both titillates and terrifies herself—and which, Naipaul implies, can end only in sadistic violence.

But apart from the consistent diversion of epic telos by a more fundamental drift toward scenic repetition or even the leitmotif of fatalistic degradation, such richly descriptive passages also assume, in bold contrast to the narrative aridity and thematic degeneration surrounding them, a kind of willed autonomy of the descriptive that Baguley, like other commentators, cites as a primary feature of literary naturalism: "Naturalist discourse, then, frequently tends toward the picturesque, towards *ekphrasis*, in passages that seem all the more detached from the main development of the plot, by the contrast with the surrounding inartistic realities" (Baguley 1990: 192).

In a brilliant narratological reconsideration of Naipaul's "forgotten

---

[5] *Germinal* ends as it begins in the vernal stirrings of the Revolutionary Calendar's month of Germinal, a setting which simultaneously recalls the execution of Georges Danton and his Indulgents during the grimmest days of the Reign of Terror.

novel...singular in its misogyny as well as its critique of a 'misguided socialism,'" Toral Jatin Gajarawala argues that in a narrative "where real guerrillas never materialize, and political revolution is a fictional abstraction, it is descriptions of landscape that hold a charged textual potential" and in which the Lukácsian opposition of narration and description is given a significant turn (Gajarawala 2012: 289). Rendered the object of colonial history, the colonized is forced to submit to a "regime of ekphrasis—'still life'—while the settler is associated with the 'epic' and the 'odyssey'"—historical acts, Gajarawala reminds us, that also assume the form of literary genres (2012: 293). Description is thus "left for those who are irrelevant, who do not change, who are immobile; it is those who cannot be described, who can only perform narrative acts, that the novel follows" (Gajarawala 2012: 295). Citing Naipaul's moments of ekphrasis as strategically menacing rather than objectively inert, however, Gajarawala distinguishes his work from Zola and the "realist prototype"—in which, she argues, description carries out the epistemological operations of discovery and categorization—and observes, citing the novel's trenchantly ironic reversals, that Naipaul's "narrative predilections are modernist" (2012: 297). Like Bewes and Suleri, then, Gajawarala proposes, against reflexive denunciations of the author's racism, classism, and misogyny, "that Naipaul's politics might be read diagonally" as obtaining within the logic of form and chiefly within scenic description, which she views as surpassing a delimiting realism (2012: 298).

Gajawarala's recovery of the novel for a postcolonial narratology turns on the recognition that the landscape descriptions enact a strategic deconcealment in which Jane's voyeuristic "will to see" is unveiled as the purposeful misrecognition of colonial ideology itself (2012: 299). The narrative's apocalyptic preoccupation with the impinging originary world may thus be attributed less to Naipaul as author than to the characterological construction of Jane, whose presiding worldview (insisting on its own distracted neutrality) is remorselessly expunged in the novel's climactic violence. Even before this, however, the narrative's description repeatedly ironizes Jane's derisive pronouncements on the island and its people, which, Gajarawala reminds us, are as historical as they are narrative: "Nothing that happened here could be important. The place was no more than what it looked" (Naipaul 1990: 46).

If Jane is correct in this, then *Guerrillas* is made a variant on the postcolonial anti-pastoral in the tradition of Olive Schreiner or (in its postmodern variety) J.M. Coetzee. But as Gajarawala points out, Jane's assessment is fatally flawed, as illustrated in her naïve misreading of Thrushcross Grange itself (2012: 299):

> Near this, and half into the forest, was a red tractor: it looked as abandoned there as those rusting motorcars in the tall grass below the embankment of the highway. The field looked abandoned as well. But presently Jane saw three men, then a fourth, working at the far end, camouflaged against the forest. (Naipaul 1990: 7)

As Roche soberly indicates, however, "That's laid on for us. Or laid on for you. It's their official rest period now. No one works in the fields at this time of the afternoon" (Naipaul 1990: 7). But Jane's *méconnaissance* (a kind of inverse Bovaryism) is gradually dispelled as what initially appears as objectively distanciated description reveals its focal origin in the limited subjective perspective of Jane herself, who, upon leaving the commune, claims to have no point of view, a statement of no little narratological and ideological significance (Naipaul 1990: 22).

Against Jane's glib pronouncement of the island's antisymbolic transparency, however, nothing in this scene is as it first appears:

> The tractor, the fields, appear abandoned, but they are not. There are men working, but they are camouflaged. Even their camouflage, however, is an elaborate ruse of discipline and productivity performed for the white visitors. The true nature of the masquerade, however, is only revealed in the final moments of the novel, when Jane is viciously attacked in the walled off forest, in view of the motorcars, in the 'abandoned' field from which Bryant emerges, camouflaged, her body thrown into the infertile furrows. Literally moments afterwards, Roche appears, to enquire after the tractor. (Gajarawala 2012: 300)

The ironic function of such descriptive passages does not necessarily lead us, as Gajarawala insists, beyond the compass of Zolian realism—as Harrow's important reassessment of that author demonstrates. Harrow's account produces a "prospective Zola," whose aesthetic, directed toward the uncertain future as much as toward the Second Empire, avails itself of modern and even postmodern methods of representation: "hybridity, indeterminacy, irony, *mise en abyme*, and self-reflexivity" (Harrow 2010: 17). Zola's "propensity to descriptive hypertrophia and repetition" shears the planar momentum of plot in order to clear space for the allochronic appearance of metaphor, metonymy, analogy, and pastiche, all opening up or disrupting the "linear telos" and totalizing agenda of what Harrow terms a "panoptic" naturalism (Harrow 2010: 98, 136). In Zola, she argues, the universalist stridencies of naturalism's documentary impulse are *internally* resisted by a particularist "drive to equivocation, fissure, irony, hybridity, ellipsis and self-reflexivity" that paradoxically emerges from Zola's own penchant for descriptive detail (Harrow 2010: 208).

Affect and the Unnarratable Present

Even Harrow, however, finds Zola wholly singular in this regard, insisting that such figurations are proleptic departures from what she rather undialectically defines as an orthodox or "straightforward Naturalist recuperation," within which Zola's novels enact a self-reflexive "oscillation between totalizing and fracturing impulses" (Harrow 2010: 17). But perhaps such tensions are less the expression of Zola's exceptional artistic foresight than the elementary substance and dynamism of literary naturalism itself. Such a view approaches that of Jameson, who situates his richly dialectical meditation on the precarious moment of the realist novel, with its irreducible epistemological and aesthetic animating tensions, "by grasping realism as a historical and even evolutionary process in which the negative and the positive are inextricably combined, and whose emergence and development at one and the same time constitute its own inevitable undoing, its own decay and dissolution" (Jameson 2013: 6). This founding opposition or structural antinomy distills through a succession of resolutions or levels into "the two chronological end points of realism" already familiar to us from Lukács: narration, in which reality is organized according to a consecutive temporality, and ekphrasis or scene, in which this temporal continuum is countered by the affective intensities of an immediate (and, for that reason, unnamable) present (Jameson 2013: 10–11).

Realism might thus be said to embody a parallax figure that grasps the temporal experience of modernity along both its irreconcilable diachronic and synchronic axes. In this way, Jameson reworks Lukács's binary formulation by suspending its bias against both naturalism and modernism and displacing an archly tendentious subjectivism within a more generously dialectical account of formal and periodic literary history. Literary naturalism, as we have already observed, may then be recognized as the earliest moment in a process of ekphrastic autonomization in which scene pulls itself free from narrative continuity and expresses from within the progressive chronologies of realism itself the entropic anxieties of an arrested present now *felt* as such.

Indeed, for both Harrow and Jameson, Zola's key innovation is linked to his rendering of the sensual body. In Harrow's account, Zola's descriptions of the corporeal (the laboring body in particular) trouble the normative gaze of naturalism through magnifications, distortions, and figural reversions that self-consciously implicate the act of linguistic representation. Jameson, on the other hand, far less interested in exempting Zola from the naturalism that he helped to codify, suggests that the achievement of the Rougon-Macquart series lies principally in its array of melodramatic resolutions to the realist crisis of plot in which the atemporal intimations of affect are registered within the epic temporality of the family saga. As Jameson observes, "Zola's narratives are what happens to individuals and their destinies when their récits fall into the force-field of affect and submit to its dynamic, in a situation in which the two forces, the two temporalities, are still for one last moment more or less equal in their power and influence" (2013: 76).

Zola's described bodies thus offer more than mere figural reprieve from the objectivist chronometrics of the naturalist narrative and extend down into the subcutaneous structures of narrative itself, absorbing and virally converting its temporal calibrations into expressions of hereditary affliction. Zolian naturalism is therefore reducible neither to scientific scrutiny nor to a "secret or nascent modernism" but may be understood as the distention of the realist narrative by the insurgent pressures of affect (Jameson 2013: 73). Seen this way, the representational and epistemological tasks that naturalism sets itself are far more complex than the positivistic model that Gajarawala describes. In *Guerrillas*, she writes, unlike in the novels of Zola, "description is not productive of concrete knowledge" (Gajarawala 2012: 299); however, as Jameson discovers in the Zolian "codification of affect," neither is description assigned such an unimaginative duty in that author.

Bewes's account of postcolonial shame is instructive here as well, for he anticipates the affective character of what I am calling postcolonial naturalism when, reflecting on the physical mortifications prominent in the novels of Coetzee, he suggests that the "shame event is neither ethical, nor discursive, nor conceptual, but sensuous, corporeal" (Bewes 2011: 153). We might productively regard such "uninstantiatable" sensuality as fully continuous with Jameson's understanding of affect as the phenomenology of "nameless bodily states" that exceed established classifications of psychology or physiology (Bewes 2011: 32). While Bewes writes that "the paradox of shame is not that it cannot be instantiated, but that it disappears at the moment of its instantiation" (2011: 77), Jameson similarly observes of affect's conversion into named emotion that "the nomination of an experience makes it visible at the very moment that it transforms and reifies it," so that it no longer exists as such (2013: 36). Affect, like shame, must therefore signify only itself. The moment it collapses into named emotion or symbolically approximates its object, it effectively ceases to exist—just as shame, in seeking to bear witness, can only ever do so as the rueful "experience of its own inadequacy" (Bewes 2011: 3).

Inasmuch as Bewes's discussion of Naipaulian shame involves the self-conscious casting aside of established paradigms—"If you want to write serious books...you must be ready to break the forms," Naipaul once advised a young writer (qtd. in Wood 2008)—we might expect to find in his novels evidence of the affective intensities whose growing autonomy Jameson discerns in Zola, a writer documenting a post-imperial epoch not wholly dissimilar to Naipaul's own, in which the living radicalisms of the past (the Paris Commune in Zola's case) are symbolically interred. Complementing the moments of ekphrastic punctuation in *Guerrillas* and underscoring its reinvention of the liberated Zolian sensorium is the recurrence of sensory experiences without immediate or fully discernible cause, purpose, or agent.

In *Guerrillas*, the senses take on a painfully aroused sensitivity, recording the choking perpetual pall of smoke and bauxite dust, the menacing shadows and surprising bursts of light, and the sound of distant, disembodied voices: "...in that hidden gully there was a regular traffic of people on foot, wild people, disordered and unkempt, who chattered as they passed, briskly, in groups, morning and evening, going to and coming from she knew not where" (Naipaul 1990: 51). If the gully is indeed "hidden" from Jane's vantage on the Ridge, the "unkempt" appearance of the "wild people" and their brisk pace are the products of her paranoid or romantic imagination, intent on providing a positive identification ("guerrillas") for an otherwise uninstantiable affective sensation. That is, in attempting to make sense of her surroundings, Jane has recourse only to narrative stratagems that are already too late.

Out of such failures grows the increasing density of affect. In the novel's opening pages, against the infernal backdrop of the perpetually smoking hillsides, Jane and Roche make their way to Thrushcross Grange: "The asphalt-road was wet-black, distorted in the distance by the heat waves. The grass verges had been blackened by fire, and in some places still burned. Sometimes, above the noise of the car, Jane and Roche could hear the crackle of flames which, in the bright light, they couldn't see" (Naipaul 1990: 4). Here again, initial appearances deceive: the incongruously "wet-black" road is a momentary perspectival mirage. But, as we find in this passage's final sentence, not all such misperceptions are so easily corrected; just as frequently, sensory impressions remain—like the presence of the titular guerrillas themselves—merely speculative and evoke less the text's admonishment of naïve perception than the unascribable intensities of affect, which cannot fully be credited, as Gajarawala suggests, to the neocolonial voyeurism of Jane.

That Jane, who claims no point of view, has an unreliable perspective is repeatedly made explicit, as when she compares her disenchantment with Roche to the surprise she felt at seeing the sunlight upon first waking at midafternoon in the dark, louvered bedroom on the Ridge: "So this morning Jane awakened, as she had awakened in the middle of that first day, to the darkness of the room with the redwood louvers and to the knowledge that she had made an error, that she had once again seen in a man things that were not there" (Naipaul 1990: 49). The sun-struck roof of the long hut at Thrushcross Grange is "dazzling and hot to look at; it barely projected over the wall and cast no shadow" (Naipaul 1990: 7); Jane, whom Roche suddenly regards as "white enough to be unreadable" (Naipaul 1990: 7), first finds the hut cool and dark before quickly emending that sensation on the next page as her perception adjusts to its interior space: "Jane was aware that the corrugated iron was radiating heat. And the hut was more open than she had thought, was really full of light" (Naipaul 1990: 9). But the sequence of perceptual corrections here again gives way to something like the dissolution of perception itself and the unmaking of the milieu by the intrusion of a nameless originary world:

> The oblong windows showed a colorless sky. But Jane had a sense now of more than heat; she had a sense of desolation. Later, on the Ridge, in London, this visit to Thrushcross Grange might be a story. But now, in that hut, with the junked office equipment on the table, the posters and black pinups from newspapers on the walls, with the boys on the metal beds, with the light and the emptiness outside and the encircling forest, she felt she had entered another, complete world. (Naipaul 1990: 11)

What might formerly have been the substance of narrative is here suspended between narrative and affect, the latter threatening to subsume the former in its immediate and totalizing meaninglessness.

Even the ironic reversal indicated by Gajarawala (with its underlying anagnorisis) has at this point lost all critical purchase, surrendering even the most sardonic grip on meaning. Roche's smile, wherein Jane will spy traces of already-present decay, holds other disappointments as well: once "so full of melancholy and irony, issuing out of the largest vision of the world," it has been reduced to "only a fixed, meaningless irony," one that expresses impotent "sarcasm, frustration, pettishness" (Naipaul 1990: 13). Every attempt to forge significance, to enact the historicizing vocation of narrative, is met with the dumb insistence and scenic immediacy of the primordial and affective. Even the futile industry of the commune, attempting to carve history from the indiscriminate bush, appears already a forgery, a conceptually barren plagiary. Led by Jimmy along a narrow, weed-choked path, shamefully befouled with human excrement, to a small field momentarily reclaimed from the greedy forest, Jane observes of his efforts to grow cash crops: "As if in a parody of nineteenth-century plantation prints, which local people had begun to collect, the boys, with sullen, downcast eyes, as though performing an unpleasant duty, were planting tomato seedlings which, as fast as they were set in their dusty little holes, quailed and drooped" (Naipaul 1990: 14). Here, there can be neither parodic appropriation nor ironic surplus. Narrative and history have reached an ignominious and inevitable finality.

The End of History, or, "No One Will Do Anything New"

Guerrillas is thus primarily—right down to its minimal fictionalization of "Michael X and the Black Power Killings in Trinidad"—a novel about the failure of the new, about the structural preclusion of conceptual futures by the exhausted syntax of the determined milieu. In only the novel's second paragraph, we are introduced to a Dantean originary landscape of unremitting and irredeemable blight, the pure scene of which will recur insistently throughout the novel to disrupt narrative momentum with a trammeling regularity:

> The sea smelled of swamp; it barely rippled, had glitter rather than color; and the heat seemed trapped below the pink haze of bauxite dust from the bauxite loading station. After the market, where refrigerated trailers were unloading; after the rubbish dump burning in the remnant of mangrove swamp, with black carrion corbeaux squatting hunched on fence posts or hopping about on the ground; after the built-up hillsides; after the new housing estates, rows of unpainted boxes of concrete and corrugated iron already returning to the shantytowns that had been knocked down for this development; after the naked children playing in the dust of the straight new avenues, the clothes hanging like rags from back yard lines; after this, the land cleared a little. And it was possible to see over what the city had spread: on one side, the swamp, drying out to a great plain; on the other side, a chain of hills, rising directly from the plain. (Naipaul 1990:3)

The naturalist themes of paralyzing torpor, failure, and inevitable degeneration are reinforced here by their stylistic complement or formal condition: anticipating both temporal and spatial foreclosure, the anaphoric "after" functions as the grammatical imprimatur of destiny, locating its object in a time and space already and unalterably described. Indeed, having established this pattern of spatial, historical, even syntactic enclosure, one might well anticipate the following paragraph's first sentence: "The openness didn't last for long" (Naipaul 1990: 3). The relentlessly forlorn and intrusive landscape is "eroded," "closed and airless" (Naipaul 1990: 99), "scorched," "collapsed" (149), "choked" (163), "blanched" (178), and "sterile" (237), ever threatening to hurl the ambiguous achievements of national independence back into the smoldering ruination of prehistory.

The fragile milieu of *Guerrillas* is an asphyxiating world of depleted promise no longer capable of restraining the originary impulses that threaten its obliteration. The shallow liberal sympathies of Jane and Roche have arrived, as always, too late to save it. In a flash of receding gum line high in the corner of Roche's ready smile Jane finds a nauseating trace of death-in-life: "It was like a glimpse of teeth in a skull, like a glimpse of a satyr; and she felt it was like a glimpse of the inner man." This "little sign that foreshadowed the future" confirms Jane's feeling that "she had come to a place at the end of the world, to a place that had exhausted its possibilities" (Naipaul 1990: 45). However much the novel seeks to upset the naivety of Jane, she is not alone in her despairing pessimism. Roche, whose liberal idealism has been sacrificed to (or perhaps fully realized in) the new corporate hegemony, recites the daily mantra, "I've built my whole life on sand," and faced with the recognition that "he had no political dogma and no longer had a vision of the world made good," he can "neither act nor withdraw; he could only wait" (Naipaul 1990: 87).

Yet Naipaul's target here extends beyond the paternalistic stratagems and self-consolations of western liberalism, implicating the historical failure of the postcolonial nation state (perhaps the nation state more generally) to make good on its emancipatory promise. During an evening gathering on the Ridge, Roche listlessly affirms that "Human ambition is limitless," while cabinet minister Meredith Herbert acknowledges the situational constraints placed on such notions of heroic subjectivism: "But capacity is restricted" (Naipaul 1990: 141). To illustrate the objective limits constraining the utopian imaginary, Herbert conducts an impromptu thought experiment: before providing his audience with the parlor game's central question, he announces that he has already written down the one answer that they will all inevitably provide. With instructions to be as imaginative and as specific as possible, Jane, Roche, and Harry, another wealthy resident of the Ridge, are then asked to write down how they would spend an entire day provided that they could be and possess anything they desire. When Jane balks at the game's extemporaneous demand, claiming, "I will have to think about it," Meredith declares it an excellent response that merely proves his point. After listening to Harry describe his idyllic day in a Toronto office followed by an evening of yoga, swimming, dinner and drinks with friends, Meredith's prediction is revealed: *"The life being described is the life the speaker lives or a life he has already lived. The setting may change, but no one will make a fresh start or do anything new"* (Naipaul 1990: 144).

As Selwyn R. Cudjoe observes, the fiction of Naipaul's late period is characterized by its fatalistic disregard for the developmental possibilities of the Third World, which he imagines as "condemned to a life of ignominy and backwardness, which cannot be prevented" (Cudjoe 1988: 166). Positioning himself as the indifferent chronicler of this irreversibly tragic history, the Naipaul of *Guerrillas* becomes "an apocalyptist of the Third World," whose grimmest prophecies are enthusiastically received by the West as testaments of fact (Cudjoe 1988: 166). Yet, it is imperative that we complement Cudjoe's insight here by observing that the paralysis of imagination diagnosed by Herbert's exercise is specifically that of the ruling class and an impotent Western liberalism. Thus, perhaps the novel's insistence on entropy and failure should not be read as entirely pessimistic or anti-utopian in the usual sense but as the uncompromising act of space-clearing negation that is the very precondition of utopian thought to come (a point explored more thoroughly in chapter four).

Such a possibility directs us back to Deleuze. In identifying the impulse-image of cinematic naturalism with the compulsions of the Freudian *death instinct*, Deleuze refers us to his earlier gloss on the concept in *Difference and Repetition* (1968). Positing that death is not the negation of Eros but its paradoxically indistinguishable and foundational complement, Deleuze argues here that "death cannot be reduced to negation, neither to the negative of opposition nor to the negative of limitation"; death is rather "like the last form of the problematic, the source of problems and questions, the sign of their persistence over and above every response" (Deleuze 1994: 12). As Lacan defines it, the reiterative compulsion of the death drive "challenges everything that exists" and expresses "a will to create from zero, a will to begin again" (Lacan 1992: 12).

If *The Enigma of Arrival,* which inaugurates Naipaul's late period, may be said to chronicle his encounter with the death drive ("I began to be awakened by thoughts of death, the end of things...it was only out of this new awareness of death that I began to write" [Naipaul 1987: 343–344]), it is in the transitional novel *Guerrillas* that the narrative possibilities of the death drive are fully discovered. We might therefore consider the possibility that the naturalist poetics of death, dissipation, and repetition has as its object not simply the biological cycle of life and death (from which a pessimistic social commentary can then be extrapolated) but the *second* or absolute death of the symbolic, which "liberates nature from its own laws and opens the way for the creation of new forms" (Žižek 1989: 134). Here, Naipaul's formal dilemma—which Bewes characterizes as a "direct presentation not of the 'decline' but of the 'coming to pure self-consciousness' of the novel form as such" (Bewes 2011: 99)—locates its historical determinate.

In "Third-World Literature in the Era of Multinational Capitalism," Jameson describes the crisis of the radical postcolonial intellectual, "bearing a passion for change and social regeneration which has not yet found its agents," as "also very much an aesthetic dilemma, a crisis of representation" occasioned by the displacement of the "visible trappings of colonial occupation" with the featureless dynamics and mercurial flows of a new global dispensation (Jameson 1986: 81). This post-independence quandary, wherein "once again no political solutions seem present or visible on the historical horizon," he likens to Lu Xun's fable of the windowless iron house, the sleeping inhabitants of which are blissfully unaware of their imminent suffocation, and the moral/formal dilemma of the artist who would alert them to their doom (Jameson 1986: 75). The formal effect of this realization is thus the end of narrative or of the kind of narrative called realism.

Independence achieved, the demiurgic realism of anti-colonial nationalism proves insufficient to address the unnamed condition of globalization. Trapped between this moment of realism and the emergence of new forms (irrealism, science fiction, and other modernisms) that would confront a reconfigured Empire, naturalism propagates. If European naturalism is not merely a subcategory of realism but a new type of narrative emerging from within it, replacing the secure sentimentalism of a hegemonic class aesthetic with the paranoid fantasies of a now-precarious bourgeoisie, then postcolonial naturalism might well be the narrative produced by the failed revolution of what Fanon called the national bourgeoisie. In assuming the role of "manager for the companies of the West and turn[ing] its country virtually into a bordello for Europe" (Fanon 2004: 102), the national bourgeoisie neglects the crucial fact that, lacking all access to the transnational levers of economic power in a transformed global system, the "bourgeoisie of the underdeveloped countries is a bourgeoisie in spirit only" (2004: 122), mimic men impotent but for the proximal force they wield over the masses of whom they are in perpetual fear.

The failure of narrative that is *Guerrilla*'s foremost formal and thematic preoccupation thus functions as the acknowledged limit-point of a kind of historical thinking: a recognition that discretely nationalist, anti-colonial resistance no longer addresses with any comprehensive efficacy the emergencies of transnational capital—a recognition that, after the global volatility of the early 1970s and the consequent refunctioning of postwar institutions like the International Monetary Fund and the World Bank, was painfully recognized by developing national polities. That Naipaul's response is one of bourgeois dread and contempt diminishes neither its critique of Third Worldism's limitations nor its symbolic and technical grasp of Empire's contemporary mutation. As Jameson reminds us,

> if it is the material substructure, the social situation that takes precedence over mere opinion, ideology, the subjective picture that one has of himself, then we may be forced to conclude that under certain circumstances, a conservative, a royalist, a believing Catholic can better seize the genuine forces at work in society than a writer whose sympathies are relatively socialistic. (Jameson 1971: 202)

Such a recognition is in fact the "ultimate force of Lukács's comparison between Balzac and Zola," for where the dynamism of the former is a consequence of his "historical luck to have witnessed not the later, fully evolved and finished capitalism" but its gradual emergence in France, the fatalistic melodrama of the latter is the product of a mature system "in which the only reality of human existence seems to be blind routine and the drudgery of daily work, forever the same day after day" (Jameson 1971: 201). If realism is conditioned by "the possibility of access to the forces of change in a given historical moment," naturalism, for which the ascendance of the descriptive mode signals that "some vital relationship to action and to the possibility of action has broken down," names a narrative as well as a historical closure (Jameson 1971: 201). The postcolonial naturalism of *Guerrillas* therefore marks out the absolute horizon of Bandung-era anti-imperialism and the exhaustion of a familiar grammar of resistance. It therefore offers a pitiless self-reproach ("the people who spoke of crisis were themselves placid, content with their functions, existing within their functions, trapped, part of what they railed against" [Naipaul 1990: 43]) even as it indicates the negative potential of an uncertain awakening: "He could write no more. He wakened from his dream to the emptiness about him..." (60).

Chapter 2

Neither Us nor Ours
The Dialectic of Hysteria and the Beautiful Soul in the Novels of Lewis Nkosi

> *Their problem—though not, of course, their subject—is finding a public role, not a private self. If European intellectuals, though comfortable inside their culture and traditions, have an image of themselves as outsiders, African intellectuals are uncomfortable outsiders, seeking to develop their cultures in directions that will give them a role.*
> —Kwame Anthony Appiah (1992: 121)

> *The* moi, *the ego of modern man, as I have indicated elsewhere, has taken on its form in the dialectical impasse of the* belle âme *who does not recognize his very own* raison d'être *in the disorder that he denounces in the world.*
> —Jacques Lacan (1977: 70)

In a recent consideration of the role played in the African novel of postcolonial disillusionment by the reactionary subject formation that Hegel names the "Beautiful Soul," Andrew Adkins argues that writers like Chinua Achebe deploy the latter to satirize a postcolonial subjectivity caught between tradition and modernity, colonial culture and national independence. Citing Lazarus's contention that anticolonial African intellectuals were frequently "predisposed to a messianic and middle-class specific conception of decolonization as a revolutionary process," resulting in an overvaluation of the "emancipatory significance of independence" (Lazarus 1990: ix), Adkins offers that the Beautiful Soul, which withdraws into abstract solitude from what it perceives as the evil of the external world, "might describe in helpful ways those African literary protagonists who—whether or not they echo their authors—struggle with brands of self-loathing and self-absolution in the face of modernity's gaps of inadequately realized change"

(Adkins 2017: 399). Adkins thus finds in the protagonist of Chinua Achebe's *No Longer at Ease* (1960), published in the year of Nigeria's independence, the Beautiful Soul negotiating "a Nigerian modernity overrun with cultures of bribery, nepotism, and tribalism" (2017: 399). Achebe's Obi struggles with the conflicting expectations of tradition and the new demands of the nationalist elite and recounts "his downfall and Nigeria's botched independence through a sardonic self-acquittal" (Adkins 2017: 399).

However, insomuch as Adkins (or perhaps Achebe) presents the Beautiful Soul as a matter of secondary character type, to be described at a distance, rather than as an elementary and untranscendable dilemma inherent to representation itself, his analysis remains confined to the Beautiful Soul syndrome that it undertakes to diagnose. Such an elevation of the isolated imago of the Imaginary is predicated on a displacement or repression of the Symbolic that, for Lacan, lies at the heart of neurosis.[1] Turning to Lewis Nkosi's polarizing Apartheid novel *Mating Birds* (1986), this essay argues that, in the context of the postcolony, the Beautiful Soul may more productively be thought of as what Lacan calls a "dialectical impasse" in the moment between formal independence and the registering of globalization's unprecedented alienations. The aesthetic expression of this impasse, I further claim, is the genre of postcolonial naturalism, a provisional form defined by the tension between the subjective poles of the hysteric and the Beautiful Soul.

In his influential discussion of American literary naturalism, Walter Benn Michaels interprets the naturalist aesthetic as the formal manifestation of an irreducible double identity, one caught in the interpellative machinery of the market and the logic of the commodity. In this naturalist "economy of selfhood," the composition of identity through "means of inscription into consumer culture" produces an anxious subjectivity, read retroactively as subjectivity *tout court*, that is "permanently under construction," a self that must ceaselessly and anxiously produce and consume itself as the very precondition of its precarious selfhood (Michaels 1987: 27–28). Thus, Michaels claims,

---

[1] Lacan writes: "The problem of the neurotic consists in a loss of the symbolic reference of the signifiers that make up the central points of the structure of his complex. Thus, the neurotic may repress the signified of his symptom. This loss of the reference value of the symbol causes it to regress to the level of the imaginary, in the absence of any mediation between self and idea" (qtd. in Fredric Jameson 1988. "Imaginary and Symbolic in Lacan," in *The Ideologies of Theory Vol.* 1 [Minneapolis: University of Minnesota Press], 83).

naturalism might best be described as the intersection of irresolvable antinomies of identity and difference, "as the working-out of a set of conflicts between pretty things and curious ones, material and representation, hard money and soft, beast and soul" with the crucial proviso that naturalism does not thematize these tensions so much as it *formally* embodies and exemplifies them (1987: 172–173).

Inasmuch as the "characteristic concerns of naturalism"—"appropriation, legitimation, the need to end representation, and the desire to represent" (Michaels 1987: 27)—recall the similar representational dilemmas of the hysteric, whose crisis of self-control is rooted in "the nonidentity of self with either body or soul," Michaels regards naturalism as the preeminent literary expression of hysteria (25). Like hysteria, naturalism "is above all obsessed with manifestations of internal difference or, what comes to the same thing, personhood" (Michaels 1987: 22). Impelled by the "possibility of identity without difference, it is provoked by its own images into ever more powerful imaginations of identity by way of difference" (Michaels 1987: 22).

Hysteria is thus "an exemplary disease" for Michaels's consideration of naturalism in that it posits a selfhood that is non-identical with either the body or the soul, a self that, borrowing from William James, Michaels describes as "neither us nor ours" (1987: 23). Producing somatic symptoms that are nevertheless physiologically undetectable, hysteria is "*in* the body...without being *of* the body" and functions as a paradoxical condition/effect attending the problem of embodiment and representation/mediation as such (Michaels 1987: 23). Compelled by the need to script the self, the discourse of the hysteric functions, in Lacanian terms, as the "speaking riddle" put repeatedly before the big Other: "Tell me who I am" (Wajman 2003).

In demanding the Other to respond with a concrete or embodying identification, however, the hysteric thereby reveals the lack in the Other. For no particular, finite manifestation can satisfy the hysteric's insistence that the Other produce this exhaustive knowledge of self. The hysterical question thus encodes a "double gesture: on the one hand, it uncovers the Other's lack, yet on the other hand, the hysteric offers herself completely as a plug to cover up the void in the Other" (Gherovici 2014: 59). Paradoxically, it is the hysteric's self-sacrificing devotion to the "absolute Other," a search for a primal father or more "perfect Master," that rejects the identities proffered by the Other and exposes as false its particulate evidence of universal knowledge (Gherovici 2014: 59). As Patricia Gherovici glosses Lacan, the hysteric, as epitomized in Freud's exemplary case of Dora, exhibits an "alienating redoubling:"

> On the one hand, she sees herself as the passive victim, and identifies with this role; this is how she presented herself to Freud, and this is how she consciously believed things were operating. On the other hand, her unconscious identification is with a structure that enables her to assume this role. (Gherovici 2014: 60)

That is, in assuming the passive role, the hysteric obscures the extent to which her self-satisfied abjuration of the world is predicated on an unacknowledged imbrication with its architectures of power.

The hysteric's act of simultaneously defying and safeguarding the Other's authority therefore reveals a dialectical torsion between, on the one hand, the force of an irresolvable, destabilizing demand upon reality and, on the other, a duplicitous retreat into the cynical subjectivity that Hegel names the "Beautiful Soul" (Hegel 1977: 384). In Hegel's account of the historical manifestation of Spirit, the Beautiful Soul marks the stubborn antithesis between immediate subjectivity and objective reality, or between thought and action underwritten by moral conscience. Ascribing to itself a transcendent moral duty, the Beautiful Soul locates truth in its absolute and immediate self-certainty. Hegel contends that the Beautiful Soul founds its moral exceptionalism on the claim that "I act morally when I am conscious of performing only pure duty and nothing else than that; this means, in fact, when I do not act" (1977: 386). Abstracting pure thought from engaged socio-material being, this pristine consciousness "lives in dread of besmirching the splendor of its inner being by action and existence" and "flees from contact with the actual world" (Hegel 1977: 400). However, such self-protective involution ultimately endangers and attenuates the self: "In this transparent purity of its moments, an unhappy, so-called 'beautiful soul,' its light dies away within it, and it vanishes like a shapeless vapour that dissolves into thin air" (Hegel 1977: 400).

In his important reconsideration of the hysteric, Lacan refigures Freud's problematic contention that Dora colludes in her own victimization with the Hegelian concepts of the Beautiful Soul and the dialectical reversal. If the Beautiful Soul denounces as corrupt and deplorable the world from which it withdraws, the dialectical reversal exposes the subjective limitations of this view and reveals the way in which the Beautiful Soul is complicit in or authors the very corruption that it abhors. Because, as Lacan claims, "a letter always arrives at its destination," the Beautiful Soul, having sought refuge in pure thought, is forced to confront the objective consequences of its actions in a way that exposes its enclave subjectivity to the very dialectic of History that it works so hard to evade (Lacan 2007: 30).

As Jameson puts it in his own Freudian invocation of Hegel, "History is therefore the experience of Necessity," and the consequent determinations of the former persist in spite of the Beautiful Soul's arch disavowals:

> Conceived in this sense, History is what hurts, it is what refuses desire and sets inexorable limits to individual as well as collective praxis, which its 'ruses' turn into grisly and ironic reversals of their overt intention. But this History can be apprehended only through its effects, and never directly as some reified force. This is indeed the ultimate sense in which History as ground and untranscendable horizon needs no particular theoretical justification: we may be sure that its alienating necessities will not forget us, however much we might prefer to ignore them. (1981: 102)

In its aspect as Beautiful Soul, then, the hysteric colludes with the iniquity of the world with which it pharisaically disidentifies precisely by positing history as that from which it can neatly abstract itself.

Indeed, Lacan goes so far as to associate the Beautiful Soul with Hegel's preeminent agent of evil, the "Law of the Heart," in whom the self-assurance of the retiring moral perspective claims for itself the force of Historical Necessity and acts accordingly upon the world. In this "frenzy of self-conceit," the Law of the Heart universalizes the individual's "inmost law" as the "law of all hearts," thereby sanctioning the ruthless suppression of anything opposed to it (Lacan 2017: 209). Yet the discourse of the hysteric, in its emphatic overidentification with the Other, also presents the latter with the impossible demand and is not, in that aspect, reducible either to the self-exempting Beautiful Soul or the psychotic Law of the Heart.

Achebe's novel, Adkins suggests, satirizes "the ineffectuality of the beautiful soul's refined anomie" as well as the postcolonial tendency toward "cynicism and moralism as widespread. . . responses to failed political visions" (Adkins 2017: 407). According to Adkins, Achebe's satire of the Beautiful Soul lays bare what Achille Mbembe terms the "conviviality" of colonial power relations, "encircling subjects under the same unconscious, mutually dis-empowering episteme" (Adkins 2017: 408). While Mbembe's approach certainly "avoids facile distinctions between victims and victimizers, oppression and resistance, challenging the beautiful soul's self-exempting politics of blame while asking us to exchange morality and moralism for ethics and implication," as Adkins rightly claims, it does not account for the formal procedure, the critical self-exemption that could enable such a satirical response in literary expression (2017: 407).

In Lacanian terms, that is, it might be said to sidestep the stubborn fact of the Symbolic and the formal problem of representation, adopting the empiricist pretensions of what Frank Lentricchia describes as naturalism's "secretarial imagination" (1968: 28). But as Lacan's most celebrated slogan has it, "*the unconscious is the discourse of the Other,*" which is to say that it is inscribed in the Symbolic (Lacan 1972: 39). In fact, in reading the Beautiful Soul as a secondary, characterological feature rather than one of elementary form, such an approach merely duplicates the subjectivist (Imaginary) exceptionalism of the Beautiful Soul. Any critique of the latter must therefore be an immanent one obtaining within and sensitive to the contradictions and antinomies of form itself. Any presumption of ethical self-exemption remains, as Lacan instructs, firmly within the symptomal binary logic of the Imaginary (1989: 55).

On the other hand, if the colonial power relation is, in fact, convivial, capillary, and *unconscious*, how much more so are the ramified ministrations of postcolonial power and transnational capital under globalization's comprehensive dislocation and refunctioning of time, space, culture, class, and identity? Fanon suggests in *The Wretched of the Earth* that colonialism effectively places the colonized in a position that we at once recognize as that of the hysteric—forced "to constantly ask the question: Who am I in reality?" (2004: 182). The postcolonial subject, encircled by the unconscious, unlocalizable, and disempowering episteme of a new historical situation, however, can address the hysteric's question only to an already obsolete, irremediably diffuse Big Other: that of an erstwhile colonialism.

The postcolonial intellectual is thus caught in hysterical naturalism's intractable antinomy, insisting on pure identity without difference, provoked by ever more insistent visions of identity by way of difference. Yet, as Michaels suggests, the naturalist writer as hysteric does not (and cannot) merely thematize these irresolvable conflicts from the outside; rather, his work inhabits and exemplifies them in the manifold textures of its formal expression—history functioning here in Jameson's precise sense as both ground and untranscendable horizon, as the objective precondition for speaking and as the intolerable constraints imposed upon the utterance. And, as I have suggested of Naipaul, such expressions are not obliged to the subjective attitude or custodial vigilance of the writer (as Beautiful Soul) but are rather the living crystallizations of a dynamic and dialectical historical process.

Therefore, if Achebe's critique remains, in its recourse to satirical meta-language, caught within the self-exempting horizon of the Beautiful Soul, this is less an indictment of the author's imaginative failure than an illumination of the postcolonial dilemma that produces it, in which resistance and critique find themselves suddenly without a defining object and incommensurate to an unfamiliar historical circumstance, oscillating between principled, if objectless engagement (hysteria) and self-acquitting irony or resignation (the Beautiful Soul). Michaels's appeal to hysterical naturalism, in which the repudiation of representation is matched by the lingering compulsion to represent, thus applies more satisfactorily to the nebulous condition of the postcolony under the regime of late capital than to Fanon's directly administered colonial state.

If Naipaul's late fiction demonstrates the crisis of narrative in the arrested dialectic of naturalism, then the work of South African novelist, playwright, and critic Lewis Nkosi epitomizes the intersection of postcolonial naturalism with the split discourse of the hysteric/beautiful soul. In the lyrical subjectivism of his apartheid-era debut novel *Mating Birds* (1986), the cynical retrospection on the guerrilla campaigns of the outlawed South African Communist Party and ANC's liberation army in *Underground People* (2002), and the psychoanalytic reversals of his *The Black Psychiatrist* (2001)—even in his trenchant critical appraisals of fellow South African writers—one may discern the traces of the hysteric's double-voiced discourse. Situated between a post-independence melancholy and the reckoning of globalization's volatile new dispensation, refracted through the racial politics of apartheid and its end as well as the subjective dislocations of exile, Nkosi's work articulates in its complex interplay of form and content the noble self-exemption of the Beautiful Soul and the subversive anxiety of the hysteric, to whom no satisfaction can be given and for whom no form is sufficient.

"The Seeds of Destruction": The Beautiful Soul in *Mating Birds*

Mating Birds recounts the fatal encounter of Ndi Sibiya, son of a Zulu chief, erstwhile university student activist, and aspiring writer, with Veronica Slater, a white "English girl" (about whom we know little else) on the beach at Durban in direct violation of the Immorality Act of 1927/1950 prohibiting sexual relations between white and Black South Africans (Nkosi 1986: 26). Narrated by Sibiya, who awaits execution for the rape of Slater, the novel is deliberately ambiguous on the point of the assault for which Sibiya is convicted:

> And to be quite honest, am I so sure that I am entirely blameless of the crime I am supposed to have committed? Everything happened

so quickly in that seaside bungalow that I could hardly reflect at the time how much of what happened was wholly of the girl's bidding, how much the result of my own wayward impulse. (Nkosi 1986: 5)

While the uncertainty of both the event and Sibiya's culpability might, as Nkosi claims,[4] illustrate the fundamental absurdity of the Immorality Act, in which consent could neither legitimately be asked nor given, its most immediate effect for the narrator is the impression of a naturalistic fatalism:

> What I have come to understand very clearly is how the seeds of my own destruction were planted the very first day I laid eyes on the girl lying on the sands of the Durban beach, for what happened later was surely the final ripening of those seeds and the harvesting of the grain of lustful ambition that had grown in a matter of weeks until it had matured like a powerful weed to consume my life. (Nkosi 1986: 5)

Sibiya professes, for example, no resentment toward dignitaries of the court, like the judge, who is likewise borne by the twin currents of duty and fate. Sibiya's philosophic resignation extends more broadly to the trial, the perfunctory ritual of which inspires a stoic acquiescence before what he regards as the impassive processes of destiny:

> Outside, the sun shines from a naked and indifferent sky. But inside the courtroom the indifference is cloaked with the significance of symbolic action. I am the eternal goat being prepared for sacrificial slaughter; and, of course, I'm bored with the prolonged but clearly necessary preparations for the ceremonial shedding of blood. (Nkosi 1986: 36)

The narrator thus regards the trial as an "elaborate primitive game" fulfilling an "atavistic need for ritual" before an implacable nature (Nkosi 1986: 32).

Between what he indignantly views as the prurient trial sessions and intervening interviews—"the excited curiosity aroused in my observers by the slightest revelation of anything to sexual matters borders on the morbid and unsavory" (14)—he sits in his cell in Camusian contemplation, "reading, writing, and reflecting on the human condition" (37). Prompted by Dufre, an eminent criminologist and "great Swiss doctor of mental health," who is compiling a scientific dossier of the (rather unaccountably) infamous case, Sibiya sounds traumatic personal and collective histories in order to locate the origins of his present compulsion, which he describes as the "fatal attractiveness of an ungovernable passion" (Nksoi 1986: 66) and which he experiences in his dreams as the "total surrender to an impulse older than human law, more ancient than civilization itself" (121).

Belatedly denouncing the apartheid laws of the 1950s in the very moment when the Immorality Act is being officially repealed (Michael Chapman deems the novel "an anachronism" in this regard [2013: 16]), Nkosi invokes a primeval natural order and an existentialist acquiescence to fate that appear to abrogate altogether the contingent determinations of history. Despite a vague dissatisfaction with Dufre's theory of intermittent cultural evolution ("Your civilization is at the very beginning of a long and cheerful struggle that must be waged with vigor and intelligence. Of all people, you should be an optimist, Mr. Sibiya!"), the narrator nevertheless concedes his inability to resist the universalizing eloquence of "appeals of this sort to first principles, to the eternal laws of man's existence, of his constant, indeed, uncheckable regeneration" (Nkosi 1986: 69–70).

History, Hysteria, and the Political Unconscious

Such an admission therefore problematizes Therese Steffen's exemplary reading of Dufre—whose name, as Steffen notes, is an obvious anagram for Freud—as "a Eurocentric expert who is mainly interested in confining a black man's sexual behavior in the cage of his Freudian theory" (Steffen 2005: 108). For Steffen, Dufre functions not only as the embodiment of European psychoanalytic hubris, but also rather curiously as "the political unconscious of Marx and the Marxist critic Fredric Jameson" (2005: 109). The "ironically detached" Sibiya, who "has nothing to lose but his life" (Steffen 2005: 109) is thus endowed with the exceptional ability to outstrip the Eurocentric ideology in which "everything in our age apparently leads back to the Trier on the Moselle or to Zurich and Vienna, to the *Interpretation of Dreams* and *The Communist Manifesto*" (Nkosi 1986: 17–18). In this reading, Sibiya's ironic detachment plies cultural difference to present an ambivalent critique of the totalizing framework of psychoanalysis, which is ultimately revealed as a metonymic displacement of the encompassing historical dialectic of Hegel/Marx (and Jameson). The irony here is that Sibiya strikes an exemplary figure of what Marie-Cécile and Edmond Ortigues long ago called the "African Oedipus," whose significance, they instruct, "cannot be assimilated to a characterology" but which "circumscribes the fundamental structures according to which, for society as well as for the individual, the problem of evil and suffering, the dialectic of desire and demand, are articulated" (M. and E. Ortigues 1966: 301).

Despite anxieties of Eurocentrism, the utility of psychoanalysis for African literature has by now been established, from Jonathan Crewe's measured assessment that "the language of psychoanalysis continues to supply terms for negotiating between what Rose calls the phantasmagoric identifications and the shifting realpolitik of political and cultural identity" (Crewe 2004: 149) in an African context to Ato Quayson's more general claim that Freudian concepts such as the uncanny, trauma, castration, and the unconscious offer us indispensable means to *calibrate* an immanent symptomology of the global present (Quayson 2003: 78).

Such a totalizing view is obliquely indicted in *Mating Birds*, however (perhaps by way of the British historian Hugh Trevor-Roper), in the racist burlesque of Professor Van Niekerk, who invokes a "great historian who needs no introduction to some" and who once claimed that "before the white man there was no African history," echoing Hegel's own infamous claims in *The Philosophy of History* (Nkosi 1986: 104). Like the virtuous renunciations of the Beautiful Soul, Sibiya's rejection of Freud/Hegel/Marx remains firmly, fittingly confined to the Oedipal structure of the pleasure-principle, to which he appeals as if to primordial nature. Such becomes his chief self-justification as he recollects the event of the rape:

> ...I remember that my one thought was to return, by force if necessary, to that narrow fount, to the source of all forbidden pleasure mother; he asks about my feelings toward my father. Did I ever wish to kill him, or perhaps did I not secretly hope that while my father was cutting the trunk of a tree, the tree would come crashing over his head. (Nkosi 1986: 18)

Like Freud's Dora, then, Sibiya's unresolved Oedipal complex, combined with his self-exonerating recourse to the supreme Other of natural law, suggests the figure of the hysteric. Like many of Nkosi's male characters, Sibiya is repeatedly associated with nervous unrest, of which he is both compulsive chronicler and longsuffering victim. Awaiting his fate on the dock, he finds that carefully observing the activities of the court is his only "way of dealing with the ennui that spreads like an epidemic" (Nkosi 1986: 34). Sibiya significantly neglects to disclose to Dufre the incidental encounter with a white girl in his youth that, he claims, "marked me for life," leaving a "permanent wound" (Nksoi 1986: 59). The incident in fact prefigures his literally bumping into Veronica in a tobacco shop in an "accidental embrace" that excites a "nervous agitation" (Nkosi 1986: 104); and he describes the recurrent horror of his "white, harrowing dreams" as bearing the amorphous shape of "a searing wound, like a memory of an exquisite torture undergone a long time ago but whose recollection it is hard to erase" (119).

Awaiting Veronica's daily arrival at the shore beneath a sun that threatens to "consume everything beneath it in a slow burning heat like the outbreak of a dreadful voluptuous fever," Sibyia is overcome by an anxiety that gripped his heart "like a vice" (Nkosi 1986: 129). He walks about the township to relieve his "jangling nerves" and to stave off a "lack of [his] own sense of worth and direction" and an "innate sense of uselessness" about the world (Nkosi 1986: 139). Overcome by debilitating physical lethargy, he writes that "I felt the physical discomfort as an addition to the already accumulated, though as yet unassessed, spiritual discomforts of the soul, as though I had been absorbing the hot stickiness of the humid air through my pores" (Nkosi 1986: 139).

Examining his past under Dufre's direction, Sibiya recalls his mother's "high nervous laugh" as sometimes tending toward "dry hysteria" (Nkosi 1986: 45). Upon arrival in Durban following the death of his father and the displacement of his village, he and his mother encounter Gabela, a "mesmeric" preacher/prophet of the local Church of Zion, who is "irresistible to women" and "was known to have cured many hysterical women simply by laying his huge hands on their heads and shoulders—though some said his hands wandered to forbidden places" (Nkosi 1986: 94). Such abuse is rumored to have been the cause of his mother's abrupt departure from the Church of Zion after two years, and though the details of their encounter are never divulged to the narrator, he observes that "its lasting and damaging effects on her personality were unmistakable" (Nkosi 1986: 95).

Subsequently giving way, in the narrator's eyes, to a cynical immodesty unbecoming a "self-respecting Zulu widow," his mother grows disturbingly responsive in her hysterical dereliction to the crowd of suitors who perpetually surround her:

> A current of ceaseless animation connected her to the jovial lust of men around her. Her toothy smiles, her dimpled copper-colored cheeks, her extravagantly hued skirts and brightly colored *doeks*, even her voice, which had always been so pure yet so close to hysteria, had become part of an arsenal she employed for the

conquest of the world of city men, the tight-fisted world of money, of desperate township intrigues, and numerous petty struggles. (Nkosi 1986: 96–97)

Giving up what Sabiya deems respectable work as a laundress for whites, she "succumbed to the temptation of running a *shebeen*," at which point her pursuers "buzzed like bees around a sweet-smelling but cankerous flower" until, Sabiya writes, "I could no longer feel that my home was my own" (Nksoi 1986: 97). Still, he admits, even these revelations are "digressions," "detours," "evasions," duplicitous screen memories that attempt to displace responsibility for his actions onto the figure of a morally frangible mother even while acknowledging in passing the historical circumstances that conditioned them (Nkosi 1986: 100). His efforts to cast his mother (and, later, Veronica) in the role of hysteric, thereby exonerating himself in the attitude of the Beautiful Soul, serve to belie his own status as hysterical subject.

Sibiya's narrative likewise expresses a deep, pre-Oedipal fixation on what Melanie Klein theorized as "part-objects," particularly the primordial image of the maternal breast (Klein 1975: 189). Such a refusal to perceive the "whole object" of the other in her complex personhood also resonates with the naturalist repudiation of totality in favor of disconnected, fragmentary images, what Lukács describes as "a series of static pictures, of still lives connected only through the relations of objects arrayed one beside the other according to their own inner logic, never following one from the other, never one out of the other" (Lukács 2005: 144). Scholars have repeatedly noted what Johan Jacobs calls the novel's "mammary obsession" (Jacobs 1990: 123), expressed not only in the "quick, tantalizing view" of Veronica's "pale breast with its nipple puckered into a pointed tip of frilled purple flesh" (Nkosi 1986: 145) on the beach, but also in Sibiya's memory of Cato Manor and the "pliant waists of languid girls, and middle-aged women who stared out of open windows, their rounded breasts lilting out of summer dresses" (Nkosi 1986: 138–139). Fittingly, as Andre Brink writes, "Even (and especially) his mother falls victim to his sexually-loaded observation" (Brink 1992: 18), as Sibiya's death-row account curiously lingers over his mother's "high pointed breasts" that "bounced like pears on the branch of a pear tree" (Nkosi 1986: 97); and her subsequent submission, "like a dumb suffering beast," to the sexual aggression of Big Joe, is provided with the preliminary glimpse of her bare breast (1986: 98).

The narrator clearly perceives this latter moment as both a personal betrayal and the rupturing of his milieu by an elemental force:

> Then all at once, as though a world had suddenly turned on its side, the man and the woman began to move together. In a steady, ever-increasing rhythm, they moved and moved and moved together while the world seemed to whirl around me like a gigantic spinning wheel. (Nkosi 1986: 99)

His maternal world upended, the Oedipal son subsequently transfers what he views as his mother's depraved, animal sexuality onto a remorseless, inexorable nature. The sea, which will later serve as primary conceit for and symbolic motivator of his transgressive sexual passion, he describes as "reposing in its watery bed like a slothful woman, bare to the sun and naked to the caressing breeze, with an occasional steamer plowing its course across the immense lagoon" (Nkosi 1986: 43). Yet, its stillness, like Veronica's, is "capricious and untrustworthy;" storm clouds ever threaten to condense without warning, and "raindrops as large as the breasts of a young Zulu virgin will roll down from the sky," making impassible the "swollen and turbulent river...carrying before it uprooted trees, drowned animals, and, occasionally, even the dead body of some unlucky individual" (Nkosi 1986: 43).

That Sibiya, perennial victim of woman's treacherous sexuality, is one such unlucky individual is understood. Similarly, "as if the sea had been stirred by a powerful hand," it begins to "swell and froth" in the moments prior to his mimed, "telepathic" sexual encounter with Veronica at the beach: "At intervals, the waves broke upon the shore with a roar as elemental as the beating of blood in my own feverish veins, harsh, murderous, deranged" (Nkosi 1986: 142). Inasmuch as he is thrall to Veronica's "quivering pagan motion of astounding primitive sensuality," he thus repeats the inexorable fall into a base, feminized Nature. His strategic use of naturalist metaphor renders him the powerless victim and her the animalized aggressor: "Like a river in flood," he reflects on his final entrance into Veronica's bungalow, "my lust swept me off toward that half-open door, toward the room in which the girl lay like a watchful lioness ready to spring" (Nkosi 1986: 147).

Brink effectively argues that the narrative functions as Sibiya's self-exculpatory testimony as the unfortunate dupe of feminine guile. Thus, his account increasingly takes on the tenor of both a personal pathology and the calculated self-acquittal of its narrator. The narrator stages his self-redemption through a strategic figuration of masculine sexual violence as anti-imperialist politics, but this elision is enabled, as the metaphoric turn to nature here affirms, by dissolving both these symbolic strands into the master trope of writing, the book's ultimate, self-legitimating horizon. *Mating Birds* is as much a novel about the hysterical anxieties of postcolonial literary production, of producing and consuming the postcolonial subject in language, as it is a lyrical rumination on the intimate politics of apartheid or even, as Brink has it, the self-legitimation of the exile.

This series of sublations, repeatedly enacted in the book, is summarily forecast in the narrator's first glimpse of Veronica on the beach:

> Her eyes closed, her mouth slightly open as though ground to dust by a nameless, tameless lust, she was asleep, mindless of the suffering she caused, just as she was mindless of the sun and the breeze that riffled through her rich brown hair as through the wealthy pages of a smutty book. (Nkosi 1986: 7–8)

Apart from being an instance of what Chapman calls one of Nkosi's "several purple passages about the female body," the sentence also indicates with synoptic economy the novel's defining thematic progression from the dilating horizons of female sexuality and impassive Nature to that of literary figuration, a second Nature both encompassing and metaphorizing the first. Inasmuch as the turgid prose and imprecise imagery here recall the narrator's overweening ambition to become, as he puts it, "the first truly great African writer my country has ever produced," they likewise suggest the narrator's compulsive scripting of a postcolonial subjectivity for literary consumption (Nkosi 1986: 4).

However, unlike Naipaul, in whose fiction, as Sara Suleri claims, "the writer is never exempted from the text's graphic indictment of the postcolonial world," Nkosi's narrator seeks anxious refuge in the closed helix of literary similitude, in which every object is made fungible with another, and all are finally dissolved in the self-reference of a writing that engages the object of its representation from the outside, from the exceptional aesthetic of the Beautiful Soul (Suleri 1992: 154). The maintenance of such an empiricist distance is also, again, the very hallmark of literary naturalism.

Onanistic Representation and the "Naturalist Machine"

Mark Seltzer identifies a similar process of displacement and rewriting at work in the novels of the American naturalist Frank Norris. Intervening in the late nineteenth century's "insistent anxiety over production and generation," and apropos the Foucauldian biopolitical inscription of the subject, Norris's novels contrive what Seltzer describes as a narrative machinery in which, drawing on a "thermodynamic technology of power," the opposition between biological female generativity and industrial male productivity (or between conservation and dissipation, production, and consumption) are imaginatively resolved through the interposition of what Norris names *force* (Seltzer 1986: 35). As Norris writes in *The Octopus* (1901):

> Men were naught, death was naught, life was naught; FORCE only existed—FORCE that brought men into the world, FORCE that crowded them out of it to make way for the succeeding generation, FORCE that made the wheat grow, FORCE that garnered it from the soil to give place to the succeeding crop. (qtd. in Seltzer 1986: 29)

Circumventing or appropriating the procreative "threat posed by the 'women people,'" force enables a "technique of nonbiological and autonomous reproduction, or what amounts to a mechanical reproduction of persons," or of subjects (Seltzer 1986: 33).

Norris's category of force, Seltzer argues, thus reconciles the incompatible energies of generation and dissipation, the (male) katabolic and (female) anabolic tendencies, within a regulatory mechanism that is at once the primordial generation of Nature ("Nature was, then, a gigantic engine..." [qtd. in Seltzer 1986: 29]) and the *technical reproduction* of that Nature, which renders its omnipresence narratively intelligible. As Seltzer summarily describes it, "the naturalist machine operates through a double discourse in which the apparently opposed registers of the body and the machine are coordinated within a single technology of regulation," which is none other than the naturalist novel and the emergent reticulations of power that it both maps and codifies (Seltzer 1986: 44). Thus, "creation, in Norris's final explanation, is the work of an inexhaustible masturbator, spilling his seed on the ground, the product of a mechanistic and miraculous onanism" (Seltzer 1986: 31). If force displaces a feminine nature, the "onanist-machine" of writing outflanks and redirects force within naturalism's "autonomous and masturbatory economy of production" (Seltzer 1986: 31).

Similarly, *Mating Birds* ultimately vindicates Sibiya's raping of Veronica as both an act of political defiance, sanctified through a tendentious juxtaposition with "political prisoners lustily singing freedom songs" at the novel's conclusion, *and* as the symbolic seizure of the generative technology of writing, which Veronica is made vividly to personify (Nkosi 1986: 4). Sibiya describes Veronica's appearance on the witness stand as being "as pale as a piece of paper," anticipating his later recollection of his mother's hopeful ambition to see him "driving his pen across the white page." "A real devil Ndi is going to be with a pen, you wait and see," she effuses of his intellectual potential (Nkosi 1986: 85). His desire for "attaining knowledge of some willing white woman" (Nkosi 1986: 44) is thus made analogous if not wholly continuous with his desire to "attain the magic of the white man" and the "vast empires to be conquered with nothing more powerful than a pen" (49).

That Veronica symbolizes not merely white authority, but specifically the alluring power of white writing is made clear during her court testimony. Sibiya is awed by "her ability to invent her fictions" and describes her as "an accomplished storyteller, with a considerable grasp of human psychology" (Nkosi 1986: 154). He enviously appraises her "instinctive knowledge of what constituted audience appeal," her "lively sense of timing, an ingenious and subtle faculty for creating suspense," and her virtuosic ability to craft "scenes of great climactic power;" "As a narrator," he writes, "she was quite simply magnificent" (Nkosi 1986: 124). She was, he determines, "a fantasist by nature," (Nkosi 1986: 155) and he finds himself "enchanted by the intense expressiveness of her face, which resembled the passionate absorption of an artist in a moment of self-creation" (156).

The narrative's jarring rehearsals of colonialist/racist stereotypes—as in the narrator's assertion that his jailers are curious to see his "well, yes, let us admit—oversized penis" (Nkosi 1986: 14)—are therefore seemingly redeemed as metaphoric assertions of the phallus/stylus in a comparably demiurgic invention of the postcolonial self as artist. Thus, the narrative does not so much stage the destitution of language and the dilemmas of incommensurability—the "profound silence between cultures which cannot finally be traversed by understanding," as Bill Ashcroft and others claim (2002: 85)—as it does repeatedly and anxiously refer us to its own self-generating, self-legitimating mechanics.

If Veronica symbolically embodies the tandem of white and literary authority, it is inevitable that Sibiya should direct the hysteric's query to that authority, which he comes to view as his subjective complement. Thus, he reasons, for Veronica, he is the "ultimate mirror in which she saw reflected the power of her sex and her race," just as she reflects his own, an analysis that elicits a hardy "Bravo!" from Dufre (Nkosi 1986: 74). Similarly, only Veronica can provide him with the "missing links in [his] faulty and, no doubt, hopelessly affected memory" (Nkosi 1986: 169). She has become, he admits, "the center of [his] desire, the focus of all [his] eternal longing, [his] inexhaustible passion" (Nkosi 1986: 171).

Once, reading served as one of Sibiya's "greatest delights," but following his destabilizing encounter with Veronica, in a moment when he fervently dreams of escaping South Africa, he "could hardly make any sense" of his books:

> My mind wandered, and between myself and the personages who peopled the novels I read interposed, uninvited, the lewd, mocking figure of the girl on the beach, turning over and over on her spread-out towel or rug. In my mind's eye I could see her lambent breasts flashing like white beacons behind her protective arms. (Nkosi 1986: 138)

His aphasiac loss of concentration is a crisis in subjective (and historical) self-representation that, he imagines, can be mediated only through appeal to the twin authority with which he invests Veronica. His dilemma, though, is that "it was just this girl who could not now be trusted, who had managed to weave a web of fiction so completely divorced from the truth that, paradoxically, it seemed the more credible for being so entirely a work of a diseased fabulist imagination" (Nkosi 1986: 169). The extreme subjectivism for which Sibiya condemns Veronica's testimony is, by way of projection, all the more true of his own, which seals itself within the self-referential idiosyncrasy and masturbatory self-generation of the Beautiful Soul.

No image more effectively exhibits this tendency than the crude symbolism of the titular "mating birds." Having expressed in the opening paragraph the naturalist observer's "lack of involvement in [his] own fate," Sibiya immediately relates the tendentious scene beyond the barred grill of his window:

> Sometimes a flock of birds will ascend the sky, wings beating wildly; often a pair will mate up there in freedom and open space, clinging to each other joyfully in the bright air as though for dear life. Then, no longer able to restrain himself, the male will attempt to inject his sperm into the female and he, of course, as often as not, will miss so that you can see his pale seed dripping through the air while the female giggles wildly, as is the habit of her sex. (Nkosi 1986: 1–2)

A number of elements give one pause here, not least Sibiya's claim that the birds appear "sometimes" and mate "often," assertions that are immediately contradicted in the next paragraph by the declaration that "[t]he scenario is the same every morning" (Nkosi 1986: 2). The narrator's fatalistic appeal to nature, confirming in advance both an absence of volition and his victimization by female treachery, is sufficiently transparent, and the "unruly birds" will return at the novel's conclusion to join the singing prisoners in a tableau anticipating the "near-dawn of freedom" (Nkosi 1986: 184).

Of the rather absurd image of failed copulation, Brink proposes three possible explanations: "either an extraordinary faculty of observation in the prisoner, or an incredibly copious discharge by the bird, or—most likely?—a tendency toward gross exaggeration and wild imagination in the narrator" (Nkosi 1986: 3). The most compelling possibility is, of course, the latter—not least because this image conspicuously encapsulates in its sterile or onanistic return exactly the structure (the ending concealed in the beginning) later disclosed by the narrator, casting the narrative as the object of its own masturbatory representation. Yet this system of self-reference is neither the historical dialectic of Hegel nor what Jacobs dismissively calls "a half-hearted stab at post-modernism" (Jacobs 1990: 122). Rather, the mythic infinity evoked here and throughout the novel is that of the naturalist machine, circumventing natural (female) generation and history itself and interposing its own conspicuously self-governing practice. Nkosi's novel formally embodies the Beautiful Soul, which renounces every metalanguage *save its own*. That critics remain divided over whether this is Nkosi's genius or his folly is indicative of the cultural and historical impasse to which the book gives mediatory expression.

As Brink has it, *Mating Birds* is simply the most visible of a series of Nkosi's early fictions constructed around the slippage between professedly public mediations and personal interests, in which the former become the alibi for the fictional exorcism of the latter. Recalling the title of fellow "*Drum* boy" Bloke Modisane's autobiography *Blame Me on History*, Brink wryly observes that "Blaming himself on history is precisely what the narrator of *Mating Birds* is trying to do, but without the irony Modisane applies to the endeavor" (Brink 1992: 2). Thus, Nkosi's fiction expresses the

> general dilemma of the *Drum* intellectual elite, who so often found themselves in limbo, between the black masses with whom they could no longer identify and the privileged whites. "I am the eternal alien between worlds," writes Modisane, "the Africans call me a 'Situation,' by Western standards I am uneducated." (Brink 1992: 2)

Nkosi already defines "Situation" in a 1962 essay as a "term of abuse for members of the African middle class trying to 'situate' themselves above the masses" (Nkosi 2005: 249). Nkosi's liminal position as exiled postcolonial intellectual therefore delineates the personal stakes of what Brink describes as Sibyia's "extremely subjective and one-sided account, offered as self-justification, and as indictment of the system of apartheid which has allegedly dictated the crime" (1992: 2). Indeed, recalling Steffen's unqualified claim for Nkosi's indirect repudiation of Jameson, Brink cites as the novel's "Jamesonian 'political unconscious'" Nkosi's "desperate need to vindicate his own exile" (1992: 17).

What is more, Brink claims, Nkosi inexplicably embellishes and distorts the sufficiently fraught historical period that he presumes to represent, a failing for which Brink provides the following summary emendation:

> There has never been a Death Row at Durban; South African court procedure is rather different from the account of it given in the novel; there have never been segregated lectures given at any university; quite simply, a trial of this nature *could not* have attracted the kind of attention Nkosi claims for his protagonist, whose exploits are alleged to have "captured the imagination of 'the entire civilized world.'" (Brink 1992: 16)

While it is no doubt true that such glaring inaccuracy and artistic license betray the self-justification of the exile, such a subjectivist explanation—itself a symptom of the Beautiful Soul dilemma—hardly satisfies the determinate conditions of History as both ground and untranscendable horizon.

If Nkosi's more immediate intent, conscious or otherwise, is to legitimate his relevance as exiled intellectual, such recognition, when confined to the binary terms of the Imaginary, does little to reveal *the motivation of the device.* In fact, Nkosi himself comes much nearer the mark in a review of Nadine Gordimer's apocalyptic vision of black uprising, *July's People* (1981), when he reflects on the likelihood that the climax of South Africa's three-hundred-year anticolonial struggle might not manifest in the revolutionary upheaval everywhere anticipated, but in "a rather banal muted whimper, a finale in which the fundamental economic structures of society would remain largely uncontested" (Nkosi 2005: 320). From here he offers an oblique but telling invocation of Hegel:

> Ambushed by history, deprived of the moral and material support of the socialist camp by the fall of the Soviet Union and its satellite states, a negotiated peace between a lame government and weary liberation movements was probably the next best thing, but the

South African novel of unbridled apocalyptic desire was equally thwarted in its secret longing for a cataclysmic, cathartic climax. The negotiated peace enacted what Doris Somer, writing about South America, described as "a premature end of history." (Nkosi 2005: 320)

While the above reflection was published in 2001, just prior to his own belated and sardonic meditation on revolution in *Underground People* (2002), Nkosi's review of Gordimer's novel originally appeared in 1983 and demonstrates a properly historical, even prescient, grasp of the postcolonial situation, much as predicted in Fanon's theorization of a national bourgeoisie.

It is precisely within this historical context, one perspicuously observed by Nkosi himself, that the withdrawal into naturalist aestheticism may be understood. The ouroboric formal and ethical logic of *Mating Birds*, according with the subjectivist retreat of the Beautiful Soul, may therefore have more to do with Nkosi's structural position within a postcolonial, middle-class "Situation," alienated from the masses and caught in the historical interstice between colonialism and global capital, than with the exile's anxious production of self; or rather, the latter may be seen as the subjective expression of the former's determinate historical substrate. Only by sustaining the dialectic of the subjective immediacy of the Imaginary and the pervasive architecture of the Symbolic (the psychic *and* the social) can we, with Quayson, abandon "any simple notion of literature as mirror" and begin to perceive it "as a variegated series of thresholds and levels, all of which determine the production of the social as a dimension within the interaction of the constitutive thresholds of literary structure" (Quayson 2003: xii).

Revelation or Revolution? The Personal and the Public in *Underground People*

Such hysterical self-reflexivity prompts Andries Oliphant's claim that it is impossible to read Nkosi's fiction apart from his "withering comments on the aesthetic deficiencies of black South African fiction of the 1960s," indeed that Nkosi's "critical writing, which belongs to the metafictional order of literary discourse, is palpable in his fiction" (Oliphant 2005: 13). Of special relevance for *Underground People* is the author's sustained polemic against South African "solidarity criticism" and its prescriptive aesthetic of social realism, which he likens to "journalistic fact parading outrageously as imaginative literature" (Nkosi 2005a: 246). Rejecting what he calls solidarity criticism's "ideological blackmail," in which a work's literary merit is held commensurate with its explicit resistance to the apartheid state, Nkosi's literary criticism advocates instead a sedulous *interiority*, through which the "inert matter" of social reality is set into productive tension with the dynamic imagination of the writer (Harris 1994: 36). Immediate experience is thereby replaced with an abstract phenomenology of experience and approximates what Nkosi, drawing on Robert Langbaum, calls "revelation" (Nkosi 2005b: 247). Nkosi's endorsement of the latter is most evident in the ironic novel of guerrilla resistance, *Underground People*, of which he remarks:

> I was really attempting to deal with the private and the public within the same novel. I was conscious of the fact that, as Black South African writers, we have always been so much more committed to the public sphere in the stories we write that we neglect to see how certain pressures of the personal, of the private life, can affect ways in which we perceive the political. (Nkosi 2005b: 248)

Underground People thus understands itself as a novel about the impingement of the private upon the public, a corrective to the vulgar historicism of solidarity criticism and its social realist orthodoxy. Discarding what he sees as the universal pretensions and formal/social typicality of contemporary South African fiction, Nkosi wagers that "actual insight into human tragedy may lie beneath this social and political turbulence" (Nkosi 1962: 3). Thus, this late novel offers a unique development of the subjectivist dynamic in Nkosi's fiction and the naturalist novel.

Scholars have been quick to note among Nkosi's sometimes unsparing appraisals of his literary contemporaries a pronounced predilection for "modern works of literature," specifically Joyce, Kafka, and Dostoevsky, coupled with a stereotypical dismissal of South African literature's "primitiveness" (Nkosi 2005b: 246). Yet it is also worth observing that his criticism is equally informed by a naturalist class anxiety that insists, as its foremost aesthetic precept, on the isolated individual and exceptional interiority. Citing as the source of his displeasure a "certain dullness of phrase, much like the ponderous speech of a dull-witted person" in the work of Ezekiel Mphalale, Nkosi scorns his stylistic choice of successive simple clauses in striking terms: "The texture of the prose had the feel and look of sweaty labour, much like the stains of honest sweat on the cloth-cap of the toiling proletariat, but hardly congenial for being honest" (Nkosi 2005b: 250). Incongruously, of communist writer

Alex La Guma, he observes that it is precisely La Guma's "enthusiasm for life as it is lived" that appeals:

> his stories and novels are sagging under the weight of real people waging a bloody contest with the forces of oppression; and, credibly, they celebrate their few moments of victory in sex, cheap Cape wine and stupid fights. The rooms they inhabit smell of decay, urine and sweat; they share them with "roaches, fleas, bugs, lice." Their only triumph is that they are human—superlatively human; and this is their sole claim upon our imagination. (Nkosi 2005a: 253)

So long, that is, as the masses are "credibly" pitiable and dissolute, politically incoherent in their atomized, "superlatively human" suffering, they are subjects fit for literary representation. Upon first meeting La Guma, Nkosi observes that he "seems cold and austere, what you probably expect a dour, very committed left-wing writer to be" (Nkosi 2005a: 257). Nksoi characterizes La Guma as "conservative and uncritical" in his "pious regard for everything Soviet;" and, while Nkosi posits that "doctrinaire" and "creative" are wholly incompatible terms, he nonetheless finds that La Guma suffers none of the insipidity that he condemns in Mphalale (Nkosi 2005a: 257, 260). Tellingly, then, what distinguishes La Guma's work in Nkosi's estimation is a "bare-limbed economy" that "owes a lot to a naturalist like Zola and the spare masculine rigour of Hemingway; La Guma "see[s] clearly" and "records faithfully," such that he seems to be "holding a movie camera on Hanover Street" (Nkosi 2005a: 262, 263).

This masculine, documentary aesthetic, however—one that ultimately directs its indictment toward South African society and the system of capitalism—finally gives Nkosi pause. He objects, for instance, to La Guma's insistence on social typology over psychic interiority, insisting that "[p]eople's failures are, after all, individual" (Nkosi 2005a: 264). In fixing its critical lens on the mere facts of social existence rather than "the interior life of his characters," Nkosi claims that La Guma's fiction "*tells* everything...but *illuminates* nothing" (Nkosi 2005a: 264). Thus, like other practitioners of social realism, La Guma "falls into the trap of giving us only glimpses of the vast machinery of political suppression, rather than of the more significant workings of human character" (Nkosi 1962: 3).

Hysterical Subjectivism and the Specter of History

In *Underground People,* Nkosi attempts to redress this imbalance in favor of the individual and psychic interiority. Like *Mating Birds*, *Underground People* may be read as an exemplary work of hysterical naturalism. We find the inept, anti-heroic protagonist Cornelius Molapo—"an incompetent teacher of languages and a dabbler in poetry and politics" as well as an avid reader of Hegel, Fanon, and, fittingly, Henry James—"emotionally shattered" by recent separation from his serially unfaithful wife (Nkosi 2002: ix, 48). Summoned by Joe Bulane, central committee member of the National Liberation Movement (a fictional coalition of the ANC and SACP, both outlawed in 1950), Molapo is tasked with serving as party liaison and director of a resistance operation in the rural township of Tabanyane, where a corrupt and authoritarian sub-chief is colluding with government officials to yield ancestral territories for industrial and white residential development. Knowing that the operation itself is wholly futile, the NLM nevertheless hopes that the inevitably repressive response from the Pretoria Government will galvanize broad support for the movement (Nkosi 2002: 52). An ancillary benefit for the NLM leadership is the removal of Molapo from Johannesburg, where his fiery, frequently drunken, scandalously public criticisms of the Movement and his "constant exposition of a kind of nationalism in the place of a broad international socialism" have grown irksome (Nkosi 2002: 52).

However, now "a complete emotional wreck," Molapo is reluctant to accept the assignment and make good on his revolutionary rhetoric (Nkosi 2002: 52). Showing "signs of nerves" and self-professedly "broken," Molapo admits, "Psychologically, I would be the weakest link in the chain of the Movement's general strategy" (Nksoi 2002: 48). Racked by "nervous excitement," "agonizing tension," "fevered agitation," "terror," and "anxiety," Molapo experiences "such anguish and sense of loss," however, that exile from Johannesburg also presents the possibility of "a kind of deliverance" (Nkosi 2002: 89–90). Like Sibiya, Molapo is plagued by dreams of his mother—"a silent figure wearing ragged clothes and watching him accusingly from the bank of a river" (Nkosi 2002: 88)—whom he correspondingly conflates with his deceitful wife: "Maureen and Margot rolled into one sack, the man had later punned lasciviously to himself" (89). And, like Sibiya, he projects Maureen's treacherous femininity onto the natural world in terms that correspond to masculine, if not colonial, oppression: "she became then a trail lost in the hot swampy jungles and dark misty forests, a sort of mystical kingdom at the core of a continent that remained inscrutable, very dark, very unconquerable" (Nksoi 2002: 58).

Other major characters also suffer what the novel explicitly calls "a tendency toward hysteria" in markedly naturalistic terms (Nkosi 2002: 103). There are, for example, white South African exile and international civil servant Anthony Ferguson's "deep apprehension," "nameless fear," and incestuous "emotions too illicit to entertain" (Nkosi 2002: 101, 111, 103). Ferguson is frequently overcome with physical lassitude and waves of swooning dizziness. Similarly, Tabanyane's De Kock, a "part-time police-farmer" charged with apprehending Molapo and struggling with agricultural mechanization, the influx of international capital, and the flight of labor to urban centers, suffers "crushed self-esteem" and "wretched humiliation," which he compulsively recalls "as a person might do when running the tip of his tongue over a chipped tooth, frightened of the pain but drawn irresistibly to the exposed nerve" (Nkosi 2002: 78–79). Catching sight of his reflection in a barroom mirror, De Kock "saw reflected there a waning of physical strength" and "the blurred contours of fear—the most suppressed and unacknowledged fear" (Nkosi 202: 82–83). De Kock's wife, Nellie, likewise "bore the marks of her own emotional impoverishment and defeat like a broken animal, sustained only by a sort of inhuman resignation" (Nkosi 2002: 78).

This mixture of nervous despair and resignation to natural impulse can likewise be found in its preoccupation (as in so many works of postcolonial naturalism—like Ayi Kwei Armah's *The Beautyful Ones Are Not Yet Born*) with the excremental. In Tabanyane, Molapo watches a silent figure on the edge of a field emptying his bowels and hurriedly cleaning himself with a stone before "gazing at the far horizon with an air of hopelessness" before the despondent reverie of each man is broken by the warbling of an "invisible bird," which seems sardonically to proclaim "man's perennial surrender to the call of nature" (Nkosi 2002: 165). In his discussion of Achebe, Adkins cites Warwick Anderson, who observes that a colonialist discursive distinction between European purity and native pollution maintains "'corporeal distinctions between colonizers and colonized,' painting the latter as promiscuous defecators who 'lacked the self-control characteristic of white men, and therefore required guidance toward self-government of body and polity'" (qtd. in Adkins 2017: 401). A native "acclimation to excreta" corresponds with his "incorrigible barbarity" in surrendering control to natural imperatives. The latter scene thus recalls Molapo's hysterical response to Bulane's revelation of Maureen's infidelity: "Cornelius's bowels moved and quite involuntarily, he farted, and Bulane spat in disgust" (Nkosi 2002: 53).

While *Underground People* rehearses many of the naturalist motifs of *Mating Birds*, however, they are more explicitly coordinated in relation to the fundamental quandary of the personal versus the public, a structural dilemma that is reproduced at several scales: rural versus urban, national versus international, affective versus rational, and historical versus natural. This central antinomy is made most explicit in Joe Bulane's effort to convince Molapo to take the Tabanyane assignment. During their tense interview, Molapo is struck with the sensation, "drawn from some inexhaustible silence at the centre of industrial chaos, of time standing still: the illusion that nothing was changing and nothing would ever change" (Nkosi 2002: 46). Against feelings of "temporary disembodiment," he struggles to "regain the echo and pulse of his own existence against a tide of public indifference" (Nkosi 2002: 46). Bulane counters Molapo's hysterical crisis of self with appeals to the collective cost of his inaction, claiming that "in comparison with the exploitation and suffering of our people, personal problems are of no consequence" and that "[o]nly struggle will endow your life with meaning where before there was nothing but futility and 'perpetual emptiness'" (Nkosi 2002: 47). Molapo insists, in turn, that Maureen and his personal crisis are "more important than all your struggling masses put together" (Nkosi 2002: 47).

The exchange culminates in Bulane's dramatic revelation that Maureen has not only been notoriously unfaithful to Molapo but has been repeatedly unfaithful with Bulane himself. The veracity of Bulane's confession remains uncertain, but its ironic effect is clear: if "[p]rivate emotion, fantasy, romantic idealism, all these were enemies of the dedicated revolutionary," as Bulane claims, they also provide the psychological leverage that he exploits to persuade Molapo, a fact of key consequence for the novel's conclusion (Nkosi 2002: 52). While Molapo reluctantly yields and accepts the mission to Tabanyane, at the heart of their exchange remains the articulation of an irresolvable impasse: "'But without love,' Cornelius protested, 'what good is political struggle'"; and "'Without freedom,' JB shouted angrily, 'what good is love?... Whoever heard of slaves falling in love?'" (Nkosi 2002: 55).

For Raffaella Vancini, Nkosi's unflattering characterization of the opportunist Bulane is expressive of "the deep hostility that he has always felt towards aspects of socialist and communist ideology in general" (Vancini 2005: 202). Therefore, the climax of Molapo's character arc is his decision to reject the NLM's stratagem of world revolution and to lead the Tabanyane people in a local struggle against the expropriation of their lands. As she contends: "Molapo will learn that politics, whether concerning the NLM or the government, are in some ways always corrupt, far removed from the ideals implicit in the fight for liberation" (Vancini 2005: 207). Moreover, she observes, "It is when

Molapo detaches himself from any external dependency that the true liberation struggle begins" (2005: 207). "Liberation" is here read as coextensive with the tenants of classical liberalism in which "freedom" is located on the side of the local/individual/internal. Thus, Vancini views *Underground People* as fully consecutive with Nkosi's passionate call some thirty years earlier for "a new mood of self-reliance" in African politics and Black resistance to apartheid ("On South Africa:" 30). Without "a radical change" in what Nkosi specifies as internal or "psychological terms," the liberation movement is doomed to failure; thus, he concludes, "A successful South African Revolution cannot be launched from abroad," indicating a domestic national enclosure as the logical complement to the subjectivist one (Nkosi 1971: 30).

But Nkosi's position is also amenable to a diametrically opposed interpretation. Monica Popescu holds that, however wary Nkosi remains of communism, it is Molapo's demonstrated fidelity to the Trotskyist doctrine of "permanent revolution" and his leftist critique of the Marxist-Leninist party line that runs him afoul of the NLM central committee. In this way, Popescu argues, Nkosi, who accepted a lectureship at the University of Warsaw in 1987, is able to "transcend the reductive binaries of the Cold War and the orthodoxy that all things communist or from the Soviet Union were necessarily good" and to open space for an alternative, perhaps not unlike the Fourth International itself (Popescu 2016: 71). By contrast, the chain-smoking Comrade X dismisses Molapo's faith in peasant-led revolution by citing their lack of education, their myopic focus on immediate material needs, and thus their fundamental conservatism. The peasants, he declares, are "the most counterrevolutionary class!" (Nkosi 2002: 71). Fittingly, this claim is echoed by X's structural counterpart, Jocelyn Baird—financial advisor to Daling International and leader of a global team of investors conducting clandestine meetings with the NLM—who holds that the natives are "natural capitalists" and need only the incentive of potential wealth (Nkosi 2002: 125).

However, the novel also resists any neat congruency with either a Trotskyite or Fanonian condemnation of bourgeois revolutionism by confirming Comrade X's assessment in the figure of Tabanyane's Princess Madi, who is described as a "diehard conservative in everything but her people's right to land and self determination" (Nkosi 2002: 173). She is openly dismissive of the NLM's socialist doctrine of common ownership and elitist pretensions to "world revolution;" her motivation is the local "'restoration' of these rights [to land and self determination], and not revolution" (Nkosi 2002: 173). Her stance thus recalls that of Mark Brody, Ferguson's future brother-in-law and a wealthy businessman whose fortune was made in buying up abandoned gold mines. Praising the government's sober attempts at redressing the social inequities of apartheid, he exhorts, "Not revolution, but reform" (Nkosi 2002: 120). Despite her reluctance, Madi's cooperation with Molapo is obtained through the pacifist Reverend Stephens's nervous assurance that "the NLM has many tendencies of which the Marxist-Leninist is only one" and that the "nationalist wing is certainly the strongest" (Nkosi 2002: 174).

Madi, whose consummate nobility of character is never questioned, thus inhabits the private (rural, national, natural) end of the novel's thematic antinomy, while the NLM and its global capitalist co-conspirators are equally consigned to the public (urban, international, historical). But permanent revolution, as theorized by Trotsky, entails the structural integration of rural peasant with urban proletarian resistance and, concomitantly, the recognition that the productive forces of global capitalism "can no longer be reconciled within the framework of the national state." As Trotsky writes in 1929,

> The socialist revolution begins on the national arena, it unfolds on the international arena, and is completed on the world arena. Thus, the socialist revolution becomes a permanent revolution in a newer and broader sense of the word; it attains completion only in the final victory of the new society on our entire planet.

Therefore, if Molapo's orientation migrates in the direction of Madi, as it seems clearly to do, he relinquishes any prior commitment to the precepts of permanent revolution in favor of an insular localism that would lump Trotskyism together with both Marxism-Leninism and global capitalism, each as aspects of a pernicious internationalism.

This stark opposition between the local and global informs the terms of Madi's pointed question: "Are you a communist, Mr. Molapo?" (Nkosi 2002: 185). For Madi, communists are defined by their internationalist agenda, their commitment to "serving the interests of a foreign power" over those of native peoples (Nkosi 2002: 185). Molapo counters that the NLM is "a national front organization" distinguished chiefly by its internal diversity and dialogic method (Nkosi 2002: 184). Pressed further, he outlines his personal orientation within the movement to Madi, whose "ample bosom, astonishingly well-shaped, rose and fell as if she were an ardent young girl, eager to be inducted into the mysteries of the Liberation Movement" (Nkosi 2002: 185). With the exchange abruptly and inexplicably charged with erotic interest, Molapo opts not to discuss party platforms; rather, "he chose to speak only of himself:"

'Your Royal Highness, I don't know what communism is. I know only what the South African Government says it is. Those of us who demand justice, those of us who clamour ceaselessly for equal pay for equal work; those of us who demand the implementation of the democratic principle of one person one vote; those of us who fight for the freedom of movement and association, and for a fair share of the land and wealth which comes from this land; those of us who all want South Africans, black and white, to marry whom they like and live where they like, those are the people the Government calls communists and they are people the Government has banned, banished, imprisoned, tortured, murdered and maimed in the name of the suppression of communism. If asking for the security of limb and property, if asking for the right of our people to be fairly represented in the political institutions of our country and to have the security of employment is communism, then I am a communist.' (Nkosi 2002: 185–186)

Regardless of whether or not his definition adheres to any consensus understanding of communism, the speech has the effect of securing Madi's cooperation and aid, which, she admits, she was determined to grant all along. But perhaps more importantly, it initiates a romantic intimacy—heralded by "a slow languid movement with her heavy hips, the weight of her breasts almost tangible in the sighing shift of the petticoat beneath her uniform" (Nkosi 2002: 187)—that exorcizes from Molapo's mind the enervating specter of his failed marriage. The novel thus oscillates between the positions of Molapo and Bulane, love and politics, or it rather presents the former as the elementary substance of the latter. Molapo's salvific sense of renewed political purpose is made inextricable from his restored capacity for sexual love.

Personal versus Political at the End of the World

Obliquely but repeatedly invoked as the crux of this private/public quandary is the figure of Hegel and the historical dialectic. As we are often reminded, Molapo dutifully reads *Phenomenology of Spirit* each night before bed ("Hegel and marital problems! What could be more normal!" [Nkosi 2002: 11]). Yet, he reads in a wholly random and desultory manner, "without pleasure, slowly, like a man in a trance, already on the edge of self-forgetfulness, ready to enter that night in which every cow is black" (Nkosi 2002: 166). Whether that "night" is the welcome insensibility of sleep or the more general stupefaction of Molapo's uncritical devotion to the European philosopher, the text does not indicate. Finding him asleep the next morning, Princess Madi peruses the worn, heavily underlined copy of the *Phenomenology* and is unimpressed: "Obviously, the book contained a lot of nonsense," and its "casual remarks" about the dialectical unity of opposites "were so obvious they did not seem to her to be profound truths at all" (Nkosi 2002: 178).

Such a curt dismissal of the dialectic would seem to support Vancini's claim that the novel "invalidates" the Marxist theory of historical materialism, attested by Nkosi's own profession that the novel undertakes to explore the possibility of

> contingency in history—how an odd happening that has nothing to do with say what a Marxist would consider to be the forces of history shaping events, but what one might call an accident in history could determine the course events take. (qtd. in Vancini 2005: 209)

"Contingency" stands here for the private, individual, interior, or affective, those elements that would appear insignificant to the molar mechanics of history or the grand destines of its collective agents, yet are, for Nkosi, equally determinate, if not more so.

In the novel's hysterical rendering of affect we can also identify a countercurrent to private withdrawal, however, one that refuses the private consolations of the interior for the uncertain anxieties of history. The natural world repeatedly provokes an objectless angst in Nkosi's characters in a kind of extended pathetic fallacy. Directly invoking *Mating Birds*, Nkosi's Tanbanyane guerrillas listen as "[s]omewhere in the trees a bird sang with an inadmissible desire that made the men think of spring and young love; but beyond this they felt an ache for something they could not name" (Nkosi 2002: 200). In the "massed darkness" of the forest, "tree trunks rise like ghosts out of an immemorial African past," and the black silence is "horrifying in its primordial muteness" (Nkosi 2002: 202). Cornelius's men fall "prey to acute anxieties," and their watch in the forest produces a "strain on the nerves" (Nkosi 2002: 205); the men "who had trusted the wilderness as they trusted their own mothers, now that it possessed secrets from which they were excluded, felt towards it nothing but fear and distrust" (Nkosi 2002: 206). Finding a burning cigarette butt on the dark forest floor, the guerrilla Ngo, a farm hand now struggling to find work, remarks that, while their fathers "tilted their spears against an enemy that could be seen," his generation is left to confront ghosts who, "when they are challenged, melt into darkness" (Nkosi 2002: 206). In the twilight, awaiting their planned assault on the Tanyabane police station, Molapo's men "felt as though their nerves were pulled by invisible wires" (Nkosi 2002: 266). Similarly, Ferguson, setting out to find Molapo and the guerrillas, has "the extraordinary sensation of being hemmed in on all sides by forces he did not understand" (Nkosi 2002: 300).

As the novel makes explicit, however, the absent cause (object) of this hysterical anxiety is inexorably historical, not natural. Ngo must battle spectral foes because the mechanization and modernization of agriculture, driven by international investment, have eliminated jobs. Similarly, De Kock's troubles are credited to the rising costs of mechanization and mass migration of manual labor to the cities (Nkosi 2002: 80). And like the guerilla fighter Ngo, De Kock is forced to reckon with his own waning physical strength, which he finds reflected in futile searches for the shadowy revolutionaries. Indeed, Bulane remarks to Ferguson that the native, as the product of imperial discourse itself, exists if at all *"by virtue of remaining outside vision"* (Nkosi 2002: 293).

Meanwhile, Bulane secures the NLM's compromising files overseas in Chase Manhattan Bank, while Jocelyn rationally calculates the unsustainable cost of apartheid, reflecting that the "collapse of the economy is a more terrifying prospect than blood mixing" (Nkosi 2002: 128). In a novel impelled by Conradian obscurity and relentlessly tenebrous natural landscapes, within which characters repeatedly seek in vain for clarity of visual, moral, and historical perception, Brody points out that a "lot more is going on under the surface than meets the eye" (Nkosi 2002: 121). As he says to Ferguson with arresting conviction: "What were once unquestionably solid coalitions are rapidly dissolving. New alliances are being formed. And to tell you the truth, no-one knows where the country is headed" (Nkosi 2002: 121). Jocelyn agrees that South Africa is experiencing "what will be seen by future generations as a historic turning point in our country's affairs," one that can be discerned in the present only as "the shape of what would be a possible idea:" a rapprochement between the NLM and the Government, the release of NLM leader Dabula Amanzi (the novel's fictional Nelson Mandela), the cessation of armed resistance and emergency, and the drafting of a new constitution. Of course, the events dimly anticipated by Jocelyn had already transpired by the time Nkosi was publishing his long-unfinished novel, and mediation between Black revolutionaries, the ANC, the South African bourgeoisie, and the institutions of multinational capital had already taken place. South Africa thus transitioned from an apartheid state into a new, integrated order in which the rigidities of an internal colonialism were rendered amenable to the unpredictable flexions of globalization.

Thus, we come to the novel's concluding standoff between Molapo and Bulane and the personal/political antinomy that they define. Having arrived in Tabanyane, Molapo "had the sensation of having arrived at the end of the world," which, the narrator affirms, is just what Tabanyane is: the last settlement between Johannesburg and the border, an apocalyptic "landscape similar to that projected in films after an imagined nuclear disaster but never seen in reality or properly grasped psychologically" (Nkosi 2002: 155). Here, at the revelatory end of the known world on the eve of an uncertain "historic turning point" beyond colonial and Cold-War polarities, Nkosi sets opposite the private and the public, the international and the local. With racial apartheid's formal dismantling, the release of Mandela, and the ANC's capitulation to economic apartheid—the tragic consequences of which can be witnessed, to take only a singular example, in the 2012 massacre of striking Marikana mineworkers—the old domestic demands for justice have nominally been met, and former international radicalisms have almost wholly surrendered to the agents of global capital.

Having journeyed to Tabanyane to warn Molapo of the forces being assembled against his doomed local insurrection, Bulane confronts a defiant revolutionary who now invokes the moral authority of the masses against the bureaucratic complacency and venality of those party apparatchiks "who will always betray the people" (Nkosi 2002: 304). Seeing that he is immovable, Bulane turns to leave only to be halted by Molapo, who, raising his rifle, remarks that officers who abandon their men are routinely shot. Bulane, however, rejects the political pretense of Molapo's threat: "You're out to settle scores. It's because of Maureen, isn't it? You want to take revenge because I once screwed your wife" (Nkosi 2002: 306). The two men thus form a neat chiasmus in which their views are transposed, and the novel leaves unresolved this tension between personal and political, internal and external.

Molapo alerts Ferguson that he is about to execute Bulane and thus commit a human rights violation when gunfire sounds all around them, such that even the narrator is uncertain who fires first: Molapo, the guerrillas, or De Kock's approaching men. In the chaos of battle, De Kock grabs Ferguson and tells him to return to England because "[i]n South Africa, the war has only just begun" (Nkosi 2002: 306), a curious closing statement given that, on one hand, Nkosi has criticized Gordimer for exactly such apocalyptic prognostication; and, on the other, he— unlike Gordimer—knows full well the historical outcome of this would-be revolution, which is as he predicted long before: "a rather banal muted whimper, a finale in which the fundamental economic structures of society would remain largely uncontested." Thus, the inconclusiveness of the novel refers not to the South African state of emergency and the approaching end of apartheid but to a contemporary recalibration of capitalist imperialism and the crisis of the nation state in the void left by the Cold War's end. At this impasse, Nkosi gives nature the last, ambivalent word: "And from the summit of an isolated yellowwood, a dove started to coo quite mindlessly" (Nkosi 2002: 306). The conspicuous symbol of peace from *Mating Birds*, which there affirms the literary and moral self-legitimacy of its narrator, here signifies hysterical indeterminacy in the face of a history that can only be read as inscrutable nature.

Nkosi as Sublime Hysteric

In a brief meditation on the dialectic of Truth and Knowledge, Žižek recalls Lacan's cryptic description of Hegel as "the most sublime of hysterics." It is an error, Žižek claims, to view the relationship of knowledge to truth as a progressive one, with each provisional or particular figure of knowledge supplanted by increasingly more proximate ones in a kind of Kuhnian evolution until a final coincidence with Truth is obtained. Against such a mechanical teleology, Žižek argues, Hegel sees truth as already coincident with the search for truth; thus, "the insufficiency of knowledge, its apropos of the truth, radically indicates a lack, a non-achievement at the heart of truth itself" (n.d.: n.p.). The hysterical question, which "burrows a hole in the Other," is therefore resolved only by a dialectal reversal in which the question is revealed to be its own answer.

Žižek illustrates this point by drawing on Adorno's observation about the absence of a contemporary definition of society: either society is perceived as an "organic Whole that transcends particular individuals," or it is perceived as "a relationship between atomized individuals." This conceptual deadlock would seem to preclude a general definition of society and condemn us to the parsing of multiple, contradictory theorizations incapable of grasping their object and thus to Thatcher's doleful conclusion that society does not exist. The dialectical reversal intervenes at precisely this impasse, Žižek writes, to reveal ways in which the contradiction that seems to obstruct knowledge is rather its very manifestation:

> the different definitions of society do not function as an obstacle, but are inherent to the thing itself; they become indicators of

actual social contradictions—the antagonism between society as an organic Whole as opposed to atomized individuals is not simply gnoseological; it is the fundamental antagonism which constitutes the very thing that one wants to comprehend. (n.d.: n.p.)

We can similarly regard Nkosi's juxtapositions of the personal and political, natural and historical, rural and urban, national and global in precisely these terms: not as the corrective preference for one over the other but as the hysterical attempt simultaneously to think both at a moment when the poles of familiar landscapes—the nationalist anticolonial and antiapartheid movements—have been effaced by the dislocating force of economic globalization. It is therefore in its formal expression of this structural transformation, rather than in the passionate provincialism of Molapo, that *Underground People* can be said to approximate the "permanent revolution" of the hysteric at the threshold of capital's real subsumption. Taken together, *Mating Birds* and *Underground People* can therefore serve as figures that map the subjectivist inclination—its limitations as well as its immanent contradictions—within the evolving practice of postcolonial naturalism.

Chapter 3

Heredity and Horizon in the Postcolonial Bildungsroman
Rhys, Cliff, and Adiga

An accounting of postcolonial naturalism is obliged to consider what might well be its most ubiquitous and therefore hegemonic exhibit. In considering the paradox of the postcolonial Bildungsroman—in which the narrative of development seeks expression under material conditions of the grimmest systematic underdevelopment—Maria Helena Lima asks why a genre that has "become virtually defunct in the European context" should have such a "new and viable identity 'overseas'" (Lima 1993: 435).[1] The predicament of postcoloniality—its cultural diremptions, temporal and spatial dislocations, and, above all, its subordinate structural position in the late capitalist world-system— might be said to produce conditions in which neither aspect of the contradictory self-actualizing and socializing dual vocation of the traditional Bildungsroman can be effected. As Simon Hay frames the problem of the apparent paradox between the terms *Bildung* and *postcolonial*, "How can the hero's process of 'development' work? How do postcolonial protagonists 'come of age' if in the Bildungsroman generally 'coming-of-age' means ascending to the ranks of the bourgeois imperialists?" (Hay 2013: 321). This chapter will examine ways that the postcolonial Bildungsroman remains caught between the naturalist imperatives of heredity (the preservation of Being) and the radical possibilities of horizon (Becoming). This dilemma, which is an objective and historical one, holds despite the political attitudes of the work or author in question. Thus, in either an arguably conservative writer like

---

[1] Lima's account refuses the supercilious developmentalism of the term "truncated *Bildungsroman*" and complicates somewhat José Santiago Fernández Vázquez's influential claim that "one of the reasons why postcolonial writers turn to the *Bildungsroman* is the desire to incorporate the master codes of imperialism into the text, in order to sabotage them more effectively," enabling her to reimagine the postcolonial Bildungsroman as a form enacting a more ambivalent symbolic decolonization (Lima 1993: 435).

Jean Rhys, a radical writer like Michelle Cliff, or a liberal writer like Aravind Adiga, we find a similar narrative and ideological quandary.

For Hay, one answer relevant for us here can be discerned in the postcolonial Bildungsroman's dialectical sublation of realist narration and naturalist description along with its preservation of a progressive impulse in the latter (2013: 341). Alternatively, Lima argues that the harmonious reconciliations between self and society, soul and convention, individual advancement and blind class interest that Franco Moretti famously recognizes as the primary ideological imperatives of the classical form are, in the postcolonial Bildungsroman, foreclosed in advance even as they are compulsively or ironically restaged. In either case, the successful integration and affirmation of the subject in accordance with bourgeois ideals are thereby revealed as structural impossibilities in a kingdom of brute necessity that is paradoxically the material precondition for the (selective) realization of these abstract ideals of freedom and morality elsewhere. Interrogating the contradictions and limitations of the European paradigm of the *Bildung* (in both its nationalist and universalist pretenses), postcolonial writers like Jamaica Kincaid therefore strategically lay claim, Lima argues, to an inherited form that is altogether incommensurate to its object of representation. As such, it "dismantles conventional notions of genre" and "destabilizes the conventions of identity traditionally found in the culture of the first world" even as it "helps to reproduce the cultural imperialism that inevitably separates the Third World intellectual from the community and culture of his or her birth" (Lima 1993: 455).

Though it reveals the inescapable dilemma of imperialist cultural inheritance, such an emphasis on the postcolonial Bildungsroman's ironic or ambivalent performativity by way of the cultural process that Lima names "generic transculturation," might nonetheless risk acceptance of bourgeois exoticism at its word (1993: 433). As Jed Esty's remarkable study of modernism's fictions of arrested development attests, the narrative of frustrated or deferred *Bildung* defines the historical situation of colonialism's uneven development at either phenomenological or experiential pole. This constitutive unevenness demonstrates that the "culture of the first world" is far from singular or homogenous and is not without its own internally asynchronous histories of overt domination as well as hegemonic interpellation. Thus, Esty writes,

> Modernism's untimely youths—Woolf's Rachel Vinrace, Conrad's Lord Jim, Joyce's Stephen Dedalus—register the unsettling effects of the colonial encounter on the humanist ideals of national culture

that had always, from the time of Goethe and Schiller, determined the inner logic of the *Bildungsroman*. (2011: 25)

While the "semicanonical, semiperipheral" novels of Jean Rhys or Elizabeth Bowen indicate a moment in which "the logic of cultural difference seems increasingly to structure antidevelopmental plots," Esty argues that such a turn also nonetheless "indexes a broader shift in the modernist era as social antagonisms are increasingly coded in terms of cultural (especially racial) difference" (2011: 31, 32). The evolutionary and developmentalist impetus of bourgeois realism, with its symbolic reconciliation of individual and national destinies, thus gives way to a "more static anthropological grid of cultural differences" (Esty 2011: 33). At the level of form, the progressive temporality of the nation meets its anti-narrative limits in the currents of global modernity as plot succumbs to scene, a trajectory already familiar to us as that of naturalism. Here, then, the deployment of difference functions as a symptomatic transference that expresses through the logic of narrative the fundamental contradictions of an evolving world-system even as it transcodes those tensions into the terms of biological and cultural determinates.

Modernism and the Cultural Logic of Empire

As Jameson contends, it is precisely the disjunctive formal architecture of empire that structures the broad delineation and interior manifold of a modernist writing that emerges as a crisis formation within the metropolitan national imaginary. Empire is characterized by a metropolitan experience in which "a significant structural segment of the economic system as a whole is now located elsewhere, beyond the metropolis, outside of the daily life and existential experience of the home country;" the modernist cultural and aesthetic concomitant of this situation thus produces a "cognitive mapping" sensitive to the radical distention and disjunction of the social space of the nation and the narrative enclosures that sustain its primary idiom (Jameson 1990: 50–51).

In the metropolitan expression of E.M. Forster's *Howards End*, for example, Jameson identifies this anti-narrative presence in the unsettling encroachment of "infinity"—"the bad opposite of place"—upon the familiar landscape of the English countryside. While any direct confrontation with the reality of what will later be known as the Third World is typically repressed in these modernist works and rewritten in terms of rival imperialist state cultures, a practice that Jameson describes as the "masking of one axis of otherness by a very different one," this strategic substitution is also representative of the determinate tension or conceptual aporia out of which modernism might be said historically to emerge (1990: 49). From this perspective, modernism quite simply *is* the formalization of an irresolvable contradiction between the domestic locus and the enigmatic "grey placelessness" of the infinite, which is nothing less than the extimate truth of the former uncannily revisited upon itself:

> Modernism is itself this very hesitation; it emerges in this spatial gap within Forster's figure; it is at one with the contradiction between the contingency of physical objects and the demand for an impossible meaning, here marked by dead philosophical abstraction. (Jameson 1990: 55)

Jameson's modernism is therefore the dim and fitful grasping of the Real of the occulted historical situation of empire (the lie told by Marlow to Kurtz's Intended *and* the unnarratable colonial horror that it conceals captured together in a single, complex figuration) from within the Symbolic securities of the lived domestic experience, which can then persist only in the Möbius structure produced by this representational impasse.

The raw material of modernism is the daily experience of the national totality (the privileged domain of realism) imaginatively sundered from and therefore haunted by the necessarily spectral presence of its material conditions located in the colonies. Therefore, a direct encounter with colonial violence, such as in a Third-World text, will not provide what Jameson elsewhere calls the aesthetic "satisfactions of Proust or Joyce" simply because "there the face of imperialism is brute force, naked power, open exploitation" rather than the oblique glimpse of empire's anamorphic death's head (Jameson 1986: 58). As Fanon characterizes this dilemma, which is both epistemological *and* representational, "the *fellah*, the unemployed man, the starving native do not lay a claim to the truth; they do not say that they represent the truth, for they *are* the truth" (2004: 13). The absence of imperialist ideology's mediating structures in the colonial context annuls the necessity of modernism's representational innovations. Thus, only with the tentative registration of globalization's new architectures of domination in the period of post-nationalist melancholy—when the ideology of redemptive national cohesion itself has been shattered by way of its fulfillment—can the postcolony be said to express aesthetic modernism, at least as Jameson defines it.

Modernism and the Postcolonial Exotic

While the primary concern of Esty's project is "British-sphere modernism within a wider global history of the novel in general and the Bildungsroman in particular," he nevertheless proceeds to suggest that the paradigm he elaborates can also be extended to postcolonial literatures (2011: 34–35). In what is admittedly a "provisional connection," Esty's account perhaps too hastily subsumes the postcolonial into a prior, European modernist model of untimely youth in what he describes as a "functional alignment between Anglophone modernism's suspicion of linear time and an anticolonial project that casts doubt on Western or Eurocentric models of development" (2011: 201–202). The first of these tendencies is spatio-temporal and universal—hence historical and narrative—while the second ambivalently yields to differences of spatio-cultural particularity (not of global capital but of "the West" or "Europe")—hence mobilizing atemporal and descriptive or anti-narrative inclinations.

Esty's analogic extension hinges on the claim that the postcolonial Bildungsroman "establishes a dialectical rather than an antinomial relation between world-historical development aimed at a shared destiny and a world of static, anthropologized differences splayed on a planetary grid" (2011: 202). The postcolonial Bildungsroman therefore symbolically mediates, in Esty's admittedly fleeting and tentative account of it, the intractable theoretical deadlock "between a singular-modernity model that projects a global *narrative* of modernization and an alternative-modernities model that *describes* a detemporalized map of raw cultural difference" (2011: 196, emphasis added)—hence, the old opposition between narration and description appears again.

But while Esty's modernist and postcolonial models of arrested temporality may be structurally analogous, the latter admits a determinate culturalism that simply inverts the logic of the former, thereby replicating what Vasant Kaiwar describes as the Orientalizing logic predominant in postcolonial theories of difference:

> The career of one of the keywords of postcolonial thought, "difference," is instructive in this regard. When it enters the postcolonial lexicon, it quickly acquires connotations of exoticism, untranscendable otherness, and the like, which immediately links it with a long-standing tradition of Orientalism. (2014: 107)

If modernism is the practice of representing the traumatic Real of material history within the abstract enclosures of national culture, the postcolonial, by this account, marks an ambivalent retreat into the timeless redoubt of cultural difference (Being).

So, although Esty's two models of the Bildungsroman, the modernist and postcolonial, share a formal symmetry, the latter has more in common, I claim, with that alternative aesthetic of arrested development—between a late realism in crisis and an oppositional modernism—from which Esty's account explicitly attempts to differentiate itself: namely, aesthetic naturalism. As he writes,

> What we conventionally understand as the transformation of the Bildungsroman into the naturalist fiction of disillusionment (with its logic of fixed social hierarchies, broken destinies, and compensatory but socially eccentric artistic visions) may also have had a geopolitical dimension—ascertainable in the incongruous temporalities of nation and empire and the emergence of eternal adolescence as a formal mediation of the two. (Esty 2011: 6)

The work of "symbolic reconciliation" undertaken, for example, in Kipling's *Kim*, therefore "fares no better in colonial precincts than in the industrialized zones of high naturalism" (Esty 2011: 11). Esty repeats this equation in the extension of the figure of unseasonable youth in the British novel of 1860–1930 to that of the post-1945 postcolonial novel. Claiming that the impetus of subjectivation with which Moretti credits the classical Bildungsroman "did not simply wither on the vine of high naturalism," Esty simultaneously asserts that the "novel of unseasonable youth and high naturalism is an alternative response to the growing aesthetic inadequacy of the novel to progress in an age of imperial-finance capital" (2011: 233, 66). The "crucial differences" between the two, he argues, lie in both their "geographical frames of reference" and in their critical modalities (2011: 67). On the one hand, the novel of unseasonable youth takes up the conflicted space of "colonial encounter" over that of naturalism's fatalistic metropolitan decadence; on the other, it preserves a dialectical rather than "purely antinomial" expression of the "still-progressive elements of middle-class realism" (2011: 67).

Yet, if modernism is a crisis of bourgeois realism arising from its oppositional margin, it is in fact the formal manifestation of the margin as such within an interior having heretofore expressed itself as a universal. Accordingly, insomuch as it partakes of realism's residual progressivism, modernism does so from precisely this tenuous and double-valanced position at the margin—neither fully inside nor outside the totality that it undertakes to critique. The national bourgeoisie of the postcolony, whose cultural self-expressions and "geographical frames of reference" provide the aesthetic parameters and abstract content of postcolonial literature, does not so much mark the margin of difference that it pronounces for itself (read strictly as geo-cultural or identitarian) as it does reflect both an intensive and extensive diffusion of a system for which the former national horizon has become simultaneously a fetter for some and a ruse for others. Whatever progressivism lingers in the unseasonable youth of modernism is thus supplanted in the postcolony by either an outer world of insidiously alienating development, arrogating to itself an evolutionary inevitability, or an interior world of immemorial, civilizational Being grounded in culture/biology.

The "developing" nation is thereby beleaguered on either front, as we find in Nkosi, by the specter of Nature in both its first and second aspects. Meanwhile, the postcolonial nation, structurally unable to manifest the destiny of the classical Bildungsroman, is caught between the *actual* margin of the potentially revolutionary masses (whose political difference is summarily recast as cultural identity) and the nameless, placeless void of the new Empire from which the hard-sought victory of national independence is found to provide neither security nor respite.

Therefore, the "radical postcolonial nationalism as a process of *Bildung*," the cultural formulation and catalyst of which is the Bildungsroman in its demiurgic or what Pheng Cheah calls its *epigenetic* aspect—figuring the emergent nation in terms of organic maturation—gives way in the postcolony and the rise of the neoliberal empire to expressions like Nuruddin Farah's The Blood in the Sun Trilogy, Ninotchka Rosca's *The State of War,* and Armah's *The Beautyful Ones Are Not Yet Born* (Cheah 2003: 240). Such works, though "marked by despair" and steeped in "melancholy irony," nevertheless take up the vocation of national allegory and the fraught realization of national *Bildung* (Cheah 2003: 245). While Cheah finds oppositional literary projects of national *Bildung* to persist in the "idea that a radical national culture of the people contains the seeds for the reappropriation and transformation of the neocolonial state" (2003: 245)—thereby enacting what Hugh Charles O'Connell importantly terms a "weak utopianism" (O'Connell 2012: 371)—they also "no longer possess the same confidence in the inevitable progress of history, the unfaltering consciousness of time characterizing the organism's self-recursive causality" (Cheah 2003: 245).

Though Bloch might remind us here that utopian hope is never reducible to confidence, this "frustration of teleogical time, with its accompanying despair," leads nevertheless to the Naipaulian realization of Armah's protagonist, who, upon hearing of the coup against Nkrumah's government, is "not burdened with any hopes that new things, really new things, were as yet ready to come out" (qtd. in Cheah 2003: 246). Giving due heed to Cheah's crucial cautioning against "reducing the Bildungsroman to a product of the educated bourgeoisie and an ideological superstructure of capitalism and its mythology of individualism," we can nevertheless perceive in this frustrated teleology a continuity with the encompassing naturalist crisis of narrative. In the Bildungsroman, this crisis is expressed as the overwhelming of (realist) narrative horizon by (naturalist) heredity, or of emergent nationalism's organicist development by the prescription of genetic destiny.

It is in response to the thwarting of narrative and of temporality—both expressed in and imposed by an aesthetic regime of naturalism—that radically extended narrativizations like Farah's The Blood in the Sun trilogy and Pramoedya Ananta Toer's majestic Buru Quartet might be said to take up the chronotope that Peter Hitchcock calls postcolonial "long space." For Hitchcock, long space entails the figuration of durational history in a moment in which time, space, and narrative—or progressive *history* itself—have become problems rather than self-evident means of dynamic social transformation and the realization of national *Bildung* (Hitchcock 2010: 4). That is not to say that oppositional, emancipatory, or transformational narratives of postcolonial national *Bildung* are impossible under the conditions of the neoliberal state within transnational capital, but simply that any such narrative of development, whether reactionary or progressive, unfolds within the closed temporality of naturalism and is therefore encumbered by its structural logics, which it must either confirm, contest, or revise.

Jean Rhys and the End of the Road

The tension between the irreconcilable impulses of development and underdevelopment, universal and local, narrative and anti-narrative, history and nature is dialectically sustained, Esty argues, in Jean Rhy's *Voyage in the Dark* (1934), a novel of "interwar modernism" informed by "a crepuscular historical phase where the emergent logic of postcolonial nationalism signals the break-up of the old European empires" (2011: 160–161). Esty attempts to offer an alternative avenue out of the scholarly deadlock in which Rhys—whom Kamau Brathwaite memorably describes in a reply to Peter Hulme as "the Helen of our wars" (1994: 69)—is regarded as both a "postcolonial writer producing a counterdiscourse to the established power of British imperialism" and alternatively as an imperial nostalgist with plantocratic sympathies (2011: 164). Rhys's fiction embodies, he suggests, the contradiction "between the modernizing, developmental discourses of emancipation-and-empire and the exoticizing, underdeveloping practices of patriarchy and imperialism" (Esty 2011: 164).

The result is a fraught formalization (the "metabildungsroman") in which the progressive plot impulse of the classical Bildungsroman is subducted beneath the "static, regressive, accelerated, syncopated" temporalities of the postcolony's uneven development (Esty 2011: 164, 165). *Voyage in the Dark* thus produces a hermetic "world without end" in which the linear momentum of narrative and destiny has irrevocably stalled in "a dark perpetual present of disorientation and disintegration" (Esty 2011: 166). Rhys's narrative momentum succumbs to an "eviscerated temporality" with sentences that either struggle to muster a predicate—and thus yield only an affective "litany of recurrent sensations that harrow Anna and press her inside a thick, foggy, medium of static time"—or otherwise lapse into "flat, repetitive, subjectless statements strung together in a way that turns narrativity itself inside out" (Esty 2011: 167, 174–175). Space, time, and syntax contract and lose distinction, and the novel relentlessly depresses plot into "a series of cinematic and spatial dissolves" (Esty 2011: 169).

If the overwhelming of plot and syntax by scene and affect is familiar to the reader of postcolonial naturalism, this resemblance is also not lost on Esty, who notes that Anna's negotiation of and ultimate subsumption by urban space suggests a "thoroughgoing naturalist plot that extends beyond the passive, disillusioned heroes of Flaubert into the downtrodden heroines of Zola" (2011: 169). Nor does he fail to note that in the novel's opening pages, Anna is found reading Zola's *Nana*, "her anagrammatic precursor in sexual victimhood" (2011: 170). In the novel's extended evolutionary biological conceit ("Feelers grow where feelers are needed and claws where claws are needed" [Rhys 1982: 107]), Esty finds a "naturalist strand of modernist writing" in the vein of Kafka that attends to the re-organization of the subject by way of sexual and racial difference. Caught in the vortex of a "deep economic naturalism," former "narratives of self-fashioning" submit to a general process of reification manifest in Anna's subjective enthrallment to fashion and the "reduction of the body to signifiers of race, citizenship, and sexuality" (Esty 2011: 175). What Esty describes as "the biopolitical dimensions of Rhys's naturalism" are therefore defined by their "reframing of social marginality and social antagonism in terms of biologized categories of difference" (2011: 178).

What, then, should forbid our classifying *Voyage in the Dark* as an exemplary work of naturalism *per se*? If it is merely the "geographical frame of reference"—rendered chiefly in Rhys as "biologized" difference—that distinguishes the devolutionary abandonment of narrative from modernism's defiant voyage out, then Esty's account risks replicating the exoticist posture of its object. If the universals of History (whose undergirding is none other than the law of the dialectic) meet their limits in the incommensurable fragment of local and biologically encoded identity, how can the subversions enacted by the latter be anything other than antinomian by definition? A clue lies in the fact that, as Esty points out, the novel's sterile "nonfuturity" precisely mirrors that of a moribund Dominican white ruling class unable to reproduce itself in a "post-emancipation, post-plantation, postcolonial world" (2011: 177). Esty claims that the immobilized plantocratic class, as represented by Anna, simultaneously "cannot avail itself of the language of national emergence" in a culture that is "not yet a postcolony, let alone a nation" (2011: 177). Consigned to anachronic repetition, it inhabits a now unproductive space that is "out of step with a model of continuous integration and capitalist development" in a rapidly changing world-system "in which progress and modernity are themselves almost endlessly deferred for the peripheral subject" (Esty 2011: 177).

Narrative Derangement and Reactionary Fiction

Yet, the language of national emergence (that is, the narrative sensibility most associated with a progressive or demiurgic *realism*) certainly remained available to those Dominicans—subjects defining another periphery altogether—who joined the cause of the Representative Government Association (RGA) in the fight for enfranchisement and independence in the inter-war period during which Rhys composed *Voyage in the Dark*. Formed in 1919, by 1924, the RGA had already gained one third of the elected seats in Dominica's Legislative Assembly; by 1936, two years after the publication of *Voyage in the Dark*, it had attained half. With a leadership largely comprised of returning servicemen and supported by the "submerged black working class," the RGA was widely feared and despised by a predominately white ruling class rapidly losing its economic and political power to both resistance at home and a capitalist system slowly evolving beyond the geopolitical constraints of the former colonial system abroad (Proctor 1973: 275).

To this insurgence from below Rhys's fiction thus balefully opposes narrative dissipation and the sterile specter of eternal return, tropes of futility and predestination long deployed by the agents of counterrevolution and central to the formation of literary naturalism; that is, in the face of an emergent historical reality without a concept, the novel dramatizes tragic submission to the inexorable current of (d)evolutionary determination. In this way, Rhys squares the circle on the temporal and developmental impasse that Esty's study identifies: momentum, perhaps, but a cyclical momentum driven by the pitiless dictates of a static, ever-renewing, but untotalizable nature—a bad infinity.

Zola's ambitious post-revolutionary project, the 20-volume Les Rougon-Macquart, accomplishes a nearly identical feat. In response to the collapse of the Second Empire and the punctuating paroxysm of the Paris Commune, Zola set out to chronicle the history of the Second Empire by way of the family saga, an approach that not only grounds the grand narrative of History in the local, cyclical drama of the family but that also exhausts the temporal dynamics of revolution in an extended apology for the liberal *via media* of the present, which suffers neither imperial decadence nor radical excess and is, moreover, secured by appeal to the ahistorical determinations of the natural world. The effect, if not the aim, of Zola's project is then to fortify his present social order against the haunting figure of a decadent familial destiny "derailed by its own momentum" and simultaneously to distance it from "the fatal convulsions that accompany the birth of a new world" (Zola 1893: n.p.).

That is, in Zola both the fitful recrudescence of the *ancien régime* and the present wave of revolutionary upheavals—for which the Paris Commune is both harbinger and lodestar—are equally consigned to the absolute past of the brave new world of the late nineteenth century in the fraught interstice between the Paris Commune and the Bolshevik Revolution. If the percussive violence of the Commune and its bloody suppression prompted Zola (as it did his historian interlocutor and fellow positivist Hippolyte Taine), it also serves as the conclusion to his pitiless and positivistic social anatomization. Having neutralized the twin threats of reaction and revolution in an extended apology for the present, he can then claim for the experimental method a utopian ambition:

> We shall enter upon a century in which man, grown more powerful, will make use of nature and will utilize its laws to produce upon the earth the greatest possible amount of justice and freedom. There is no nobler, higher, nor grander end. (Zola 1893: n.p.)

If *Voyage in the Dark* cannot yet avail itself of the utopian language of national emergence in 1934, the anti-Bildungsroman *Wide Sargasso*

Sea (1966) undeniably can. Rhys abortively began the novel as early as 1938 and desultorily composed it in the postwar decades spanning Bretton Woods, Bandung, and the welter of anticolonial independence struggles. In fact, she witnessed firsthand the strides made by the RGA during her brief, two-month visit to Dominica in 1936, her first and only return to the island after her original departure in 1907.

There is ample evidence that the political unrest that Rhys encountered on this return trip powerfully and directly informed her fictionalized recollections of Dominica in *Wide Sargasso Sea*. As Hulme observes,

> Jean Rhys returned to a West Indies on the edge of political turmoil. A sugarworkers' strike in St. Kitts the previous year heralded a period of labour disturbances, with political overtones: this was the decade when the great trade union leaders like Grantley Adams (Barbados), Alexander Bustamante and Norman Manley (Jamaica) were coming to prominence. There had been riots in St. Vincent and St. Lucia before the end of 1935. Marcus Garvey's reputation was at its height: he would visit Dominica in 1937, a visit arranged by a local supporter, the writer J. R. Ralph Casimir (Andre, pp. 22-25). The very month Rhys left England (February), there had appeared a prophetic volume called *Warning from the West Indies* (Macmillan). (2000: 39)

Hulme identifies as the most salient political event of Rhys's girlhood in Dominica the institution in 1898 of the Crown Colony Government, which provided direct administration to colonial territories through appointed royal governors. In 1932, on the cusp of a wave of West Indian revolt, members of the RGA elected to Dominica's local legislature resigned in protest for self-governance.

What is most interesting for me in Hulme's influential reading is the way that Rhys's fiction, like Zola's or Naipaul's, responds formally and stylistically as well as thematically to the threat of revolt. Such reactions can best be illuminated by comparison with her notorious story, "The Imperial Road," which was rejected by her editor Diana Athill for being "too anti-negro in tone" (qtd. in Hulme 2000: 23). The story's plangent imperial nostalgia and the utter obliviousness of its Creole female protagonist to local race and class resentments in its 1936 setting clearly refract the political turbulence of the 1970s. Such disturbances were in fact reported to Rhys by her friend and fellow writer Phyllis Shand Allfrey. Although Allfrey helped found the Dominica Labour Party, her 1953 novel *The Orchid House* similarly laments both the circumstances of the fallen plantocracy amid the ascent of the "coloured" class and the island's decadently ruinate beauty.[2] If the road is what Hulme describes as a "pre-eminent sign of modernity," both the *trace* and material conduit of commercial and policiary mobility, Rhys places her 'Imperial Road,' or at least its pristinely idealized girlhood memory, in direct opposition to a native ruination. Contemporary political unrest is thus consistently undermined by way of its elision with natural processes of entropy and degeneration.

The ideological and imperialist opposition of civilization to nature is already apparent, however, in *Wide Sargasso Sea* in the proximate identification of Antoinette Cosway with inordinate wildness and of the unnamed Rochester with rational civilization. As Hulme also notes, *Wide Sargasso Sea* anticipates the central themes of "The Imperial Road" in the novel's opening sentences, when the narrator Antoinette reflects: "When I asked her [mother] why so few people came to see us, she told me that the road from Spanish Town to Coulibri Estate where we lived was very bad and that road repairing was now a thing of the past" (Rhys 1999: 9). Following Tia's taking of Antoinette's dress, which prompts Christophine's sharp reproval ("She run wild" [Rhys 1999: 15]), Antoinette recalls her mother's lament that they are "marooned" (the misappropriated term derived, as is frequently glossed in the novel's criticism, from the Spanish *cimarrón*, meaning "wild" or "untamed" and originally applied to livestock). After her first dream of walking in the forest with a shadowy and hateful companion and in response to her mother's long absences from Coulibri and sudden, mysterious bursts of gaiety, Antoinette retreats to the older and wilder interior of the estate:

---

[2] As Hulme writes,
   Dominica had become an Associated State of the Commonwealth in March 1967 but was still not fully independent (it became so in November 1978). Its political radicalism, especially in the early 1970s, was often associated with strong anti-white sentiment. A US tourist was killed in 1974, as were a Canadian couple who had settled in Dominica. A Rastafarian-style Dread group, largely peaceful, attracted a hysterical response, not least from the Dominica Labour Party government of Patrick John (though Allfrey opposed the draconian legislation —the Prohibited and Unlawful Societies and Associations Act, enacted in November 1974) . . . . Some of Rhys's responses to Allfrey's reports on the madness of those years in Dominica probably find their way into "The Imperial Road," events recalled from 1936 and read through the filter of 1976. (2000: 38)

I took another road, past the old sugar works and the water wheel that had not turned for years. I went to parts of Coulibri that I had not seen, where there was no road, no path, no track. And if the razor grass cut my legs and arms, I would think 'It's better than people.' Black ants or red ones, tall nests swarming with white ants, rain that soaked me to the skin—once I saw a snake. All better than people. (Rhys 1999: 16)

Similarly, the unnamed Rochester is informed by a black porter upon arrival in Dominica, "This a very wild place—not civilized," a description that he later amends: "Not only wild but menacing. Those hills would close in on you" (Rhys 1999: 40). He frequently observes the "very bad" roads and the "hostile" forest but has significant difficulty distinguishing the certain lineaments of the one from the sinister derangement of the other:

A track was just visible and I went on, glancing from side to side and sometimes quickly behind me. This was why I stubbed my foot on a stone and nearly fell. The stone I tripped on was not a boulder but part of a paved road. There had been a paved road through this forest. (Rhys 1999: 62)

However, Baptiste denies that any "*pavé* road like the French made in the islands"—certainly an oblique reference to the "imperial road"— ever existed in the forest (Rhys 1999: 63). The lack of clearly demarcated roads, as the material trace of an imperialist hierarchical order and lost plantocracy, thus provokes a corresponding epistemological disequilibrium: "The path was overgrown but it was possible to follow it. I went on without looking at the tall trees on either side. Once I stepped over a fallen log swarming with white ants. How can one discover truth I thought and that led me nowhere" (Rhys 1999: 62).

Rochester's reflections therefore rehearse the European trope of the Caribbean natural landscape as "richly but degeneratively tropical, frightening, fecund, even pathological," tendentiously juxtaposed against the rational civilization of the metropole (Tiffin 2005: 201). But as Helen Tiffin further observes, the privileged representation of the Caribbean lapsed paradise in European representations of the islands is the intermediary image of the "fallen garden," evocative of the plantation deprived of its sustaining labor and having fallen back into natural or pre-colonial disorder. The lapsed garden's mediating symbolic function in Rhys is achieved through its strategic identification with the uncultivated Caribbean landscape in Antoinette's fiery self-immolation, as Tiffin writes:

...Rhys's refraction and inversion of the values of landscape imagery in Jane Eyre enables the Caribbean landscape, not the "temperate" English countryside, to be the one accepted. The garden at Coulibri seemed to the child, Antoinette, to be, at times, the abode of evil; but by gladly embracing as her own—not the white plantation garden but the Afro-Caribbean legend of the flamboyant tree— with all its European associations of heat, fire, excess— Antoinette jumps from an imprisonment in the temperate "ideal" to embrace her Caribbean "natural" and cultural world. (2005: 205)

Mary Lou Emery similarly reads the evocation of the garden and the flamboyant tree at the book's conclusion as the redemptive embracing of a "wild" cultural and racial diversity over and against a vigilantly discriminative and homogeneous European civilization. Antoinette's "return to the Caribbean in her final vision unites her with all of its peoples—the transplanted English and white Creoles of her family, but also the older native races, and finally the blacks from whom her 'real' life had inevitably estranged her" (Emery 1999: 58). Evoking the figure of Anancy, Emery observes: "Transformed into the flying trickster, Antoinette spins her web, lifting her soul above the flames, burning like the Pleiades in a constellation of all the peoples of the Caribbean" and identifies with "the history of the blacks of the island, learning from them traditional means of resistance" (1999: 59).

Setting aside the problem of this tactical elision—which perhaps too handily unifies the imperiled interests of a displaced Creole planter class with an abject Black Other via mutual opposition to European white male cultural authority—the space of resistance is here reduced to a tragically suicidal return to nature at precisely the moment when Dominica and the wider Caribbean were struggling mightily toward political solidarity and independence. Alongside Dominica's entrance into the short-lived West Indies Federation in 1958 and the rise to prominence of the socialist Dominica Labour Party in the elections of 1962, the island also felt the influence of the U.S. Black Power movement in the late 1960s and early 1970s, culminating in the formation of the Movement for a New Dominica and the controversial murder trial of 'dread' activist Desmond Trotter in 1974.

Allfrey, who resumed an intense correspondence with her old friend Rhys in 1973 after a twenty-year silence, had by that time suffered the public indignity of expulsion from the DLP. Believing the ouster to be racially motivated as well as in response to her public protests against Chief Minister and Premier Edward Oliver Le Blanc's legislative silencing of the press's criticism of the DLP, Allfrey founded the Dominica

Freedom Party—whose reactionary, conservative platform was seen by many Dominicans as representing the interests of the former white plantocracy and current merchant class and which subsequently helped usher in a decade of neoliberal reforms. She likewise founded the DFP's opposition newspaper, *The Star*, to which Rhys subscribed. Allfrey even enlisted Rhys's aid in promoting in the pages of *The Star* the DFP's preference for delayed political independence "in order that the full implications of independence could be explained to the people" (qtd. in Paravisini-Gerbert 1998: 15). Indeed, it is tempting, despite customary assertions of Rhys's disinterest in politics, to consider the public career of Allfrey alongside the congruent political implications of *Wide Sargasso Sea*, a parallel that might explain Allfrey's reaching out to Rhys, with much-belated congratulations on her last novel, after such a protracted silence and during the period of her own growing alienation from the Black radical resistance movement and her feverish activity in support of the conservative DFP.

What is more, this tragic impasse not only arrests the historical momentum of anti-imperialism/anti-capitalism (and the aesthetic corollary that Jameson identifies with the demiurgic practice of narrative realism), but it also fatalistically returns the reader to the absolute narrative confines of the very Bildungsroman whose titanic gravity Rhys's novel ostensibly struggles to escape. Antagonizing and enlarging the sympathetic scope of *Jane Eyre* while simultaneously surrendering to its extensive demesne, *Wide Sargasso Sea* concludes, as Spivak notably contends, by restoring a re-domesticated 'Bertha' to the fictional world of *Jane Eyre*; the "cardboard house" in which she finds herself imprisoned is thus in reality "a book between cardboard covers" (Spivak 1985: 244). For Spivak, the arrested narrative of *Wide Sargasso Sea* manifests the "epistemic fracture" of imperial culture itself and dramatizes the impossibility for the subaltern (figured in the marginalized presence of Christophine) to speak to effect (1985: 246). Thus "bound by the reach of the European novel" and the fact that "the hegemonic definition of literature is itself caught within the history of imperialism," Rhys's feminist anti-Bildungsroman marks, despite its custodial investments, the abortive "limits of its own discourse," a theme further materialized, as Spivak notes, in Rochester's "letter which should have been written" (Spivak 1985: 246) but was not and the letter he writes, with omissions, but does not send: "And I wondered how they got their letters posted. I folded mine and put it into a drawer of the desk. As for my confused impressions they will never be written. There are blanks in my mind that cannot be filled up" (Rhys 1999: 39, 45).

Thus, in Rhys as in Naipaul's *Guerrillas*, a Black Power-inspired anticolonial resistance is depressed into an unnarratable state of nature. Here, however, the tragic defiance of Rhys's white Creole protagonist finds doleful consummation and symbolic consolation in the foreclosure of narrative horizons by inherited form. Just as Antoinette cannot escape the fate of her mother's madness—which replicates in its turn the hereditary "derangement of the brain and heart" suffered by Zola's family matriarch in *The Fortune of the Rougons* (1871) and revisited upon her many descendants (qtd. in Hill 2020: 62)—the novel's fiery dénouement is prescripted and predestined. Its derangement of narrative figures the end of history and the end of the road.

"You Must Learn Once and For All Who You Are": Negotiating Heritage and History in Michelle Cliff's *Abeng*

That Michelle Cliff's debut novel *Abeng* (1985) bears a self-conscious kinship to Rhys's *Wide Sargasso Sea* has been well established. Mary Lou Emery and Belinda Edmondson have each noted how Cliff critically revises the scene in which Tia strikes the young Antoinette with a stone such that it is the light-skinned protagonist Clare Savage who, in her closing dream, throws the stone that injures her black friend, Zoe. For Edmondson, this critical inversion indicates that "Cliff is rewriting an *historical* relation of black and white West Indian women not only to link their cultural identities but to acknowledge the white woman's relation to power" (Edmondson 1993: 183). Cliff's *Abeng* and its sequel *No Telephone to Heaven* therefore "extend and re-evaluate the pre-occupations of Jean Rhys's *Wide Sargasso* Sea," which Edmondson designates as Cliff's clear "literary forebear" (1993: 182).

Clare's task is also Cliff's: negotiating with inheritance in a way that enables new forms of Becoming. Where Rhys's fiction might be said to "reveal simultaneous attraction to and fear of Afro-Caribbean society," seeking refuge in the resultant ethical and cognitive as well as narrative ambiguities and aporias outlined above, Cliff's duology powerfully evinces the fact that, as Edmondson puts it, "an understanding of black consciousness is crucial to resolving the complexities of being a white colonized subject, and more importantly is empowering not only to black people in the Caribbean, but to white people as well" (1993: 186). Thus, she claims, "Clare must first understand and acknowledge this unequal power dynamic before she can be (re)integrated with the society, with her history, and consequently her paradoxical identity" (Edmondson 1993: 183).

This fraught and fitful process of shameful self-cultivation, social (re)integration, historical exhumation, and the formation of revolutionary consciousness is one routed through a complex genealogy. Clare's struggle is "not simply with a white creole tradition but also with the European literary canon itself, which freezes the colonized subject in an eternal relation of subject/object" (Edmondson 1993: 184). To that end, *Abeng* reverses the ideological valence of Rhys's retelling of *Jane Eyre* in what amounts to a literary negation of negation or the staging of an anti-anti-Bildungsroman. If *Wide Sargasso Sea* dramatizes the failed integration of Antoinette Cosway into colonial English society, thereby producing a gendered ethical critique of the social order of empire and the structural impossibility of the colonized subject's capacity to make her way in the world, Cliff's novels radically engage the shortcomings of their literary progenitor while preserving, if not redeeming, the active core of its revisionary and anti-imperialist critique.

For Simon Gikandi, the novel's signal achievement in this regard is established through a repudiation of the modernist grand narrative and a concomitant affirmation of the postmodern fragment, a refusal conditioned by a post-independence recognition of the limits of inherited form. Gikandi writes that "if Caribbean discourse during the period of decolonization appropriated the narrative strategies of high modernism to resist an ecumenical European notion of history," the deflationary period following the realization of national independence "made clear that attempts to appropriate and revise the European language and topoi were already a mixed blessing" (1992: 231–232). The densely self-conscious intertextuality of *Abeng*, Gikandi claims, functions simultaneously to evoke the colonial archive and to disorient the reader from entrenched forms of modernism in a "dual mediation of the Caribbean experience" in which the novel "echoes, revises, and sometimes amplifies both colonial discourse and its more immediate anticolonial precursors" (1992: 237).

Thus, Cliff's intertextual mediations are both dependently parasitic and openly subversive in relation to the texts (including *Wide Sargasso Sea*) and the forms (chiefly the Bildungsroman) that they interpolate. Characterized by Gikandi as the "schizophrenic text" of a postcolonial "split consciousness" suspended between a hegemonic colonial language and an antagonistic vernacular, the motivating tension in Cliff's novel arises "from the author's consciousness of her troubled relationship with her colonial *heritage*" as well as from the masculine preeminence dominating the discourse of Caribbean national identity (1992: 236, emphasis added). It is precisely in this tension between the horizon of Becoming and the inheritance of Being that we can discern the inclination toward the naturalist pole.

History as Recovery and Return

In its particular embodiment of the longing for narrative/historical form, *Abeng* dramatizes the fitful recovery of a repressed matrilineal history by Cliff's young protagonist in the bones of the physical landscape as in an obscure geoglyph. Such impetus informs the opening invocation of geologic history: "The island rose and sank. Twice. During periods in which history was recorded by indentation on rock and shell" (Cliff, *Abeng* 3). For Gikandi, the effect of this "geological genesis of the Caribbean" is twofold. First, it enacts a critical negation of "traditional histories, which posit 'discovery' as the ground zero of the Caribbean experience;" at the same time, it proffers "modes of historical knowledge which are accessible to us outside previously privileged European documents" (1992: 242). In this *"annales* approach" to historical recovery, then, not only oral forms and local knowledges but also the trilobite fossil that Clare finds on the beach as well as the legendary hills and precipitous hollows of the Cockpit Country themselves serve as alternatives to narrative historicity and "part of the museum from which the desire of history rises" (Gikandi 1992: 243).

Equally discernible in this passage, however, is what Gikandi observes as Clare's penchant, inherited from her father, Boy, for exalting (and therefore reifying) history as either myth or catastrophe. As Gikandi notes, "Boy Savage has created in his daughter a sense that history has no cognitive status unless it is informed by a vision of myth and natural disaster" (1992: 244). For Boy, history as the mundane expression of collective human agency is inadmissible: "Nothing, to him, was ever what it seemed to be. Nothing was an achievement of human labour" (Cliff 1995: 50). Boy's position is that of anti-history.

However, Clare also recognizes the limits of her mother's own historical perspective, the novel's seeming alternative:

> Both Boy and Kitty were locked in the past—separate pasts to be sure, but each clung to something back there. For Boy it was Cambridge University and sugar plantations and a lost fortune. For Kitty it was what had been done to her people when they were slaves. (Cliff 1995: 128)

Kitty's debilitating orientation to the past and ancestral land/ inheritance might thus be termed *ante*-historical. Suspended between these diametrically opposed but equally ahistorical fatalisms, in which history is collapsed back into primordial nature, Clare must invent a narrative stratagem in which a schizophrenic or detotalizing historical discourse itself assumes the place "formerly reserved for character" in the inherited literary and linguistic forms of colonial legacy, a form whose most instructive analog lies paradoxically in the fragmented and unnarratable landscape itself (Gikandi 1992: 244).

In an alternative reading of the novel as an ambivalent Bildungsroman—which fulfills the form's canonic requirement of tracing the protagonist's progression from ignorance to knowledge but fails to reconcile the protagonist's desires with the shifting demands of postcolonial Jamaican society—Alfred López interprets the geologic preamble not as the grasping after an anterior alternative to imperialist historicity but as the symbolic recognition of colonialism's enduring impingement upon Jamaican historical consciousness, or of "how both the landscape and the colonized subject's body become the primary spaces or indexes on which colonial discourses leave their psychical 'indentations'" (López 2001: 175).

If Clare's task in *Abeng* lies not only in excavating and interpreting the violent inscriptions of the colonial encounter upon the landscape and her own body but also in positively identifying with the forbidden motherland, her *Bildung* is consummated in the final pages of *No Telephone to Heaven*. There, having returned to her grandmother's land with a small guerrilla outfit intent on disrupting a Hollywood production of the life of Granny Nanny, she is, as Cliff elsewhere describes it, "burned into the landscape" by deadly machine-gun fire from U.S. helicopters (1990: 265). Thus "indistinguishable from the ground," Clare achieves symbolic reconciliation with a proscribed history (Cliff 1990: 265). Cliff insists in a later essay on her autobiographical character that Clare's death, in achieving bodily incorporation with the land, should be read as redemptive rather than tragic. Indeed, her explicit model for what López describes as the book's "fiery conclusion" is Cuban artist Ana Mendieta's Silueta Series, which features land sculptures depicting the negative space of female bodily forms pressed into the earth, outlined in rocks, sea foam, tangles of vegetation, and fire. For López, the earth sculptures "invoke the uprooted, exiled, or otherwise alienated subject's desire to reinscribe their bond with the land, more specifically with homeland, the will to rewrite the marginalized self into the national identity" (López 2001: 176).

So, despite opposed interpretations of the novel's enframement by an Annales-style *total historical* conceit, Gikandi and López both arrive at a reading in which the revolutionary reclamation of history coincides with or is enabled by way of an identification with the land and in which Clare's suicidal assault on a film production in the dyad's "fiery conclusion" is celebrated as a form of historically constrained agency. Similarly, despite *Abeng*'s critical revision of the racial dynamic of *Wide Sargasso Sea*, *No Telephone to Heaven* realizes Clare's *Bildung* in yet another compulsory restaging of Bertha Mason's doomed act of symbolic resistance. This recovery of matrilineal history and the fatalistic return to the motherland are emplotted in the narrative's symbolic identification with Clare's bodily maturation such that the resistant political consciousness of the latter novel's ambiguously tragic/redemptive denouement is anticipated in the concluding revelation of Clare's first menstruation in *Abeng*. As Mary Douglas famously cautions in *Natural Symbols*, however, we should beware of "arguments couched in the bodily medium: Strongly subjective attitudes to society get coded through bodily symbols" and thereby naturalized (1996: 170).

For Jennifer J. Smith, these political/somatic parallels are problematic in that they ultimately "establish the body as a cause for, site of, means to, and limitation to political action" (2009: 144). In fact, Smith posits that *No Telephone to Heaven*, in which the pervasive image of the womb is superimposed with those of sterility and the grave, functions both as a powerful jeremiad for severed matrilineal histories and lost landscapes of the past even as it soberly "reminds us of the dangers of idealizing maternity as a site of power and invites us to consider other modes of feminist recovery" (2009: 159). Far from suggesting a radical alternative to the perpetual present of empire, then, Cliff's return to the body/motherland dramatizes the resigned non-futurity of such strategies of resistance:

> The experience of the land through the body, while it connects Kitty and Clare to a matrilineal history, also suggests that the body's connection to history and place is limited, as these forces render their bodies sites of death and reproductive loss. The reproductive and sexualized body initiates the characters into challenging norms and precipitates acts of resistance; paradoxically, the body is the agent of violence and simultaneously its greatest victim. The imbrications of menstruation, miscarriages, hemorrhages, and womb images in *No Telephone to Heaven* suggest that relying on a relationship among blood, land, and identity is always already limiting. The lack of a future in the text indicates that while we must experience place and history through the body,

the body as the sole means of connection cannot survive and it cannot suffice. (Smith 2009: 144)

Winifred Stevens of St. Ann's Bay, who discloses to Clare in the final pages of *Abeng* her own traumatic experience of a young pregnancy amid sedimented racial prejudice, describes their present dilemma under history's long shadow: "They are all gone now—the ones who did these things—gone to their reward. But the afterbirth is lodged in the woman's body and will not be expelled. All the waste of birth. Foul smelling and past its use" (Cliff 1995: 165).

Smith's reading of *No Telephone to Heaven* as a critical reassessment of *Abeng* thus departs from the consensus opinion of the latter as redemptive maternal restoration and helps to direct us toward the novel's more general anxiety over inheritance and a return to the enclosures of the body/earth. Less a triumphant reclamation of repressed history than the involuted form that the developmental (or narrative) impulse takes in the absence of a differential horizon, inheritance operates as the recursive or ouroboric naturalist limitation of Being imposed on an inventive and utopian process of historical Becoming (*Bildung*). Such a reframing helps us to perceive Cliff's earlier novel not only as a politically idealistic or naïvely celebratory archaeology of lost pasts but also as a self-reflexive interrogation of the narrative limits imposed by a new historical situation. Here, the future promised by independence remains as tragically foreclosed as the inaccessible past itself and in which the revolutionary charge, denied a horizon of difference (utopia), is run aground or diverted back into inexorable nature. The reckoning of this shameful or frustrated historical consciousness likewise informs the book's motivating *Bildung*. As Rajeswari Mohan observes,

> As a Bildungsroman, *Abeng* explores the *contest over Clare's inheritance* to explain her ambivalence about her class position and her sexuality, suggesting furthermore that the disorientation Clare experiences is indispensable for the emergence of a historical consciousness that would serve as the enabling condition of a critical and activist subjectivity. (2011: n.p., emphasis added)

Clare's burgeoning agency is therefore both conditioned and repeatedly thwarted by the specter of inheritance. Having enframed the story with the invocation of an unnarratable, Precambrian Being-in-time and Boy's contention that "[n]othing was the achievement of human labor"—a point of view that Clare cannot yet bring herself to question—*Abeng* proceeds to the Tabernacle meeting, symbolic of the

Black feminine and maternal counterpoint. Here, however, we are also confronted with the problem of inheritance. Clare observes that "the girl children were small replicas of the women" and the girls themselves are all nearly identical (Cliff 1995: 9, 11). Brother Emmanuel, who "began as he usually began," delivers his "standard preface to a sermon in which all in the room were condemned—'unto your children and your children's children'—for the sin and wretched hopelessness of their lives" (Cliff 1995: 11). The narrator regards the hymns and the ecstatic surrender of the congregation, which consists "for the most part of Black women," as animated by a collectively recognized "necessity of deliverance" by the extrahistorical intervention of the divine (Cliff 1995: 12). As for the few men in the congregation, we are told that they later find themselves beset by primeval temptations of the flesh originating in a "space... carved so long ago, carried so long within, it was a historic fact"—history here registering as the protracted sedimentation of nature (Cliff 1995: 16).

Anti-history or Ante-history? A Forced Choice

Clare, who is "the family's crowning achievement, combining the best of both sides," must plot her growth toward an agential historical consciousness by negotiating between dual fatalisms and their respective reversions to untranscendable nature (Cliff 1995: 61). The possibilities of either emancipatory consciousness or inveterate servitude are likewise posited as the unbidden inheritance of a mythic past: "In the beginning there had been two sisters—Nanny and Sekesu," Maroon and slave, and "[i]t was believed that all island children were descended from one or the other" (Cliff 1995: 18).

Resistance, which is no longer a necessary response to concrete and unique historical circumstance, is thus figured as a privilege (or curse) of birthright. As she understands it, then, Clare's dilemma—caught between Boy and Kitty, Sekesu and Nanny—is to select from between them her *true* lineage and the capacities and limitations that it imposes upon her developmental trajectory. However, despite their irreducible differences, both paths lead back to a predeterminant natural destiny that is altogether outside the narrative logic of history. The specificity of Clare's own situation is similarly threatened in the narrative by subsumption into a universalized generational conflict between parents and children. Clare's struggle, like that of "most children," the narrator informs, lies between, within, and against the personalities, values, and desires of her parents, though "nothing new," this also "makes resistance very difficult, and may even make a child believe that resistance is impossible or unnecessary" (Cliff 1995: 49). Cliff could be no more explicit about the retardant effect that the discourse of natural inheritance has upon the practice of resistance.

Accompanying Boy—whose nickname is itself an "imitation of England, like so many aspects of their lives"—on a solemn pilgrimage to the old family estate house at Runaway Bay, latterly the Paradise Plantation development, Clare is struck by the recursive pattern of the wallpaper depicting European women and children at leisure in a park setting: "The scene was repeated again and again across the wall; it was not a continuing story with a theme, like the Bayeux tapestry her father had described to her" but rather provides an insistent tableau, "a small glimpse of the background against which this part of her family had once existed." Most disturbing in the surrounding pattern's antinarrative eternal return, however, is the "danger...that the background could so easily slide into the foreground," that the spatial and temporal distinction between surface and depth, past and present, could collapse into a statically indiscriminate singularity (Cliff 1995: 25). Indeed, later reflecting on the possibility that "the walls of certain places were the records of those places—the events which happened there. More accurate than the stories of the people who had lived within the walls," Clare "began to confuse the ladies on the paper with the women in her past" and further to assume that "the women who had lived in the great house had been as white as the women on the paper" (Cliff 1995: 33).

In contradistinction to this Eurocentric re-vision of history, explicitly informed here by the imposing Bildungsroman *Great Expectations* ("Sometimes she felt sure that she would make her own way in the world—would 'be' someone, as Pip had wanted for himself" [Cliff 1995: 36]), the narrative interposes the tragic story of Mma Ali, Inez, and Justice Savage. The latter, having read with great attention the warnings of Thomas Jefferson and Benjamin Franklin against the dangers of miscegenation, set fire to his slaves in their quarters on the very eve of their emancipation. His act of desperate brutality creates the scarcely perceptible "pattern of foundation stones and thin dirt gullies Clare saw that afternoon behind the great house, rectangles remembering an event she would never know of," both confirming her earlier theory that the walls of a place record its history and indicating the inadequacy of this theory to reckon with the bloody foundation upon which the visible walls themselves are erected: "The bones of dead slaves made the land at Runaway Bay rich and green. Tall royal palms lined the avenues leading to the houses of the development" (Cliff 1995: 40).

The latter term is a signal one. The involutional story of Western "development" is, as Edward Said (or Walter Benjamin) taught us long ago, rooted in the unnarratable barbarity of colonization and enslavement. Thus is Boy's perspective "caught somewhere between the future and the past—both equal in his imagination" such that the Savage family crest's motto—"MIHI SOLICITUDO FUTURI—TO ME THE CARE OF THE FUTURE"—expresses the inertia of an arrested development or historical short circuit in which the only possible solicitude toward the future lies in a reverent preservation or mythologization of the past with which it is emphatically identified (Cliff 1995: 22, 31).

Boy's hope for salvation is therefore fittingly vested in the Calvinist doctrine of predestined Election by the "Puritan Almighty," an assurance that he extends to his daughter as a right of inheritance: "She was a true Savage, he assured her," and in a formulation that makes explicit the crippling fatalism of the doctrine, he promises, "Her fate was sealed" (Cliff 1995: 45). Even the opposition to Boy's worldview, however, remains thrall to its fatalistic axiom of inheritance. For example, Kitty's mother Mattie, who disapproved of her daughter's marriage on the suspicion that Boy was "an inheritor of bad traits," later observes of Clare's transgressions that "this wickedness must come from the girl's father's family. Misbegotten people and a misbegotten girl" (Cliff 1995: 134); or, as she later puts it, "De pickney no mus' tek on de blood" (Cliff 1995: 147).

If Boy's stunted or oblique historical mysticism is presented as a disablingly Eurocentric and masculinist inheritance to be rejected, then, the ostensibly alternative pole represented by Kitty likewise fails to free itself from the "pessimistic materialistic determinism" of naturalism (Becker 1963: 35). Clare perceives in her mother an organic connection to the Jamaican landscape that, while wholly lacking in her father, is nevertheless also grounded in an older and encompassing feminine natural law: "For her God and Jesus were but representatives of Nature, which it only made sense was female, and the ruler of all—but this she never said" (Cliff 1995: 53). If Clare has "inherited her father's green eyes,"—her "finest feature," which, we are told, Boy likewise inherited from his mother—as well as his light skin, she is also nevertheless regarded as the "dead stamp" of Kitty, who is similarly "locked in the past" (Cliff 1995: 61, 124, 128). Kitty's tragic vision, as the structural complement to Boy's triumphalist one, is equally predicated on an irresistible fatalism:

> Kitty's mistake in all this was casting her people in the position of victim, so that her love of darkness became a love conceived in grief—a love of necessity kept to herself. The revolution had been lost when the first slave ships arrived from the west coast of Africa, and she felt Black people were destined to labor under

the oppression of whiteness, longing for a better day but not equipped, Kitty believed, to precipitate the coming of a better day. Looking into the past their history could be kept alive in tongues, through speech and in songs—but too much of their future lay at the bottom of the sea in lead coffins or scattered through the earth on plantations. For all its tenderness, her vision was sad. (Cliff 1995: 128)

The ante-historical alternative proffered by Kitty against Boy's anti-historical discourse of dominance is thus one equally constrained by determinants outside the scope of human agency. Their occasional trips to the bush, treasured by Clare, "always stopped short, interrupted by the roar of the river, a sudden storm, an invasion by an army of biting ants, so tiny you didn't know they were there until they attacked" (Cliff 1995: 128). Kitty's concession that the light-skinned child must "by common law, or traditional practice" belong to the light-skinned parent is rooted in an assumption that "this, after all, was how genetics was supposed to work, moving toward the preservation of whiteness and the obliteration of darkness," and she regards as her foremost parental duty helping her daughter to "accept her destiny" (Cliff 1995: 129). To Mattie's claim that she should never have married Boy, Clare hears her mother's scarcely audible reply, "What choice did I have?" (Cliff 1995: 147).

The Anxiety of Inheritance

As with *Wide Sargasso Sea*, destiny likewise provides the primary optic through which the novel engages its literary progenitors. In addition to the book's self-conscious rewriting of *Wide Sargasso Sea* and *Great Expectations*, we also find it wrestling with the inheritance of other works like *The Diary of Anne Frank*, Walter Scott's great historical novel *Ivanhoe*, and even the influential Caribbean Bildungsromane *Beka Lamb* and *Crick, Crack, Monkey* by Zee Edgell and Merle Hodge respectively. In considering the tragically truncated Bildungsroman of *The Diary of Anne Frank*,[3] a key intertext whose racial violence haunts Clare and through which she seeks "an explanation for her own life"

---

[3] For a discussion of Frank's utilization of the literary techniques of the Bildungsroman in her revision of the diary for future publication, see O'Donnell, Daniel Paul 2011. "'I Certainly Have the Subjects in my Mind': The Diary of Anne Frank as Bildungsroman," *Canadian Journal of Netherlandic Studies* 32.2: 49–88.

(Cliff 1995: 72), she finds herself comparing the death of Anne at such a tender age to the death of a classmate from leukemia, or what her grandmother calls "Cancer of the blood," a description that causes Clare to ponder: "How did her blood turn against her?" (Cliff 1995: 68–69). Such fatalistic *betrayal by the blood* is similarly suggested by her teachers, when pressed, as an explanation for the Holocaust itself: "Jews were expected to suffer. To endure. It was a fate which had been meted out to them..." (Cliff 1995: 70). Like the Africans, then, they are a people perceived to be "flawed in irreversible ways," a presumption that Boy also expresses in justifying his preference for Rebecca over Rowena as heroine of Walter Scott's *Ivanhoe*: "Rebecca is a tragic figure. You know that great writers often create their characters with tragic flaws, so that no matter what happens, they cannot succeed. They will never win in the end" (Cliff 1995: 71, 72).

Clare is compelled to her own ambivalently tragic/triumphal destiny through a harrowing world, an originary milieu fraught with congenital affliction and the pervasive threat of pestilence, in which the body's illusory autonomy is mercilessly and repeatedly exposed as vulnerable to the forces of an antecedent and indwelling decadence. The body thus becomes another text that prescribes Being by way of inheritance. Clare symbolically links the above treacheries of the blood to other such encounters, like the episode of her classmate's epileptic seizure, "which had given her a clue to the difference between herself and the other scholarship students. Color. Class. But not in those words" (Cliff 1995: 96). Clare is disturbed by the fact that her teachers and classmates ignore the violent thrashings of the "dark girl" Doreen when she suffers a mid-class seizure (Cliff 1995: 96). When Clare expresses her consternation to her parents, they first explain epilepsy as "a curse" and "a stigma," a "terrible" and "incurable disease," one that "could travel through families" (Cliff 1995: 98). The others did not come to her aid, Kitty further clarifies, because they were behaving as "proper" ladies who were taught that it was "beneath their station" to engage too closely those who suffer "the congenital defect of poverty—or color" (Cliff 1995: 99). Silently, Clare suspects that Kitty, though certainly no proper lady, would also have declined to come forward despite her privately held sympathy for and identification with those like Doreen—the poor and the dark. The "congenital" defects of class and race are thus posited as natural maladies: ontologically constant, impervious to history.

Sanguine claims to the land are similarly complicated by the acknowledged intersection of class and race, though in strictest terms of their fatalistic compulsions and restrictions upon heroic subjectivation. When Zoe loses patience with Clare's fanciful and ill-fated trip to the bush to hunt Massa Cudjoe, she enunciates, in terms of space and identity, the unspoken classed and raced antagonisms that make their true friendship as peers impossible. To Clare's romantic protestation of a Pip-like desire to *be somebody*, Zoe offers a soberly materialist rejoinder: "Wunna no is smaddy already? Gal smaddy. Kingston smaddy. White smaddy. Dis place no matter a wunna a-tall, a-tall. Dis here is fe me territory. Kingston a fe wunna. Me will be here so all me life—me will be marketwoman like fe me mama" (Cliff 1995: 118). And the long memory of local culture would not soon forget or forgive a transgression against customarily classed, raced, and gendered roles of social interaction, the consequences of which would propagate unto the generations, "unto your children and your children's children" (Cliff 1995: 11). As Zoe points out, her children "would be *traced* if dem mama did do such a t'ing" (Cliff 1995: 118, emphasis added).

Similarly, in Zoe's emphatic enunciation of the word *territory* "over at least six syllables" Clare perceives that "the word and its meaning arched everything she said:"

> Clare felt hurt. By territory, Zoe's division of it, and by Zoe's conclusion that without a doubt their lives would never be close once they reached womanhood. This was not something that had passed between them. Zoe seemed so certain of their fates—she sounded almost like Miss Mattie in her quiet sternness. "Cancer of the blood," Miss Mattie had said. "No one is too young to die." Why did everything seem so fixed? So unchangeable. (Cliff 1995: 118)

Recalling the troubling episode with Doreen and what Clare anticipates as her mother's likely failure, following the way of the proper ladies, the pinnacle of approaching womanhood marks the site of necessary social cleavage, stratified by class and race, rather than gendered solidarity. Though Clare desperately "wanted them to be the same," Zoe reminds her that Clare's family has long owned the land on which her family struggles to exist and that the material constraints of her poverty foreclose her own claiming of any narrative of development or personal *Bildung*. To Clare's hysterical denial of this uncomfortable truth, Zoe offers the naturalistic stoicism, "Well, gal, sometime dat is jus' de way t'ing be" (Cliff 1995: 118). In such a situation, the sentimental return to the motherland is simply insufficient at best and disguises rather than discerns racial and class antagonism.

In the English tabloid received by Clare's uncle, we find the clearest intersection of the twin themes of textual and bodily inheritance. Here,

Clare and Zoe discover two otherwise seemingly unrelated sensational stories that similarly resonate with the fatalistic return to or betrayal by the body. In the first, they read of "a rare disease which only girls could contract" that alters one's biological sex from female to male. The disease, which is described as "irrevocable," Clare describes as "more like a curse" and fears that she and Zoe will unknowingly "become contaminated" by it (Cliff 1995: 103). "Imagine," Zoe marvels darkly, "wunna could turn into one man, and wunna mama cannot do no-ting" (Cliff 1995: 103). The second story tells of a five-year-old girl in Peru who gave birth to a healthy baby boy. More dubious of the second story's claims than the first because of their recent awareness of the disturbing realities of incest and rape, the girls suspect that in implying a miraculous virgin birth, the reporter attempts "to turn what had been conceived and borne in violence and tragedy into something of mystery and devotion," a critical recognition that can equally serve as a self-reflexive admonition against eagerly triumphalist readings of *Abeng* itself (Cliff 1995: 104).

What connects the two stories in the girls' minds is their shared relation to the destiny of (female) embodiment: "Both things appeared to Clare and Zoe caused by some mysterious force over which they would have no control at all. Two unwanted and sudden disasters which would change their lives totally. Two visitations about which they could do nothing;" and further, "Both things seemed beyond their grasp and it didn't much matter which they would choose, because it didn't seem to be theirs to choose. The filament which bound the two stories—that their bodies might not belong to them—tightened around the girls" (Cliff 1995: 103, 104). In what might therefore be seen as an ironic anticipation of the conclusion of *No Telephone to Heaven* (as well as a replication of both *Jane Eyre* and *Wide Sargasso Sea*), the girls seek consolation in their perceived powerlessness through an act of symbolic resistance ("the only power they had") by ceremoniously burning the newspaper (Cliff 1995: 103).

The tabloid stories also relate to Clare's burgeoning sexual consciousness and the inchoate stirrings of homosexual desire, the shameful realization of which triggers a related anxiety over her biological "duty" to preserve Boy's green eyes and to further whiten the Savage lineage by having children with a white man. Following the climactic firing of the rifle that kills Old Joe, the narrative shifts abruptly to the recollection of a "funny" distant relative known to the family as "uncle" Robert, who once scandalously brought home a "Dark American Negro" whom he claimed to be his "dearest friend" and who tried to convince Robert to come and live with him in New

York City (Cliff 1995: 125). When Clare enquires about the meaning of "funny" in this context, she is told that "it is when one smaddy is a little *off*—is one sint'ing one smaddy is born with. Him no can help himself" (Cliff 1995: 124).

Other naturalizing explanations for Robert's being "hopelessly afflicted" by homosexuality are also adduced: that it was "caused by inbreeding" or that his "mother did not wean him soon enough" (Cliff 1995: 126). Once Robert's drowning in Kingston Harbor ("drowned just as Clinton—about whom there had been similar whispers") is widely accepted by the community as an accident, the "stigma was removed," and "the family became more relaxed, telling each other that there had been an uncommonly strong riptide that afternoon" (Cliff 1995: 126). Here, appeals to natural determination and the site of the body provide neither defense nor transformative resistance; rather, they first outflank and recontain the supposed aberration, then obscure its traumatic (historical) suppression. Robert's suicide thus remains narratively unsanctioned as an act of symbolic resistance (tellingly marked here by water rather than fire) and instead describes briefly the evanescent void of Becoming as it is subsumed and obliterated within the organic constancy of vertically aligned Being.

Such Becoming or resistance-to-Being is most dramatically expressed ("She had been caught in rebellion") in the narrative arc of Clare's frustrated growth by her inadvertent shooting of Old Joe (Cliff 1995: 150). Despite their diametrically opposed identifications of the significant motivation of her actions—Kitty thinks it the inveterate arrogance of her whiteness, while Boy credits it to "the irresponsibility he felt imbued *those* people"—Boy and Kitty concur that "she was showing signs of something which had to be stopped—corrected—something which might make her wrong-headed;" indeed, Boy asks, "If she's like this now, what will she *become*?" (Cliff 1995: 148, emphasis added).

This first ambiguous act of bloodletting adumbrates, of course, its repetition in the novel's concluding image of menarche, which Clare has earlier anxiously associated with the tabloid stories in the sense that it likewise "appeared to her as the culmination of the process that was happening within and without her girl's body...something which would allow no turning back" (Cliff 1995: 106). Inasmuch as the "sweet pain" initiates her into womanhood, tethering her to a suppressed maternal and embodied history of oppression and resistance, it likewise portends, as Smith's reading suggests, of destiny, the cycle, and the genetic "duty" of childbirth and thus resonates with the novel's other anxious images of biological determination.

The blood of menstruation further materializes and confirms for the reader Clare's dim recognition—via the dream in which she strikes Zoe with a stone, drawing blood—of the primal antagonism into which history has placed her as well as of her unwitting perpetration of violence, as if both were necessary extensions of her nature. At the same time, while the novel can provide no effective resolution to the problem of the postcolonial Bildungsroman and refuses to retreat, like *Wide Sargasso Sea*, into formal compensation for these intractable dilemmas, it just as emphatically suggests in its necessary failure that to mistake that history for nature is to abandon even the hope of Becoming and of the universalizing solidarity that it labors to embody. It will be the task of *No Telephone to Heaven*, not least through Clare's galvanizing encounter with Harry/Harriet, to figure (though not yet fully to manifest) the plastic possibilities of historical Becoming through horizontally constructed and intentional, rather than vertically conferred, identity.

The White Tiger and Cynical Reason: A Liberal "Literature of Defeat"

> *Imagine an iron house having not a single window and virtually indestructible...*
> —Lu Xun (1981: ix)

As another postcolonial reimaging of *Great Expectations*, Aravind Adiga's 2008 Booker Prize-winning novel *The White Tiger* depicts its young Dickensian protagonist's ascension from low-caste abjection to affluent social respectability, an arc that is candidly credited to criminal cunning and what can only be described as vengeance murder. The novel has been lauded in the West for its astringent and unflinching confrontation with bureaucratic corruption in the Third-World state, the imported fetish of entrepreneurial capitalism, and the broader topographies of social injustice in contemporary India. As a preeminent "condition-of-India-novel" (Detmers 2011: 535), *The White Tiger* is thus touted as presenting a bitterly salutary, satisfyingly ironic corrective to "the florid exotica" (Tonkin 2008: n.p.) characteristic of much Anglophone Indian fiction—the domestic romance and especially Rushdian magical realism—as well as the colorful melodramas of Bollywood. More pointedly, as the novel's commentators repeatedly observe, Adiga's literary debut vigorously undermines both the casino capitalist wish fulfillment of Vikas Swarup's *Q&A* (2005) and the 'poverty porn' of its sensationally successful adaptation as *Slumdog Millionaire* (dir. Danny

Boyle, 2008), which has today grossed more than $378 million worldwide on its modest $15 million budget.[4]

The White Tiger is therefore most frequently understood as a chastening return to clear-eyed realism in a cultural moment for which the luxurious estrangements of prior fictional modalities seem no longer adequate or convincing. Ana Cristina Mendes appraises, for example, what she calls Adiga's "unremitting satire and gore-and-grime realism" (Mendes 2010: 283), whereas Ulka Anjaria finds in *The White Tiger* the emergent reinvention of a "new social realism, a mode that dialectically transcends early twentieth-century progressive writing and the self-conscious aesthetics of a Rushdian postmodernism in order to draw attention to social inequalities in India today" (Anjaria 2015: 114).

Enthusiastic comparisons to Dickens unsurprisingly appear with frequency in the robust critical and scholarly literature already generated by the novel. While a 2008 review in *The Economist* nominates Adiga "the Charles Dickens of the call-centre generation," for example, Andrew Reimer of *The Sydney Morning Herald* (Adiga emigrated to Australia in the 1990s) dubs him "the Dickens of Mumbai" and extols his "passionate indictment of the social and ethical bankruptcy of contemporary India" (Reimer 2011: n.p.). Suggestive of what I will here identify as a naturalist rather than strictly Dickensian realist ethos, however, Reimer further observes,

> As Adiga sees things, contemporary Mumbai is the new London of grime, lawlessness, corruption, greed, fabulous wealth and abject misery living side by side, a world in which predators always triumph, where people of integrity and goodwill are almost always gobbled up. (2011: n.p.)

Mendes convincingly resists both the reflexive tyranny of authenticity undergirding some critical dismissals of the novel's penchant to *speak for* the subaltern and the conventional positioning of *The White Tiger* as post-Rushdian realism by identifying what she calls, following Graham Huggan's theory of strategic exoticism, Adiga's "strategic inauthenticity."[5] Mendes argues that "through intentional

---

[4] *The White Tiger* itself has subsequently been adapted as a film (dir. Ramin Bahrani, 2021), which David Ehrlich describes as a "brutal corrective" to *Slumdog Millionaire*.

[5] See, for example, Younis, Abida 2017. "The Wrongs of the Subaltern's Rights: A Critique on Postcolonial Diasporic Authors," *Rupkatha Journal on Interdisciplinary Studies in Humanities* 9.3: 132–141.

self-contradiction and ironic character development, Adiga's failure to achieve (an in itself untenable) authenticity is deliberate" (Mendes 2010: 284). *The White Tiger* thus self-consciously "stage[s] 'inauthenticity' while simultaneously holding up for critical scrutiny the novel's own complicity with the marketing of an Exotic India" (Mendes 2010: 284). Far from presenting a realist alternative to Rushdie, then, Mendes claims that "like Rushdie in *Midnight's Children*, Adiga disavows any attempt to legitimize his depiction of India as 'real' by setting *The White Tiger* against a deliberately inauthentic historical background" (Mendes 2010: 287–278).

Alternatively, Anjaria *does* view *The White Tiger* as representing a literary advancement beyond Rushdie's shadow as well as that of a progressive realism. Adiga's alternative social realism depends on an aesthetic practice that she names "realist hieroglyphics." Refusing a progressive or postcolonial "politics of visibility" (reliant on what one might also wish to name a *metaphysics of presence*), Adiga's new social realism traces a "complex counterpoint between illegibility and transparency" and thereby "posits the illegibility of the image in the very moment in which that image signifies within a narrative of social rebellion" (Anjaria 2015: 115, 120). Directly repudiating Marx's notion of "social hieroglyphics"—which demands that we decipher in the appearance of reality its underlying structural logics—Anjaria contends that "it is only when literature reflects on its own unknowability that it can represent social and economic injustices and the complex routes to their restitution" (Ajaria 2015: 115).

Therefore, Adiga's new realist hieroglyphics metaphorically invoke the figure of the veil "to call into question interpretable symbols" and to enact an "aesthetics of indecipherability" that, in its inscrutability, somehow nevertheless functions to "stir the middle classes out of their political apathy" (Anjaria 2015: 115, 123, 125). While Anjaria views Adiga's emphasis on cunning unrepresentability as a novel response to the structural and phenomenological bewilderments of globalization, the primary target of the novel's "tentative unknowability" is, her reading suggests, quite simply Leftism itself (Anjaria 2015: 120). In negating representation, Adiga simultaneously and deliberately rejects the "progressivist and overdetermined logic of socialism," offering in the void left of these presumably depleted forms "not a politics but a new envisioning out of which such a politics might emerge" (Anjaria 2015: 130). The "progressive writing" against which Adiga's fiction positions itself is what K.A. Abbas defines as a practice of representation concerning "dynamic depictions of life with the purpose of changing that reality" and its authors as those who assume a "definite stand on social, and even political issues," much like the politicized solidarity criticism denounced by Nkosi (qtd. in Anjaria 2015: 133). By contrast with the interventionist aesthetic of Abbas, Anjaria holds that Adiga offers a cynical and shrewdly discerning deflation of any such emancipatory transformation of the present, which can perhaps be sardonically delineated but not in the least changed.

By thus evading the formal limitations of both realism (in either its progressive or hegemonic inclination) and modernism, which Anjaria deems equally inadequate to this task of pre-political figuration, Adiga breaks from Rushdie, who in any case "does not talk often of social injustice and who has made it repeatedly clear: 'I am not very inclined towards social realism'" (Anjaria 2015: 117). The adequation of social justice with social realism neglects, of course, the radical content of both socialism and modernism. Indeed, as Rushdie writes in *Imaginary Homelands*, upon losing his native faith during his education in England, he found himself "drawn to the great traditions of secular radicalism – in politics, socialism; in the arts, modernism and its offspring" (Rushdie 1992: 377). It is the residue of this radicalism and the demiurgic yearning that it betokens, I argue here, that is jettisoned in the emergence of postcolonial naturalism and its cynical correlates—or rather, the latter is a reactive response to the threat posed by the former.

Anjaria's crediting of social realism with the formal grasping of the economic, political, and social "problematic" of a given moment will recall for many readers the familiar Lukácsian reading of the form's critical vocation in the figural depiction of reality. For Lukács, "the contrasts of appearance and essence, of general law and the particular, of immediacy and of concept coincide in a direct impression" such that "the essential becomes visible in the appearance, the general law seems to be the cause of the particular instance" (qtd. in Reimer 2011: 238). Yet, this figural capacity, which is the primary formal impetus in what I have elsewhere called the modernist praxis of Rushdie's *postcolonial science fiction* (especially in the works *Grimus* and *Midnight's Children*), is foreclosed by the rejection of visibility and representation that Anjaria discerns in Adiga. This crisis of representation—significantly located, once again, between the aesthetic parameters of realism and modernism and bearing a decided resemblance to postmodernism—is that of a naturalist bourgeois reflex whose surest aesthetic index is the repudiation of progressive politics and the corollary cessation of narrative momentum and plot by the ascendance of descriptive stasis. Balram makes it explicit that the *tenor* of his writing to the Chinese premier is less the recounting of his own growth and dynamism as a subject (as in the mode of the classical Bildungsroman) than the revelation of the "truth" about Bangalore and entrepreneurship by way of the *vehicle* of his synecdochic life story (Adiga 2008: 4).

In a provocative reading of *The White Tiger* as a contemporary picaresque novel rather than a Bildungsroman, Jens Elze argues that both Moretti's classificatory and transformational modes of the latter (which historically vies with the picaresque as the preeminent mediation of the individual with modernity) are predicated upon an "aspirational temporality of sought-after self-assertion" that is wholly abandoned in Adiga's novel (Elze 2018: 234). Moretti's mode of classification—which entails the inclusion of the protagonist within a pre-existent structure of rights and an apparatus of political recognition—"was the concern of the decolonization Bildungsroman and the Bandung-era 'Third-World Project' that sought inclusion and global justice" (Elze 2018: 233).

The transformation mode, however, expresses in the postcolony a postmodernist or "antinomian" assertion of sheer difference that calls into question the basic legitimacy of these structures (Elze 2018: 233). The re-emergence of the picaresque in the place formerly occupied by the postcolonial Bildungsroman thus indicates for Elze the limitation of this aspirational assertion in both aspects of emergence and critique (2018: 233–234). In refuting the "isotropic temporalities of developmentalism, education, and social mobility" that define the modern *Bildung* and its contemporary mythology of neoliberalism, Adiga also thereby abandons plot—which is homologous with what Rob Nixon calls the "slow violence" of development itself—for picaresque fragmentation (2018: 226, 229).

Dickensian Realism or Zolian Affect?

Insufficiently discussed in these critical acknowledgements of the novel's rejection of Leftist politics, representation, and even narration, however, is Adiga's fidelity not to the narrative realism of Dickens nor to the anti-representationalism of postmodernism, but to the experimental method of Zola. As Stephen Moss notes in a 2017 interview, the author's

> earliest passion was 19th-century French literature, Émile Zola in particular, a "literature of defeat" (in contrast to the self-confidence of 19th-century British fiction), which spoke to a young man in a country that, he says, had spent centuries being defeated. (Adiga 2017: n.p.)

Crediting his training as a freelance journalist for "forcing myself to meet and talk to people I knew I wouldn't meet otherwise" and helping him to collect the necessary raw material to become a writer, Adiga further defines himself as having "old socialist nerves in a capitalist country." Situating his fiction in India's crisis-driven transition from Nehruvian socialism to neoliberalism beginning in 1991—a move that has dramatically intensified rather than resolved problems of economic and social inequality—Adiga, like Rushdie, also eschews the label "social realist," which, he claims, makes him "sound boring."

Identifying instead a libidinal charge motivating his interest in the economic, Adiga again invokes Zola:

> For me, macroeconomics is like sex. Social change is as intense, as passionate a subject. I don't see it as an abstract thing. It has a sort of erotic fascination or I wouldn't be writing about it. These never strike me as dry subjects. It was the same with the heroes of my childhood, Maupassant and Zola. Zola is often accused of being more interested in processes than people, and it is a danger you fall into, but nevertheless the body of work he's created is vital, tremendous. (Adiga 2017: n.p.)

Indeed, the sexual candor of Zola, whom Freud approvingly dubbed a "fanatic for truth," has been widely discussed (qtd. in Gay 1990: 108). Brian Nelson observes of the "erotic verisimilitude of his fiction" that Zola's "sexual and social themes intersect at many points" and that "the theme of sexuality is a vital shaping factor in Zola's creative vision," chiefly with regard to his thoroughgoing anatomization of classed society (Nelson 1983: 4, 48).

Adiga's work is likewise characterized by a candid vitalism in which the material labors of politics and class struggle are bracketed away as irredeemably corrupt and futile. The contradictions of history are displaced at once into carnally sordid spectacle (what Jameson recently discusses as the centrality of the body in Zolian naturalism [2020: 274]) and into an implicit moral calculus working in harmony with cyclical natural processes. Inasmuch as Adiga's representations are renditions of this libidinal Zolian vitalism, then, they bear a striking similarity to what has come to be called "ruinporn," which J.D Taylor glosses as "the arousal that comes from taking and contemplating images of decay and disaster" (Taylor 2013: 121). This contemporary phenomenon, generated almost exclusively by white, Western, middle-class photographers, is chiefly characterized by an "ironic disregard for contexts and sociological explanations" that proffers the adulterated image of degradation itself as a fully sufficient surrogate for critical analysis (Taylor 2013: 121).

The aestheticizing decadence of ruinporn is also accompanied, as the term implies, by sublimated arousal, which Taylor explains by reference to the notorious dissector of classical liberalism's obscene excess, the Marquis de Sade. In *120 Days of Sodom*, de Sade's wealthy financier Durcet explains his inability to reach orgasm in the opulent surroundings of the castle:

> there is one essential thing lacking to our happiness. It is the pleasure of comparison, a pleasure which can only be born of the sight of wretched persons, and here one sees none at all. It is from the sight of him who does not in the least enjoy what I enjoy, and who suffers, that comes the charm of being able to say to oneself: "I am therefore happier than he." (qtd. in Taylor 2013: 123)

For Taylor, ruinporn is a cultural expression of a generalized cynicism in which every possibility of resistance "is individualised and internalised … but it also erupts through the medium of the body, in stress, panic attacks, random acts of violence, skin disorders, or violent master-slave narratives to achieve orgasm amongst exhausted part-time lovers" (2013: 119). Such withdrawal of the social to the confines of the atomized body is central, I suggest, to the cynical realism of Adiga's novel.

Cloacal rather than erogenous, Adiga's frank, decadent imagery nonetheless presents the mortified body as the absolute circumference of Being, manifesting what Alain Badiou describes as *democratic materialism's* founding precept: "There are only bodies and languages" (Badiou 2011b: 19).[6] Thus, as Adiga has it, while a "poor man's life is written on his body, in a sharp pen" as a "human beast of burden," a servant is obliged to "know his master's intestinal tract from end to end—from lips to anus" (Adiga 2008: 118). The turning point for Balram in his decision to murder his master occurs when, having

[6] In his *Second Manifesto for Philosophy*, Badiou describes its fundamental "materialist postulate" as follows: "'There are only bodies and languages.' This maxim may be declared to be that of democratic materialism and the active core of dominant ideology" (2011b: 19). Badiou's critique of parliamentary democracy should not be regarded as a denunciation of democracy as such, however, for elsewhere he observes that "democracy" remains relevant so long as it manifests as "a dimension of collective freedom which subtracts itself from the normative consensus that surrounds the State;" that is, *"as long as 'democracy' is grasped in a sense other than a form of the State"* (2006: 85).

received a pittance one-hundred-rupee note from Ashok for what the latter misunderstands to be Balram's desire to marry, he follows a set of paw prints (the phantasmal trace of his guiding animus—not unlike Zola's own curious flourishes of the supernatural[7]) to the slums, where he encounters a row of defecating laborers (Warwick Anderson's "promiscuous defecators" again [qtd. in Adkins 2017: 401]), squatting "like stone statues:"

> The men were defecating in the open like a defensive wall in front of the slum: making a line that no respectable human should cross. The wind wafted the stench of fresh shit toward me.
>
> ...
>
> The stench of feces was replaced by the stronger stench of industrial sewage. The slum ended in an open sewer—a small river of black water went sluggishly past me, bubbles sparkling in it and little circles spreading on its surface. Two children were splashing about in the black water. (Adiga 2008: 222)

Tossing the note to the children, Balram joins this human *cordon sanitaire* and squats directly facing one of the men, who neither averts his gaze nor stares ahead shamelessly, but who rather grins "as if he were proud of what he was doing" (Adiga 2008: 223). When Balram shouts deliriously at the man in what is, to the latter, unintelligible English ("We'll take care of your wedding expenses," and "We'll even fuck your wife for you, Balram!"), the man begins "laughing so violently that he fell down face-first into the ground, still laughing, exposing his stained arse to the stained sky of Delhi" (Adiga 2008: 223).

Rooster Coops and Iron Houses

The frank acknowledgement of class conflict in the representation of the slum-dwelling construction workers—who, like Balram, come from the Darkness to build the city's malls, office buildings, and towering apartment complexes for the wealthy—meets its terminus in the

---

[7] Consider Zola's use of the supernatural in *La Débâcle*. See also Knutson, Elizabeth M. 2001. "The Natural and the Supernatural in Zola's in *Thérèse Raquin*," *Symposium* 55.3: 140–154.

impossibility of collective class identity.[8] This social atomization is marked here by the absurd failure of communication, the reduction to individualized and degraded bodily subjectivity (enlarged as a conceit of encompassing nature), and cynical (rather than Rabelaisian) laughter. Here, then, are the bodies and languages of Badiou's democratic materialism. Immediately following this encounter, Balram "walked into the parking lot, found an iron wrench, aimed a couple of practice blows, and then took it to [his] room," intent on fulfilling his individualist destiny as the White Tiger who ensures the durability of the Rooster Coop by becoming its rare, but necessary exception (Adiga 2008: 223).

However, Balram already adopts such a capitulatory view much earlier in the novel upon seeing his mother's funeral pyre, when his irrational hopes that her body will be held incorruptible and liberated by the gods of Benaras give way to a despairing grief from which he extracts the novel's comprehensive worldview:

> And then I understood: this was the real god of Benaras—this black mud of the Ganga into which everything died, and decomposed, and was reborn from, and died into again. The same would happen to me when I died. Nothing would get liberated here. (Adiga 2008: 15)

Balram flees the grim world-without-end that is Benaras only to discover that its suffocating enclosures extend to the whole of India, defining the contours of a Darwinian social ontology in which "there are just two castes: Men with Big Bellies, and Men with Small Bellies" and "only two destinies: eat—or get eaten up" (54). This absolute opposition recalls both the Devil's Feast of Ngũgĩ wa Thiong'o's mordantly satirical *Devil on the Cross* and, perhaps more instructively in the present context, the

---

[8] One might usefully recall here Marx's observation on the French peasantry's lack of political consciousness and the resulting election of Napoleon III:
> Insofar as millions of families live under conditions of existence that separate their mode of life, their interests, and their culture from those of the other classes, and put them in hostile opposition to the latter, they form a class. Insofar as there is merely a local interconnection among these small-holding peasants, and the identity of their interests forms no community, no national bond, and no political organization among them, they do not constitute a class. They are therefore incapable of asserting their class interest in their own name, whether through a parliament or a convention. They cannot represent themselves, they must be represented. (1852: n.p.)

cynical "Two Laws of Survival" described by the treacherous Dr. Henry Goose in David Mitchell's *Cloud Atlas*: "The weak are meat the strong do eat" and "there is no second law. Eat or be eaten. That's it" (Mitchell 2008: 489–490). The lack of a second law signifies the anti-dialectical collapse or reversion to zero-degree reality, nature red in tooth and claw, from whose pre-symbolic order there is no imaginable exit or alternative.[9]

The hermetic social architecture of this natural logic appears in *The White Tiger* as the anti-utopian figure of the Rooster Coop, the ideological enclosure of which prevents the "99.9%" from resisting their exploitative masters. This image also vividly recalls Lu Xun's paradigm of the iron house central to Jameson's infamous discussion of Third-World literature and national allegory, a reference made very nearly explicit in Balram's later appropriation of the Buddha's words, "I have woken up, and the rest of you are still sleeping, and that is the only difference" (Adiga 2008: 271). At the heart of the coop's repressive logic, the chief reason for its efficacy, is "the pride and glory of our nation, the repository of all our love and sacrifice ... *the Indian family*" (Adiga 2008: 150). Thus, it follows that "only a man who is prepared to see his family destroyed—hunted, beaten, and burned alive by the masters—can break out of the coop."

Only a singular "freak, a pervert of nature," a White Tiger—that heroically aberrant "creature that comes along only once in a generation," one one-hundredth of the population (Adiga 2008: 32)—can resist the oppressive and instinctive gravity of the family and natural law to assert the heroic primacy of self. This escape is not, however, a reprieve from the natural mandate but is rather the index of its surest confirmation, for "[t]o break the law of the land—to turn bad news into good news—is the entrepreneur's prerogative" and upholds rather than violates the encircling iron law of the Rooster Coop (Adiga 2008: 32). To the extent that it compels servants "to keep other servants from becoming innovators, experimenters, or entrepreneurs," the Rooster Coop is therefore "guarded from the inside" (Adiga 2008: 166). As Balram reflects at the novel's conclusion, having "switched sides" to become" one of those who cannot be caught in India:" "I think the Rooster Coop needs people like me to break out of it. It needs masters like Ashok—who, for all his numerous virtues, was not much of a master—to be weeded out and exceptional servants like me to replace them" (Adiga 2008: 275).

---

[9] Crucially, Adiga's rendition omits the countervailing insight of Mitchell's that "a purely predatory world *shall* consume itself" (2008: 830).

The origin of this predacious social organization, safeguarded by the isomorphic bulwarks of nation and family that provide the primary infrastructure of the Rooster Coop, lies for Balram in the ruse of independence and its democratic pretexts of social parity and universal recourse to the law. In the Raj's "days of greatness," he expounds, India was like a "clean, well kept, orderly zoo. Everyone in his place, everyone happy" under the auspices of British rule and its reinforcement of caste (Adiga 2008: 53). Independence disturbed the rational phylogeny of this menagerie and replaced it, under the aegis of democratic materialism, with the brute struggle for dominance among nominal equals:

> And then, thanks to all those politicians in Delhi, on the fifteenth of August, 1947—the day the British left—the cages had been let open; and the animals had attacked and ripped each other apart and jungle law replaced zoo law. Those that were the most ferocious, the hungriest, had eaten everyone else up, and grown big bellies. That was all that counted now, the size of your belly. It didn't matter whether you were a woman, or a Muslim, or an untouchable: anyone with a belly could rise up. (Adiga 2008: 54)

The big-bellied landlords of this simplified pseudo-Darwinian duality (importantly defined as a *caste* rather than a *class* opposition) are given animal names reflective of the "peculiarities of appetite" characterizing their respective domains of predation: the Stork "owned the river" and "took a cut of every catch of fish caught by every fisherman in the river;" his brother the Wild Boar dominated "all the good agricultural land" and grinned lasciviously at the vulnerable women in the village from his car window; the Raven, who "owned the worst land," scavenged from the poor goatherds of the hills and "liked to deep his beak into their backsides;" and the Buffalo, "greediest of the lot," controlled all the roadways and rickshaw operators, from whom he demanded a third of their earnings (Adiga 2008: 21). It is perhaps not incidental that units of the armed Central Industrial Security Force (CISF)—established in 1969 in response to the Naxal uprising in order to protect industrial installations in the Red Corridor and ultimately throughout the country—likewise bear the names of animals: Greyhounds, Scorpions, and Cobras (Roy 2011: 86).

The obverse complement to the predatory landowner is the caste of servile "human spiders," who, performing their social roles with "honesty, dedication, and sincerity, the way Gandhi would have done it," are thereby both animalized and immobilized in a state of perpetual underdevelopment: they "go crawling in between the tables with rags in their hands, crushed humans in crushed uniforms, sluggish, unshaven, in their thirties or forties or fifties but still 'boys'" (Roy 2011: 43). Prior to being randomly assigned the name "Balram" by his teacher, the narrator himself is known simply as "Munna," which is "not a real name" insomuch as it "just means 'boy'" (Adiga 2008: 10). The individualist character of this servile stasis is, Balram reflects, "bred into us, the way Alsatian dogs are bred to attack strangers," with the crucial inversion: "We attack anyone who's familiar" (Adiga 2008: 109). Undermined by the natural enmity of all against all and the repressive logic of the Rooster Coop, solidarity, like narrative, is thus canceled in advance.

Cynical Realism and the Affirmation of Being

If Zola's ambivalent social critique, compelled by the specter of genuine revolution, is finally in service of a reformist agenda in which the negative elements of bourgeois dissipation and profligate excess are ruthlessly satirized in order to salvage the ruling class's utopian capacity for "energy and order," *The White Tiger* self-consciously scandalizes mainstream "world literary" tastes with an impenitent cynicism and stark carnality only to reinscribe the unassailable grammar of the neoliberal order. Class struggle is displaced by ignominious spectacle that nevertheless offers a sentimental appeal to the liberal myth of "capitalism with a heart"—one that does not so much revoke the optimistic fantasy resolution of *Q&A/Slumdog Millionaire* as it does present its necessarily cynical complement. *The White Tiger* does not negate. Rather, in its performance of realist critique, it refortifies the neoliberal order against the threat of genuine opposition from below.

In this sense, the novel fulfills the function of "cynical reason," which Žižek, following Peter Sloterdijk, identifies as the predominant mode of ideology under contemporary capitalism. Rendering obsolete Marx's classic definition of ideology as misrecognition or false consciousness—"*Sie wissen das nicht, aber sie tun es*" [they do not know it, but they are doing it"]—and thereby nullifying traditional ideology critique, cynical reason is the product of a paradoxically "enlightened false consciousness" in which, as Sloterdijk puts it, "they know very well what they are doing, but still, they are doing it" (qtd. in Žižek 1989: 29). Strategically appropriating the subversive tenor of an authentically "popular plebeian rejection of the official culture" and its reigning solemnities—a sardonic resistance that Sloterdijk names *kynicism*—cynicism outflanks the critique of ideology. By avidly conceding its foremost suspicions, cynicism refortifies the fundamental structures that the latter undertakes to detect and oppose:

> Cynicism is the answer of the ruling culture to this kynical subversion: It recognizes, it takes into account, the particular interest behind the ideological universality, the distance between the ideological mask and the reality, but it still finds reasons to retain the mask. (Žižek 1989: 29)

What the cynical unmasks is not the dominant order but the intolerably presumptuous operation of unmasking itself.

Žižek observes that "like morality itself put in the service of immorality—the model of cynical wisdom is to conceive probity, integrity, as a supreme form of dishonesty, and morals as a supreme form of profligacy, the truth as the most effective form of a lie" (1989: 30). In its performance of cynical reason, we can therefore discern the reconciliation of the novel's seemingly opposed strands, identified above in the performance of strategic inauthenticity and in the realist hieroglyphics of its (pre- if not anti-political) alternative social realism. The novel ironically stages (while tacitly reinforcing) the logic of cultural authenticity and civilizational discourse even as it reaffirms a global socio-economic order that it contemptuously denounces.

That is, *The White Tiger* expresses a genuinely aggrieved, if vaguely generalized, account of the global neoliberal status quo not to conceive but to forfend against a properly political response by designating it as already corrupt, inept, or indecipherable. As Žižek writes, "cynical reason, with its ironic detachment, leaves untouched the fundamental level of ideological fantasy, the level on which ideology structures the social reality itself" (1989: 30). This undergirding fantasy—that of neoliberal individualism, of the "White Tiger" itself—is paradoxically sustained by way of the novel's posture of sensational, cynical renunciation.

This cynical attitude is most prominently displayed in the derisory refrain that serves as the book's distinctive motto-theme, "*What a fucking joke*," which sneeringly proclaims a worldly-wise disenchantment—*in English*—with the social pieties of democratic materialism even as it superciliously spurns the possibility of any legitimate alternative:

> The jails of Delhi are full of drivers who are there behind bars because they are taking the blame for their good, solid middle-class masters. We have left the villages, but the masters still own us, body, soul, and arse.

Yes, that's right. We live in the world's greatest democracy.
What a fucking joke. (Adiga 2008: 185)

The critique of parliamentary democracy's fealty to the big-bellied caste—while above any reasonable reproach—coincides with an ironic detachment (in the disposition of the "Beautiful Soul") that precludes the possibility of political intervention and therefore tacitly sanctions the present state of affairs by the foreclosure of alternative social horizons. Balram's incredulity toward what Ashok describes as "this fucked-up system called parliamentary democracy" is exceeded only by his arch vilification of socialism/communism, for which China ("great lovers of freedom and individual liberty" [Adiga 2008: 3]) stands as both his fictional addressee and ironic primary referent.

The novel's most prominent abridgment of progressive politics, however, lies in its satirical skewering of the "right" Communist Party of India (Marxist) in the figure of the Great Socialist. Having dominated politics in the Darkness since time immemorial—or at least beyond the reach of Balram's memory and therefore that of the novel's representational scope—the Great Socialist deftly exploits a populist agenda to enrich himself through the embezzling of public funds and the conniving consolidation of power over a network of corrupt rural landlords in order to purchase legitimacy on the national political scene. Capturing a national election toward the novel's conclusion, the caricatural Great Socialist thus ascends to even greater and more far-reaching abuses of power and public trust than before.

Adiga's critique of the thoroughgoing failure of India's electoral Left is certainly beyond dispute, and the corruption that he lays at the feet of the Great Socialist is fully consistent with that of the CPI and CPI-M. As Arundhati Roy observes in an account of her time in the forest with Maoist guerillas, the CPI has fully acceded to the eradication of trade unions, the mechanization and casualization of the labor force, and the assault on worker's rights such that "their thirty-year rule in West Bengal has left that state in near ruins;" similarly, she observes, "The repression they unleashed in Nandigram and Singur [where CPI leadership sought to dispossess local farmland for the creation of a Special Economic Zone], and now against the adivasis of Jangalmahal [under Mamata Banerjee's 'tide of development'] has furthered their alienation of the Indian masses" (Roy 2011: 198). In an attempt to curtail the unchecked power of the Great Socialist, the landlord "animals" attempt to exploit India's populist "election fever"—which is tellingly listed along with typhoid and cholera, as one of India's "three main diseases"—and found their own nominally Leftist party: the calculatedly, if absurdly named

All India Social Progressive Front (Leninist Faction) (Adiga 2008: 82). The Great Socialist is subsequently forced to negotiate an agreement with the animals, which results in further consolidation of the corrupt mainstream Left.

The Naxal Novel and Counterrevolution

Adiga dispenses not only with parliamentary Leftism, however, but also with its more radical alternatives, manifest as the various splinter groups of the banned CPI-Marxist-Leninist party—formed when they were expelled from the CPI-M for opposing the revisionist, reformist tendencies of Left parliamentarians, whom the former decried as "social fascists" (Roy 2011: 194)—but tendentially collapsed together here, as in most liberal and reactionary accounts alike, as the Maoist "Naxals." We might therefore place *The White Tiger* in the provisional canon of what Nina Martyris has usefully called "the Naxal novel" (Martyris 2014: n.p.)—ranging from the liberal account of Jhumpa Lahiri's *The Lowland* to the sympathetic rendition of Mahasweta Devi's *Mother of 1084* to the ambivalent form of Neel Mukherjee's *The Lives of Others* (discussed in the following chapter). Adiga follows the lead of both liberal and right-wing (including Hindu nationalist) accounts in strategically deploying "Naxal" as a loose hypernym with which to designate all Maoist as well as Adivasi and extra-state agents of opposition to state violence as well as capitalist interest. This elision allows Adiga's narrator to condemn—albeit with ironic equivocation—*all* Leftist opposition as Naxal terrorism.

Balram writes to Premier Jiabao of the kidnapping of the Buffalo's son by the Naxals: "they're Communists, just like you, and go around shooting rich people on principle" (Adiga 2008: 21). Balram fancies that his adversarial fellow servant Ram Persad perceives his refusal to pray as evidence of a more damning association: *"Don't you pray? What are you, a Naxal?"* (66). Balram, in fact, defines his own position (and that of the Indian masses) as occupying an ideally neutral space—through appeal to a liberal humanist universalism—itself what Wegner recently describes as "the secular religion for the new imperialisms of bourgeois civilization" (2021: 52)—that is neither that of the rapacious "animals" and opportunist Great Socialist nor that of the peasant "terrorists," a descriptor that Balram repeats without irony throughout the narrative:

> The Great Socialist was as corrupt as ever. The fighting between the Naxal terrorists and the landlords was getting bloodier. Small

people like us were getting caught in between. There were private armies on both sides, going around to shoot and torture people suspected of sympathizing with the other. (Adiga 2008: 73)

However, the unofficially named "Operation Green Hunt" security offensive, marshalled by Indian paramilitary troops in the five states of the Red Corridor beginning in 2009 to suppress Maoist resistance to the appropriation of Adivasi land—armed with advanced U.S. and Israeli weapons, including drones—can by no reasonable calculus be equated with the desperate resistance tactics of the ill-equipped, poorly trained, and undernourished cadres of the peasant resistance. The recourse to a rhetorical middle ground betwixt equally intolerable extremes is a classic strategy of liberalist conservatism. President Donald Trump deployed just such a device in the aftermath of the violence at the 2017 "Unite the Right" rally in Charlottesville, Virginia, where professed Neo-Nazi James Fields drove his car into a crowd of counter-protestors, killing one and injuring nineteen. In his polarizing comments on this act of domestic terrorism, Trump strategically lumped all counter-protestors under the heading of the "alt-left" and declared that there was "blame on both sides" as well as "very fine people." Trump continued,

You had a group on one side and you had a group on the other, and they came at each other with clubs — and it was vicious and it was horrible. And it was a horrible thing to watch.

But there is another side. There was a group on this side. You can call them the left — you just called them the left — that came violently attacking the other group. So you can say what you want, but that's the way it is. (Trump 2017)

Maoism/Naxalism similarly functions here as a convenient hobgoblin toward which one can redirect (and thereby recontain) legitimate political ire.

Roy observes that despite claiming in a 2009 meeting of state chief ministers that the Maoist army was of merely "modest proportions" and therefore no significant threat, Prime Minister Manmohan Singh nevertheless proceeded to designate the Maoists "the single biggest international security challenge ever faced in our country" (2011: 3). Roy locates the reason for this reversal in Singh's June 2, 2009, warning to Parliament that "if Left Wing extremism continues to flourish in important parts of our country which have tremendous natural resources of minerals and other precious things, that will certainly affect the climate for investment" (2011: 3). Similarly, current right extremist Prime Minister Narendra Modi claimed the Naxals in 2010 as "our people," who should be reached by way of dialogue, only to state in 2018,

> The tribal children should be studying, but instead the Naxals hand them weapons and destroy their lives. Urban Naxals stay in cities and have luxurious lives, their children are well-educated, but they remote control the lives of *adivasi* children and destroy their lives.

The threat to Indian tribal peoples is therefore, by this logic, not Hindu nationalism, which posits an indigeneity superseding *Adivasi* claims to the land, nor the global capitalist interests that it has been vehiculated to serve, but the dangerous manipulations of the Naxal cadres, who prey upon the poor while enjoying lives of affluent ease.

Despite participating in this discourse, Balram encounters a street bookseller at the market in Delhi who briefly offers a potentially alternative representation of the Naxals. Perusing a sixty-rupee English magazine, Balram expresses his bewilderment both at the extravagance of the ruling class and at the fact that "they treat us like animals" (176). Furtively, the bookseller whispers something that Balram just as circumspectly asks him to repeat:

> "It won't last forever, though. The current *situation*."
> "Why not?" I moved toward the mandala.
> "Have you heard about the Naxals?" he whispered over the books. "They've got guns. They've got a whole army. They're getting stronger by the day."
> "Really?"
> "Just read the papers. The Chinese want a civil war in India, see? Chinese bombs are coming to Burma, and into Bangladesh, and then into Calcutta. They go down south into Andhra, Pradesh, and up into the Darkness. When the time is right, all of India will..."
> He opened his palms.
> We talked like this for a while—but then our friendship ended as all servant-servant friendships must: with our masters bellowing for us. (Adiga 2008: 177)

However, it is a second bookseller who will later provide the catalyst that determines Balram's fate and defines the book's ultimate political exhortation in the form of poetry by Muhammad Iqbal, the renowned Urdu intellectual and Muslim separatist who was instrumental in the formation of the state of Pakistan. When the bookseller has explained "the true history of poetry, which is a kind of secret, a magic known only to wise men," Balram observes that "the history of the world is the history of a ten-thousand-year war of brains between the rich and the poor. Each side is eternally trying to hoodwink the other side: and it has been this way since the start of time" (Adiga 2008: 217). The bookseller shares a couplet from Iqbal as a kind of shibboleth to ensure that Balram understands: *"You were looking for the key for years/ But the door was always open!"* (Adiga 2008: 216). Balram personalizes this wholly decontextualized couplet and makes it into the mantra of his effort to escape the Rooster Coop. Reciting the lines of verse becomes the only way that he can sleep at night, preparatory to his galvanizing (and supernatural) encounter with the white tiger at the zoo. Awaking from a faint that functions as a significant death and rebirth upon the encounter, Balram observes the beauty of the wildlife set suggestively against the poignant backdrop of the Old Fort's ruins:

> Iqbal, that great poet, was *so* right. The moment you recognize what is beautiful in this world, you stop being a slave. To hell with the Naxals and their guns shipped from China. If you taught every poor boy how to paint, that would be the end of the rich in India. (Adiga 2008: 236)

Following this revelation, Balram determines that the key to his cage is not to be found in the violent ruse of revolution but in the cultivation of the exceptional self, one marked out by the rare sensitivity of what David Russell and Jin Gon Park have called "aesthetic liberalism."[10] The specificity of capitalist exploitation and the distinctive stages of historical materialism (indeed, it is not incidental that Balram ironically echoes the famous words of the *The Communist Manifesto*: "The history of all hitherto existing society is the history of class struggles") are wholly dehistoricized and *flattened* into an eternal contest between rich and poor. But these categories are presupposed as inevitable and inviolable ontologies outside history. The most exceptional individuals

---

[10] See Russell, David 2013. "Aesthetic Liberalism: John Stewart Mill as Essayist," *Victorian Studies* 56.1: 7–30; and Park, Jin Gon 2020. "Aesthetic Liberalism: Beauty and Political Action in the Age of Interest," Dissertation. New York: Cornell University. Park summarizes, "The animating claim of aesthetic liberalism is that beauty has more power to generate political virtues than rational arguments," or, as we see in Adiga, revolutionary action.

might escape to one or lapse to the other, but the categories themselves cannot be altered by any political craft.

In the novel's final pages, Balram offers a definitive reflection on the "stirrings, rumours, [and] threats of insurrection," in which the masses rise up and smash the Rooster Coop. Posing the possibility of revolt as a rhetorical question ("An Indian Revolution?"), Balram provides a cynically dismissive response: "Ha! Maybe once in a hundred years there is a revolution that frees the poor" (Adiga 2008: 260). Offering to name the leaders of four successful revolutions, he can dubiously produce only Alexander the Great, Abraham Lincoln, and Mao, while he speculates that the fourth "may have been Hitler, I can't remember" (Adiga 2008: 260). On the prospect of an Indian revolution, however, he is clear: "No sir. It won't happen. People in this country are still waiting for the war of their freedom to come from somewhere else—from the jungles, from the mountains, from China, from Pakistan. That will never happen. Every man must make his own Benaras;" and further, in a final affirmation of visceral individualism, particularized through use of the second person, "The book of your revolution sits in the pit of your belly, young Indian. Crap it out, and read" (Adiga 2008: 261).

With politics utterly discredited, the only course remaining is individual assent to (and ascent within) Rooster-Coop logic and compassionate capitalism. The novel therefore concludes with an account of Balram's management of an incident in which a driver for his transportation service (established with the money stolen from Ashok) fatally strikes a child with his car—repeating Pinky Madam's earlier drunk hit-and-run. In this case, Balram seeks to redeem the earlier error of the Mongoose by assuming, as owner of the company, personal (though not legal) responsibility for the child's death. In fact, he observes that the fault is no one's in particular but is the inevitable result of a system in which "outsourcing companies are so cheap that they force their taxi operators to promise them an impossible number of runs every night" (266–267). Neglecting to trace out the encompassing global forces that coerce the outsourcing companies to work within such narrow margins, Balram visits the family to express his regret and offer them a compensation of twenty-five thousand rupees and an employment opportunity for their remaining son, explaining, "The police have let me off. That is the way of this jungle that we live in. But I accept my responsibility. I ask for your forgiveness" (Adiga 2008: 268).

Also neglecting to acknowledge the Brechtian query, "What is the murder of a man to the employment of a man," Balram explains his motives to Mohammad Asif: "But I had to do something different; don't you see? I can't live the way the Wild Boar and the Buffalo and the Raven lived, and probably *still* live, back in Laxmangarh. I am in the light now" (Adiga 2008: 269). Thus characterizing himself as an alternative to the predatory landlords, he likewise credits himself as an agent of social transformation, ushering in a "new Bangalore for a new India:"

> Am I not part of all that is changing this country? Haven't I succeeded in the struggle that every poor man here should be making—the struggle not to take the lashes your father took, not to end up in a mound of indistinguishable bodies that will rot in the black mud of Mother Ganga? (Adiga 2008: 273)

The fact that he has murdered and robbed his way to such standing—vice, not virtue, rewarded—he justifies by asking whether or not "everyone who counts in this world including our prime minister (including *you*, Mr. Jiabao), has killed someone or other on their way to the top?" (Adiga 2008: 273). Eschewing the glory that attends mass murder ("Kill enough people and they will put up bronze statues to you near Parliament House in Delhi" [Adiga 2008: 273]), Balram claims that "All I wanted was the chance to be a man—and for that one murder was enough" (274). His own act of desperate violence, sanctioned by the naturalized logic of the Rooster Coop, is therefore redeemed as an act of individual emancipation, while collective, revolutionary, or radically democratic resistance is proscribed as either immoral or improvidently futile.

However, as both Taylor and Badiou respectively assert, democracy need not be reduced to an empty symbolism in which a "vote at the ballot box or attempting to live a meaningful life outside of corrupt and hostile political and economic intervention is a joke, a tawdry fantasy" (Taylor 2013: 14). Taylor opposes the alienations of what he calls "negative capitalism" to the possibility of a social democracy predicated on "an uncomfortable abandonment from the cool safety of cynicism," the latter of which "prevents us from trusting a credible alternative" by "liberat[ing] the modern individual from the burdens of taking responsibility for transforming society" (2013: 39, 104). Similarly, for Badiou, who also rejects a merely emblematic democratic materialism, "we will only ever be true democrats, integral to the historical life of peoples, when we become communists again" (Badiou 2011a: 15). In its cynical denial of democratic possibility, *The White Tiger* manages a unique synthesis of Moretti's dual categories: here, the Bildungsroman's critical and oppositional disposition of transformation is seized and incorporated into that of classification so that the latter is scorned even as it is maintained as the only realistic possible outcome.

This cynical realist effect is in some sense, then, the superlative expression of the naturalist postcolonial Bildungsroman: symbolically reconciling the contradiction intrinsic to its borrowed European form in such a way that the horizon of difference to which it responds is subsumed precisely to the extent that it is acknowledged and thus neatly canceled. Secured against the genuine threat of Becoming, it is free to exult in the caustic irony and complacent disdain of Being *in the name of Becoming*. As Taylor writes, "cynicism shields itself from the 'naivety' of universal laws to a depressive self-protection within the ironic treatment of language." He continues, "In a cynical era, utopia is replaced by ruin and catastrophe; cheerful and cheeky truth-seeking affirmation is replaced with a cold, hard-lipped demoralisation and retreat into narcissism" (2013: 105). A cynical detachment from the social and a sneering suspicion of the collective as utopian therefore entwine with "an internalisation of the self-seeking consumerist and money-motivated ideals of the economic politic of neoliberalism" (Taylor 2013: 107).

Hence, Balram's concluding fantasy of "founding a school full of White Tigers, unleashed on Bangalore" and his expressed desire to have children are the closest the novel can approach to a sentiment of revolution: not as transformation, but as *replication* and the commission of inheritance, the genetic protraction of the present into an undifferentiated future (Adiga 2008: 275). Balram's is a world without non-identical horizon in which the individual integrates into what Deleuze describes as the *dividual* order of the control society, where the seeming autonomy and free mobility of the individual, necessary for the flexible accumulation of global capital, is a requisite feature of her total subjugation (Deleuze 1992: 5). The transformation of individual actor into dividual subject, especially in the space of the postcolony, where empire and its few extant alternatives yet walk unveiled, means that making one's way in the world now entails collapsing the differential interiority and mobility that Moretti discerns in the classical Bildungsroman. Instead, this contemporary expression rewrites individual yearning as the cynical affirmation of a static social reality and flat exteriority and ironically recodes classification *as* transformation, arrested development *as* world-wise development, and cynical description *as* narration.

This recognition, as we find with Naipaul, need not lead us back to a weak subjectivism and the ethical condemnation of one writer or text and favoring of another, but rather to the perception of an encompassing field of historical influence that conditions, provokes, limits, and distorts any such aesthetic expression—the determinations of which field can be detected in writers with drastically divergent subjective sensibilities or political motivations, whether radical, reactionary, or progressive. The radical writer (like Michelle Cliff) must navigate, map, confirm, or contest these forces fully as much as the reactionary (Rhys) or liberal-progressive writer (Adiga) in order to narrate ways in a world from which the prospective horizon, as Bloch puts it, has been omitted.

Chapter 4

Future Perfect and the Impossible Present
Two Faces of Postcolonial Anti-Utopianism

It's all impossible, everything between us, every possibility imaginable or unimaginable, is impossible.
—*Neel Mukherjee*, The Lives of Others (2014: 178)

Their evocation of the solidity of their object of representation—the social world grasped as an organic, natural, Burkean permanence—is necessarily threatened by any suggestion that the world is not natural, but historical, and subject to radical change.
—*Fredric Jameson*, The Political Unconscious (1981: 193)

The saturation of postcolonial narrative horizons by inertial Being and the cynical renunciation of utopia simultaneously accord with another of literary naturalism's most prominent modes of expression or motivating temperaments: that of the anti-utopia. Less formally consistent and generically coherent than the narrative utopia, anti-utopia persists as what Lyman Tower Sargent describes as "a constant but generally unsystematic stream of thought" haunting utopian aspiration at its foundation (1994: 134). In one of the most thoroughgoing and influential considerations of this somewhat elusive concept, Trinidad-born sociologist Krishan Kumar describes anti-utopia as "a malevolent and grimacing *doppelgänger*" that "has stalked utopia from the very beginning," disrupting the totalizing social dreams of the latter with menacing visions of its inevitable failure or futility (Kumar 1987: 99). More than utopia's negative twin, anti-utopia also serves as a necessary supplement that guards utopianism against its own constitutive impetus to absolute closure or spatio-historical secession. If, therefore, as Bill Ashcroft observes, "Postcolonial utopianism began with anti-colonial utopias that focused on the prospect of an independent nation" (2016: 4), this very aspiration soon gives rise to a secondary anxiety in which "the somber realities of post-independence political life began to be felt" and in which

> utopian nationalist dreams of the anti-colonial liberation struggles were doomed to disappointment, bound, as the newly independent nations were, to the political structures of the colonial state, and a political system largely incompatible with cultural realities. (2016: 5)

Following the deflation of pre-independence nationalist fervor in the wake of its realization, then, emerges an alternative form of utopian thought. Here, the "critical dimension of utopianism began to replace the ideological elements of pre-independence utopias," centering on what is latterly recognized as the problem of nationhood within an incipient globalization and figuring an array of alternatives to the narrative of nationalist ascension and coherence (Ashcroft 2016: 97). Rather than countenance this impulse as anti-utopian, Ashcroft extends to the registration of post-nationalist skepticism Tom Moylan's important concept of the *critical utopia,* which Moylan identifies as emerging in the 1970s science fiction of writers like Joanna Russ, Ursula Le Guin, Marge Piercy, and Samuel Delaney (crucially, voices that speak from a variously gendered, sexed, raced or politically oppositional margin). Faced with the various failures and compromises of 60s global radicalism, critical utopianism debunks utopia as a program or static blueprint even as it emphatically preserves, reinvents, and reaffirms utopia as principle and open-ended process of social transformation (Moylan 2014: 10).

Hugh Charles O'Connell similarly locates a postcolonial variant of utopia in what he names "weak utopianism"—derived from both Benjamin's *weak messianism* and Derrida's concept of the *messianic without messianism*—which O'Connell characterizes as a "utopianism from the abyss." This weak utopianism enacts in the midst of the undeniable and unrelenting floodwaters of the present what Donna Haraway calls a "staying with trouble" that is neither a capitulation to the grim and unrelenting circumstances of the status quo nor a naïve faith in the possibility of its imminent transcendence (O'Connell 2012: 123). This heavily qualified utopianism, despite its dubious outlook, nevertheless stands opposed to the consensus "strong anti-utopianism" that O'Connell defines as the pervasive contemporary

> belief or feeling that there is no outside to capitalism, that it is impossible to imagine futurity (the future as qualitatively different

from the present capitalist world-system), and a corresponding belief that any alternative would only be worse. (2012: 123)

Kumar defines anti-utopianism in highly comparable terms while also invoking the "longstanding clash between Augustinian and Pelagian traditions within western thought" and the credo of an irredeemable, *postlapsarian* human nature:

> The anti-utopian need not believe in original sin, but his pessimistic and determinist view of human nature leads him to the conviction that all attempts to create the good society on earth are bound to be futile. Utopian strivings will lead to violence and tyranny. The anti-utopian takes certain melancholy pleasure in the recital of failed and aborted reforms and revolutions. (1987: 100)

However, while anti-utopianism frequently undergirds a conservative, reactionary, or counterrevolutionary agenda,[1] Kumar further argues that the "anti-utopian temperament was not always or only tied to a conservative ideology" and is in fact frequently found to accompany the discontented, diverted, or impeded ambitions of former utopians:

> We might even say, stretching the point only a little, that the anti-utopia is largely the creation of men for whom it represented the dark obverse of their own profound and passionate utopian temperament. Their anti-utopias are born of a sense of frustrated and thwarted utopianism. Neither in their individual lives nor in the world at large do they see any prospect of the utopia they so desperately wish for. (1987: 104)

Anti-utopianism thus "reveals itself as the anguished cry of a single divided self," duplicating with dialectical consistency the double-valence of utopianism/anti-utopianism within its own conceptual horizon (Kumar 1987: 104).

Antonis Balasopoulos further advances Kumar's understanding of a complex anti-utopianism by outlining an expanded typology of five distinct varieties: the satirical, the dogmatic fictional, the dogmatic non-fictional, the pre-emptive, and the critical anti-utopia. What I am here calling (by way of Kumar) the twin valences of postcolonial

---

[1] He notes, for instance, that Edmund Burke's *Reflections on the Revolution in France* has provided a "philosophical rationale for anti-utopian conservatism for nearly two centuries" (Kumar 1987: 104).

anti-utopianism correspond roughly with, on the one hand, a partial admixture of the satirical and dogmatic fictional variations and, on the other, the critical anti-utopia. Satirical anti-utopias, Balasopoulos writes, "attack previous works or intellectual traditions by exposing them as impractically and unrealistically 'Utopian'" and "show no interest in substituting what they expose as folly with more rational or functional alternatives" (Balasopoulos 2006: 61). Dogmatic fictional anti-utopias indicate the "catastrophic potential of the Utopian impulse" and "assume a fundamentally unchangeable, ahistorical definition of what is 'natural' to mankind" (Balasopoulos 2006: 61). Conversely, critical anti-utopias—which are seldom, if ever, associated with conservative political positions—"are opposed to Utopianism, but without either upholding the desirability of the current social order or rejecting the prospects of radical social change" (Balasopoulos 2006: 63). While Balasopoulos finds that the satirical and dogmatic fictional varieties have waned in equal measure with the utopian narratives upon whose energies they necessarily depend, one might argue that they yet persist in those national cultures where revolutionary struggle itself endures in whatever constrained or attenuated form as a social potentiality.

As Wegner points out, what Moylan calls the "anti-utopian temptation" that is ever present in the genre of the dystopia can be traced to the form's "roots in the traditions of literary naturalism" (2002: 120). It is therefore no coincidence, Wegner maintains, that the majority of properly dystopian fictions are written by "authors who understood their politics to be left of center, if not explicitly socialist—something equally the case for many of the great nineteenth-century practitioners of literary naturalism, including Gissing, Émile Zola, and Theodore Dreiser" (2002: 120). We ought therefore to supplement the critical or weak utopianism that Ashcroft and O'Connell find operative in postcolonial narratives with these nuanced accounts of its apparent counterpart and, in some instances, perhaps discover that the former terms can more accurately be said to rename tendencies and ideological formations already present in the latter.

Cautioning against the undialectical binary reductivism of "a relatively simple play of oppositions in which the enemies of Utopia can easily be sorted out from its friends" (Jameson 1996: 54), Jameson likewise argues that even in the moment of globalized or late capital in which "the times are propitious for anti-Utopianism" (1996: 53), it nonetheless remains the case that "the most powerful arguments against Utopia are in reality Utopian ones, expressions of a Utopian impulse *qui s'ignore*" (1996: 54–55). Beginning, like Kumar, with Burke and his counterrevolutionary descendants, Jameson traces the lineage of anti-utopianism to the "implacable postmodern critique of high modernism itself as repressive, totalizing, phallocentric, authoritarian, and redolent of an even more sublime and inhuman hubris than anything Burke could have attributed to his Jacobin contemporaries" (Jameson 1996: 53).[2] With its characteristic antipathy for totality and vigilant equation of the latter with political totalitarianisms of both right and left, postmodernist thought rehearses "a very old (but hitherto Western) Cold-War and ... market rhetoric about hubris and human sinfulness (our old friend human nature again)" in order emphatically to caution against "the Burkean Jacobinism and the Stalinism implicit and inevitable in any Utopian effort to create a new society, or even in any fantasy of doing so" (Jameson 1996: 54).

Committed to Ernst Bloch's notion of utopia as the ineradicable and universal surplus hope-content vivifying a human predisposition toward the Not-yet conscious, Jameson seeks alternatively to map a dynamic dialectics of utopia/anti-utopia in which each tendency is to be found in and substantiated only through the expression of its putative other. In a passage that recalls his insistence on a historicizing, formalist method that can detect the presence of a properly historical consciousness in the work of a subjectively conservative writer, Jameson remarks on the similar importance of recognizing the utopianism inherent in anti-utopian negation:

> If indeed one believes that the Utopian desire is everywhere, and that some individual or pre-individual Freudian libido is enlarged and completed by a realm of social desire, in which the longing for transfigured collective relationships is no less powerful and omnipresent, then it can scarcely be surprising that this particular political unconscious is to be identified even there where it is the most passionately decried and denounced. (Jameson 1996: 55)

---

[2] In *Archaeologies of the Future*, however, Jameson does productively call for a distinction between, on the one hand, the narrative utopia and its dystopian "negative cousin"—both of which are informed by a "positive conception of human social possibilities"—and, on the other, the anti-Utopia. Like Orwell's exemplary texts, the latter is rooted in "a conviction about human nature itself, whose corruption and lust for power are inevitable" and is ultimately "informed by a central passion to denounce and warn against Utopian programs in the political realm," though this distinction does not negate, in my view, Jameson's earlier emphasis on the dialectic of utopia/anti-utopia (2005: 198–199).

Thus, amidst a generalized political alienation and a fully justified disdain for actually existing "utopian" projects—which are now the exclusive provenance of the alliance of corporate interests with instrumental state sovereignty[3]—the authentically utopian impulse can most readily be detected in an arch skepticism, that is, in "the fear and anxiety before Utopia itself" (Jameson 1996: 61).

Rather than passively await the resurgence of positively charged "new visions of the future, such as are bound to appear when the outlines of a new global order and its postnational class system have become stabilized" and therefore available for immediate representation, Jameson instead invites us to undertake, in the lived opacity of the present, "a rigorous look at everything we fantasize as mutilating, as privative, as oppressive, as mournful and depressing, about all the available visions of a radical transformation in the social order" (1996: 61). Such critical intolerance for utopia, Jameson further maintains, is, upon closer inspection, often revealed to be a sublimated anti-institutionalism in which we can further discern "the more fundamental object" of corporate capitalism itself, much as in the ersatz cognitive mapping of the conspiracy film (1996: 63).

However, as Jameson repeatedly suggests, this misdirected repudiation of utopia-as-institution is by and large a postmodernist and First-World one; as he further notes, there is "no more pressing task for progressive people in the First World than tirelessly to analyze and diagnose" the anxiety aroused by utopia, just as the phantasmatic but omnipresent bureaucracies of capitalist oligarchy constitute "the only experience people in the West have had of omnipotent and impersonal power structures" (1996: 63). Putting aside the purely culturalist charges of essentialism or chauvinism,[4] such a geopolitical framing does not fully countenance the variability and vicissitudes of the global "postnational class system" that Jameson also recognizes, however. My contention here is that attention to the divergent expressions of

---

[3] This is largely true with a few scintillating exceptions, such as the ongoing project of American science fiction writer Kim Stanley Robinson, notably his Mars (1992–96) and Science in the Capital (2004–07) trilogies and his *Ministry for the Future* (2020), and Yanis Varoufakis's *Another Now* (2020).

[4] The salient critique here is, of course, to be found in Ahmed, Aijaz 1987. "Jameson's Rhetoric of Otherness and the 'National Allegory'," *Social Text* 17: 3–26. Rpt. in Ahmad 1992. *In Theory: Classes, Nations, Literatures* (London: Verso), 95–112. See the important reassessment of the debate in Lazarus, Neil 2011. *The Postcolonial Unconscious* (Cambridge: Cambridge University Press), and Jameson's more recent response in *Allegory and Ideology* (New York: Verso, 2019).

ressentiment found in the postcolonial anti-utopia can help us to track this emergent complex not by way of First-World postmodernism (nor, as we shall see, by the melancholic arc of postcolonial tragedy) but by way of postcolonial naturalism, which bears sometimes striking similarities to the former, particularly with regard to its intolerance for the totalizing project of utopia.

The proposition of the present chapter is therefore to situate the political expression of anti-colonial nationalism within the cultural practice and periodizing schema of realism, which, as Anna Kornbluh recently argues, constructs (via its own passion for totality) "utopian models of possible socialities" (Kornbluh 2019: 156). This realist utopian project is primarily the progressive and demiurgic impetus of the national bourgeoisie in its struggle for political independence and the invention of a national culture,[5] however much of its rhetorical appeal is to that of general emancipation. Once the goal of formal independence is realized in the postcolony, however, and the developmental aims of the national bourgeoisie are revealed to be structurally untenable under the emergent dispensation of economic globalization and its refunctioning of national sovereignty, the national bourgeoisie finds itself trapped between the urgent demands of "the people" in whose name it has legitimated its ascendance and the now-decentered and liquid sovereignty of the new global Empire. The structural flexions and phenomenological derealizations of this new dispensation will demand the mobilization of altogether novel forms of representation, both political and cultural. The postcolonial period is thus that of a realism-in-crisis, in which the bourgeois narratives of national cohesion and progressive self-determination are undermined by the realization that the palliatives of cultural unity cannot exorcize the specter of class antagonism in a global capitalist system.

As Jameson maintains in his reading of British naturalist writer George Gissing, the "conceptual and organizational framework" of naturalism is, in fact, "not that of social class," which is thoroughly repressed and unthinkable as such, but rather "the notion of 'the people,' as a kind of general grouping of the poor and 'underprivileged' of all kinds, from which one can recoil in revulsion, but to which one can also, as in some political populisms, nostalgically 'return' as to some telluric source of strength" (1981: 189). The naturalist text thus oscillates

---

[5] For more on the importance of the narrative utopia to the project of the nation state, see Wegner, Phillip E. 2002. *Imaginary Communities: Utopia, The Nation, and the Spatial Histories of Modernity* (Berkeley: University of California Press).

between "revulsion and fascination" with 'the people' just as it balances between attitudes of philanthropic and conciliatory reformism and paranoid and renunciatory political despair (1981: 189).

This double-aspect also informs the two faces of anti-utopia, which can be distinguished by their respective orientations toward and objects of *ressentiment*. On one hand is projected both the envy of the underclasses toward their social superiors and the "private dissatisfactions" of progressive intellectuals who, driven by personal failure and resentment (much like Mulapo in Nkosi's *Underground People*), agitate social unrest; on the other, we find the registration of the bourgeois class anxiety from which this first expression originally derives (Jameson 1981: 202). As Jameson notes, "the theory of *ressentiment*, wherever it appears, will always itself be the expression and the production of *ressentiment*," or of what he terms an *"authentic ressentiment"* (1981: 203). Thus, however much it is motivated by Sartrean bad faith, the naturalist (anti-utopian) expression nevertheless bestows form to the very class consciousness that it would otherwise actively repress from thought.

In fact, Wegner questions whether "anti-utopia is a position that any human being can inhabit for very long and if such a pure form of an assault on the utopian imaginary exists" at all (2002: 123). If the anti-utopian posture of pure negation is finally unsustainable *à la longue*, Wegner suggests that its dark spectacle of repudiation typically reveals itself as tacitly in service of what Karl Mannheim calls the *conservative utopia* in which, "not only is attention turned to the past and the attempt made to rescue it from oblivion, but the presentness and immediacy of the whole past becomes an actual experience"—a description that could certainly apply to the postcolonial novel's attempt to excavate a "usable past" amid the vertiginous realities of the new global Empire (qtd. in Wegner 2002: 123).

In this chapter, I read two postcolonial narratives within the intersecting frameworks of naturalist *ressentiment* and anti-utopian renunciation that resist placement within either a "weak" or "critical" utopian paradigm but that also register in their variously resigned or reactionary alienations an authentic *ressentiment* within the protracted moment of postnationalist melancholy. In Neel Mukherjee's widely celebrated Naxal novel, *The Lives of Others* (2014), the radical Maoist uprising is delegitimated and recontained not only through the invocation of terrorist violence but also through an Orwellian narrative stratagem of circular or closed temporality and the primacy of affect. Next, in *The Children of Sisyphus* (1968) by Orlando Patterson—the Jamaican novelist and sociologist whom London's *Daily Telegraph* once dubbed "The Caribbean Zola" and whose monumental study *Slavery and Social Death* (1982) is frequently invoked as centrally influential in the late emergence of Afro-Pessimist thought[6]—we find an engagement with the immediate aftermath of Jamaican independence and the bleak foreclosure of emancipatory horizons. Here, I suggest, we find another face of anti-utopianism, one that expresses an active nihilism that refuses the consolations of hope in the name of a political longing that is both without recourse to the progressive realisms or utopianisms of the past and without the representational resources necessary to map its present dilemma except in terms of negation.

The "Great Circularity": Mukherjee's *The Lives of Others*

Everyone is hectically denying the existence of favourites, of special affections and allegiances and alliances within a larger group of siblings, or between parents and children, while, just under the surface, the empty drama of equality is torqued to its very opposite by the forces of conflicting emotions and affinities. The Ghosh family unwittingly followed this paradigm with slavishness.
—*Neel Mukherjee*, The Lives of Others (2014: 105)

Does that mean that the world is wherever one is? Is that not the most accurate and strictest of all definitions of self-centeredness? Does that mean that there is no escape from the self? After chanting to ourselves millions of times, <u>Change yourself, change the world</u>, is this the outcome—failure?
—*Fredric Jameson*, The Political Unconscious (1981: 240)

In a manner that the *New York Times Book Review* favorably compares to Tolstoy and that *Kirkus Reviews* extols as "Victorian in its solidity," Neel Mukherjee's Booker Prize short-listed *The Lives of Others* executes an expansive and seemingly unsparing critical anatomy of late twentieth-century Indian social conflict, which, more reminiscent of Zola than Tolstoy,[7] is anchored in the extended family saga. If Tolstoy remains

---

[6] See Wilderson, Frank 2020. *Afropessimism* (New York: Liveright), 40; and Sexton, Jared 2011. "The Social Life of Social Death: On Afro-Pessimism and Black Optimism," *InTensions*: 1–47.
[7] I suggest the more apt comparison with Zola notwithstanding the applicability of either the "Anna Karenina Principle" to Mukherjee's incestuous,

(as his ardent reader Virginia Woolf ultimately found him to be[8]) largely allegiant to the traditional and patriarchal lineaments of the family, Mukherjee's commodious generational saga seems, as Nivedita Majumdar observes, contrarily "invested in exposing a particularly dark underside of familial life" (2021: 119). As Majumdar further describes *The Lives of Others*, "Commonplace matters of illicit romance, sibling rivalry, maternal broken hearts, envious and plotting sisters-in-law, deceitful brothers, and anguished children constitute the multigenerational saga of the Ghosh family," a dubious litany to which one might also add the more sensational matters of exploitation, rape, fraud, theft, false incrimination, murder, suicide, sadism, and coprophilia (2021: 119).

The limitation of Mukherjee's evocation of the family is therefore less to be found in any residual Tolstoian sentimentality (there is no trace, for example, of the latter's idyllic maternal figures) than in the emphatic suggestion that a *natural* predisposition to corruption, frangibility, and degradation fatally restrains any individual or collective effort to transcend these innate limitations, which, like original sins, are visited upon one generation after another, world without end. As Majumdar observes,

> The deficiency of *The Lives of Others* is not that its portrayal of the dark underbelly of social and familial life falls short in any way. To the contrary, the portrayal is incisive and brilliant. The issue with this novel is that it doesn't get past that underbelly. (2021: 119)

Indeed, the inability of the Ghoshes (and the family's satellite characters) to escape by their own volition the shadow of this fatalistic bane is the book's most prominent and explicit theme.

From the novel's brutal prologue, we are thrown into a world of absolute predestination, one that is instantiated both thematically and formally. We are briefly told the story of exploited and hopelessly indebted tenant farmer Nitai Das. Faced with the imminent starvation of his family, he is forced to choose what he perceives as the more merciful option of, first, murdering his wife with a sickle ("The head isn't quite severed, perhaps he didn't strike with enough force, so it hangs by the still-uncut fibres of skin and muscle and arteries as she collapses with a thud" [Mukherjee 2015a: 3]) and, second, killing his three

---

vituperative, and broadly dysfunctional Ghosh family or the wife's assertion in Tolstoy's "Family Happiness:" "You call it love, but I call it torture" (561).

[8] See Dalgarno, Emily 2004. "A British *War and Peace*? Virginia Woolf Reads Tolstoy," *Modern Fiction Studies* 50.1: 129–150.

children. After decapitating his son with one stroke, he "squeezes and squeezes and squeezes" his middle child's throat "until her protruding eyes almost leave the stubborn ties of their sockets and her tongue lolls out and her thrashing legs still," then suffocates the infant, silencing her "weak, runty mewl," before drinking a jerrycan of Folidol insecticide, a dreadfully common method of suicide among the poor of rural India (Mukherjee 2015a: 3).[9] He is compelled to this despairing extreme, the lurid details of which are gratuitously lingered over in the narrative description, by the realization that he could no longer discern in the eyes of his children the familiar longing of hunger, hope for the cessation of pain, or even a glint of "puzzled resentment;" instead, the narrator remarks, "now there is nothing, a slow, beyond-the-end nothing" (Mukherjee 2015a: 2).

The recognition that settles Nitai Das's grim resolve is thus one of inexorable fate: "Who can escape what's written on his forehead from birth?" (Mukherjee 2015a: 3). The doomed, long-suffering servant of the Ghosh family, Madan, who is claimed informally as "part of the family" and "like our eldest son," will repeat this very sentiment after he is betrayed and framed for the theft of Purnima's jewelry by Supratik for the purpose of funding a Naxalite urban campaign: "Ma, what can I say, what's written on the forehead will come to pass" (Mukherjee 2015a: 439).

The narrator further indicates the futility or hypocrisy of the rhetoric of social equality in recounting Madan's reflexive deference to the children. From the time of their infancy, he addresses them by appending the honorific "Da" and "Moni" to indicate an elder brother or sister (Mukherjee 2015a: 319). Thus, Madan-Da's honorary family membership notwithstanding, the "invisible membrane separating the two worlds never got breached," as though "the design of things, which was meant to remain unchanging, ever so, was ceaselessly invigilating a flexible barrier that could be moved only so far and no further" (Mukherjee 2015a: 319). Despite or because of what Supratik laments as this "unbridgeable gap between the lives of these people and of our kind," he will later journey to the village of Majgeria, which appears on the list of communities most potentially receptive to the Maoist message for the "one big reason" that it is the hamlet where Nitai Das murdered his family and killed himself the previous spring (Mukherjee 2015a: 104). With the capture of Supratik and the morbid spectacle of his

---

[9] See Karunarathne, A., Bhalla, A., Sethi, A. et al. 2021. "Importance of Pesticides for Lethal Poisoning in India During 1999 to 2018: A Systematic Review," *BMC Public Health* 21. https://doi.org/10.1186/s12889-021-11156-2.

torture and death at the hands of the state followed by the suicide of Madan and the second epilogue's anticipated death of 1,500 passengers aboard a train that will be derailed by Maoist insurgents in 2012 using techniques originated by Supratik ("his gift to future comrades"), the novel comes full circle, its mythic repetition graphically symbolized in the images of the lunar cycle depicted without commentary throughout the novel.

This concluding anticipation of an act that *will have happened*—subsequent to the action of the novel but just preceding the reader's own present in 2014—is itself repeatedly anticipated in the occasional imposition of the future perfect tense, one of what A.S. Byatt's review of the novel calls the "various time-bombs that suddenly change the way we see the book's whole world." This tense shift abruptly reframes the narrative diegesis from the vantage of a future that already perceives the ultimate futility of the characters' unwitting struggles in the present. Meditating on his inability to bridge the existential chasm separating him from the villager for whose emancipation he is determined to fight, Supratik writes: "And yet I'm no closer to that man. Most importantly, I haven't been able to answer that big question: what idea did he have of the story of his life, not only of the past and the present, but also of what was to come?" (Mukherjee 2015a: 178).

On the following page, the narrator directly responds to the open-ended and present uncertainty of Supratik's quandary with the confident foreknowledge of future eventualities: "Many years later, as he faced his own dissolution, Prafullanath *was to remember* a distant afternoon when his father took him to see the Elphinstone Bioscope..." (Mukherjee 2015a: 179, emphasis added). The recollection itself is described as an "undead" apparition from a metaphorical book of memories containing "an infinite number of self-renewing pages" that cannot be eradicated and that return to taunt and mock any attempt to efface their supervisory content (Mukherjee 2015a: 179). And while Prafullanath labors in vain to escape this phantom grip of the past, he is thereby oblivious to the future prefigured in his own failed efforts to be free of that past. Likewise, upon Purba's fortuitous marriage to Somnath, "Prasanta, *who was later going to be sorry* to see Purba go, experienced the dazed detachment someone feels when events they ignited go far beyond any reasonable trajectory they had imagined" (Mukherjee 2015a: 353, emphasis added). This, then, is the novel's overriding message: one should tread carefully, lest one's purblind efforts to improve the current situation initiate a cascade of events that bring about unforeseeable misery.

Naturalism's Foreshortened Worlds and the Future Perfect

In a recent reflection on the "foreshortened worlds" of what anthropologist Philippe Descola also calls "naturalism" (here defined as "Western modernity's characteristic disagreement—its hygienic division—between nature and culture"), Pedro Neves Marques rehearses Afrofuturist Kodwo Eshun's suggestion that the logic of empire is "managed by both a preemptive and a predictive power" that Marques identifies with the future anterior or future perfect tense. As he puts it, "The future anterior orients the present toward a predetermined goal, while also rereading the past in its image" (Marques 2019: n.p.). That is, the future perfect seems to evacuate the present of its tensed possibility and to subordinate it to an already completed outcome. This interpretation would seem incompatible with the claim of Alain Badiou that the utopian force of what he calls a truth process lies in its capacity to "authorize[ ] anticipations of knowledge concerning not what is but *what will have been if truth attains completion*," hence his requirement that "truth judgements be formulated in the future perfect" (Badiou 2004: 127).

In fact, Andrew Milner cites these passages from Badiou in a critical reassessment of George Orwell's *Nineteen Eighty-Four*, a work that bears, I argue, a significant kinship with *The Lives of Others*. For Milner, the *subjunctive* future perfect is, even where it is not "empirically present," always "the logically informing tense of dystopia" in that it evokes possible future events "that will not necessarily have eventuated" (Milner 2013: 135). The immediate context of Milner's claim (and thus his primary example of this narrative effect) is the ongoing scholarly debate over the ideological charge and formal categorization of *Nineteen Eighty-Four*.

Against Jameson and Raymond Williams, who each regard Orwell's most famous novel as an anti-utopia that cancels utopian possibility, Milner attempts to identify the text's intent to prompt and imaginatively enable social transformation, which would qualify it, in his reading, as what Lyman Tower Sargent and Tom Moylan call a "critical dystopia."[10] If the novel is read as an anti-utopia, then it can be said

---

[10] Moylan defines the concept as "a textual mutation that self-reflexively takes on the present system and offers not only astute critiques of the order of things but also explorations of the oppositional spaces and possibilities from which the next round of political activism can derive imaginative sustenance and inspiration" (2000: xv). Whether or not *Nineteen Eighty-Four* provides the latter is the crux of debates over the novel's formal status and ideological charge.

to foreclose political and imaginative horizons of possibility and inscribe a fatalistic outlook underwritten by an arch dismissal of the working class Proles, in whom it nominally locates hope, through a comprehensive and enfeebling theory of human nature. Thus, for Jameson, "the force of the text (and of *Animal Farm*) springs from a conviction about human nature itself, whose corruptions and lust for power are inevitable, and not to be remedied by new social measures or programs, nor by heightened consciousness of impending dangers" (Jameson 2005: 198).

For Milner, however, such an assessment fails to grant due significance to the marginal supplement in which Orwell preserves some measure, albeit abstract, of utopian alterity. First, Milner underscores the novel's conspicuously singular footnote located in chapter one ("Newspeak was the official language of Oceania") for its retrospective gesture toward the narrative from which it thus asserts a critical distance, or what Milner calls "narrative externality in form, but historical internality in fictional content" (2013: 134). Next, he builds upon the insight of Margaret Atwood, who likewise notes that the Appendix on "The Principles of Newspeak"

> is written in standard English, in the third person, and in the past tense, which can only mean that the regime has fallen, and that language and individuality have survived. For whoever has written the essay on Newspeak, the world of Nineteen Eighty-Four is over. Thus, it's my view that Orwell had much more faith in the resilience of the human spirit than he's usually given credit for. (Atwood 2005: 337)

In addition to the mere repetition of the footnote's past tense, however, Milner also points to the presence in the essay's temporal framing of the subjunctive future perfect tense, which opposes the foreclosed temporality of the novel's dismal ending with what *"would have happened"* (2013: 135).

Invoking Williams's influential discussion of utopian "tenses of imagination" and his assertion that William Morris's *News from Nowhere* provides a "true subjunctive" that is altogether absent in Orwell's vision, Milner argues that *"Nineteen Eighty-Four* cannot be considered in any real sense an anti-utopia, but must rather be judged a critical dystopia in the full sense of the term" (2013: 135). While instances of the subjunctive future perfect tense do occur in the Appendix, however, these are incidental to the narrative's dominant past tense and simply recount past speculations that have not in fact come to pass.[11] For all that, the dominant temporal framework of the Appendix remains, as Atwood notes, the past tense, as in the opening sentence: "Newspeak was the official language of Oceania and had been devised to meet the ideological needs of Ingsoc, or English Socialism" (2005: 299).

Moreover, in an approving summary and elaboration of Milner's reading, Sean McQueen writes,

> Whether Newspeak and, thus, the Party, fell by means of revolution, theodicy or hubris is not apparent; whether it represents the same revisionist history perpetuated by the Party or its successors is unlikely, but not unthinkable. It does not represent, as Williams and Jameson would wish, a proper description of socialist alternatives, but rather, *a return to Oldspeak, and thus normalcy*. (McQueen 2014: 76, emphasis added)

To Darko Suvin's recent claim that it is "indefensible to assume some deep plot by Orwell that this [verb tense] should add a totally different perspective to the Winston story by situating a collective happy ending in its future" (Suvin 2022: 272), we must also at once add that if Orwell's differential horizon is merely the return to "normalcy" and the indicatively familiar linguistic and social formations (standard English, individualism) of the present, then the double closure effected by the Appendix only reconfirms the narrative's status as anti-utopian in its refusal to figure the subjunctive possibility of an alternative that is not merely restorative.

This Orwellian digression can help us to distinguish between the radically transformative future perfect tense privileged by Badiou—for whom the revolutionary intervention of truth reorders the domain of the known or knowable from the impossible vantage of a future eventuality—and the future perfect tense deployed by Mukherjee, which seeks rather to foreclose that very possibility. Whereas for Badiou, future realization is invoked as a concrete counterfactual with which to militate against a statically dominant present order, for Mukherjee, considerations of present action from the vantage of an

---

[11] Milner cites only two instances from the novel of the subjunctive future perfect, neither of which convincingly appears to "provide its chronological frame:" "Orwell writes that it 'was expected that Newspeak would have finally superseded Oldspeak ... by about the year 2050' and that 'within a couple of generations even the possibility of such a lapse would have vanished .... When Oldspeak had been once and for all superseded, the last link would have been severed'" (135).

already completed future rather neutralize those actions in advance and, deeming them both foolish and futile, reassert the suffocating immobility of the present as inexorable fate. And like Orwell, whose socialist commitments were tempered by and often set at odds with the naturalist aesthetic and intellectual cynicism that he so admired in a writer like Gissing, Mukherjee's anti-utopian temperament is rooted deeply in a philosophy of fatalistic nature. As a latter-day heir to Orwell, Mukherjee might therefore be seen as both affirming Orwell's observation that "every revolutionary opinion draws part of its strength from a secret conviction that nothing can be changed" (1958: 190) while nonetheless revealing the ideology of its inverse form: *every conviction that nothing can be changed draws part of its strength from the revolution that it seeks to abolish.*

Narrative Logic and Revolutionary Recontainment

In contemplating the opaque interior life of her son (the incommensurability and unknowability of "the other" emerging unsurprisingly as one of the novel's foremost "postcolonial" themes), Supratik's mother Sandhya absentmindedly spills lamp oil and—given her belief that "nothing falls outside a particular design"—is overcome with fear that she has offended Lakshmi, goddess of wealth, and therefore jeopardized her son: "The very contiguity of her worries about Supratik and the oil spill makes her think that the minor accident is heaped with meaning about some imminent evil related to her son, maybe some danger that is about to befall him," a premonition that the book's conclusion will fatefully realize (Mukherjee 2015a: 30). Similarly, Prafullanath finds himself trapped in a version of what Supratik will name the "great circularity" (Mukherjee 2015a: 199) as he prepares to punish Somnath in "a baleful mimicry of an action from another life," unwittingly begetting his own trauma and shame unto the next generation of Ghoshes:

> The distance of more than thirty years foreshortened to nothing; the bad blood was flowing in the new one too, no escape was possible. Inheritance was everything, and he and his had got nothing except the negatives: cheated out of wealth and property, stalked by decadence and bad character. (Mukherjee 2015a: 287)

As he will later observe of his son, "'Everything was ordained by fate. Or it is all in the blood. Bad blood will tell one day .... I feel I have just been a conducting pipe between the bad in the past and the bad in the future'" (Mukherjee 2015a: 350).

Despite his practiced fidelity to the Maoist doctrine of revolutionary transformation from below, Supratik is likewise susceptible to this logic, as he later reflects: "Events fall into a pattern that we can only discern retrospectively. We credit ourselves with far more agency than we actually possess. Things happen because they happen" (Mukherjee 2015a: 38). This cynical renunciation frequently contradicts and even countermands Supratik's revolutionary zeal, as when he contemplates greed as "something about human nature I'd never been able to understand." As he reflects, "Greed ate the soul. Sometimes I felt that the haves in our society became giant magnets and, following some law of physics or astronomy transposed to human affairs, sucked in more and more, enlarging their states" (Mukherjee 2015a: 99). Either this acquisitiveness is wholly subjective (individual greed rather than social structure), or it is determined by nature. In neither case is space made for countenancing or intervening into historical processes of political economy. Indeed, he questions the efficacy and purpose of any opposition to such natural laws: "This was the way the world was, so why did I refuse to acknowledge and accept this truth?" (Mukherjee 2015a: 99).

In contemplating the disparity between landlord and tenant in the distribution of the crop, he later elaborates on this theory of natural accumulation and the principle of the "great circularity" (Mukherjee 2015a: 199): "The world ran on this law, and only on this. Some magnetic field began to develop around those who had a little something— power or money or influence or friends, you name it—and the more these things accrued, the more that magnetism increased .... It was like gravity: everything flowed, and could only flow, in one direction" (Mukherjee 2015a: 196). It is no accident that this principle of proleptic circularity also describes the narrative rationale of the novel's own closed totality, for which the occasional intrusion of the future perfect tense serves to indicate a teleological temporal and consequential terminus.

The fulcrum of the novel's critical exposition of both destiny and the middle-class Indian family lies, of course, with the young revolutionary Supratik, the favored son of the Ghosh dynasty at its apex, who attends the prestigious Presidency College in Calcutta, where he, like many students of his station in his generation all over the world— though particularly so in the Calcutta of 1967–73—comes to a bitterly critical realization of his own middle-class privilege. This emergent consciousness leads ultimately to his support of the Naxalite peasant insurgency against the Indian state. Thus, we might read the novel's scathing critique of Bengali middle-class values—one fully shared with its central character, who is also the only one to speak directly in first person—as providing a sympathetic identification with "the people." Against this, Mukherjee's brutal counterrevolutionary morality tale takes on the appearance of some sensible middle ground, acknowledging the legitimacy of the aggrieved while also indicating the dangers of taking demands for equality and social justice too far, which is to say too practically.

The radicalization of Supratik—his evolution from the unhappy consciousness of liberal guilt in his youth (railing against the family's material excess and their treatment of the poor) to direct involvement with the Maoist revolutionaries—is traced in a series of epistles to an unnamed addressee, his uncle's widow, for whom he has conceived a passionate, though prohibited romantic infatuation. As he ruefully confesses to her of his callow activist efforts,

> Yes, I was a communist activist from my very first year in Presidency College, but there is a large gap between being an activist out of the idealism that comes from books and, conversations, the fire of youth, and being one because you have lived through the depredations that life has thrown at you. (Mukherjee 2015a: 34)

So, while he was already "doing politics" as a "bright, short-lived star" of the Students' Federation of the CPI(M), Supratik soon develops a shameful awareness of the "invisible shadow" of privilege and of how "unbloodied my hands were, how full my stomach" when contrasted with the striking workers with whom he proudly declares solidarity (Mukherjee 2015a: 36). Having come to view the CPI(M) as a strategic, state-sanctioned bulwark against genuine social transformation, Supratik is revolted by the hypocrisy and thus primed for the emergence of the radically new, the impossible possibility of what Badiou calls the Event and Bloch the Novum:

> While the spectre of erstwhile revolutionaries becoming Establishment figures within the folds of that great betrayer, the CPI(M), was painful and intolerable, something else was taking shape, something that was going to explode like a thousand suns in an unsuspecting sky—Naxalbari. (Mukherjee 2015a: 38)

Of course, this hopefulness, directly at odds with the fatalism outlined above, is largely confined to the letters (distinguished from the narrative proper in both point of view and typography) that Supratik writes though does not post—recalling the abortive letters that Spivak notes in Rhys. The formal discontinuity in the work between the third-person and epistolary narratives therefore gives formal expression to the ideological dilemma for which it emerges as a symptom of the novel's anxiety over time and agency.

While the epistolary chapters provide abundantly descriptive detail of rural Bengal and the desperate lives of the peasant inhabitants, the formal discontinuity itself is suggestive of an ideological torsion and of the novel's deeper political unconscious. Majumdar notes that in limiting the rural perspective to that of the naïvely romantic and immature Supratik, the novel effects an abstract portrayal of peasant life "in which the burden of an impoverished representation could be placed on a particular character, rather than on the narrative itself" (Mukherjee 2015a: 122).

Mukherjee's strategic firewall also performs a curious (perhaps symptomal) dialectical inversion, however, in which the virtue of subjective interiority that it repeatedly attempts to privilege is denied to the first-person epistolary form in which its expression ought most nearly to be found. When, after a long and unaccountable absence, Supratik returns home for a wedding in the novel's concluding chapters ("He scintillates with the glamour of terror. Or so it seems to him"), he wrestles with what are presented as the irreducibly opposed loyalties of familial love and revolutionary commitment. Attempting to maintain an aloof distance, he is nonetheless moved by the sight of his mother and her longsuffering love for him, a temptation that he tries mightily to resist: "Emotion is a luxury, he knows; like all revolutionaries he cannot draw the correct line between emotion and sentimentality" (Mukherjee 2015a: 419).

The revolutionary—our omniscient narrator thus informs is the product of a fatal misapprehension and misalignment of the relation between inner and outer, emotional and material realities, the implications of which Supratik discerns in his father if not immediately in himself. Having acknowledged the "soul-staining" shame and guilt of his comrade Badal's death, he thinks of his father's "confected luxury of shame" over Supratik's political activity, which has made it impossible for him "to show his face to the outside world" (Mukherjee 2015a: 422):

> It struck him again, with vivid force, that all this talk of 'the outside world' turned round one thing only: what the outside world made of your own life. You were forever at the centre of things, the subject of the sentence; it was not the outside world you were thinking of, but where *you* stood in regard to that world. (423)

Supratik's utopian aspiration is "set on the shiny new moon of a new, ideal order, not on the soiled coin, which can be scrubbed to a gleam, lying at his feet," however, he is equally oblivious to the signs of his brother Suranjan's drug addiction, a revelation that forces him to confront the limitations of his "ability to separate himself out of his own self" and retreat into an abstract idealism that the narrative insists that we read as the projection of sheer egoism (Mukherjee 2015a: 457). Following a brief, melancholic reflection over his sleeping brother on the limits of one's ability to know the other—"because one can never enter that insuperably private world of the sleeper, regardless of how intertwined the lives are of observer and observed"—he is arrested by the police and taken away for Mukherjee's harrowing rendition of Orwell's Ministry of Love, where the narrative exposes and purges Supratik's utopian hubris.

Ressentiment and the Legacy of Room 101

Supratik's strategy of compartmentalization thus meets its practical and formal limits in the novel's culminating torture scene. Having abandoned the epistolary conceit with Supratik's return home, the omniscient narrative now assumes absolute control, reconciling inner and outer spaces through formal fiat. In attempting to steel himself against what may follow by means of dissociation from his physical circumstances, Supratik comes to an awareness of his mind as "a different creature, really; embodied inside him but a separate presence" (Mukherjee 2015a: 468). Torn between identifying and disidentifying with the political actions for which he will be punished, he oscillates between poles of "'Salvation' and 'Despair'" and comes to think of his interior and inviolable self as merely a medium for the conflict of "two abstract principles" wholly independent from his interior, hence *true* self (Mukherjee 2015a: 469). Again, the narrative performs a solipsistic ideological inversion in which the material, historical world is an abstract ideal, while the interior subjective world is substantial and more deeply consequential (reversing Marx's own inversion of Hegel). Supratik's fatal error, the novel insists, lies in his forsaking the latter for the former.

When his bloodlessly urbane interrogator (like Orwell's O'Brien, "He was the tormentor, he was the protector, he was the inquisitor, he was the friend" [Mukherjee 2015a: 244]) asks that Supratik tell him "[s]omething private," he proceeds to probe the young middle-class revolutionary's motives, which prompts Supratik's idealistic reply that he fights for "those who have nothing" so that "their expendable lives needn't be fodder, generation after generation" (476). It is here that Supratik's ultimate hypocritical betrayal, the framing of Madan for the theft of his aunt's jewels, is dramatically revealed to the reader. Though the narrator has already demonstrated foreknowledge of all outcomes, this one is suppressed for exactly this dramatic and edifying effect (Supratik earlier thinks only in passing of "the ticking time-bomb of the jewelry theft") (Mukherjee 2015a: 460). Supratik's shocking confession also sheds new light on his earlier argument with Madan, who counters Supratik's political commitments with the observation that "The world is very big, and we are very small:" therefore, the faithful old servant gently proposes, "Being kinder to your near and dear ones—isn't that a bigger thing than doing good for the unknown mass of people?" (Mukherjee 2015a: 426).

Supratik's vexed response, citing Madan's own hypocrisy with regard to his son Dulal (whose efforts at labor organizing in the Ghosh's factory is viewed by the family and by Madan himself as traitorous disloyalty), is precipitated both by a "cold fury that he is being given a lesson in political morality by the family's cook" and by his security in the knowledge that "Madan-da will not answer back because his station in life has not taught him how to" (Mukherjee 2015a: 427). The magnitude of Supratik's hypocrisy is therefore realized in the novel's disclosure that even his reckless political commitments are merely sublimated expressions of class envy.

Confronted with the paralyzing shame of this revelation, "questions of feelings and principles and inhuman betrayal" return to Supratik without recourse to either the abstract political calculus of his prior self-justifications or the first-person narrative in which they have heretofore been expressed (Mukherjee 2015a: 477). Reflecting on his childhood memories with Madan and thus the depth of his treachery, Supratik's sense of self is mortified but also thereby clarified and purified as discrete from the outer world. Like Winston Smith, who is also confronted with the fragility of his political commitments as well as with their hypocrisy (as in Winston's professed willingness to throw sulfuric acid in a child's face in the cause of the revolutionary Brotherhood), Supratik undergoes a similar forced conversion, the result of which is the renunciation of political commitment for individualist sympathetic indifference.[12] Faced with the recognition that his fervently

---

[12] Of Orwell's preference for the politically neutral and autonomous intellectual, Wegner observes, "The grim lesson in all this is clear: the political represents the negation of ethical conceptions of good or evil

espoused principles are as harmful as they are hypocritical and hence hollow, Supratik must, like Winston, learn that "[i]n the face of pain, there are no heroes" (Orwell 1961: 239).

Under extreme duress, Supratik is thus led to wonder, "How could he ever have imagined that ideology, revolution, the needs of others, abstractions, all these, combined or individually, could have been weightier than the simple business of self-preservation, of the sheer physicality of pain?" (Mukherjee 2015a: 482). Once the temptations of such "abstract" commitment have been brutally driven out of him in an utterly salacious torture sequence culminating in the flaying of his upper thigh in the shape of a hammer and sickle, he experiences "a gratuitous vision, no longer yoked to the dry words of propaganda...a vision of the future" in which the figurative seeds he has sown will have grown into a sanctuary forest, providing cover and sustenance for all who need them.

At precisely this moment of "proleptic hopefulness" (Mukherjee 2015a: 489), he thinks—just as Winston does—of his mother and contemplates her warning against spurning the material blessings of Lakshmi and the possibility of begging her forgiveness before he is shot in the back of the head at the forest's edge, and his narrative comes to an abrupt end in the circular fulfillment of both his mother's earlier premonition and the conclusion promised to Winston but deferred (or metaphorized) in Orwell's own narrative: "Everything is cured sooner or later. In the end we shall shoot you" (1961: 274). Wegner argues that Winston's "utter abnegation at O'Brien's hands is also a form a 'salvation'" in which he is "redeemed once and for all from the temptations of political power" (2002: 227). Here, however, the malign consequences of Supratik's own "thwarted efforts to overcome the terrible reality of his present—a failure shared, without exception, by every one of Orwell's fictional protagonists" and a direct "link between Gissing's naturalist fictions and Orwell's work"—outlive the doomed revolutionary and continue to harry the reader's present with a politically motivated, violent *ressentiment* against which the reader is encouraged to remain vigilant (Wegner 2002: 227).

The primacy of self in Mukherjee's novel is thus aligned with a general suspicion of or intolerance toward the political, and it is

> because any form of overt political action ultimately degenerates into an expression of an instrumental will-to-power. The only way the intellectual can avoid such a danger is by maintaining his autonomy from any political group formation. Ironically, then, Winston Smith's utter abnegation at O'Brien's hands is also a form of 'salvation': in being rendered completely powerless, Winston Smith is redeemed once and for all from the temptations of political power" (2002: 227).

here that we must seek the novel's *authentic ressentiment*. While Majumdar observes that Mukherjee "maintains equal ironic distance from oppressors like the capitalist Ghoshes and from the struggles of their oppressed workers," this posture of objectivity is, she finds, fully complicit with neoliberalism in its "fundamental ideological premise that there cannot be an alternative to the present order" (2021: 130). Of the novel's unsparingly bleak vision, Majumdar further observes that if it were simply "confined to comprehensive social and moral wretchedness, completely lacking in hopeful glimmers, it would qualify as a powerful dystopia" (2021: 127). A more apt generic term for such an uncompromising assault on social possibility, as suggested above, however, is the *anti-utopia*, which, as Wegner suggests, cannot sustain its attitude of pure negation without the undergirding of an implicit alternative.

Thus, as Majumdar rightly claims, Mukherjee "does invest in a specific kind of possibility" that she locates in "a vision of individual success, untainted by either interpersonal or social dynamics," the exemplary case for which is Sona, the young math prodigy whose exceptional talents earn him a scholarship to Stanford University and, as we learn in the novel's first epilogue, the Fields Medal (2021: 128). In tendentious contrast to Supratik, Sona is "dissociated from the real world" and invested purely in isolated mathematical abstraction: "There is an innocence about him which the world has not been able to touch" (Mukherjee 2015a: 498). For Majumdar, the novel's celebration of Sona's singular success, in providing a stark counterpoint to the fate of Supratik as well as to the lethal legacy of his revolutionary misdeeds as depicted in the second epilogue, "amounts to a straightforward approval of neoliberal logic" (2021: 129).

The novel's privileging of the private domain of affect over the egotistical world of political action should also be seen in this light, such that the conservative utopian horizon evoked alongside the novel's anti-utopian assault on the public/political is the reigning order of neoliberalism, which upholds the entrepreneurial prerogatives of the individual as its highest ideal, one suggested on the inscription of the Fields Medal itself: "Then he reads again, '*Transire suum pectus mundoque potiri.*' To rise above oneself. That will do. That is enough" (Mukherjee 2015a: 499).

As David Harvey reminds us, however, neoliberalism names not only an economic but also a *political* project undertaken by the global corporate capitalist class when its existence came under direct threat during the late 1960s and early 1970s. Responding to a welter of anti-imperialist uprisings in the Third World as well as to the resurgence of Leftist movements in Western Europe and even the emergence of a Democratic Congress in the United States that, as Harvey has it, was "radical in intent," neoliberalism solidified a counterrevolutionary political strategy that was defined in part by the outward eschewal of the practice of politics as such (Harvey 2016: n.p.). This, then, is the true *ressentiment* of Mukherjee's naturalist anti-utopia: the counterrevolutionary delegitimating of politics and the social itself in an internationally best-selling "socially symbolic act."

That Mukherjee's message of counterrevolutionary alarm is received by his intended readership is evidenced not only by the accolades heaped generously upon the novel in the West but also by the aforementioned "Neel Mukherjee's Top 10 Books About Revolutionaries," which, appearing subsequently in *The Guardian* in 2015, might also serve as a kind of coda to *The Lives of Others*. Mukherjee's selections share what he calls a "scepticism – and, in the case of V.S. Naipaul, open contempt – towards any movement for progressive change." It thus comes as no surprise to see Naipaul's *Guerrillas* listed in passing here, though Mukherjee ultimately selects the author's late novel *Magic Seeds* (2004) due to the fact that its protagonist, "like Supratik in my novel, joins a Naxalite/Maoist guerrilla group in a forest in India;" however, as he writes, "it's the late 1970s and the fraying of the movement and its inevitable descent into compulsive violence, its ideals corrupted and debased, is what interests Naipaul" and, we can surmise from his list, Mukherjee as well.

Indeed, he defines his sole criterion of selection as follows:

> A common theme in most of these books is how revolutionary action is foredoomed to failure and revolutionaries are either deluded, or wrong, or both; at worst, they are psychopaths and criminals. Idealism seems to be vitiated the moment it is translated into (usually misguided) action. (Mukherjee 2015b: n.p.)

In addition to Naipaul's novel, Mukherjee selects Dostoevsky's *The Possessed*, which he justly calls a "scathing denunciation of idealistic, utopian revolutions;" Turgenev's novel of Populist serf uprising *Virgin Soil*, which extends sympathy to its revolutionary "*malgré lui*" largely because he "never really believes in the movement" and is appropriately regretful "when disaster ensues from his political action, as he has always known it would;" and Conrad's *The Secret Agent*, which "asks deep questions about the morality of terrorism, and how revolutionary ideals and idealism are always already compromised."

Other entries include Nadine Gordimer's *Burger's Daughter*, which questions the role and responsibility of white Afrikaner anti-apartheid activists; Leonardo Sciascia's *The Moro Affair*, offered with the caveat that there are "no revolutionaries in this book, only terrorists;" Doris Lessing's *The Good Terrorist*, which asks, "Why did so many of the ultra-left movements of the Sixties and Seventies turn to terrorism?"; and the graphic novel *Sally Heathcote, Suffragette* by Mary Talbot, Kate Charlesworth, and Bryan Talbot. Regarding Manini Chatterjee's novel of the much-neglected chapter of Indian anti-colonial resistance, *Do and Die: The Chittagong Uprising, 1930-34*, Mukherjee finds the account of the revolt most notably "affecting because it failed." The only novel on his list that offers an unqualifiedly sympathetic account of revolutionary opposition from below is Mahasweta Devi's *Aranyer Adhikar*, a fictional retelling of the nineteenth-century anti-colonial guerrilla campaign led by tribal religious leader Birsa Munda, which Mukherjee describes as "rousing and ultimately tragic" (Mukherjee 2015b: n.p.).

The latter is a particularly curious choice for Mukherjee given that Devi is also author of two of the most powerfully affecting fictional portrayals of the Naxalite movement, *Mother of 1084* and the novelette *Operation?—Bashai Tudu* (not to mention the powerfully defiant short story "Draupadi"). In fact, each of these narratives provides a diametrical counterpoint to the formal and ideological bent of *The Lives of Others*. Where the latter offers an expansive multi-generational family saga that ultimately capitulates before what Patrick Wright calls the "morbidity of heritage" (qtd. in Gilroy 2006: 100) and the more urgent imperative of counterrevolution, the former radically restrict their temporal horizons to a single day in which a quest for knowledge regarding a lost revolutionary brings, as Sourit Bhattacharya writes, "the revolutionary cause into the heart of the domestic sphere" and "powerfully weds the personal with the political in the revolutionary imagination" (2020: 114).

Mukherjee's novel does precisely the opposite in prizing the corrupt political away from the authentic, personal sphere. Devi's novels grapple with and ultimately uphold the still-vital legacy (the universalizing truth) of the Naxalite movement in the questing protagonists themselves rather than linger obscenely, as Mukherjee's novel does, over the mortification of the Naxalite body—irredeemable victim of a foolhardy idealism. Thus, while Mukherjee's narrative tracts ineluctably toward its fatally predetermined, consummating expurgation, Devi's is rather characterized by what Bhattacharya calls the defiant "non-death of the insurgent," whose tragic demise refuses to become an object lesson for counterrevolutionary acquiescence and whose cause endures principally in *and for* the living (2020: 131).

There are any number of other novelistic accounts of revolution that one might consider here, but Devi's will suffice to reveal the anti-utopian ideological agenda animating Mukherjee's own "novel of the people." As Jameson observes in his reflection on the emergence of naturalism as a crisis response to revolutionary insurgency, the bourgeois realist writers, whom he calls "'shepherds of Being' of a very special, ideological type" are thereby compelled into a "repudiation of revolutionary change and an ultimate stake in the status quo" such that they then deploy in their experimental fictions

> a host of containment strategies, which seek to fold everything which is not-being, desire, hope, and transformational praxis, back into the status of nature; these impulses toward the future and toward radical change must systematically be reified, transformed into 'feelings' and psychological attributes [...]. (Jameson 1981: 193)

Conversely, he notes "for the conscious political revolutionary, he or she must be the object of a very special kind of naturalizing operation" of the sort that we find applied to Supratik in *The Lives of Others* (Jameson 1981: 193–194). In this special case, "the protagonist in question will be the one who is alienated in a very special way, namely by *déclassement* and by that form of class treason which is fascination with or aspiration to the status of those on the other side of the class line," which is precisely Supratik's fatal misstep (1981: 195).

Furthermore, Mukherjee's insistence on the primacy of the authentically internal/psychological rather than the abstractly and egotistically material thus neatly fulfills the function of the ideologeme that Jameson finds most prevalent in the naturalist novel: *ressentiment*, which seeks "to account in a 'psychological' and nonmaterialistic sense for the destructive envy the have-nots feel for the haves and thus account for the otherwise inexplicable fact of a popular mass uprising" (1981: 201). In outflanking the utopian desire of transformational non-being, the naturalist thwarting or renunciation of desire makes it appear "as though the whole system of success and failure has been determined from the outset by a narrative strategy which may thus be read as something like the final form of *ressentiment* itself" (Jameson 1981: 205). The envy attributed to the desiring class (as well as to the class traitor) is "dialectically transformed" into a revelation of the very class consciousness that it was conceived to suppress and deny (Jameson 1981: 205). Here, then, we discern not only the naturalist genealogy of Mukherjee's novel but also the distinctive abnegation that is particular to the anti-utopia.

Tragedy, Subtractive Nihilism, and Anti-utopia in *The Children of Sisyphus*

'Negation negates itself,' he used to murmur to himself whenever he completed reading the sonnet, never failing to revel in the esoteric absurdity of his own paradox. Yet he was sure that in the wisdom of what was communicated, whatever it was, there was a kind of tragedy. Perhaps he should have sought no further. All that was being expressed was that to be wise is to be tragic. To perceive the truth of existence is to perceive an unutterable tragedy.

'Speak not of Heaven, Brother Ezekiel, but of hell; the thought of eternal bliss is a thousand times more frightening than all the brimstone you can give me.'
—Orlando Patterson, *The Children of Sisyphus* (1968: 74, 210)

If *The Lives of Others* demonstrates one facet of anti-utopianism in the repudiation of the desire for revolutionary transformation and the concomitant naturalization of the status quo, Orlando Patterson's *The Children of Sisyphus* reveals another visage altogether. This aspect is born of what Kumar calls a "frustrated and thwarted utopianism" in which the desperately sought social alternative of decolonization has been both realized and simultaneously evacuated of its surplus hope content, leaving the tragically marginalized inhabitants of the postcolonial state tragically bereft (Kumar 1984: 104).

Invocations of the postcolonial tragic have become *de rigueur* since David Scott's highly influential discussion of narrative emplotment in his *Conscripts of Modernity*. Scott argues that anticolonialism's political and moral impetus structured a particular kind of narrative relation between past, present, and future, one predicated on and governed by the "distinctive story-potential" of the romantic plot (Scott 2004: 7). Anticolonial romance narratives thus tend to be triumphal "narratives of overcoming, often narratives of vindication" and "have largely depended upon a certain (utopian) horizon toward which the emancipationist history is imagined to be moving" (Scott 2004: 8). The anticolonial romance corresponds to the cultural period that we have identified with "fighting phase" realism.

Yet, Scott writes more recently that "in the wake of the global historico-political and cognitive shifts" of the decades following formal independence, the utopianism of the romantic plot is no longer commensurate with the demands of the present and should be replaced by a critically applied tragic mode of emplotment (2004: 799). Within the parameters of the tragic, the anticipated futures of anticolonialism have been consigned to the past, while the postcolonial present is apprehended as a time "marked by irreversible transformation" and "the exhaustion or dead end of the old emancipationist stories (nationalist ones, socialist ones)" (Scott 2014: 806). Thus, as Scott further observes,

> In the tragic we are given a picture of human undertakings that end in irreparable misery and colossal suffering, not because this is all that human life amounts to but because there is a keen moral insight concerning our limits and our excellences to be had in starting off with the recognition that well-intended human purposes often have unintended consequences, are never invulnerable to chance, and are sometimes undermined by forces (from within or without) over which we have little conscious control. (2014: 800)

He recommends Patterson's *The Children of Sisyphus* as an exemplary expression of this tragic postcolonial vision, which "raises fundamental questions about the narrative of progressive temporality that undergirds and drives" the imperatives of anticolonial nationalism and its lasting relevance for postcolonial exigencies (Scott 2014: 802). While Scott's insight regarding the hermeneutic value of postcolonial tragic emplotment offers an immensely useful and enabling historicizing intervention (prompting the crucial question, "What if the futures anticipated by the past are now themselves a part of the past?" [2014: 799]), the Romantic/Tragic binary itself ultimately rests on an aesthetic rationale that nevertheless risks a simplifying and undialectical abridgement of the locally and globally striated class interests at work in the cultures of both anti-colonial nationalism and its postcolonial successors. Simply put, for what class position or class fragment is the postcolonial moment tragic, and to what extent does the form's pivotal anagnorisis—as a moment of critically enlarged consciousness—represent a meaningful deviation from the romantic *Weltanschauung* that precedes it?

If the epic "is tasked with the conjuration of a Hegelian 'Spirit of the People' as a 'history of the winners,'" as Samuel Durrant puts it, the tragic modality conversely "enables a traumatized body of people to survive the 'phenomenal erosion' of time that constitutes the precipitate experience of colonization" (2012: 95–96). Thus, Durrant argues, Chinua Achebe's *Things Fall Apart* presents, on the cusp of Nigerian independence, a tragically foredoomed hero "whose actions will turn out not to have been actions at all, in the active, history-changing sense, but rather modes of suffering, ways of fulfilling his—and his people's—tragic destiny, ways of fulfilling a certain prophecy" (2012: 96). However, in Durrant's reading, Achebe's tragic capitulation to fate—as both a critical and symptomatic *"reenactment* of postcolonial modernity"— also nevertheless projects "the sublime image both of his people's alienation and of their redemption" in its foreclosure of an oppositional return to tradition (Durrant 2012: 113).

Such ambiguity likewise informs Scott's tragic reading of *The Children of Sisyphus*, in which an apparent attitude of pessimistic resignation is simultaneously a generative site. Here, the aims and limits of national sovereignty and cultural identity are scrutinized by way of a tragic staging of constrained agency against the forces of insuperable ruination and grief and an absolute temporality of pitiless immanence. But Durrant's deployment of the tragic as a "[l]oser's epic" is instructive for its invocation of "the people" and its sense of communal destiny (2012: 96). If, as Scott puts it, the postcolonial state and its inhabitants are modernity's conscripts, then the tragic mode offers a means not to transcend the enfeebling circumstances of the present but to reimagine and redefine the categories and conceptual schemas (such as "the people") used to enlist them. In this sense, the tragic is for Scott (who invokes Lucien Goldmann[13]) paradoxically *utopian* in the sense that it manifests "a provisional *wager* we make with hope against despair" (2014: 806).

Tragedy and the Shadow of Fate

However, in addition to countenancing the limitations of cultural nationalism's teleological histories, Scott's tragic model also contravenes, as suggested above, more radical forms of alterior agency. He describes the world of Patterson's novel, for example, as

---

[13] As Jameson recently observes, however, Goldmann's own theorization of the tragic is motivated less by utopian aspiration than class *ressentiment*: "The study was pathbreaking insofar as Goldmann took as his category of analysis not class but a class fraction: and he linked the Jansenist 'structure of feeling' (a concept of Raymond Williams's from much the same period) to the failure of this class fraction to achieve social dominance" (2022: 565). What's more, Jameson further suggests that "today we might also perhaps want to understand his work as an anticipation of the role of melancholy in affect theory" (2022: 565), all formal features that I read here as evidence of the naturalist aesthetic and the anti-utopian impulse.

> a structure of anomic, Sisyphean repetition, a world of endemic conflict in which the meagerness of meaning and the poverty of economic resources strip social and psychological life down to the real and metaphoric bone and so leave human action especially exposed to the vagaries of irreversible contingency and vulnerable to the unpredictable machinations of moral evil. In such a world it is scarcely possible not to choose badly, no matter what the context of choice. (Scott 2014: 806)

For this originary milieu of Hobbesian asociality—what Patterson famously calls "natal alienation"—or inherited social derangement, Scott observes that "neither the liberal-nationalist narrative of social cohesion nor the revolutionary narrative of class emancipation captures adequately the paradoxes of promise and betrayal, expectation and dissolution, that distort the postcolonial nightmare world" within which Patterson's characters futilely strive for a quantum of dignity, if not an impossible liberation (Scott 2014: 806). The narrative of revolutionary class emancipation is then displaced by cultural and moral considerations on one hand and absurdist resignation on the other. This elision is consistent in Patterson's thought as both a fiction writer and a sociologist, and it perhaps accounts for the broad appeal of Patterson's thought for contemporary Afropessimist as well as both white liberal and conservative reactions.

In a lengthy and characteristically astringent review of Patterson's *Rituals of Blood: Consequences of Slavery in Two American Centuries* (1998), Martin Kilson goes so far as to describe the eminent sociologist's work as "cannon fodder for white conservatives" and castigates what he describes as "Patterson's metamorphosis from a black Marxist intellectual of Caribbean background to the ranks of black conservative intellectuals" (Kilson 2001: 81). Citing E. Franklin Frazier's *The Negro Family in the United States* (1939) as a more satisfactorily materialist accounting of African-American social development, Kilson argues that African-American social evolution "can only be seriously probed one way, *namely through contextual interaction with the dominant processes of a racist American capitalist society*" (2001: 84).

More measured than Kilson's provocation that Patterson's work expresses "deep and twisted black-rejectionist feelings, near-Negrophobic tendencies" that are "packaged in a black-friendly veneer" is Edward Kamau Brathwaite's nevertheless pointed appraisal of Patterson's defining earlier work, *The Sociology of Slavery* (1967), the very title of which, Brathwaite contends, presents its reader with a "challenging generalization" (1968: 331). Indeed, Brathwaite locates the primary flaw of Patterson's work in the weakness of its historicism relative to the stridency of its social-scientific theoretical framework: "torn between his history and his sociology," Brathwaite writes, Patterson "is forced to simplify his history, giving it a static quality" (1968: 332). Most troubling for Brathwaite is the fact that Patterson's governing precept of a "disintegrated, debased society" actively distorts and limits any capacity to countenance resistance:

> In fact, by concentrating exclusively on the 'Quashie personality trait' (the submissive/trickster type of slave), Dr. Patterson is unable, when he comes to it, to provide a convincing explanation of the high frequency of slave rebellions in Jamaica. 'The ultimate answer to the question. . . lies—strictly speaking—outside the framework of the sociologist. . .' (p.260). And thus, Camus's *The Rebel* is allowed to have the final word. (Brathwaite 1968: 337)

Brathwaite's invocation of Camus is telling and of obvious significance for a reading of *The Children of Sisyphus*. Indeed, the eminent existentialist's rejection of radical hope casts a long shadow over Patterson's own depictions of social struggle and its limits, a point to which I want shortly to return.

While Scott's account of Patterson's "tragic vision" reveals the exhaustion of predominately emancipatory narratives, especially those of bourgeois nationalism, Eric Pieto's reading of the novel's representation of urbanism in the light of Kingston slum clearances offers a complimentary, yet distinctive approach. Pieto notes that Patterson emphasizes "the gravitational pull of the Dungle, understood as a place that allows no one to escape"—save the young Rosetta, whose educational opportunity can be redeemed only through renunciation of her own family, race, class, and culture. He finds that the novel's unrelenting disillusionment with given emancipatory/utopian horizons is, in fact, a rejection of consolatory escapist fantasy and a call for novel forms of resistance:

> In this light, Patterson's novel would have to be read not as a tragic, fatalistic or resigned statement, but as a call to stand and fight—where one is [...]. The real mistake made by the characters in Patterson's novel, then, would be to believe that the only way to transcend their degraded condition was to move on to a better place, whether an idyllic past, an idealized motherland, salvation in the afterlife, or a more desirable neighborhood. (Pieto 2016: 55)

Similarly, Sherie Marie-Harrison claims that the novel's much-criticized "pessimism conveys both a lived contemporary reality and the futility of buying into the national narrative of success via self-sufficiency and self-determination" at the same time that its "engagement with the more fatalistic facets of national self-determination tells us about the relationship between localized and global economic policy" (2017: 92).

Absurdism, Totality, and Anti-utopianism

But such gestures to fatalism and disavowals of the utopian must also be read, as Brathwaite's comment suggests, alongside Patterson's prominently acknowledged chief intertext, Albert Camus's 1942 essay *Le mythe de Sisyphe*, in which the French-Algerian philosopher asserts the imperative of hopelessness in a fundamentally absurd existence. As he puts it in "Summer in Algiers," "[c]ontrary to popular belief, hope equals resignation. And to live is not to resign oneself" (Camus 1970: 80). The problem of the absurd, which is located neither in the subject nor in the objective world a priori, arises only when one's passion for totalizing meaning, what Camus describes as the "nostalgia for unity, that appetite for the absolute," is forced to reckon with the natural "impossibility of reducing this world to a rational and reasonable principle" (1955: n.p.). This insistence on the ineluctably absurd and the preeminence of an unknowable, unalterable, and irrational nature lies at the heart of Camus's break from the Algerian Communist Party and his bitter alienation from his former friend and comrade Jean Paul Sartre in the pages of *Les Temps modernes*.

If, for the former, meaninglessness is the axiomatic horizon of being, which one must choose either to accept or not, for the latter, meaning is located in the process and product of strenuous human intervention continuous with the living dialectic of history. That is, as Sartre memorably puts it *pace* Hegel, "Reason is neither a bone nor an accident" (2004: 30). Camus's definitive statement in this regard is his 1951 treatise *The Rebel* in which he extends the absurdist paradigm elaborated in *The Myth of Sisyphus* to the problematic of political revolt. Appalled by the violence of the Bolshevik Revolution and its aftermath, Camus advocated what amounts to a reformist anarcho-syndicalism underpinned by a liberal philosophy of, as he put it, "live and let live" predicated on the refusal of "absolute justice"—the Robespierrean excesses of which, in suppressing natural contradiction, thereby necessitate the abrogation of human freedom (Camus 1962: 219, 252). Thus, he writes, "[t]he slave starts by begging for justice and ends by wanting to wear a crown. He too wants to dominate" (Camus 1962: 32). Camus's view is fundamentally anti-utopian, as he makes explicit in *The Rebel*: "Utopias have almost always been coercive and authoritarian. Marx, in so far as he is a Utopian, does not differ from his frightening predecessors, and one part of his teaching more than justifies his successors" (1962: 176).[14]

The affinities of Camusian absurdism with literary naturalism have only scarcely been acknowledged. J.H. Matthews proposes Edmond de Goncourt's *La fille Élisa* and Zola's *L'Assommoir*, both published in 1877, as key influences on Camus's *L'Étranger* (1942) (Matthews 1968: 241), while Joyce Hamilton Rochat has identified the warm stream of "romantic-naturalism" (as distinct from the cool stream of Zolian "realistic-naturalism") in Camus's aesthetic and philosophical project (Rochat 1971: 14). Said famously reproves Camus, whom he significantly compares to the anti-utopian Orwell (who, again, is deeply influenced by Gissing), not only for the remotely objective reportorial style often associated with naturalism but also for what (sharpening Conor Cruise O'Brien's original insight) he terms Camus's *unconscious colonialism* (Said 1993: 173):

> Like Orwell's work and status in England, Camus's plain style and unadorned reporting of social situations conceal rivetingly complex contradictions, contradictions unresolvable by rendering, as critics have done, his feelings of loyalty to French Algeria as a parable of the human condition. (1993: 185)

What interests me here, however, beyond the demonstrated sequence of literary/ideological influence (Goncourt and Zola > Gissing and Orwell > Camus > Patterson) is Patterson's comparable anxiety over the revolutionary potential of the masses and the suggestion of individualized, affective accommodations to the present as preferable to militant, collective resistance from below. In Patterson's estimation, as in Orwell's, the masses lack a proper political consciousness and are reduced to obliviously suffering and therefore safely pitiable bodies.

---

[14] He further writes that "every kind of socialism is Utopian, most of all scientific socialism. Utopia replaces God by the future. Then it proceeds to identify the future with ethics; the only values are those which serve this particular future. For that reason Utopias have almost always been coercive and authoritarian. Marx, in so far as he is a Utopian, does not differ from his frightening predecessors and one part of the teaching more than justifies his successors" (Camus 1976: 176).

Active Nihilism

Scott asserts that the historical rupture of decolonization might have presented a moment of conflict between opposed forces and the fitful emergence of a new structure of feeling in which Camus could perceive the conditions for the reemergence of the tragic (2014: 801). One must also note that while Camus denounced the imperialist violence of the French, he notoriously opposed the Algerian struggle for independence and, indeed, revolutionary resistance as such. Conversely, while Sartre's commitment to revolutionary possibility led him to a much-criticized defense of both the Soviet purges and the tactical violence of terrorism, it also bolstered a passionate support for anticolonial resistance, as can be found in his endorsement of the FLN and culminating in his incendiary 1961 preface to Fanon's *The Wretched of the Earth*, published only three years before *The Children of Sisyphus*.

In an insightful application of Badiou's "politics of conflict" to the historical scene of Jamaican resistance from the Morant Bay Revolt to the present, Colin Wright suggests that the seemingly intractable terms of the Camus/Sartre binary define an antinomy that, in its very irresolvability, paradoxically provides the most useful resource for renewed anti-imperialist praxis. Citing Slavoj Žižek's useful distinction between *subjective*, *objective*, and *symbolic* forms of violence, Wright argues that while Camus gives exclusive priority to "epiphenomenal" expressions of subjective violence (as in a riot or coup), Žižek follows Sartre in revealing forms of oppression encoded in sanctioned forms of representation and the opaque, putatively neutral structures of the social status quo (Wright 2013: 309).

The pervasive violence of the latter is "so thoroughly embedded in the political and economic institutions of everyday life that it is not merely invisible to us, but is paradoxically experienced as the guarantor of stability, security, continuity" (Wright 2013: 309). However, for Wright, who also recognizes in Žižek's theory of objective violence a reflection of Sartre's own concept of the *practico-inert*, both thinkers might likewise err in excessively romanticizing revolutionary violence and creative destruction. Like Camus, then, they each overemphasize *subjective* violence, albeit from the opposite direction.

The Camus/Sartre opposition thus presents a false or forced choice between "politics" (implicitly defined in terms of Camusian liberalism) and "violence" (in terms of Sartrean terror). By way of Badiou's assertion that the relation between the two terms is neither that of exteriority ("the liberal logic of security, violence on the outside of politics") nor immanence ("the Jacobin logic of Terror, violence as homogenous with politics"), Wright suggests an alternative form of violence (Wright 2013: 313). In its "destruction of the old coordinates by which violence was defined and judged," this new violence displaces the "Statist localization of violence within a spectrum of legitimacy-illegitimacy" by which we may assess good and bad forms: that is, conservative or reactionary violence attached to the structural logic of the status quo and the "'good' violence of innovative praxis" (Wright 2013: 314).

Rejecting an undernuanced "old romance of creative destruction" (Wright 2013: 318) and individuated acts of violence committed against the body, this progressive violence must take on the form of a sustained social disruption that replaces both a terroristic nihilism and a "passive, or reactive, nihilism" with what Badiou calls an "active nihilism" (Badiou 2007: 65). This active form "attempts to hold onto the passion for the real without falling for the paroxysmal charms of terror" and opposes the parochial logic of merely reactionary negation with the detection of "minimal difference" and the positive substantiation of "the void." Importantly, the latter is not *nothing* but is rather the foundational exception, the uncounted or unnamed being that goes unacknowledged within the ontological calculus of the situation or status quo. Badiou writes that the aim of such subtraction, vis-à-vis the void, is

> to exhibit as a real point, not the destruction of reality, but minimal difference. To purify reality, not in order to annihilate it at its surface, but to subtract it from its apparent unity so as to detect within it the miniscule difference, the vanishing term that constitutes it. (2007: 65)

In Wright's reading, the radical culture of Rastafari has cultivated precisely this subtractive or active form of nihilism throughout its decades-long history: in its opposition to European fascism, its support for Third-World revolution, and not least in its principled counterpoise to both the forces of twentieth-century and neoliberal capital and the urban gang violence that has, since the 1950s, been both a consequence and a strategic pillar of the fierce contest for state power waged between the JLP and PNP (Wright 2013: 331). Indeed, Wright recognizes in the radical culture of Rastafari "a mode of militant fidelity to the black subject-body that emerged from [Paul] Bogle's peasant army at Morant Bay" (2013: 274). Explicitly rejecting the "'whacky cult' caricature" of the movement, he further writes,

> Far from an irrational millennial cult or a music-centered subculture, Rastafari is an extremely rich and sophisticated

response to slavery, colonialism, the class-race nexus in postcolonial Jamaica, and indeed the deeply racialised nature of today's economic, cultural and political globalization. (Wright 2013: 274)

In fact, Wright directly credits the millennialist cult caricature to "Kingston-based sociologists in the 1960s," for whom the movement was merely "a form of desperate escapism on the part of maladjusted youths from the ghettoes, not much different from turning to the bottle" (2013: 273). In a footnote identifying these sociologists, Wright cites—along with Vittorio Lanternari (who places Rastafari amidst a miscellany of other global nativist or prophetic religions oriented around messianic liberation[15])—Patterson's *The Children of Sisyphus* as a primary source for this disabling misrepresentation.

Indeed, Patterson's representation of Rastafari is especially striking in contrast with many of his contemporaries. George Lamming, for instance, observes in 1980 that "Rastafari has extended from a small and formerly undesirable cult into a dominant force which influences all levels of national life; and it has done so against formidable odds, political harassment and general condemnation." Apropos both Kilson's rebuke of Patterson and Wright's indication of Rastafari's militant black subject-body, Lamming further remarks, "The Rastafari has dramatised the question that has always been uncomfortable in Caribbean history, and the question is where you stand in relation to blackness" (1990: n.p.).

While Patterson's widely influential definition of slavery as "the permanent, violent domination of natally alienated and generally dishonored persons" displaces the conventional priority granted to slavery's materialist origins with those of cultural and discursive authority, it is in contrast to his great Caribbean intellectual contemporary, friend, and frequent interlocutor Walter Rodney that Patterson's elision of material history—and of historical agency—is made most glaringly evident. In the 1979 co-authored essay "Slavery and Underdevelopment," published less than one year prior to Rodney's assassination, the two thinkers present a starkly revealing contrast in their respective approaches to the structural complementarity of these phenomena.

For Rodney, priority is given to the historical circumstances of underdevelopment, for which slavery serves as both an agent and an effect:

---

[15] See Lanternari, Vittorio 1963. *The Religions of the Oppressed: A Study of Modern Messianic Cults* (New York: Knopf).

Slavery—as institution, as epoch, as mode of production—acquires its significance in the formulation from an awareness of the implications of inequality and dependence in the modern world. Failure to grasp the multiple manifestations of underdevelopment as a contemporary phenomenon inevitably leads to an obscuring of the historical issues. (Rodney and Patterson 1979: 275)

To Rodney's historical materialist account, which locates the rationale for the trans-Atlantic slave trade in Western capitalist structural necessity, Patterson counters with "an inclination to take a rather broader view of underdevelopment, and not to identify it necessarily with what Wallerstein calls the modern world system, or with capitalism" (Rodney and Patterson 1979: 287). Thus, he writes of slavery, in Foucauldian terms, that "fundamentally it is not an economic institution" but is instead "a relation of power, which immediately debases" (Rodney and Patterson 1979: 288). Therefore, he observes, "the slave order of power can exist within the context of many different kinds of mode of production" (Rodney and Patterson 1979: 289).

For instance, in addition to indicating evidence of underdevelopment in pre-capitalist Sudan and Sahel, Patterson notes that Islamic imperialism and other cultures of slavery prior to the arrival of Europeans may even have compromised resistance to the latter.[16] Therefore, he avers, underdevelopment, like slavery, "is not exclusively related to capitalism" but may be rooted in oppressive social structures that antedate it (Rodney and Patterson 1979: 287). This leads Patterson to a minimizing of the role of capitalism in his claim that the socially "disintegrative" effects of slavery as a deracinating, dishonoring, and disempowering cultural institution have contributed to what he observes to be a contemporary "incapacity to organise, and an unwillingness to organise on a community level" that have considerable implications for underdevelopment (Rodney and Patterson 1979: 291). Such conditioned asociality—as the *cultural* legacy of the historically displaced social institution of slavery—is therefore to blame, Patterson concludes, for Jamaica's postcolonial political and economic failures:

---

[16] Patterson's discussion of Islam and anti-black racism is particularly inconsistent in *Slavery and Social Death* and may also be seen as demonstrating the anti-Arab influence of Camus, who feared what he characterized as the "Arab imperialism" of the Algerian struggle. Sartre, too, it must be remembered, infamously refused to advocate the anti-colonial cause of Palestinians. See also Bashir, Haroon 2019. "Black Excellence and the Curse of Ham: Debating Race and Slavery in the Islamic Tradition," *ReOrient* 5.1: 92–116.

> Hence the failure of the Manley government's co-operative policy in Jamaica. Hence the failure of urban policies which assume that the urban working class will organise on a co-ordinated basis. Hence the Rastafarian ideology, which, in spite of the fact that it constitutes in some ways an ancient form of class consciousness, is nonetheless external in its orientation—as external, as removed and, ultimately, as non-integrative as is the bourgeois orientation to Europe and North America. (Rodney and Patterson 1979: 292)

It is indeed difficult not to perceive in such "broad view" conclusions shades of the victim-blaming that Kilson alleges above. Moreover, it is in view of such ambivalent invocations of "the people" as both a "telluric source of strength" and an irrational figure of anomic, archaic threat that what Scott, Pieto, and Harrison laud as the novel's critique of nationalism and the state should be considered.

For the historical materialist Rodney, Rastafari is conversely "a profound response to the racial repression of capitalism" and the latter's specifically transformative imperial scaffolding. He traces the former's roots not only to Garveyism but also (like Wright) to the reaction against Italy's fascist invasion of Abyssinia in 1935, the 1938 Jamaican labor uprising, support for Kenya's 1953 Mau Mau Rebellion, and the wave of urbanization brought on by the Jamaican rural population's displacement at the hands of U.S.-owned mining companies in the scramble for the island's rich bauxite deposits (qtd. in Campbell 2007: 2). Thus, for Rodney, Rastafari is in no way, as it is for Patterson, a superannuated curiosity of ancient class consciousness but is instead astutely and imperatively contemporary; furthermore, the global orientation that Patterson scorns as a political weakness is, in Rodney's view, further evidence of the movement's conscious rejection of bourgeois nationalism's chauvinist myopia for the expansive orientation of a principled internationalism. That Patterson identifies the latter internationalism with that of a global capitalist class is a telling elision insomuch as it rests upon a cultural nationalism that his novel otherwise seems to cast into doubt.

In this juxtaposition with Rodney, then, Patterson's contrary apprehension of material history and Rastafari reveal the particular lineaments of a thwarted bourgeois nationalist utopianism—both as it is expressed in *The Children of Sisyphus* and as it evolves over the course of his intellectual career—such that we can agree simultaneously with critics of this novel's pitiless fatalism and with those who commend the book's generative indication of historical limits or, more ambiguously, constrained social possibility. Despite its representation of the Rastas as naïve millenarians—a portrayal that in fact owes its popularity to the famous 1960 *Report on the Rastafarian Movement in Kingston*[17]—the novel also credits them with perspicacious insight into the passage to neo-imperialist or economically and culturally leveraged forms of domination.

Ambition, Masochism, and Other Original Sins

Brother Solomon's assertion that they are now bound by "a different kind of slavery, a more subtle kind" is exemplary of the novel's registration of this transformed imperial sovereignty:

> So now him whip is poverty and his claim to superior culture and the Slave Driver is the dirty black lackeys who lap up his myths and the Slave Master is the filthy white capitalists from abroad. Development! Economic development, that is the new Sermon on the Mount, Brother. (Patterson 2012: 60–61)

Later, in his introduction to the university student come to express solidarity with the Rastas, whom the narrator repeatedly and unironically calls "cultists," Brother Solomon remarks that student support "was largely futile since they had to depend on the middle and upper classes" and that the "farce of independence," the student's proposed subject, had already been revealed to the Rastas "through the unperverted scriptures of the Bible and the Holy Key, which they were able to interpret because of the divine influence of the holy weed" (Patterson 2012: 125). When the student passionately inveighs against mental slavery, the "pathetic self-hate and subservience to English culture," and "the crafty myths of multiracial harmony and democracy" as "the true heritage of colonialism," however, he is hailed by the congregation, who declare him "[a]nother Solomon" and a true "descendent of Negus" (Patterson 2012: 125–126).

Immediately following this acknowledgment of economic and cultural subordination, however, is a hortatory "divine injunction" to patience and

---

[17] Commissioned by University of the West Indies Vice Chancellor Sir Arthur Lewis and authored by Rex Nettleford, Roy Augier, and M.G. Smith, the report considerably improved relations between the Rastas and the wider community. However, it also certified "popular misconceptions on ganja; centralised the personality of Haile Selassie, spoke of the group fantasy or millenarian cultism, distorted the history of the movement and in the end warned the State about the potential of links between the Rastafari and Marxists" (Campbell 2007: 105).

a repeated invocation of what emerges as the novel's primary motif of original sin. Thus, we are told, "It was the sin of impatience on the part of their forefathers which had condemned them to Babylon" (Patterson 2012: 127). Solomon, in fact, opens the meeting with what appears to be an accustomed call and response: "'Brethren!' he screamed, 'why is I here? Why is we here?'" to which the congregation automatically replies, "'Cause we forefathers sin, Brother!'" (Patterson 2012: 121). In affirmation of this response, Solomon recites Lamentations 5:7: "Our fathers have sinned and are not: and we have borne their iniquities" (Patterson 2012: 122). The penalty for this primordial transgression, the crowd rehearses in unison, is "Slavery! Slavery to the white man" (Patterson 2012: 122). Thus, what might appear a critically cognizant recognition of the precipitate relation between objective material history, slavery, and the legacies of empire is here rendered as primordial guilt. Viewed in light of Patterson's claim that antecedent practices of enslavement and native underdevelopment weakened African resistance to European imperialists, such invocations of sin and guilt shed light on the primary political contexts and ideological significations of the novel.

Patterson in fact returns to this link in his recent study of what he calls Jamaica's "paradoxical" and "tragic" postcolonial failings alongside the island's notable cultural achievements. He remarks that while Jamaica has produced a culture of pious religiosity, it is also "one of the most violent, reckless, and *downright sinful of nations*" (Patterson 2019: 2, emphasis added).[18] While the word "tragic" appears liberally throughout the study, its appearance here alongside the repetition of "reckless" is especially instructive: "The tragedy of radical change is that you can't implement it without able managers; but such reform, accompanied by reckless revolutionary rhetoric, is exactly what is guaranteed to send the bureaucrats fleeing" (Patterson 2019: 17). The tragic, the reckless, the violent, the radical, and the sinful are thus suggestively aligned in a way that helps to illuminate the confounding politics of Patterson's early fiction.

Dinah's metamorphic experience at the Revival Zion Baptist of God Church similarly turns on the presumption of original sin and evinces the

[18] In a brief reflection on his time working in Michael Manley's administration, Patterson harshly criticizes the Prime Minister's "compulsive womanizing," noting that "it was Manley's good fortune that the sexually promiscuous and conjugally challenged nation he ruled adored him for his carnal recklessness," the latter a descriptor that he repeatedly associates with political radicalism. In a further reading of the political through the lens of personal morality, Patterson claims that "Manley's relations with women were a vital clue to the nature of his political behavior" (2019: 318).

theme of sadomasochistic desire that undergirds the novel's presentation of the Jamaican suffering body. Upon her initial visit to the church, Dinah finds inscribed on a wooden sign the following: "THE WAGES OF SIN IS DEATH," upon which the letter 'K' has been mysteriously added between the 'S' and the 'I,' neatly replicating (or perhaps ambiguously critiquing) the association of race with hereditary iniquity (Patterson 2012: 158). The congregation remains uncertain whether the letter, "not written by human hand," is "a sign from God showing that he had not forgotten his poor black pickneys" or indicates a curse from Rutibel, "the fallen angel and Satan's closest assistant" (Patterson 2012: 158).

This moral ambivalence is key for the novel's presentation of tragic desire and the compulsion to *Até*, named for the Greek goddess of reckless folly, madness, and ruination and marking (in Lacan's influential reading of *Antigone*) the traumatic limit of the existing Symbolic order. Struck by the "sweet, gurgling, rushing agony" of the ecstatic congregation's hymns and the "excruciating release" that they provoke, Dinah is convinced by the charismatic Shepherd John to renounce the world and join his church as a Daughter of the First Order. She must first undergo a series of ritual ablutions and sanctifications beginning with a meditation on her sins. Despite her earnest efforts, however, she struggles to identify her sins, rejecting the notion that they might be as petty as prostitution or anger and hate: "Sin could not have come that easily and could not be thought away that easily. There must be something more powerful in its evil. There must be some tormenting pain in its extinction" (Patterson 2012: 168).

Falling into a rapturous faint at the next communion service, Dinah awakes to find herself lying on a bed before Shepherd John, who stands naked over her holding a tamarind switch. Commanded to disrobe, Dinah leans over the bed and receives the whipping with a penitent eagerness in which the guilt of sin manifests a longing for punishment as the source of erotic pleasure: "Yet as the pain rooted into her she felt a ticklish tinge in its quivering. No sooner had she felt it than it destroyed itself and filled her instead with a terrifying joy;" thus, "[l]ong after he had stopped beating the last remnants of evil spirits from her she was still relishing the warm, vibrating ecstasy of the flagellation" (Patterson 2012: 182). This is followed by their ritual lovemaking in which Dinah experiences both an enlargement of consciousness and an annihilation of self that "dissolved her into an infinite awareness of a passing self-destruction," and which she experiences as rapturous surrender (Patterson 2012: 183).

But this experience is actually the culmination of a series of episodes in which the narrative observes in Dinah a masochistic impulse toward de-subjectification and submission. In fact, Brother Joseph simply functions here as an iteration of Cyrus, who, upon Dinah's first encounter with him, "forced her to submission," and she finds that she is both revolted and "compelled to it" (Patterson 2012: 40). Later, during their ferocious lovemaking—which, as in Nkosi, is ambiguously indistinguishable from rape—she relishes the "delicious rebellion against her will" and the "intense negation of her being" that she feels in submitting to him as object of desire. Her fear, she realizes, is not so much a dread of her attacker as of her own ambivalently recalcitrant will: "She wanted to escape, and she wanted to escape only so that he could hold her back, so that she could hate him more and further terrify herself in her desire for him" (Patterson 2012: 42). So, while "he raped her, [and] he mauled her," Cyrus simultaneously "gushed her being with complete rapture" (Patterson 2012: 43).

Dinah's propensity to seek pleasure in abuse and degradation is not limited to acts of sexual submission, however. When she later obtains a job cleaning the home of the white, middle-class Mrs. Watkins, whose casual derision initially incites her to anger, she realizes that she is similarly compelled to submit to her racial and class authority:

> A strange, humiliating awareness came upon her. She tried to throw it off. It could not be true. But her very anxiety to deny its truth revealed how true it was. She was going to the kitchen because she wanted to go, because she had to go, because in her fear of Mrs. Watkins she felt a compelling urge to be near her and at her command. (Patterson 2012: 140)

The novel's surprising turn to themes of sado-masochistic violence, ritual punishment, and self-abasement, taken alongside the recurring theme of carnal sin, seem to follow Freud's own observation that the masochistic impulse is primarily born of an unconscious guilt, which, through the introjected parental authority of the superego—assuming "the dark power of Destiny"—compulsively seeks satisfaction through punishment, neglect, displeasure, and general self-abnegation (Freud 1961: 168). Dinah's narrative arc thus appears to repeat the theme of original sin established by Brother Solomon and to portend the foreclosure of narrative and social horizons in the Sisyphean return to the Dungle as both the inescapable locus of hereditary degradation and tragic acquiescence to fate as the consequence of failed individual responsibility.

As Kwame Dawes contends in his 2012 introduction to its republication, more than a "deterministic narrative of cruel circumstance,"

Patterson's novel is "committed to honouring his characters' potential for freedom even within such confines;" therefore, he writes, "If his characters fail, Patterson pays them the compliment of suggesting that they must take some responsibility for their failure; that the barriers to their declared goals are as much embedded in their mentalities as in external circumstance" (Dawes 2012: 17). The invocation of subjective responsibility and guilt to address a circumstance in which it is nevertheless, as Scott contends, "scarcely possible not to choose badly, no matter what the context of choice," marks the fundamental political and ethical impasse of the novel and, in its recourse to Camusian absurdism, begins to suggest the figure of its *authentic ressentiment* (Scott 2014: 806).

The "Horror of the Rabble"

In addition to Patterson's critique of an emergent neoliberalism's new imperial networks of opaque sovereignty, dramatized both in the speech of Brother Solomon and in the prostitute Mary's vicious encounter with a drunken U.S. sailor (who, after taunting her with "Yankee dollars," assaults her while humming "The Star Spangled Banner" [Patterson 2012: 152]), the novel also directs critical attention, as indicated by the scholars discussed above, to the limitations of cultural nationalism and its implication within state-sanctioned structures of inequality. Driven by an insatiable and troubling longing (the same compulsion that drove her to leave Cyrus and the Dungle and which might be usefully associated with the excessive, *inhuman* desire of Antigone), Dinah visits the unemployment office at the Ministry of Labour. The latter is housed in "the converted mansions of the old plantocracy," symbolizing the persistence of the old regime in the newly independent state as well as the latter's complicity with the emergent dispensation (Patterson 2012: 104). There, she finds herself part of a similarly restless crowd being addressed by a member of the People's Workers' Movement. The crowd falls into angry disagreement regarding the relative corruption of the PWM and its opposition, the Jamaica National Party, a thinly fictionalized reference to Jamaica's two dominant parties: the Jamaica Labour Party (JLP) and the People's National Movement (PNM).

A young man with a "pigeon chest" decorated with a brass badge distinguishing him as "a member of some league of the unemployed" imperiously shouts down the crowd, rebuking their myopic party loyalties. Indicating the spuriously utopian promises of both parties, he derisively ventriloquizes, "'Put me in power an' I will give you paradise.'

An' the only paradise I know is when I had to go an' haul me little sister from Paradise Street whore house" (Patterson 2012: 106). The PWM man counters that he comes bearing "tidings of great joy" from the "dearly beloved leader" and "prophet" Seymore Nathaniel Montesaviour, who intends to purge the Civil Service of the JNP supporters allegedly conspiring to deny employment to the masses (Patterson 2012: 106). The ludicrous, charismatic Montesaviour is likely a naked satire of Alexander Bustamante, though his affiliation with the PWM (which would seem to suggest the PNM) rather than the JNP (which more nearly recalls Bustamante's JLP) signifies a comprehensive critique of the two-party system itself as well as the postcolonial state. Indeed, the narrative might seem in this regard fully to endorse the materialist critique of cultural nationalism voiced by the impassioned youth:

> He poured his wrath upon the politicians, those merciless, selfish, opportunistic pack of tricksters; he reviled the middle classes, ambivalent, hypocritical, puritanical sons of bitches who licked the asses of the white upper class while they pretend to live in peace and harmony with them; he raged against the upper classes, the thieving merchants and their four hundred per cent profits, their bribery of the politicians, their contempt for the masses, whom they had fooled, through their control of the Press, into believing that they held power in their country under the treacherous farce of democracy. (Patterson 2012: 110)

However, the narrative expresses an equal, though more circumspect discomfort with (if not arch contempt for) the gathered masses themselves, whose excessive anger and politically incoherent demands threaten that system. Upon arrival, fearing that the agitated assembly that she finds there is on the verge of becoming a "mob" ("She sensed the tautness, the rising passion..."), Dinah momentarily "los[es] herself in the collectivity" before a large woman stamps on her toe, the disruptive pain breaking the dangerous enchantment and restoring her to a proper sense of discretely embodied selfhood (Patterson 2012: 104). Dinah recognizes above all "the anger and the longing, the hope and the despair" that animates the assembly's desperate, if politically aimless desire, but after listening to their internecine squabbling, she ultimately pities them and again "separated herself from the crowd" (Patterson 2012: 104, 108).

Her superior distance from the others, whom she now regards as "little pieces of garbage thrown aside by their worlds," she rationalizes with the curious notion that the complete poverty of the Dungle produced the much more desirable sense that "there was no poverty" (Patterson 2012: 108). Recalling the original sin of impatience to describe these "fallen" masses, many displaced from their rural homes and striving for better circumstances, the narrative expounds: "In the Dungle you could be easy, you could be patient, you could even be happy in your complete loss of hope," the pernicious nature of hope and the necessity of accepting hopelessness as the key to reconciling oneself with an imperfect and irrational world here reaffirmed as the novel's foremost theme and moral/political imperative (Patterson 2012: 108).

The association of an absurd search for totalizing meaning with the iniquitous nature of the mob is, in fact, established by the novel's twin epigraphs: the first, from Camus's *The Myth of Sisyphus*, concerns the absurdity of the "wild longing for clarity" in an "irrational" and "measureless" universe, while the second, taken from the book of *Isaiah*, invokes the prophet's vision of Babylonian exile as punishment for Israel's impiety and wickedness. Moreover, Dinah's metaphoric reference to garbage here directly recalls the belabored dissociation of the garbage-man Sammy in the novel's sordidly lyrical prelude. Navigating the crowded city and approaching the infernal space of the Dungle with their laden wagons of refuse, Sammy and his two co-workers are "like condemned men being hauled by the asses to a fate unknown, unthinkable;" they are "wretched and lost" and "[a]bandoned to a fate" that is no more believable for having been fully anticipated (Patterson 2012: 27).

"Embedded in their fate," bound to a path without history or future, "[s]eeming to pass, yet forever present," Sammy and his companions find most disconcerting of all the yearning and accusatory gazes of the ever-watchful poor: "They are too many, the faces of the city" and "every glance of their eyes a terrifying punch of humiliation" (Patterson 2012: 28). To protect himself from such direct encounter, Sammy attempts to cultivate an egoistic withdrawal by "grasping frantically upon every incident, every object that would mercifully hide him from the consciousness of the moment" and transmuting every threatening external stimulus into a sense memory to serve as "the vehicle to the past of his childhood" (Patterson 2012: 30). When these strategies of denial and narcissistic interiority prove ineffective, Sammy seeks consolation in absurdist disavowal:

> He had to forget. He would tell himself that he would not face them again. It was all a façade, anyway. All a meaningless, ghastly façade. And so it didn't matter what he convinced himself to believe. They weren't there. Those things. Those creatures of the Dungle.

No, they weren't human. If anyone told him they were human like himself he would tell them that they lied. Those eyes peering at him. Deep and dark red and hungry for what he carried. And for his own blood, too, he was sure. No, he had to forget. Only by forgetting could he possibly bear the burden of the moment [...]. (Patterson 2012: 30)

Taking the trail alone into the heart of the Dungle to the place where he disposes of food refuse, Sammy is revolted by the "ugly, inhuman," well-nigh Morlockian appearance of the slum dwellers and unaccountably disconcerted by the presence of Brother Solomon and the Rastafarian "cultists," whose dreadlocks and beards "always reminded him of a picture of Satan" (Patterson 2012: 34). As he approaches the open field where he will dump the food, he notes, too, that the "gathering herd had grown into a mob," and when he begins shoveling the fly-blown offal into the dirt, the crowd descends in a "mad, raging, screaming, laughing, angry, hungry scramble" (2012: 34). The indiscriminate "wolf-pack" of men and women, children and dogs fight fiercely with fists, claws, and teeth for the noxious, disinfectant-covered scraps, with which they hungrily flee back to their makeshift hovels (Patterson 2012: 35).

Afterwards, pausing at the entrance to the Dungle, Sammy casts his eyes back upon the tableau, which, now emptied of inhabitants, appears a "freakish, infernal beauty" in the way the towers of filth rise up in "frozen flight" from the Luciferian "menace of the sea" that ever threatens to engulf them in blue oblivion (Patterson 2012: 36). This "wide, vacuous, lingering, yet perpetual beauty" is disturbed only by a tenacious flock of crows, which the narrator's imaginative penchant for the diabolic here conceives as "fallen angels defiling what seemed no more capable of defilement, intensifying all the macabre beauty of the scene" (Patterson 2012: 37). Having thus metaphorized and aestheticized the site of human suffering as both a scene of otherworldly perdition and a postlapsarian *nature morte*, Sammy fixedly returns his gaze to the top of his donkey's head, intent on the reassuring circuit of the changeless present, and begins his journey homeward.

To the extent that the novel largely shares Sammy's paranoid mix of fear, pity, and contempt, the object of its express *ressentiment* is easily enough located in an anxiety over the haunting apparition of the underclasses, their foolhardy demands and compensatory fantasies of abstract liberation. Sammy's absurdist stoicism thus seems to oppose the impassioned attempts either to impose reason on an irrational world or to seek it elsewhere. But the echo of Sammy's narrative in Dinah's encounter at the labor ministry stands out as curious because of the way that Dinah there applies the terms of Sammy's defensive strategy to the spontaneous assembly. She likewise dismisses the crowd as politically disorganized and self-interested but *in surprising contrast* to the Dungle, which she deems comparably more peaceable because less provoked by injurious hope (Camus again).

The appropriation is also significant for repeating the connection between the two characters revealed in Sammy's narrative. There, we learn that, despite his revulsion for the people of the Dungle, Sammy has repeatedly hired Dinah's services as a prostitute while his wife is away at church. He assuages the quick pang of remorse that the memory causes by noting Dinah's exceptionality:

> In any case, he didn't consider Dinah a whore, she was so different from the rest. Not a bit like the others you picked up on Harbour Street. She was really somebody to go to when too many worries start to pour down on your head. She had character, that Dinah. And she wasn't a whore, even if she lived in the Dungle with one of those Rastafarians, even if other men bought her body every night. (Patterson 2012: 29)

Recalling that Mary, driven by the desperate need to provide her daughter with good food and decent clothes for her pending social ascent, engages the drunken U.S. sailor on Harbour Street, we are invited here to doubt both Sammy's assessment of Dinah's virtuous exceptionalism and his self-justifying rationale. Both elide the transactional, material fact of their relation with a dubious and self-serving moralism. In fact, read alongside his solipsist and resolutely presentist blinkers against an encounter with the importunate poor, Sammy here exemplifies the self-ennobling sequestration of the *belle âme* (as Sartre also alleged of Camus). This recognition opens up the possibility that the novel stages a complex and deeply conflicted double negation in which, as Brother Solomon observes, "*Negation negates itself*" and in which Camusian perseverance is deployed against itself in a figure of active or subtractive nihilism (Patterson 2012: 74). Insomuch as the novel shares Sammy's point of view, then, it indicts its own politics of representation.

Death Drive, or, the Refusal of False Hope

Framing Dinah's anxiety about absorption into the collective is the fact that she is driven by an excessive "ambition" that compels her to challenge each successive sphere of social existence/confinement. Having fled her masochistic bondage to Cyrus and the Dungle to move in with Alphanso, a Special Constable and former client who becomes infatuated with her, Dinah tries to convince herself that this new domestic life and relative social ascendance "filled some long-lasting gap in herself" and that she is undergoing a process of ameliorative civilization (Patterson 2012: 76). Almost immediately, however, she discerns in the displeasure of the Jones Town locals over the presence of a Dungle prostitute in their midst the material substrate of the civilizational affect:

> Exposed continuously to the joys and ease of a good life, to the secretaryship of an Anglican Church—an Anglican church, god up above, that had to do with Missis Queen and all that—to the security of owning a house, to good food and lots and lots of other civilized people, it had all been a bit too much. This high-handed, stupidly domineering attitude, she conjectured, seemed a kind of disease that only the civilized enjoyed. (Patterson 2012: 84)

In an attempt to emulate the deliberately narrowed perceptual horizons of Sammy and to suppress the destabilizing "freak" desire inside her, Dinah "determined to hide herself from herself" (Patterson 2012: 103). However, the restless impulse "to go yet farther" subsequently leads her to the labor office, where she fights the temptation to join the angry collective, and eventually to employment cleaning in the home of Mrs. Watkins in St. Andrews. Dinah is "revolted" not only at the thought of servile obedience to middle-class "brown people," but more generally at the very necessity of selling one's labor: "Why should anybody work for anybody else at all? It was such a nasty, bitchy world, but she would lick it yet" (Patterson 2012: 136). Even in the throes of the masochistic "paradox that perplexed her soul," Dinah impudently confronts Mrs. Watkins by calling her name and holding her gaze without shrinking, recognizing in the ferocity of the lady's commands the corresponding call of her own internal longing, a recognition that drives her to Shepherd John, where the novel's theme of masochistic submission culminates in the ritual abuse discussed above before her fatal wounding by Shepherd John's jilted followers and the foredoomed return to the Dungle (Patterson 2012: 144).

Dinah's brief confrontation with Mrs. Watkins, during which their asymmetrical class positions collide with their shared womanhood, is a crucial moment of reversal regarding the novel's unsettling masochistic theme and its central tragic anagnorisis:

> She wanted to be facing Mrs. Watkins always, she wanted to hear her bark at her, she wanted to be commanded, to be pushed, to

be kicked, because it was her, Dinah's, command, her pushing, her kicking, even if they came from another person. Her soul raged with humiliation and bitterness, but in the humiliation and bitterness, there was the sheer pleasure of pain. (Patterson 2012: 144)

Dinah's insight is not merely the oblique realization that she has internalized the latter's superegoic authority such that the consequent guilt complex of the servant demands the perverse satisfaction of derision and abuse. Her recognition is rather the key to discerning the link that I wish to posit here between the novel's apparently fatalistic cancellation of agency and its negative performance of an active nihilism under the formal heading of the anti-utopia.

Freud observes that the danger of moral masochism, a secondary derivative of the more elementary erotogenic masochism, "lies in the fact that it originates from the death instinct and corresponds to the part of that instinct which has escaped being turned outwards as an instinct of destruction" (Freud 1961: 170). Moral masochism is thus the internalization or self-direction of the destructive impulse of the death drive, which, as Žižek has it, seeks in its unrelenting passion for the Real "the radical annihilation of the symbolic texture through which the so-called reality is constituted" (1989: 132). Refusing the "natural cycle of generation and corruption," the death drive "liberates nature from its own laws and opens the way for the creation of new forms of life *ex nihilo*" (Žižek 1989: 134). It is thus in the compulsion of the death drive to annihilate a reality posited as a naturalized presupposition, Žižek contends, that "human *history* differs from animal *evolution*" or nature (1989: 135). Dinah's ambitions cannot therefore find satisfaction in the novel, which instead ruthlessly negates by way of an active nihilism every perceivable avenue of (false) hope. As in Mukherjee, individual scholastic excellence provides the opportunity for one character, the young Rossetta, to elude what Brother Solomon regards as the comic cycle of fate, but here the price for such a transgression of social precinct (which precisely inverts that of Supratik) is the utter dereliction of family, race, and class.

Having admitted to his forgery of the letter promising deliverance to Ethiopia, Brother Solomon defends the deception by claiming that it is only through the deflation of the redemptive fantasy, or what Lauren Berlant has in a more recent context called "cruel optimism,"[19] that a measure of peace may be attained in the paradoxical hope of hopelessness: "the thought of eternal bliss is a thousand times

---

[19] See Berlant, Lauren 2011. *Cruel Optimism* (Durham: Duke University Press).

more frightening than all the brimstone you can give me" (Patterson 2012: 210). In addition to a Camusian reconciliation with fate, his words here also resonate with Afro-pessimist thinker Calvin Warren's recent call for "black nihilism"—which he, like Badiou, also calls *"active nihilism"* (Warren 2015: 233). As a form of "political apostasy," Warren's black nihilism rejects the ever-deferred liberal promise of the Political and its "utopian vision of a 'not-yet-social order,'" which, predicated on a valorized concept of struggle, "perpetuates black suffering by placing relief in an unattainable future ... that offers nothing more than an exploitative reproduction of its own means of existence" and is ultimately undergirded by a "political metaphysics that depends on black-death" (Warren 2015: 243).

Warren thus advocates what Badiou would call a subtractive form of opposition that rejects the cycle of the Political and reclaims or reinvents a form of radical (what he calls "spiritual") hope outside the constraints of the situation. For Žižek, the violence of such subtractive or active nihilism surpasses merely subjective destruction and, in refusing the terms imposed by the hegemonic field, "violently *affects* this field itself, laying bare its true coordinates" (2008: 411). Wright describes this process as a negation of or withdrawal from *"all* wordly predicates," which forces into visibility the excluded term or void, the originary suppression of which "enables all the other relational differences (including those of class and gender) that hierarchically structure a given world" (2013: 321).

It is in the absolute foreclosure of horizons by an active nihilism that we may read in the novel's intersecting themes of masochism and fatalist resignation the anti-utopianism of the second type identified by Kumar, one born of a bitterly thwarted utopianism, the emancipatory promises of which have seemingly failed or been betrayed and have thus lapsed back into a fallen natural milieu of endemic, Hobbesian strife. The ideological charge of the novel is ambivalent, therefore, as a consequence of history; its representation of Rastafari (or at least Brother Solomon) is not simply a sociological typification of millenarian naivety, but a critique of false hope and the naturalizing logic through which it must perforce speak that critique.

Brother Solomon's suicide, like Antigone's, is the result of a tragic anagnorisis of hopelessness, a percipient insight into the dilemma that Mukherjee names the "great circularity," and is honored as an act of heroism:

> Only we can see that suicide is the supreme reason. Only we have searched for meaning and could not find it. The rich are

those who've had all they want to have. They're few[...]. It is the desperately poor that are many. It is only we who see the dreary circle going round and round. (Patterson 2012: 211)

Following the novel's climactic paean to human suffering in Brother Solomon's suicide, the death of Dinah, and the brutal imprisonment and subsequent betrayal of Mary, the novel concludes with a caustically ironic critique of fraudulent or escapist hope. Having cleansed and anointed the body of Dinah, Cyrus—who seeks solace in the "deep fervour of his faith" that the Holy Emperor's ships will soon arrive and that the Emperor could restore Dinah's life—whispers the novel's closing prayer: "Tomorrow we shall meet again in paradise," thus renewing the cycle of delusion and despair (Patterson 2012: 216).

The novel's pitiless conclusion does not so much figure alternative or preferable strategies of opposition—as Harrison, Pieto, and (to some extent) Scott each claim—as it does absolutely jettison those that it regards as now futile. Patterson's anti-utopianism is therefore not, like Mukherjee's, simply a moralizing affirmation of the global status quo. Rather, in rejecting the palliatives and broken promises of prior utopianisms, the novel dramatizes something akin to Horkheimer and Adorno's critique of the liberal "rights" discourse and the imperatives to "happiness" that are foisted upon the "cheated masses"—as they observe:

> The rights of man were designed to promise happiness even to those without power. Because the cheated masses feel that this promise—as a universal—remains a lie as long as classes exist, it stirs their rage; they feel mocked. Even as a possibility or an idea they repeatedly repress the thought of such happiness, they deny it ever more passionately the more imminent it seems. Wherever happiness seems to have been achieved in the midst of universal renunciation, they must repeat that gesture of repression, which is really the repression of their own longing. Everything that occasions such repression and such repetition, however miserable it may be in itself ... draws down upon itself the destructive lust of the 'civilized,' who could never wholly fulfill and realize the painful process of civilization itself. To those who spasmodically dominate nature, a tormented nature provocatively reflects back the image of powerless happiness. (Horkheimer and Adorno 1972: 172)

Such an uncompromising negation of manufactured happiness nevertheless also includes, as Jameson notes in his analysis of this final chapter of *The Dialectic of Enlightenment*, a concomitant "envy for what is fantasized as the less alienated state of an older community or collectivity" that will produce the perverse cultural rationalization for racist, anti-Semitic violence in lieu of critical class consciousness (2007: 153).

This deep, if obliquely expressed *ressentiment* perhaps explains the novel's vexed ideological torsion and Patterson's long-time reluctance to acknowledge the provisional feats and imminent possibilities of social rebellion as well as his insistence that Rastafari represents neither the subtractive nihilism with which Wright credits the movement nor the anti-capitalist solidarity that Rodney observes, but the vestiges of an archaic class conscious. For all the novel's insight into the structural and cultural transformations of capitalist imperialism and the insufficiencies of romantic/realist nationalism to contest these new forms of oppression, it cannot finally overcome this tormented image of entrammeling nature and the class envy that undergirds it.

The novel therefore expresses the simultaneous revulsion for and sympathetic fascination with the masses that Jameson recognizes as the underlying impetus of literary naturalism. Such are the vicissitudes of this second form of anti-utopianism that it can, like Orwell's, be claimed with equal assurance by the Leftist and the Conservative even as it most frequently lends itself to the maintenance agenda of the liberal progressive, whose humanist pluralisms, in preempting the hopes of radical universalism, ultimately provide the sympathetic criteria for admittance into the reassuringly melancholic canon of postcolonial literature. It is between the poles of the two complementary but irreducible forms of anti-utopianism described above that much of what has come to constitute "postcolonial literature" is consolidated.

Conclusion
Naturalism, or, the Cultural Logic of Capital in Crisis

How could 'empirical' man think? Confronted with his own history, he is as uncertain as when he is confronted by Nature, for the law does not automatically produce knowledge of itself—indeed, if it is passively suffered, it transforms its object into passivity, and thus deprives it of any possibility of collecting its atomised experiences into a synthetic unity.

—Jean Paul Sartre,
Critique of Dialectical Reason Vol. 1 (2004: 30)

For Hill, the global transit of naturalism is defined through (or at least identified by way of) the recurrence and novel inflection of key naturalist techniques, chiefly the appearance of what he cites as the form's three principal tropes: the degenerate body, the unbound woman, and the spatial analogization of social relations in the form of typically marginalized or "bounded" milieux: the mine, the ship, the plain, the backwater, and so forth (2020: 134). Central to Hill's claim for naturalism's transnational and plural currency is the recognition that, following the abbreviated life of the form in the turn-of the-century European context, we find flourishing throughout the better part of the twentieth century "as many naturalist afterlives as there were naturalisms," *past tense* (2020: 173). From African American writers like Richard Wright in the 1940s, naturalism would thence be taken up and reinvented, Hill maintains, within widely divergent historical and national situations (Japanese, Korean, Egyptian, Kenyan, Botswanan, and so on) in the decades spanning the aftermath of World War II and the anticolonial struggles for national independence throughout the 1960s and into the 1970s. While naturalism provided the representational resources for these writers to "depict the force that social environments exert on individual behavior," they also rejected, Hill claims, the European naturalist's privileging of heredity (2020: 174).

However, Hill's contradictory insistence on this point[1] is clearly inseparable from his own effort to delineate a deductive account of a globally diverse form that circumvents prevailing diffusionist and developmentalist "arguments about imitation and catching-up" (2020: 174). Therefore, though the signifier "Zola" might frequently function in transnational naturalist fiction as the name for "a legitimating principle that could be invoked by intertextual allusion and paratextual homage," as the works discussed in the present book amply demonstrate, Hill argues that the writers who appeal to this European authority do so in heterogeneous and heterodox ways (2020: 177). In forcefully opposing the diffusionist "World Lit" model, which is ultimately reliant on a discourse of origination and imitation—effectively, an inductive flattening out of global difference—he therefore emphasizes the vitally plural propagation of naturalisms as an expression of cultural diversity: in short, "naturalism proliferated because of the multiplicity of human social life" (Hill 2020: 179). That is, Hill's model moves us from an account positing the local adoption or modification of an originary corpus of European texts and methods to one in which the identifying methods are selectively adapted, stretched, or heretically reimagined to address the variety and specificity of unique social assemblages.

This reliance on stylistic method and multiplicity threatens, however, to define naturalism according to formalist specifications that are at once too narrow and too general. If naturalism is identified by the rehearsal of a definitive tropology, however varied in application, we are left to ask why the persistence of these figures beyond the period of the 1970s does not thereby indicate the contemporary perseverance and thus enduring historical relevance, if not necessity, of the form. Works of contemporary world-literature like Bode Osanyin's *The Noble Mistress* (2000) or Chika Unigwe's *On Black Sisters' Street* (2009)—both of which should perhaps be read as direct heirs of Cyprian Ekwensi's *Jagua Nana* (1961)—might indeed suggest that the figure of Nana persists long after the end of the 1970s, as do the tropes of degenerate bodies and bounded milieux in the savage age of Empire.

Conversely, a naturalism whose specific features coincide with the "multiplicity of human social life" threatens to exceed the historicizing parameters to which Hill otherwise repeatedly alludes—such as in his contention that a "more thorough materialist analysis" than the one

---

[1] Again, he earlier notes the naturalist text's "closed circuit of heredity and social determinism that is a basic part of their social analytic" and that also "seems to exclude the possibility of change" (Hill 2020: 95).

he has space to undertake might trace, for example, "the relation of the Nana figure to the economics of women's labor" (2020: 179). This conception would instead offer up an abundance of culturally specific, "alternative naturalisms" whose very faithfulness to the method undermines the latter's continued relevance as vitally expressive form. As Hill writes, "If naturalism was essentially a method—as many of its adherents thought it was—then the embrace of the method in different parts of the world paradoxically was naturalism's undoing as a transnational phenomenon" (2020: 180). Naturalism's success in replicating its figural logic, however much each distinctive iteration bears the imprint of its culture, is therefore the root of its failure. This is indeed a paradox in that the appropriation and deployment that Hill addresses is thus haunted by the very "anxiety of influence" that his study undertakes to oppose.

The Eternal Return of Foreshortened Worlds

Yet, inasmuch as capitalism continues to shape and define our global reality, naturalism persists as an historically conditioned reflexive response, particularly to the challenge of mass movements from below or radical insurgency. Naturalism is, thus, like its historical counterpart, modernism, a cultural response to the representational crisis of realism in a moment of historical transition. Suspended between the vanishing "moment" of realism—when the bourgeoisie lay claim to the medium of literature in order to universalize its particular class interests[2]—and the estranging imperatives of postcolonial modernism—which undertakes to map the spatio-temporal deformations and political challenges of capitalist globalization—naturalism surrenders history and retreats into pre-symbolic or organic immanence.

This reactionary eschewal necessarily implicates narrative, such that we find the suppression of narrative momentum by scenic or descriptive stasis in which *World* subsumes *Way* and *Being* abrogates *Becoming*. As Nivedita Majumdar recently claims in an astringent critique of postcolonial theory in the name of radical universalism, this selective tradition's celebrated "defense of the quotidian and the marginal" and putative recovery of subaltern agency in fact more frequently "naturalize[s] domination and evacuate[s] actual instances of

---

[2] As in the social realist novels of Alfred Mendes or C.L.R. James' pre-Marxist *Minty Alley* with its focus on the sympathetic education of an intermediary middle-class, for example.

resistance" (2021: 13). Narratively, this tendency produces a climacteric disintegration of narrative itself, an arrested momentum in which underdevelopment manifests in expressive form. Ultimately, the effect is the presentation of what Pedro Neves Marques calls naturalism's "foreshortened worlds" (2019: n.p.). If modernism estranges by figuring horizonal difference or futurity into its self-conscious depiction of the present, postcolonial naturalism leaves us a world without utopia's prospective horizons, a statically determined and timeless milieu that can be represented by a language unproblematically flattened into objectively descriptive and subjective immediacy. Such a world can be mourned but not changed.

Marques observes that his own writing has for several years been haunted by the following two sentences: "There is only one planet, but there are many worlds inside of it" and "It is only white people who have the privilege of living in one world; everyone else must live in many worlds, theirs and ours (I mean, mine) in order to survive" (2019: n.p.). The first sentence registers the homogenizing distillation of "a plurality of worlds into a single, streamlined capitalist modernity," the reduction of "the gap between nature and culture," and the relegation of "other livelihoods into invisibility" (Marques 2019: n.p.). The second acknowledges the privileged subject position of the middle-class intellectual who presumes to write about indigenous and Third-World concerns.

The singularity proffered by the present global dispensation is, as many commentators have recognized, one without a future or differential horizon—one in which the world, as Naipaul would say, simply is what it is. To oppose the tendential singularity of the capitalist "World" with the sheer difference of the local, experiential, and individual/identitarian, however, is simply to fall victim to the very logic of the system in which the only totality that counts is that of global capital, a system that presents itself as the social realization of manifest (human) nature. Such a reduction occludes from view, as Marques notes, the other futures that persist in our present and that might, like Majumdar's reclamation of radical universalism, figure properly utopian alternatives to the culturalist political particularism (of the sort exploited by India's right-wing Bharatiya Janata Party, for example) that informs the naturalizing logic of much orthodox postcolonial representation. This representational and historical dilemma is registered, I have argued here, in the tension between postcolonial naturalism and modernism, which can stand as the polar cultural extremes of a protracted moment of historical transition from the old imperialisms to the new forms of economic and political domination that structure the contemporary world-system.

The recognition of naturalism as the unnamed aesthetic impulse underlying the emergence and consolidation of a field of postcolonial literary studies brings narratological and hermeneutic resources to bear on the ideological disposition of particular works. It also provides the means to orient postcolonial literary production more broadly within the periodizing field that the WReC name "world-literature," one defined, I claim, by the four cultural logics of capitalist modernity: realism-naturalism-modernism-postmodernism. Situation within this four-fold schema thus provides a means to account for the large-scale evolution of transnational form that eludes the diffusionist tendency to which Hill objects but that also avoids lapsing into a rigid formalism (the inventorying of definitive tropes) or losing meaningful coherence in the face of cultural incommensurability.

Indeed, by way of the WReC's materialist account of world-literature and Jameson's historicizing logic of cultural periodization, we perhaps come closer to Hill's own stated intention of pursuing a large-scale literary history that does not forsake the necessity of close reading (2020: xvii). Such a goal is best approached, as Jameson has long insisted, by the practice of dialectical criticism, a totalizing method that, as he nevertheless cautions, "can be acquired only by a concrete working through of detail, by a sympathetic internal experience of the gradual construction of a system according to its inner necessity" (1971: xi). Meanwhile, any provisional theory of periodization, "intolerable and unacceptable in its very nature," faces a comparable challenge in its attempt "to take a point of view on individual events which is well beyond the observational capacities of any individual, and to unify, both horizontally and vertically, hosts of realities whose interrelationships must remain inaccessible and unverifiable" (2002: 128). Such, it seems, is also the challenge specific to any meaningful cultural comparatism.

An additional merit of this periodizing aesthetic is that it also avoids the ethical tendency in some postcolonial readings to separate the "good" writers (whose identity and political views align with those of the critic or the prevailing ethos of the discipline of postcolonial studies) from the "bad" writers (whose identities might be inconvenient for theorizing purposes or whose views, like Naipaul's, might be partially or wholly repugnant). The subjectivist limitation of such an approach is two-fold: first, it isolates the text from the historical situation out of which it emerges, perceiving it solely as the product of conscious authorial intent; then, it enacts a qualitative evaluation of the text from the vantage of the critic's institutional habitus, according to which the former is either positively affirmed or imperiously discredited (or, more often, ignored). Such a criticism can itself be read as the symptomatic expression of the ethical binarism that Jameson calls "the root form of all ideology" (2009: 408).

As alternative to an ethical criticism, Jameson offers his unorthodox retooling of the Greimasian semiotic square, the structuralist dialecticism of which is both diagnostically formalist and dynamically generative. Among the merits of Greimas's system in Jameson's hands is its capacity to "substitute objective processes for largely subjective or experiential perceptions" without lapsing into a rigidly prescriptive, undialectical formalism (2009: 489). If such an approach "permits a more microscopic scrutiny of the intellectual or semic content of works normally dismissed as pure entertainment or at best mythic representation" (Jameson 2009: 489), it does so because it rejects the imperative to render aesthetic judgment for the more capacious facility to both think and represent historical contradiction.

Contradiction in this case, as ever, is overdetermined by the semic complexity of language and materiality itself, chiefly the modern disjuncture of the local/particular and the global/universal. It is this disjuncture that Hill's study of transnational naturalism attempts to bridge with a large-scale, molar reading practice that is nevertheless acutely sensitive to granular, particular difference. Similarly, the WReC authors state that any attempt to understand world-literature by way of the combined and uneven systemic logic of modernity

> must attend to its modes of spatio-temporal compression, its juxtaposition of asynchronous orders and levels of historical experience, its barometric indications of invisible forces acting from a distance on the local and familiar—as these manifest themselves in literary forms, genres, and aesthetic strategies. (2015: 17)

A theorization of postcolonial naturalism emerging from the four-fold periodizing schema outlined above attempts to advance precisely these aims by accounting for a heretofore unrecognized but broadly pervasive aesthetic practice tacitly informing what scholars like Kalpana Seshadri-Crooks have long recognized as postcolonial studies' defining inclination to the melancholic, one which is "induced paradoxically by its new-found authority and incorporation into institutions of higher learning" (2000: 3). As she observes, the institutional recognition of postcolonialism's discursive authority is predicated on what might well be a "conciliatory" performance of imperialist critique. Establishing "criteria for political self-legitimation" that simultaneously presume "the impossibility of representing the Third World as an anti-imperialist constituency, especially in the face of the retreat of socialism," such institutionally sanctioned critical gestures ultimately present a "peculiar immobility as an effective oppositional force" (Seshadri-Crooks 2000: 3).

Similarly abandoning political agency to the incontestable laws of nature, naturalism presents itself (much as Pizer claims) as the search for individual dignity in an utterly irremediable world. In fact, this is the version of the Third World privileged in much of postcolonial studies. Of the "intermittent tendency to romanticize the uncommitted, exilic, individual vocation" of the postcolonial intellectual (specifically in Said), Lazarus observes that it reflects an "unwarranted suspicion of solidaristic intellectualism" (2011: 202) and an anxiety before the radical possibilities of the collective. As it emerged in historically comparable conditions in post-revolutionary Europe and Mexico, Meiji-era Japan, or post-civil war Lebanon, naturalism is the aesthetic expression of this anxiety. Postcolonial naturalism thus functions as a cultural formation mediating the interests of the Third-World bourgeoisie and the dangerous masses in whose name it speaks—presenting a safely post-historical, pitiable vision of cultural otherness whose sympathetic authenticity is coextensive with its reassuringly disempowered abjection.

At the same time, postcolonial naturalism's melancholic (objectless) aspect nevertheless presents something like the death drive's desire for or registering of the Symbolic order's terminal limit, in this case the order constituted by bourgeois anti-colonial nationalism, which expresses aesthetically as a species of realism. If postcolonial modernism registers unevenness and the simultaneity of the non-simultaneous, absorbing into its own narrative structure the lived discontinuity of a singular modernity, postcolonial naturalism manifests the entropic degeneration and "necessary failure" of prior emancipatory resolutions to address the postcolonial situation. If the account here is correct, we can expect the foreshortened worlds of naturalism to continue appearing in the wake of capital's spasmodic librations wherever hegemonic realisms are imperiled by forces at the uneven, ever-insistent margin.

Works Cited

Adiga, Aravind 2017. "Aravind Adiga: 'I Was Afraid the White Tiger Would Eat Me Up Too,'" Interview with Stephen Moss. *The Guardian*. https://www.theguardian.com/books/2017/aug/25/aravind-adiga-books-interview-selection-day-the-white-tiger. Accessed 18 May 2021.
— 2008. *The White Tiger* (New York: Free Press, 2008).
Adkins, Alexander 2017. "Chinua Achebe's Beautiful Soul," *The Cambridge Journal of Postcolonial Literary Inquiry* 4.3: 398–408.
Anjaria, Ulka 2015. "Realist Hieroglyphics: Aravind Adiga and the New Social Novel," *Modern Fiction Studies* 61.1: 114–137.
Ashcroft, Bill, Gareth Griffiths, and Helen Tiffin 2002. *The Empire Writes Back*. 2nd edn. (New York: Routledge).
Ashcroft, Bill 2016. *Utopianism in Postcolonial Literatures* (Oxford: Routledge).
Atwood, Margaret 2005. *Curious Pursuits: Occasional Writing 1970–2005* (London: Virago).
Azuela, Mariano 1963. *Two Novels of the Mexican Revolution*. Trans. Frances Kellam Hendricks and Beatrice Berler (San Antonio: Trinity University Press).
Azuela, Salvador 1963. "Influence of Emile Zola on Mariano Azuela," in *Two Novels of the Mexican Revolution*. Trans. Frances Kellam Hendricks and Beatrice Berler (San Antonio: Trinity University Press), ix–xi.
Badiou, Alain 2007. *The Century*. Trans. Alberto Toscano (Cambridge: Polity).
— 2011a. "The Democratic Emblem," in *Democracy in What State?* (New York: Columbia University Press).
— 2004. *Infinite Thought: Truth and the Return of Philosophy*. Trans. Oliver Feltham and Justin Clemens (London: Continuum).
— 2006. *Metapolitics* (New York: Verso).
— 2011b. *Second Manifesto for Philosophy*. Trans. Louise Burchill (Malden: Polity Press).
Baguley, David 1990. *Naturalist Fiction: The Entropic Vision* (Cambridge: Cambridge University Press).

Balasopoulos, Antonis 2006. "Anti-Utopia and Dystopia: Rethinking the Generic Field" Online. https://www.academia.edu/1008203/_Anti_Utopia_and_Dystopia_Rethinking_the_Generic_Field_. Accessed January 2021.

Bewes, Timothy 2011. *The Event of Postcolonial Shame* (Princeton: Princeton University Press).

Berman, Jaye 1986. "V.S. Naipaul's *Guerrillas* as a Postmodern Naturalistic Novel," *Perspectives on Contemporary Literature* 12: 29–34.

Bhabha, Homi 1984. "Representation and the Colonial Text: A Critical Exploration of Some Forms of Mimeticism," in *The Theory of Reading*. Ed. Frank Gloversmith (Brighton: Harvester), 93–122.

Bhattacharya, Sourit 2020. *Postcolonial Modernity and the Indian Novel: On Catastrophic Realism* (New York: Palgrave).

Brathwaite, Kamau 1968. "Jamaican Slave Society, A Review," *Race & Class* 9.3: 331–342.

— 1994. "A Post-Cautionary Tale of the Helen of Our Wars," *Wasafiri* 20: 5–11.

Brink, André 1992. "An Ornithology of Sexual Politics: Lewis Nkosi's *Mating Birds*," *English in Africa* 19.1: 1–20.

Byatt, A.S. 2014. "*The Lives of Others* by Neel Mukherjee Review—Marxism and Tradition in 1960s India," *The Guardian*. May 14. Online. Accessed 7 October 2021.

Campbell, Horace 2007. *Rasta & Resistance: From Marcus Garvey to Walter Rodney* (Hertford: Hansib).

Camus, Albert 1955. "The Myth of Sisyphus," in *The Myth of Sisyphus and Other Essays*. Trans. Justin O'Brien. Web. https://people.brandeis.edu/~teuber/Albert_Camus_The_Myth_of_Sisyphus_Complete_Text_.pdf.

— 1962 [1942]. *The Rebel*. Trans. Anthony Bower (New York: Penguin).

— 1970 [1936]. "Summer in Algiers," in *Lyrical and Critical Essays*. Ed. Philip Thody. Trans. Ellen Conroy Kennedy (New York: Vintage), 80–92.

Carter, Angela 1997. *Nothing Sacred: Selected Writings*. Ed. Jenny Uglow (London: Chatto and Windus).

Casanova, Pascale 2001. "Not Worth the Prize: Naipaul in Denial," *Le Monde Diplomatique*. English Ed. http://mondediplo.com/2001/12/13naipaul.

Chapman, Michael 2013. "The Ambiguities of Exile: Lewis Nkosi, Literary Critic," *English Academy Review* 30.1: 6–21.

Charles, David 2017. *Émile Zola et la Commune de Paris: aux origines des 'Rougon-Macquart'* (Paris: Classiques Garnier).

Cheah, Pheng 2003. *Spectral Nationality: Passages of Freedom from Kant to Postcolonial Literatures* (New York: Columbia University Press).

Cheng, Chu-chueh 2006. "Anachronistic Periodization: Victorian Literature in the Postcolonial Era or Postcolonial Literature in the Victorian Era?" *Postcolonial Text* 2.3: 1–13.

Cliff, Michelle 1995 [1984]. *Abeng* (New York: Plume).

— 1990. "Clare Savage as a Crossroads Character," in *Caribbean Women Writers: Essays from the First International Conference*. Ed. Selwyn Cudjoe (Amherst: University of Massachusetts Press).

Coundouriotis, Eleni 2014. *The People's Right to the Novel: War Fiction in the Postcolony* (New York: Fordham University Press).
Crewe, Jonathan 2004. "Black Hamlet: Psychoanalysis on Trial in South Africa," in *South Africa in the Global Imaginary*. Eds. Leon de Kock et al. (Pretoria: University of South Africa Press), 136–153.
Cudjoe, Selwyn R. 1988. *V.S. Naipaul: A Materialist Reading* (Amherst: University of Massachusetts Press).
Dawes, Kwame 2012. "Introduction," *The Children of Sisyphus* (Leeds: Peepal Tree Press), 5–23.
Deleuze, Gilles 1986. *Cinema 1: The Movement Image*. Trans. Hugh Tomlinson and Barbara Habberjam (Minneapolis: University of Minnesota Press).
— 1989. *Cinema 2: The Time Image*. Trans. Hugh Tomlinson and Robert Galeta (Minneapolis: University of Minnesota Press).
— 1994. *Difference and Repetition*. Trans. Paul Patton (New York: Columbia University Press).
— 1992. "Postscript on the Societies of Control," *October* 59: 3–7.
Detmers, Ines 2011. "New India? New Metropolis? Reading Aravind Adiga's *The White Tiger* as a 'condition-of-India' Novel," *Journal of Postcolonial Writing* 47.5: 535–545.
Douglas, Mary 1996. *Natural Symbols: Explorations in Cosmology*. 2nd edn. (New York: Routledge).
Duneer, Anita 2020. "American Literary Naturalism's Postcolonial Descendants," *Studies in American Naturalism* 15.1: 49–74.
Durrant, Samuel 2012. "Surviving Time: Trauma, Tragedy, and the Postcolonial Novel," *Journal of Literature and Trauma Studies* 1.1: 95–117.
Edmondson, Belinda 1993. "Race, Privilege, and the Politics of (Re)Writing History, An Analysis of the Novels of Michelle Cliff," *Callaloo* 16.1: 180–191.
Elze, Jens 2018. "Genres of the Global South: The Picaresque," in *The Global South and Literature*. Ed. Russel West-Pavlov (Cambridge: Cambridge University Press): 223–234.
Emery, Mary Lou 2014. *Jean Rhys at "World's End": Novels of Colonial and Sexual Exile* (Austin: University of Texas Press).
Esty, Jed 2011. *Unseasonable Youth: Modernism, Colonialism, and the Fiction of Development* (Oxford: Oxford University Press).
Fanon, Frantz 2004 [1961]. *The Wretched of the Earth*. Trans. Richard Philcox (New York: Grove Press).
French, Patrick 2008. *The World Is What It Is* (New York: Knopf).
Freud, Sigmund 1961 [1924]. "The Economic Problem of Masochism," in *The Standard Edition of the Complete Psychological Works of Sigmund Freud*. Trans. James Strachey (London: Hogarth).
Gajarawala, Toral Jatin 2012. "Fictional Murder and Other Descriptive Deaths: V.S. Naipaul's *Guerrillas* and the Problem of Postcolonial Description," *Journal of Narrative Theory* 42.3: 289–308.
Gay, Peter 1990. *Reading Freud: Explorations and Entertainments* (New Haven: Yale University Press).

Gherovici, Patricia 2014. "Where Have the Hysterics Gone? Lacan's Reinvention of Hysteria," *ESC* 40.1: 47–70.

Gikandi, Simon 1992. *Modernism and Caribbean Literature* (New York: Cornell University Press).

Gilroy, Paul 2006. *Postcolonial Melancholia* (New York: Columbia University Press).

Goncourt, Edmond de and Jules de 1900. *The Journal of the de Goncourts: Pages from a Great Diary, Being Extracts from the Journal des Goncourt* (New York: T. Nelson).

Gupta, Kanchan 2009. "*Slumdog* is About Defaming Hindus," *The Daily Pioneer*. Jan. 25. Web. http://dailypioneer.com/152164/Slumdog-is-about-defaming-Hindus.html. Accessed 19 April 2021.

Harris, Janice 1994. "On Tradition, Madness, and South Africa: An Interview with Lewis Nkosi," *Weber Studies* 11.1: 25–37.

Harrow, Susan 2010. *Zola, The Body Modern: Pressures and Prospects of Representation* (Oxford: Legenda).

Harvey, David 2016. "Neoliberalism is a Political Project," *Jacobin*. Jun. 23. Web. https://www.jacobinmag.com/2016/07/david-harvey-neoliberalism-capitalism-labor-crisis-resistance/. Accessed January 2022.

Hay, Simon 2013. "*Nervous Conditions*, Lukács, and the Postcolonial Bildungsroman," *Genre* 46.3: 317–344.

Hegel, G.W.F. 1977 [1807]. *Phenomenology of Spirit*. Trans. A.V. Miller (Oxford: Oxford University Press).

Helgesson, Stefan 2022. *Decolonisations of Literature: Critical Practice in Africa and Brazil After 1945* (Liverpool: Liverpool University Press).

Hill, Christopher 2020. *Figures of the World: The Naturalist Novel and Transnational Form* (Evanston: Northwestern University Press).

— 2009. "The Travels of Naturalism and the Challenges of a World Literature," *Literature Compass* 6.6: 1198–1210.

Hitchcock, Peter 2010. *The Long Space: Transnationalism and Postcolonial Form* (Chicago: University of Illinois Press).

Horkheimer, Max and Theodor W. Adorno 2001 [1944]. *The Dialectic of Enlightenment*. Trans. John Cumming (New York: Continuum).

Hulme, Peter 2000. "Islands and Roads: Hesketh Bell, Jean Rhys and Dominica's Imperial Road," *The Jean Rhys Review* 11.2: 23–51.

— 1994. "The Locked-Heart: The Creole Family Romance of *Wide Sargasso Sea*," in *Colonial Discourse, Postcolonial Theory*. Ed. Francis Barker, Peter Hulme and Margaret Iversen (Manchester: Manchester University Press), 72–88.

Jacobs, Johan 1990. "Lewis Nkosi: Mating Birds," *Critical Arts* 5.2: 119–124.

Jameson, Fredric 2020. *Allegory and Ideology* (New York: Verso).

— 2013. *The Antinomies of Realism* (New York: Verso).

— 2005. *Archaeologies of the Future: The Desire Called Utopia and Other Science Fictions* (New York: Verso).

— 1970. "The Case for George Lukács," *Salmagundi* 13: 3–35.

— 2022. "Criticism and Categories," *PMLA* 137.3: 563–567.
— 1979. *Fables of Aggression: Wyndham Lewis, the Modernist as Fascist* (Berkeley: University of California Press).
— 1988. "Imaginary and Symbolic in Lacan," in *The Ideologies of Theory Vol. 1* (Minneapolis: University of Minnesota Press), 75–115.
— 2007 [1990]. *Late Marxism: Adorno or the Persistence of the Dialectic* (New York: Verso).
— 1971. *Marxism and Form* (Princeton: Princeton University Press).
— 1990. "Modernism and Imperialism," in *Nationalism, Colonialism, and Literature* (Minneapolis: University of Minnesota Press), 43–66.
— 1981. *The Political Unconscious* (Ithaca: Cornell University Press).
— 1991. *Postmodernism, or, the Cultural Logic of Late Capitalism* (Durham: Duke University Press).
— 1992. *Signatures of the Visible* (New York: Routledge).
— 2002. *A Singular Modernity: Essay on the Ontology of the Present* (New York: Verso).
— 1986. "Third World Literature in the Era of Multinational Capitalism," *Social Text* 15: 65–88.
Kaiwar, Vasant 2014. *The Postcolonial Orient: The Politics of Difference and the Project of Provincialising Europe* (Leiden: Brill).
Kilson, Martin 2001. "Critique of Orlando Patterson's Blaming-the-Victim Rituals," *Souls*: 81–106.
Klein, Melanie 1975. "Narrative of a Child Analysis," in *The Collected Works of Melanie Klein* (London: Hogarth).
Knight, Denise D. 2000. "Charlotte Perkins Gilman and the Shadow of Racism," *American Literary Realism* 32.2: 159–169.
Kornbluh, Anna 2019. *The Order of Forms: Realism, Formalism, and Social Space* (Chicago: University of Chicago Press).
Kramer, Hilton 1976. "Naipual's Guerrillas and Oates's Assassins," *Commentary* https://www.commentarymagazine.com/article/naipauls-guerrillas-and-oatess-assassins/.
Kumar, Krishan 1987. *Utopia and Anti-Utopia in Modern Times* (Oxford: Blackwell).
Lacan, Jacques 2007. *Écrits* (New York: W.W. Norton).
— 2017. *The Formation of the Unconscious: The Seminar of Jacques Lacan, Book V.* Ed. Jacques-Alain Miller. Trans. Russell Grigg (Cambridge: Polity).
— 1989. "Kant with Sade," trans. James B. Swenson, *October* 51: 55–75.
— 1992. *The Seminar of Jacques Lacan Book VII: The Ethics of Psychoanalysis, 1959–1960*. Ed. Jacques-Alain Miller. Trans. Dennis Porter (New York: W.W. Norton and Company).
— 1972. "Seminar on 'The Purloined Letter,'" *Yale French Studies* 0.48: 39–72.
Lamming, George 1990. "Statement on the Rastafari," *Daily News*, Jamaica, Sept. 28.

Lazarus, Neil 2011. *The Postcolonial Unconscious* (Cambridge: Cambridge University Press).
— 2007. "Realism and Naturalism in African Fiction," in *African Literature: An Anthology of Criticism and Theory*. Eds. Tejumola Olaniyan and Ato Quayson (Oxford: Blackwell), 340–344.
— 1990. *Resistance in Postcolonial African Fiction* (New Haven: Yale University Press).
Lefebvre, Henri 1991. *The Production of Space*. Trans. Donald Nicholson-Smith (Malden: Blackwell).
Lima, Maria Helena 1993. *Decolonizing Genre: Caribbean Women Writers and the Bildungsroman* (College Park: University of Maryland Press).
Link, Eric Carl 2004. *The Vast and Terrible Drama: American Literary Naturalism in the Late Nineteenth Century* (Tuscaloosa: University of Alabama Press).
London, Jack 2006 [1908]. *The Iron Heel* (New York: Penguin).
López, Alfred 2001. "(Un)concealed Histories: Whiteness and the Land in Michelle Cliff's *Abeng*," *MaComère* 4: 173–183.
Lukács, Georg 1970. "Narrate or Describe?" in *Writer and Critic and Other Essays*. Ed. and trans. Arthur Kahn (London: Merlin), 110–148.
— 2002 [1950]. "The Zola Centennial," in *Studies in European Realism* (New York: Howard Fertig).
Majumdar, Nivedita 2021. *The World in a Grain of Sand: Postcolonial Literature and Radical Universalism* (New York: Verso).
Marie-Harrison, Sheri 2017. "Global Sisyphus: Rereading the Jamaican 1960s through *A Brief History of Seven Killings*," *Small Axe* 21.3: 85–97.
Marques, Gabriel Pedro 2019. "Parallel Futures: One or Many Dystopias," *e-flux*. Online. Accessed 12 October 2021.
Martyris, Nina 2104. "The Naxal Novel," *Dissent*. Fall. https://www.dissentmagazine.org/article/the-naxal-novel. Accessed 21 May 2021.
Marx, Karl 1993 [1871]. "Address of the General Council of the International Working Men's Association on The Civil War in France, 1871," in *Civil War in France: The Paris Commune* (New York: International), 36–82.
— 1852. "The Eighteenth Brumaire of Louis Bonaparte," Marxists.org. 2022. https://www.marxists.org/archive/marx/works/1852/18th-brumaire/ch07.htm Accessed 7 February 2021.
Marx, Karl and Frederick Engels 2022 [1848]. "Manifesto of the Communist Party," in China Miéville, *A Specter Haunting: On the Communist Manifesto* (Chicago: Haymarket).
Matthews, J.H. 1968. "From Naturalism to the Absurd: Edmond de Goncourt and Albert Camus," *Symposium: A Quarterly Journal in Modern Literatures* 22:3: 241–255.
McQueen, Sean 2014. "Future Imperfect: Mass and Mobility in Williams, Orwell, and the BBC's *Nineteen Eighty-Four*," *Key Words: A Journal of Cultural Materialism* 12: 74–92.

Mendes, Ana Cristina 2010. "Exciting Tales of Exotic Dark India: Aravind Adiga's *The White Tiger*," *The Journal of Commonwealth Literature* 45.2: 275–293.
Michaels, Walter Benn 1987. *The Gold Standard and The Logic of Naturalism* (Berkeley: University of California Press).
Milne, Drew 2002. "The Beautiful Soul: From Hegel to Beckett," *Diacritics* 32.1: 63–82.
Milner, Andrew 2013. *The Location of Science Fiction* (Oxford: Oxford University Press).
Mitchell, David 2004. *Cloud Atlas* (New York: Random House).
Mohan, Rajeswari. "The Excavation of History in Michelle Cliff's Fiction," *Otherness: Essays and Studies* 2.1. Online. https://www.otherness.dk/fileadmin/www.othernessandthearts.org/Publicatioss/Journal_Otherness/Otherness__Essays_and_Studies_2.1/9._Rajeswari_Mohan.pdf. Accessed 7 February 2021.
Moretti, Franco 1987. *The Way of the World: The Bildungsroman in European Culture* (New York: Verso).
Moylan, Tom 2014. *Demand the Impossible: Science Fiction and the Utopian Imagination*. Ed. R. Baccolini (Bern: Peter Lang).
— 2000. *Scraps of the Untainted Sky: Science Fiction, Utopia, Dystopia* (New York: Routledge).
Mukherjee, Neel 2015a. *The Lives of Others* (New York: Norton).
— 2015b. "Neel Mukherjee's Top 10 Books About Revolutionaries," *The Guardian*. Jan 14. Online. Accessed 2 November 2021.
Naipaul, V.S. 1989a [1979]. *A Bend in the River* (New York: Vintage).
— 1987. *The Enigma of Arrival* (New York: Vintage).
— 2003. "A Handful of Dust: Cheddi Jaggan and the Revolution in Guyana," in *The Writer and the World* (New York: Vintage), 485–502.
— 1989 [1961]. *A House for Mr. Biswas* (New York: Vintage).
— 1990 [1975]. *Guerrillas* (New York: Vintage).
— 1980. "Michael X and the Black Power Killings in Trinidad," in *The Return of Eva Peron* (New York: Knopf), 3–91.
Nelson, Brian 1983. *Zola and the Bourgoisie: A Study of Themes and Techniques in* Les Rougon-Macquart (New York: Barnes & Noble).
"New fiction: Aravind Adiga His master's Voice" 2008. *The Economist*. Nov. 11. Web. www.economist.com/books-and-arts/2008/09/11/his-masters-voice. Accessed 2 May 2021.
Nkosi, Lewis 1962. "African Fiction Part 1," *African Report* 7.9: 3–6.
— 2005a. "Alex La Guma: The Man and His Work," in *Still Beating the Drum: Critical Perspectives on Lewis Nkosi*. Eds. Linda Stiebel and Liz Gunner (Amsterdam: Rodopi), 257–266.
— 2005b. "Fiction by Black South Africans," in *Still Beating the Drum: Critical Perspectives on Lewis Nkosi*. Eds. Linda Stiebel and Liz Gunner (Amsterdam: Rodopi), 245–256.
— 1986. *Mating Birds* (New York: St. Martin's Press).

— 1971. "On South Africa: The Fire Some Time," *Transition* 38: 30–34.
— 2005c. "The Republic of Letters After the Mandela Republic," in *Still Beating the Drum: Critical Perspectives on Lewis Nkosi*. Eds. Linda Stiebel and Liz Gunner (Amsterdam: Rodopi): 311–330.
— 2002. *Underground People* (Oxfordshire: Ayebia Clarke).
Nkrumah, Kwame 1965. *Neo-Colonialism: The Last State of Imperialism* (Bedford: Panaf Books).
Norris, Frank 1986 [1901]. *The Octopus: A Story of California* (New York: Penguin).
O'Connell, Hugh Charles 2012. "A Weak Utopianism of Postcolonial Nationalist *Bildung*: Rereading Ayi Kwei Armah's *The Beautyful Ones Are Not Yet Born*," *The Journal of Postcolonial Writing* 48.4: 371–383.
Oliphant, Andries 2005. "Mammon and God: Reality, Imagination and Irony in *Underground People*," in *Still Beating the Drum: Critical Perspectives on Lewis Nkosi*. Eds. Linda Stiebel and Liz Gunner (Amsterdam: Rodopi), 187–196.
Ortigues, Marie-Cécile and Edmond 1966. *L'Oedipe africain* (Paris: Plon).
Orwell, George 1961 [1949]. *Nineteen Eighty-Four* (New York: Signet Classic).
— 1958 [1937]. *The Road to Wigan Pier* (New York: Harcourt, Brace, & World).
Paravisini-Gerbert, Lizabeth 1998. "Jean Rhys and Phyllis Shand Allfrey: The Story of a Friendship," *Jean Rhys Review* 9.1–2: 1–24.
Parry, Benita 2004. *Postcolonial Studies: A Materialist Critique* (London: Routledge).
Patterson, Orlando 2012 [1968]. *The Children of Sisyphus* (Leeds: Peepal Tree Press).
— 2019. *The Confounding Island: Jamaica and the Postcolonial Predicament* (Cambridge: Belknap Press).
— 2018. *Slavery and Social Death: A Comparative Study* (Cambridge: Harvard University Press).
Payne, Robert 1960. "Caribbean Carnival," *The Saturday Review*. Jul. 2: 18–19. http://www.unz.org/Pub/SaturdayRev-1960jul02-00018.
Pieto, Eric 2016. "Informal Urbanism and the Hard Question of the Anthropocene," *Journal of West Indian Literature* 24.2: 46–62.
Pizer, Donald 1984. *Realism and Naturalism in Nineteenth-Century American Literature* (Carbondale: Southern Illinois University Press).
Popescu, Monica 2016. "Lewis Nkosi in Warsaw: Translating Eastern European Experiences for an African Audience," in *Postcolonial Perspectives on Postcommunism in Central and Eastern Europe*. Eds. Dorota Kołodziejczyk and Cristina Şandru (New York: Routledge), 64–75.
Proctor, Jesse Harris 1973 [1963]. "British West Indian Society and Government in Transition 1920-1960," in *The Aftermath of Sovereignty: West Indian Perspectives*. Eds. David Lowenthal and Lambros Comitas (New York: Anchor).
Quayson, Ato 2003. *Calibrations: Reading for the Social* (Minneapolis: University of Minnesota Press).

Raiser, Philip 1974. "Grist for the Mill: James Joyce and the Naturalists," *Contemporary Literature* 15.4: 457–473.
Reimer, Andrew 2011. "The Dickens of Mumbai," *The Sydney Morning Herald*. Jul. 9, https://www.dropbox.com/scl/fi/a45hhduar58me81gby1vi/Postcolonial-Bildungsroman.docx?cloud_editor=word&dl=0&wd-Pid=5a70aab6. Accessed 5 March 2021.
Rieser, Max 1957. "The Aesthetic Theory of Social Realism," *The Journal of Aesthetics and Art Criticism* 16.2: 237–248.
Rhys, Jean 2016 [1979]. *Smile Please: An Unfinished Autobiography* (New York: Penguin).
— 1982 [1934]. *Voyage in the Dark* (New York: Norton).
— 1999. *Wide Sargasso Sea* (New York: Norton).
Rochat, Joyce Hamilton 1971. "The Naturalistic-Existential Rapprochement in Albert Camus's L'étranger and Paul Bowles' Let it Come Down: A Comparative Study in Absurdism" (Diss. University of Michigan).
Rodney, Walter 2019. *The Groundings with My Brothers*. Eds. Asha T. Rodney and Jesse J. Benjamin (New York: Verso).
Rodney, Walter and Orlando Patterson 1979. "Slavery and Underdevelopment," *Historical Reflections* 6.1: 275–292.
Roy, Arundhati 2011. *Walking With Comrades* (New York: Penguin).
Rushdie, Salman 1992. *Imaginary Homelands* (New York: Penguin).
Said, Edward W. 2000. "After Mahfouz," in *Reflections on Exile* (Cambridge: Harvard University Press).
— 1993. *Culture and Imperialism* (New York: Vintage).
Sargent, Lyman Tower 1994. "The Three Faces of Utopianism Revisited," *Utopian Studies* 51: 1–37.
Sartre, Jean Paul 2004. *Critique of Dialectical Reason Vol. 1*. Trans. Alan Sheridan-Smith (New York: Verso).
Schwarz, Roberto 2005. "A Brazilian Breakthrough," *New Left Review* 36: n.p. https://newleftreview.org/issues/ii36/articles/roberto-schwarz-a-brazilian-breakthrough.
Scott, David 2004. *Conscripts of Modernity: The Tragedy of Colonial Enlightenment* (Durham: Duke University Press).
— 2014. "The Tragic Vision in Postcolonial Time," *PMLA* 129.4: 799–808.
Seltzer, Mark 1986. "The Naturalist Machine," in *Sex, Politics, and Science in the Nineteenth-Century Novel*. Ed. Ruth Bernard Yeazell (Baltimore: Johns Hopkins University Press), 116–147.
Seshadri-Crooks, Kalpana 2000. "At the Margins of Postcolonial Studies: Part I," in *The Pre-Occupation of Postcolonial Studies*. Eds. Fawzia Afzal-Khan and Kalpana Seshadri-Crooks (Durham: Duke University Press), 3–23.
Smith, Eric D. 2012. *Globalization, Utopia, and Postcolonial Science Fiction: New Maps of Hope* (London: Palgrave).
Smith, Jennifer J. 2009. "Birthed and Buried: Matrilineal History in Michelle Cliff's No Telephone to Heaven," *Meridians* 9.1: 141–162.

Spivak, Gayatri Chakravorty 1988. "Can the Subaltern Speak?" in *Marxism and the Interpretation of Culture*. Eds. Cary Nelson and Lawrence Grossberg (Basingstoke: Macmillan), 271–313.

— 1985. "Three Women's Texts and a Critique of Imperialism," *Critical Inquiry* 12.1: 243–261.

Steffen, Therese 2005. "The Desire of Knowledge, or, the Body in Excess: Lewis Nkosi's Play 'The Black Psychiatrist,'" in *Still Beating the Drum: Critical Perspectives on Lewis Nkosi*. Eds. Lind Stiebel and Liz Gunner (Amsterdam: Rodopi), 103–126.

Subrahmanyam, Sanjay 2008. "Another Booker Flop," *London Review of Books*. https://www.lrb.co.uk/the-paper/v30/n21/sanjay-subrahmanyam/diary. Accessed 12 March 2021.

Suleri, Sara 1992. *The Rhetoric of English India* (Chicago: University of Chicago Press).

Suvin, Darko 2022. *Disputing the Deluge: Collected 21st-Century Writings on Utopia, Narration, and Survival*. Ed. Hugh C. O'Connell (New York: Bloomsbury).

Taylor, J.D. 2013. *Negative Capitalism: Cynicism in the Neoliberal Age* (Winchester: Zero Books).

Tiffin, Helen 2005. "'Man Fitting the Landscape': Nature, Culture, and Colonialism," in *Caribbean Literature and the Environment: Between Nature and Culture*. Eds. E. DeLoughrey, R.K. Gosson, and G.B. Handley (Charlottesville: University of Virginia Press), 199–212.

Tonkin, Boyd 2008. "Wizards of Oz Surf into Fictions Front Ranks," *Independent*. Nov. 28. Web. n.p. https://www.independent.co.uk/arts-entertainment/books/features/general-fiction-wizards-of-oz-surf-into-fiction-s-front-rank-1037794.html. Accessed 17 April 2021.

Trotsky, Leon 1929. *The Permanent Revolution and Results and Prospects*. Web.

Trump, Donald 2017. "President Donald Trump on Charlottesville," YouTube. Web. https://www.youtube.com/watch?v=JmaZR8E12bs. Accessed October 2021.

Vancini, Raffaella 2005. "Beyond the Literature of Protest: Lewis Nkosi's *Underground People*," in *Still Beating the Drum: Critical Perspectives on Lewis Nkosi* (Amsterdam: Rodopi), 197–218.

Vázquez, José Santiago Fernández 2002. "Recharting the Geography of Genre: Ben Okri's *The Famished Road* as a Postcolonial Bildungsroman," *The Journal of Postcolonial Literature* 37.2: 85–106.

Wajman, Gérard 2003. "The Hysteric's Discourse," *The Symptom* 4. https://www.lacan.com/hystericdiscf.htm.

Warren, Calvin 2015. "Black Nihilism and the Politics of Hope," *The New Centennial Review* 15.1: 215–248.

Warwick Research Collective 2015. *Combined and Uneven Development: Towards a New Theory of World Literature* (Liverpool: Liverpool University Press).

Wegner, Phillip E. 2002. *Imaginary Communities: Utopia, the Nation, and the Spatial Histories of Modernity* (Berkeley: University of California Press).
— 2020. *Invoking Hope: Theory and Utopia in Dark Times* (Minneapolis: University of Minnesota Press).
— 2021. "The Jameson Files," Unpublished Manuscript.
— 2009. *Life Between Two Deaths, 1989-2001: U.S. Culture in the Long Nineties* (Durham: Duke University Press).
— 2014. *Periodizing Jameson: Dialectics, the University, and the Desire for Narrative* (Evanston: Northwester University Press).
— 2002. "Spatial Criticism," in *Introducing Criticism at the 21st Century*. Ed. Julian Wolfreys (Edinburgh: Edinburgh University Press), 179–201.
Weinberg, Henry H. 1979–80. "Zola and the Paris Commune: The 'La Cloche' Chronicles," *Nineteenth-Century French Studies* 8: 79–86.
Wood, James 2008. "Wounder and Wounded: V.S. Naipaul's Empire," *The New Yorker* Dec. 1. http://www.newyorker.com/magazine/2008/12/01/wounder-and-wounded.
Wright, Colin 2013. *Badiou in Jamaica: The Politics of Conflict* (Melbourne: Re.press).
Xun, Lu 1981 [1922]. "Preface to *Call to Arms*," in *The Complete Stories of Lu Xun*. Trans. Yang Xianyi and Gladys Yang (Bloomington: University of Indiana Press), v–x.
Zahlan, Anne R. 1994. "Literary Murder: V.S. Naipaul's *Guerrillas*," *South Atlantic Review* 59.4: 89–106.
Žižek, Slavoj 1992. *Enjoy Your Symptom* (New York: Routledge).
— n.d. "The Most Sublime of Hysterics: Hegel with Lacan," trans. Rex Butler and Scott Stephens. *Lacan.com*. Web.
— 1989. *The Sublime Object of Ideology* (New York: Verso).
— 2000. *Tarrying with the Negative: Kant, Hegel, and the Critique of Ideology* (Durham: Duke University Press).
— 2008. *Violence* (London: Picador).
Zola, Émile 1964 [1880]. "The Experimental Novel," in *The Experimental Novel and Other Essays*. Trans. Belle M. Sherman (New York: Haskell House), 1–54.
— 2004 [1885]. *Germinal*. Trans. Roger Pearson (New York: Penguin).

Index

9/11 and the World Trade Center Attacks 45

Abbas, K.A. 131
Abida, Younis
  "The Wrongs of the Subaltern's Rights: A Critique on Postcolonial Diasporic Authors" 130n5
absurdism 182–183, 193
Abyssinia 188
Achebe, Chinua 65–66, 69–70, 88, 178–179
  No Longer at Ease 66
  Things Fall Apart 178
Adams, Grantley 110
Adhikar 175
Adiga, Aravind 27, 35, 99–100, 129–135, 138, 142–143, 146
  the Naxal novel 143, 158
  The White Tiger 27, 129–133, 135–143, 143, 145–150
Adivasi 142–145
Adkins, Andrew 65–66, 69–70, 88, 136
Adorno, Theodor 5–6, 10, 48, 96, 201
The Dialectic of Enlightenment 202
  happiness 201
  liberal rights 201
  see Horkheimer, Max
affect 55–57, 133

vs. political action 73
see also political action
Africa 18, 23–24, 34–35, 65, 71, 74, 78, 81–86, 88, 90, 92–96, 123, 125, 190, 203
  African fiction 23
African-American 180
African National Congress (ANC) 71, 87, 94–95
Afrikaner 174
Afro-Caribbean 113, 115
Afro-Pessimism 159, 180, 200
Afrofuturism 163
Ahmed, Aijaz 156n4
al-Daif, Rashid 22
Alexis, Paul 15
Algeria 182–184, 187
  Algerian Communist Party 182
Algiers 182
national allegory 11, 27, 105, 138, 156
Allfrey, Phyllis Shand 110–111, 113–114
  The Orchid House 110–111
alternative modernities 3
America 2, 15–16, 26–28, 66, 78, 84, 127, 156, 180, 188, 203
American Federation of Labor 16
Anderson, Warwick 88, 136
  promiscuous defectors 136
Anglophone novel 143
  modernism 103

223

Indian 129
Anjaria, Ulka 130–132
Anna Karenina Principle 159
  see also Tolstoy, Leo
Anna 107, 108, 157
anti-history 121
anti-utopianism 22, 26, 31, 36–37, 45, 61, 138, 151–155, 158–159, 165–166, 173, 175, 177, 179, 182–183, 200–202
  Rooster Coop as a figure of 137–140, 146–148
  see also Adiga, Aravind
anticolonial nationalism 8, 11, 20, 45, 65, 97, 103, 177–178
Antigone 191, 193, 200
Antônio, Cândido 24
apartheid 66, 71, 73, 78, 83, 85, 90–91, 94–97
Appiah, Kwame Anthony 65
Apter, Emily 3n5
Arendt, Hannah 24
Armah, Ayi Kwei
  The Beautyful Ones Are Not Yet Born 88, 105–106
Ashcroft, Bill 80, 151, 152, 154
Athill, Diana 110
Atwood, Margaret 164, 165
Augier, Roy 189
Azevedo, Aluísio 17
Azuela, Mariano 22, 29–34
  The Underdogs 22, 29–31, 33
  reactionary politics 29–34
  relation to Zola 30
Azuela, Salvador 30

Badiou, Alain 135, 137, 148, 163, 165, 168, 184–185, 200
  Second Manifesto for Philosophy 135n6
  democratic materialism 135, 137
  Event 168
Baguley, David 14–15, 18–19, 41, 52
Bahrani, Ramin 130
Balasopoulos, Antonis 153–154

Balzac, Honoré de 42, 63
Bandung-era 46, 63, 110, 133
Banerjee, Mamata 142
Bangalore 133, 148, 149
Bashir, Haroon
  "Black Excellence and the Curse of Ham: Debating Race and Slavery in the Islamic Tradition" 187n16
Becoming 17, 35, 99, 115, 117, 120, 128–129, 137–138, 149, 205
  see also Being
  see also Bildungsroman
Being 17, 20, 35, 99, 104–105, 117, 120, 125, 128, 135, 140, 149, 151, 176, 205
  resistance to 128
Being-in-time 120
Bellamy, Edward
  Looking Backward: 2000–1887 15, 16
Bengal 142, 168–169
Benjamin, Walter 122, 152
  weak messianism 152
  see Derrida, Jacques
Benson, Gale 47, 48
Berlant, Lauren
  cruel optimism 199
Berler, Beatrice 30
Berman, Jaye 46, 47
Bewes, Timothy 40, 48–53, 56, 57, 62
Bhabha, Homi 20, 24, 43–44, 46, 49–50
The Bharatiya Janata Party 206
Bhattacharya, Sourit 175
Bible 189
  Lamentations 190
Bildung 35, 99–100, 105–106, 118–199, 120, 126, 133
  relationship to postcoloniality 99–100
Bildungsroman 28, 35, 99–101, 103–107, 114, 116, 118, 120, 122, 124, 129, 132–133, 148–149

Great Expectations 122
The White Tiger 133
see Cliff, Michelle
Black Optimism 159
see Afro-Pessimism
Black Other 113
Black Power 35, 59, 115
Black South Africans 71, 85
Bloch, Ernst 5, 105, 150, 155, 168
novum 168
Bogle, Paul 185
Bollywood 129
The Bolshevik Revolution 109, 182
Bong, Joon-ho 27–28, 29
Parasite 27–28, 34
Booker Prize 129, 159
see Adiga, Aravind
see Mukherjee, Neel
Botswana 25, 203
Bovaryism 54
Bowen, Elizabeth 101
Boyle, Danny 129–130
Slumdog Millionaire 129–130, 140
Brathwaite, Edward Kamau 106, 180–182
Brazil 5
Brecht, Bertolt 4, 147
Verfremdungseffekt 4
Bretton Woods 110
Brink, Andre 76–78, 82–83
Brody, Mark 90, 94
Brontë, Charlotte
Jane Eyre 113–114, 116, 127
Brontë, Emily
Wuthering Heights 51
Burke, Edmond 151, 153–155
Reflections on the Revolution in France 153
Jacobinism 155
Bustamante, Alexander 110, 194
Byatt, A.S. 162

Calvinist predestination 123
Campbell, Horace 188, 190

Camus, Albert 72, 181–184, 187, 193, 195, 197, 200
L'Étranger 183
Le mythe de Sisyphe (The Myth of Sisyphus) 182, 195
The Rebel 181–183
Cândido, Antônio 24, 25
capitalism 1–7, 9–13, 20–21, 25, 28–29, 36, 62–63, 70–71, 84, 86, 88, 90–91, 94–97, 99, 103–104, 106, 108, 114, 129, 134, 140, 143, 145–149, 152–154, 156–157, 173, 180, 185, 187–189, 202–203, 205–207, 209
Caribbean 27, 112, 113, 115, 116, 117, 124, 158, 180, 186
Carranza, Venustiano 31–32
Casanova, Pascale 1, 40, 48
Casimir, J.R. Ralph 110
Central Industrial Security Force (CISF) 139
Chapman, Michael 73, 78
Charles, David 19
Charlesworth, Kate 175
Charlottesville, Virginia 144
Chatterjee, Manini 175
Do and Die: The Chittagong Uprising, 1930–34 175
Cheah, Pheng 23, 35, 105–106
Cheng, Chu-chueh 39
Chevrel, Yves 2
Le Naturalisme: Étude d'un mouvement littéraire international 2n1
Chibber, Vivek 37
China 142, 146–147
Chinese 132, 145
Christian Socialists 15
see also Bellamy, Edward
Cleary, Joe 7
Cliff, Michelle 35, 99–100, 115–120, 122, 150
Abeng 35, 115–120, 127
No Telephone to Heaven 35, 115, 118–120, 127, 129

postcolonial Bildungsroman
 99, 120
Coetzee, J.M. 53, 56
Cold War 2, 7, 45, 90, 95–96, 155
Communist Party India (CPI) 142
 Marxist (CPI-M) 168, 142–143
 CPI-Marxist-Leninist 143
Conrad, Joseph 45, 94, 100, 174
 Heart of Darkness 102
 The Secret Agent 174
Constitutionalist Army 31
Coundouriotis, Eleni 18, 24, 26
 "Narrate or Describe" 18n13
Creole(s) 110, 113, 115
Crewe, Jonathan 74
Crown Colony Government 110
Cudjoe, Selwyn R. 61, 126
cynical realism 135–140
cynicism 28, 69, 135, 140–141, 148–149, 166

Daily Telegraph (London) 158
Dalgarno, Emily
 "A British War and Peace? Virginia Woolf Reads Tolstoy" 160n8
Danton, George 52
Daoud, Hassan 22
Darwinism, social 15–16, 137
Dawes, Kwame 192
death drive
 see Freud, Sigmund
 see also Lacan, Jacques
Delaney, Samuel 152
Deleuze, Gilles 34, 48–50, 61, 149
 death instinct/drive 61–62
 Difference and Repetition 61
 impulse-image 34, 49–50, 61
 originary world 49
 "Postcript on the Societies of Control" 149
Democratic Congress (in the U.S.) 174
Derrida, Jacques 152
 messianic without messianism 152

 see also Benjamin, Walter
Descola, Philippe 163
Devi, Mahasweta 143, 175
 Aranyer Adhikar 175
 Mother of 1084 175
 Operation?—Bashai Tudu 175
dialectic(ism) 6–9, 14–15, 19–20, 25, 41–42, 55, 65–66, 68, 70–71, 73–74, 82, 84, 92–93, 96, 100, 103–104, 106, 108, 130, 138, 153–155, 169, 176, 178, 182, 202–203, 207–208
The Diary of Anne Frank 124–125
 as Bildungsroman 124n3
Díaz, Porfirio 31
Dickens, Charles 40, 43, 129–130, 133
 Great Expectations 122, 124, 129
Dirlik, Arif 20
dogmatic anti-utopianism 153–154
Dominica 35, 108, 110–114
 Dominica Freedom Party (DFP) 114
 Dominica Labour Party (DLP) 35, 110–111, 113
 Dominican Legislative Assembly 108
 Prohibited and Unlawful Societies and Associations Act 111
 Representative Government Association (RGA) 108
Dostoevsky, Fyodor 6, 85
 The Possessed 174
Douglas, Mary
 Natural Symbols 119
Dread 111
Dreiser, Theodore 15, 154
Dreyfus Affair 41
Du Bois, W.E.B. 11
Duneer, Anita 26–28
Durrant, Samuel 178–179

The Economist 130
Edgell, Zee
 Beka Lamb 124

INDEX

Edmondson, Belinda 115–116
Egypt 203
Ehrlich, David 130
Ekwensi, Cyprian 23, 204
  Jagua Nana 204
Eliot, T.S.
  The Waste Land 10
Elze, Jens 133
  see *The White Tiger*
  see also Bildungsroman
Emery, Mary Lou 113, 115
Engels, Friedrich 17
  see also Marx, Karl
England 39, 95, 110, 122, 132, 183
English 101, 113, 116, 126, 136, 145, 164–165, 189
English Socialism 165
Eros 61
Eshun, Kodwo 163
Esty, Jed 35, 100–101, 103–104, 106–109
eternal return 50, 108, 122, 205
Ethiopia 199
Eurocentrism 73–74, 103, 122, 123
Europe 2, 62, 174, 188, 209
European(s) 2, 5, 7–8, 10, 14–15, 19, 21–22, 25, 62, 65, 73, 88, 93, 99–100, 103, 106, 112–114, 116–117, 122, 149, 185, 187, 190, 203–204
exoticism 100, 103, 107–108, 129–131
  see also Huggan, Graham

Fanon, Frantz 8, 11, 26, 52, 62, 70–71, 84, 87, 90, 102, 184
  The Wretched of the Earth 70, 184
  see also Sartre, Jean Paul
Farah, Nuruddin 105
  The Blood in the Sun Trilogy 106
Fields, James 144
First-World 11, 45, 156, 157
Fisher, Mark
  Capitalist Realism: Is There No Alternative? 29

Fiske, John 15
Flaubert, Gustave 107
Folidol 161
Forster, E.M
  Howard's End 101–102
Foucauldian 78, 187
Fourth International 90
framing 197
France 63
  Northern 30
Franco-Prussian War 30
Franklin, Benjamin 122
Frazier, E. Franklin
  The Negro Family in the United States 180
French 19, 24, 48, 112, 133, 137, 183, 184
French Algeria 182–183
Freud, Sigmund 34, 61, 67–69, 73–74, 134, 155, 192, 199
  death drive 40, 61–62, 197, 199, 209
  Dora 67, 68, 74
  Interpretation of Dreams 73
  masochism 199
  see also Lacan, Jacques
Froude, James Anthony 39–40

Gajarawala, Toral Jatin 53–54, 56, 58
Gandhi, Mahatma 139
Ganguly, Debjani 23
Gaonkar, Dilip Parameshwar
  Alternative Modernities 3n4
Garvey, Marcus 110
Garveyism 188
Gay, Peter 134
Gherovici, Patricia 67–68
  see also Lacan, Jacques
  see also Freud, Sigmund
Ghosh, Amitav 25–26, 159, 160–161, 167, 171
  The Calcutta Chromosome 26
Gikandi, Simon 116–118
Gilman, Charlotte Perkins 15–17, 19
  Herland 16

Gilroy, Paul 175
Gissing, George 16, 40, 154, 157, 166, 172, 183
Goethe, Johann Wolfgang von 1, 101
Weltliteratur 1
Goldmann, Lucien 179
Goncourt, Edmond de 15–17, 19, 24, 183
Germinie Lacerteux 15
La fille Élisa 183
"the rabble" 19
Goncourt, Jules de 15–17, 19, 24
Germinie Lacerteux 15
"the rabble" 19
Gordimer, Nadine 83–84, 95, 174
Burger's Daughter 174
July's People 83
Gothic 44, 46
Greek 191
Greimas, A.J. 12–13, 208
The Guardian 17, 174
Guin, Ursula Le 152
Guma, Alex La 86

Haraway, Donna 152
Harrow, Susan 47, 54, 55
Harvey, David 173–174
neoliberalism 174
see also neoliberalism
Hassan, Ihab 27
Hay, Simon 35, 99
Head, Bessie 23, 25, 28, 34
A Question of Power 25
When Rain Clouds Gather 25, 34
Hegel, G.W.F. 26, 35, 65, 68, 69, 73–74, 82–83, 87, 92, 96, 170, 178, 182
Beautiful Soul 26, 35, 65–66, 68–71, 74, 76, 78, 81–84
Law of the Heart 69
Phenomenology of Spirit 92–93
The Philosophy of History 74
Spirit 68, 92
Helgesson, Stefan 24–25
Hemingway, Ernest 86

Hendricks, Frances Kellam 30
Henshall, Ken
"The Puzzling Perception of Japanese Naturalism" 22n15
Herbert, Meredith 60–61
Hill, Christopher L. 1–3, 12, 17–18, 20–23, 42, 115, 203–205, 207–208
Hindu 143, 145
Historical Necessity 69
Hitchcock, Peter 106
Hitler, Adolf 147
Hobbesian 180, 200
Hodge, Merle
Crick, Crack, Monkey 124
Holden Philip
"The 'Postcolonial Gothic': Absent Histories, Present Contexts" 46
Hollywood 118
Holocaust 125
Horkheimer, Max
see Adorno, Theodor
Huggan, Graham
strategic exoticism 130
Hugo, Victor
Les Misérables 19
Hulme, Peter 106, 110–111
hysteria 34, 65, 67, 71, 73, 75, 87–88, 96
hysterical subjectivism 87

Ibsen, Henrik 14
idealism 18, 174
Immorality Act of 1927/1950 71–73
see Nkosi, Lewis
India 129–131, 134, 137–139, 142–143, 145–146, 148, 161, 174, 206
Parliament 144, 148
Indian 27–28, 48, 129, 138, 142–145, 147, 159, 167, 175
Indulgents 52
see also Danton, Georges
Industrial Workers of the World (IWW) 16
inheritance 40–41, 100, 115, 117–118, 120–126, 149, 166

International Monetary Fund (IMF) 63
Iqbal, Muhammad 145–146
Isaiah 195
Islam 187
Israel 144, 195
Italy
 invasion of Abyssinia (1935) 188

Jackson, K. David 4
Jacobin 155, 184
Jacobs, Johan 76, 82
Jamaica 110, 118, 123, 158–159, 181, 184, 186, 187, 188, 190–191, 193
 Jamaica Labour Party (JLP) 185, 193–194
 Jamaica National Party (JNP) 194
James, C.L.R 205
 Minty Alley 205
James, Henry 87
James, William 67
Jameson, Fredric 3, 5–16, 19, 21–23, 27, 36–37, 42, 44, 51, 55–57, 62–63, 66, 69–70, 73, 101–102, 114, 134, 138, 151, 154–158, 163–165, 176, 179, 201–202, 207–208
 Archaeologies of the Future 155n2
 cognitive mapping 11, 20, 101, 156
 empire 101
 "The Existence of Italy" 9, 12
 Fables of Aggression 11
 modernism 5, 101–102
 'the people' 157–158
 periodization 9, 12, 21, 23
 political unconscious 37, 73, 83, 155, 169
 The Political Unconscious 151, 159
 ressentiment 157–158
 Signatures of the Visible 9
 "Third-World Literature in the Era of Multinational Capitalism" 11, 62
Jangalmahal 142
Jansenism 179n13

Japanese 20, 22, 209
Japanese Naturalism
 see Naturalism
Jefferson, Thomas 122
Jesus 123
Jiabao, Wen 143, 148
Johannesburg 87, 95
John, Patrick 111
Jones Town 198
Jonestown (Guyana) 48
Joyce, James 5, 10, 14–15, 22, 27, 85, 100, 102
 A Portrait of the Artist 14
 Dubliners 14
 Ulysses 14
June Rebellion (1862) 19

Kafka, Franz 85, 107
Kaiwar, Vasant 20, 37, 103
Karunarathne, A., Bhalla, A., Sethi, A. et al. 161
Kenya 188, 203
Khoury, Elias 22
 Little Mountain 22
Kilson, Martin 180, 186, 188
Kincaid, Jamaica 100
Kingsley, Charles 39
Kingston 126, 181, 189
Kingston Harbor 128
Kipling, Rudyard
 Kim 104
Kissinger, Henry 40
Klein, Melanie 76
Knight, Denise 17
Knutson, Elizabeth M.
 "The Natural and the Supernatural in Zola's in Thérèse Raquin" 136n7
Korea 20, 27, 203
Kornbluh, Anna 157
Kramer, Hilton 45
Krupp 4
Kumar, Krishan 151, 153–154, 177, 200
Kurtz
 see Conrad, Joseph

Lacan, Jacques 13, 61, 65–70, 96, 191
    Big Other 67, 70
    dialectical impasse 66
    Hegel as 'sublime hysteric' 96
    Hegelian Beautiful Soul 69
    Hegelian Law of the Heart 69
    the Imaginary 7, 13, 34, 66, 70, 83–84
    the Real 13, 102–103, 199
    the Symbolic 12, 13, 62, 66, 70, 84, 102, 199
    see also Antigone
Lagos de Moreno (Mexico) 30–31
Lahiri, Jhumpa
    The Lowland 143
Lakshmi 166, 172
Lamming, George 186
Lang, Felix
    The Lebanese Post-Civil War Novel: Memory, Trauma, and Capital 22
Langbaum, Robert
    'revelation' 85
    see also Nkosi, Lewis
Lanternari, Vittorio, Lanternari 186
    The Religions of the Oppressed: A Study of Modern Messianic Cults 186n15
Lawrence, D.H. 14, 15
Lazarus, Neil 6, 20, 23–55, 37, 45, 65, 156, 209
    Into Our Labors: Work and its World-Literary Perspective 6n8
Le Blanc, Edward Oliver 113
Lebanese Civil War 22
Lebanon 209
Lefebvre, Henri 28
Leftism 15, 22, 131, 133, 142–144, 174, 202
Lenin, Vladimir 10
    Imperialism: The Highest Stage of Capitalism 10
Lentricchia, Frank 70
Les Temps Modernes 182
Lessing, Doris
    The Good Terrorist 175

Lewis, Sir Arthur 189n17
Lewis, Wyndham 10–11
Lima, Maria Helena 35, 99–100
Lincoln, Abraham 147
Link, Eric Carl 15–16
London, Jack 15–17, 19, 58, 130, 158
    The Iron Heel 16
    the people of the abyss 16–17, 19
López, Alfred 118
Lukács, György 6, 18, 23–24, 33–34, 39, 41–42, 53, 55, 63, 76, 132
    "The Zola Centenary" 39

Machado de Assis, Joaquim Maria 4, 5
Madero Revolution of 1911 30
Mahfouz, Naguib 23
Majumdar, Nivedita 160, 169, 173, 205, 206
Malik, Michael Abdul 47–48, 50
Mamdani, Mahmood
    Good Muslim, Bad Muslim: America, the Cold War and the Roots of Terror 2
Mandela, Nelson 94, 95
Manley, Michael Norman 110, 188, 190
Mannheim, Karl 158
Mao Zedung 147
Maoist(s) 142–144, 158, 161–162, 167–168
    see also Naxalite(s)
Marie-Harrison, Sherie 182, 188, 201
Marinetti, Filippo 10, 14–15
Marques, Pedro Neves 163, 206
    foreshortened worlds 163, 206, 209
Marquez, Gabriel Garcia 25
Martyris, Nina 143
Marx, Karl 17, 41–42, 50–51, 73, 131, 137, 140, 170, 183
    The Communist Manifesto 17, 73, 146

French peasantry and class
    consciousness 137
The German Ideology 41
Marxism 73, 93, 180, 189
Marxism-Leninism 90–91
masochism 189, 199–200
    see also Freud, Sigmund
Matthews, J.H. 183
Mau Mau Rebellion (1953) 188
Maupassant, Guy de 134
    Mbembe, Achille 69
McQueen, Sean 165
Meiji Restoration 22
Meiji-era Japan 209
Mendes, Alfred 205
Mendes, Ana Cristina 130–131
Mendieta, Ana
    Silueta Series 118
Mexican Revolution 29, 33
Mexico 209
Michael X
    see Malik, Michael Abdul
Michaels, Walter Benn 66–67,
    70–61
Milner, Andrew 163–165
Mitchell, David
    Cloud Atlas 138
modernism 4–11, 14, 20–22, 25, 27,
    29, 34, 37, 48–49, 55–56, 62, 82,
    100–106, 108, 116, 130, 132–133,
    155, 205–207, 209
modernities (alternative) 3, 103
modernity 1, 3, 5–6, 11, 25, 47, 55,
    65–66, 101, 103, 108, 111, 133, 157,
    163, 177, 179, 206–209
Modi, Narendra 145
Modisane, Bloke
    Blame Me 82
Mohan, Rajeswari 120
Morant Bay Revolt 184–185
Moretti, Franco 1–3, 100, 104, 133,
    148–149
Morris, William
    News from Nowhere 164
the Moselle 73
Moss, Stephen 133

Movement for a New Dominica 113
Moylan, Tom 152, 154, 163
    critical utopia 152
Mphalale, Ezekiel 85–86
Mukherjee, Neel 17–18, 36, 143,
    151, 158–160, 165–166, 168–170,
    172–176, 199–200
    The Lives of Others 18, 36, 143,
        151, 158–160, 163, 174–176, 177
    "Neel Mukherjee's Top 10 Books
        About Revolutionaries" 18, 174
    great circularity 36, 159, 166–167,
        200
Mumbai 130
Munda, Bursa 175
Munif, Abdelrahman
    City of Salt 27n18
Mwangi, Meja
    Going Down River Lazarus 23

Naipaul, V.S 34, 36, 39–40, 42–50,
    52–53, 57, 60–63, 70–71, 78, 105,
    110, 115, 149, 174, 206
    A Bend in the River 39
    "A Handful of Dust: Cheddi
        Jagan and the Revolution in
        Guyana" 48n3
    A House for Mr. Biswas 43–44, 51
    An Area of Darkness 40
    The Enigma of Arrival 39, 49, 61
    Guerrillas 34, 36, 39, 44–54,
        56–63, 113–116, 127, 174
    Magic Seeds 174
    "Michael X and the Killings in
        Trinidad" 47–48, 59
    Miguel Street 42–43
    and *Tehelka* 48
Nandigram 142
Napoleon III 137
    see also Marx, Karl
National Liberation Front (FLN) 184
    see Sartre, Jean Paul
National Liberation Movement
    (NLM) 45, 87
Nationalist Clubs 15
    see also Bellamy, Edward

Natural 136
Naturalism 1–4, 12, 14–17, 19–29, 33–34, 36–37, 39–42, 44–46, 49–50, 52, 54–56, 61–63, 66–67, 70–71, 78–79, 87–88, 97, 99, 101, 104, 106–107, 109, 123, 132, 135, 151, 154, 157, 163, 167, 183, 202–209
   Argentine 2
   Brazilian 2, 17
   narrative entropy 16, 23–24, 28, 40, 50, 55, 61, 209
   postcolonial 1, 21, 23–25, 27–29, 34, 36–37, 39–40, 45, 56, 62–63, 66, 71, 88, 97, 99, 107, 132, 157, 206, 208–209
   and postmodernism 27
Nature 16, 77–79, 105, 123, 203
Naxal(s) 139, 143, 145–146, 158
Naxalite(s) 36, 161, 167, 174–175
   see also Maoist(s)
Ndebele, Njabulo 23
Necessity, Historical 69
Nehru, Jawaharlal 134
Nelson, Brian 134
neoliberalism 36, 133–134, 149, 173–174, 193
Nettleford, Rex, et al.
   Report on the Rastafarian Movement in Kingston 189n17
New York City 128
Nigeria 66, 178
nihilism
   active nihilism 36, 159, 184–185, 199–200
   subtractive nihilism 177
Nixon, Rob
   slow violence 133
Nkosi, Lewis 34–35, 65–66, 71–74, 78, 82–87, 89–90, 93–97, 105, 132, 192
   The Black Psychiatrist 71
   Mating Birds 35, 66, 71, 74, 77, 79, 82, 84, 87–88, 93, 96–97
   Underground People 87–97, 158

Nkrumah, Kwame 11, 106
   and neo-colonialism 11
Nobel Prize
   Naipaul, V.S. 40
   Kissinger, Henry 40
Norris, Frank 15, 17, 78, 79
   The Octopus 79
North America 26, 188
novum
   see Bloch, Ernst

O'Brien, Conor Cruise 183
O'Connell, Hugh Charles 105, 152, 154
O'Donnell, Daniel Paul 124
Obejas, Achy
   Ruins 27n18
Oedipal (structure/complex) 74, 77
Oedipus 73
Oliphant, Andries 84
Operation Green Hunt 144
Ortigues, Edmond 73–74
Ortigues, Marie-Cécile 73–74
Orwell, George 22, 34–35, 155, 158, 163–166, 170–172, 183, 202
   Nineteen Eighty-Four 163–165
   Animal Farm 164
   Homage to Catalonia 22, 34
Osanyin, Bode
   The Noble Mistress 204
the Other 10, 67–70, 74, 88, 96, 113, 128, 174, 189

Pacheco, Jorge 45
Pakistan 146, 147
Paravisini-Gerbert, Lizabeth 114
Paris Commune 19, 30, 57, 109
Park, Jin Gon 146
   aesthetic liberalism 146
Parry, Benita 37
El Paso, Texas 32
Patterson, Orlando 36, 158, 177–183, 186–190, 193, 201–202
   and Até 191
   as 'The Caribbean Zola' 158

The Children of Sisyphus 36, 158, 177–179, 181, 184, 186, 188
Rituals of Blood: Consequences of Slavery in Two American Centuries 180
The Sociology of Slavery 180
Payne, Robert 42
Pelagian (Christianity) 153
'the people' 16, 19, 24, 157–158, 168, 179, 188
   the Goncourt brother's figuration as "the rabble" 19, 193
   see also London, Jack
People's National Movement (PNM) 193–194
People's National Party (PNP) 185
Peru 127
Piercy, Marge 152
Pieto, Eric 181, 188, 201
Pizer, Donald 26–27, 40, 209
Pleiades 113
political action 18, 24, 199, 170, 172–173
   vs. affect 173
   see also affect
Popescu, Monica 90
Port of Spain 43
postcolonial naturalism
   see Naturalism
postcolonial science fiction 8
   see Smith, Eric D.
postmodernism 9–13, 22, 25, 27, 130, 132–133, 157, 207
   and postcolonialism 11–12, 20, 27
Pretoria 87
Proles 164
Proust, Marcel 102

Quayson, Ato 11, 74, 84

Raiser, Philip 14
Rastafari(an) 36, 111, 185–186, 188–189, 196–197, 200, 202
realism 4–9, 11–14, 18, 20, 22–25, 28–29, 34–35, 37, 39–43, 49–50, 53–55, 62–63, 84, 86, 101–102, 104, 108, 114, 129–133, 135, 140–141, 157, 159, 177, 205, 207, 209
Red Corridor 139, 144
Reign of Terror 52
Reimer, Andrew 130, 132
representation 15, 78
   onanistic 78
   naturalist 41, 66, 71, 78, 81, 132
   (crisis of) realist 4, 7–9, 34
Representative Government Association (RGA) 108
ressentiment 16, 36, 157–158, 170, 172–174, 176, 179, 193, 196, 202
Rhys, Jean 35, 99–101, 106–116, 115, 169
   "The Imperial Road" 110–111
   Voyage in the Dark 106–110
   Wide Sargasso Sea 35, 109–129
Rivera, José Eustasio
   The Vortex 34
Robinson, Kim Stanley
   Mars Trilogy 156n3
   Science in the Capital Trilogy 156n3
Rochat, Joyce Hamilton 183
Rodney, Walter 186–188, 202
Romantic/Tragic 178
Rosca, Ninotchka
   The State of War 105
Roy, Arundhati 142, 144, 189
Rushdie, Salman 25, 129–132, 134
   Grimus 132
   Imaginary Homelands 132
   Midnight's Children 131–132
Russ, Joanna 152
Russell, David 146
Russian Revolution of 1905 16

Sade, Marquis de 135
   120 Days of Sodom 135
Sahel 187
Said, Edward 7, 22, 45, 122, 183, 209
   Orientalism 45, 103
St. Kitts 110

St. Lucia 110
St. Vincent 110
Sargent, Lyman Tower 151, 163
Sartre, Jean Paul 158, 182, 184, 187, 197, 203
  Critique of Dialectical Reason Vol. 1 203
  relation to Palestinians 187
Satan 191, 196
Saudi Arabia 27
scenic description 40, 50, 53
Schiller, Friedrich 101
Schreiner, Olive 53
Schwarz, Roberto 4, 5
Sciascia, Leonardo
  The Moro Affair 175
science 8, 29, 156
science fiction 8, 29, 62, 132, 152, 156
Scott, David 177–181, 184, 188, 193, 201
  Conscripts of Modernity 177
Scott, Walter 124–125
  Ivanhoe 124–125
Second Empire 54, 109
Selassie, Haile 189
Seltzer, Mark 78–79
Seshadri-Crooks, Kalpana 208
Sexton, Jared 159
Shaw, George Bernard 14
Shimazaki, Tōson
  Spring 18
Shizenshugi
  see Japanese Naturalism
Singh, Manmohan 144
Singur 142
Sinha, Indra
  Animal's People 27–28
Sisyphean 180, 192
  see Camus, Albert
  see also Patterson, Orlando
Skerritt, Joseph 47
slavery 158, 180, 187, 190
Sloterdijk, Peter 36, 140
  cynical reason 36
Smith, Eric D. 8
  Globalization, Utopia, and Postcolonial Science Fiction: New Maps of Hope 8
Smith, Jennifer J. 35, 119–120, 128
Smith, M.G. 189
socialism 15, 53, 87, 131–132, 134, 142–143, 165, 183, 209
Somer, Doris 84
South Africa 34–35, 71, 81, 83–86, 90, 92, 94–96
  Government 92
  Marikana 95
  Communist Party 71
  Revolution 90
South African Communist Party (SACP) 87
South America 84
South Korea 27
Soviet Union 83, 86, 90, 184
Special Economic Zone 142
Spencer, Herbert 15
Spivak, Gayatri 24, 114, 169
  Vertretung and *Darstellung* 24
Stalinism 155
The Star 114
Steffen, Therese 73, 83
Stendhal 39
Students' Federation 168
subjectivism 26, 28, 35, 42, 44, 46, 50, 55, 60, 70–71, 81, 83–85, 87, 90, 97, 149
Sublime Hysteric 96
Sudan 187
Suleri, Sara 40, 48, 53, 78
surrealism 29, 34, 49–50
Suvin, Darko 29, 165
Swarup, Vikas 129
  Q&A 129
The Sydney Morning Herald 130

Taine, Hippolyte 109
Talbot, Bryan 175
Talbot, Mary
  Sally Heathcote, Suffragette 175
Taylor, J.D. 134–135, 148–149

Tengai, Tsugi
  Hatsusugata 22
Texas 32
Thatcher, Margaret 96
Thiong'o, Ngũgĩ wa 23, 137
  Petals of Blood 23
  Devil on the Cross 137
Third World 11, 21, 45, 61, 100–102, 129, 138, 173, 185, 206, 208–209
Third Worldism 63
Third-World Project 133
Tiffin, Helen 112
Toer, Pramoedya Ananta
  Buru Quartet 106
Tolstoy, Leo 159–160
  "Family Happiness" 160
Toronto 61
totality/totalization 1, 2, 3, 11–12, 14, 20–22, 24–25, 34, 50, 51, 55, 58, 73–74, 76, 102, 104, 109, 118, 151, 155, 157, 167, 182, 195, 206–207
tragedy 15, 32, 36, 61, 85, 95, 109, 113–115, 118–120, 122–125, 127, 157, 175, 177–179, 181, 184, 190–192, 198, 200
Trevor-Roper, Hugh 74
Trinidad 43, 47, 59, 151
Trollope, Anthony 39–40
Trotsky, Leon 2–3, 90–91
Trotter, Desmond 113
Trump, Donald 144
Turgenev, Ivan 45, 174
  Virgin Soil 174

United States (U.S.) 16, 45, 113, 118, 144, 174, 180, 193, 197
underdevelopment 1, 4, 99, 106, 140, 186–187, 190, 260
Unigwe, Chika
  On Black Sisters Street 204
Urdu 145
Uruguay 45
U.S. Black Power Movement 113
utopia(nism) 5, 8, 15–17, 22, 24–26, 31, 36–37, 45, 48, 60–61, 105, 109, 120, 138, 140, 149, 151–159, 163–166, 170, 173–177, 179, 181–183, 188, 193, 199–202, 206

Vancini, Raffaella 89–90, 93
Varoufakis, Yanis 156
Vázquez, José Santiago Fernández 99
Verfremdungseffekt
  see Brecht, Bertolt
Victorian 39–40, 146
Vienna 73
Villa, Pancho 31

Wallerstein, Immanuel
  world-system 6, 187
Walrand, Eric
  Tropic Death 27n18
Warren, Calvin 200
Warsaw, University of 90
Warwick Research Collective (WReC) 3, 5–10, 12, 22, 29, 34, 37, 207–208
The Waste Land
  see Eliot, T.S.
Way 205
  see also Becoming
  see also Being
  see also World
Wegner, Phillip E. 11–13, 16, 45, 143, 154, 157–158, 171–173
  Life Between Two Deaths, 1989–2001: U.S. Culture in the Long Nineties 45n1
  Imaginary Communities: Utopia, The Nation, and the Spatial Histories of Modernity 157n5
Weinberg, Henry 19
Weltanschauung 178
Weltliteratur
  see Goethe, Johann Wolfgang von
the West 4, 12, 21, 45, 60–62, 82, 103, 122, 129, 134, 153, 155–156, 163, 174, 187

West Bengal 142
West India 110, 115
West Indies 110, 113, 189
West Indies Federation 113
Western Europe 5, 174
Wilderson, Frank 159
Williams, Raymond 163–165, 179
   "tenses of imagination" 164
Wilson, Edmund 14
Wood, James 57
Woolf, Virginia 100, 160
   The Voyage Out 100
World 205
   see also Becoming
   see also Being
   see also Way
World Bank 63
World-Literature 1, 3–4, 8, 12, 24, 37, 204, 207–208
World War II 20, 203
Wright, Colin 184–185, 188, 200, 202
Wright, Patrick 175
Wright, Richard 203

Xun, Lu 62, 129, 138

Zapata, Emiliano 31
Zitkála-Šá
   "The Soft-Hearted Sioux" 27

Žižek, Slavoj 36, 96–98, 140–141, 184, 199–200
   active nihilism 200
   cynical reason 36, 140–141
   death drive 199
   dialectic of Truth and Knowledge (Lacan vis-à-vis Hegel) 97–98
   violence 184
   see also Badiou, Alain
   see also Hegel, G.W.F
   see also Lacan, Jacques
Zola, Émile 15, 18–19, 24, 30, 34, 36, 39, 40–44, 47, 49, 52–57, 63, 86, 107, 109–110, 115, 133–134, 136, 140, 154, 158–159, 183
   L'Assommoir 183
   La Débâcle 30, 136
   experimental method 30, 39, 44, 49, 109, 133
   "The Experimental Novel" 39
   The Fortune of the Rougons 115
   Germinal 30,52
   Les Rougon-Macquart 109
   and the supernatural 136
   Thérèse Raquin 136
Zulu 71, 75, 77
Zurich 73